THE BATTLE

Mitsouko

AMIDST A CLASH OF EMPIRES

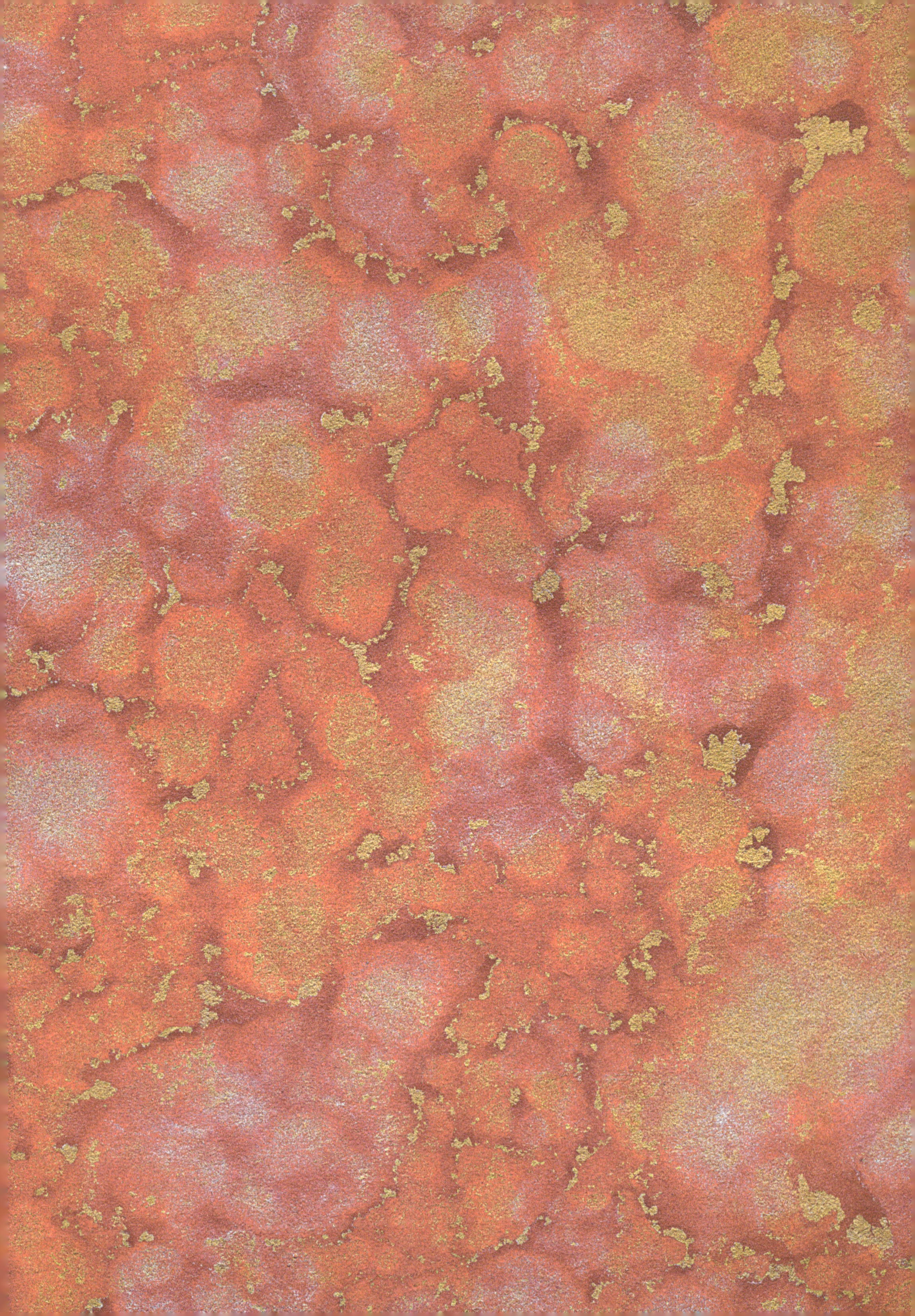

THE BATTLE
Mitsouko
AMIDST A CLASH OF EMPIRES

By

Claude Farrère

Original Illustrations by
Charles Fouqueray

Edited by
Kent Davis

Translated by
Pedro Rodríguez

DatASIA Press
MMXXV

About the Cover

French artist Charles Dominique Fouqueray (1869-1956), an official Painter of the French Navy (Peintre officiel de la Marine), drew upon his maritime experience to create 108 stunning illustrations for the 1925 deluxe limited-edition of *La Bataille*. All have been painstakingly restored and are included in this landmark 2025 English-language edition.

Sampling Fouqueray's art, graphic designer Becca Klein captures the dichotomy of Farrère's clash of East and West. The front cover shows Marquis Yorisaka commanding the battleship *Nikkō* with a vision of Mitsouko. The back depicts French artist Felze painting her portrait, prompting her prophetic words:

"…I shall be delighted that, thanks to you, my husband will have me at his side, after a fashion… A portrait is almost a double of oneself, is it not? So a double of me will be going out there, to sea, and might even witness some battles…"

Editor: **Kent Davis**
Translation: **Pedro Rodríguez**
Art Restoration: **Artsiom Yatsevich**
Text Design: **Pedro Rodríguez**

Original French transliterations of the Chinese and Japanese languages and names have been updated to modern transliterations.

DatASIA Press — www.DatASIA.us

First English Language Edition

ISBN: 978-1-934431-32-0 (paperback)
Library of Congress Pre-Assigned Control Number: 2025937523

Printed simultaneously in
the United States of America and Great Britain.

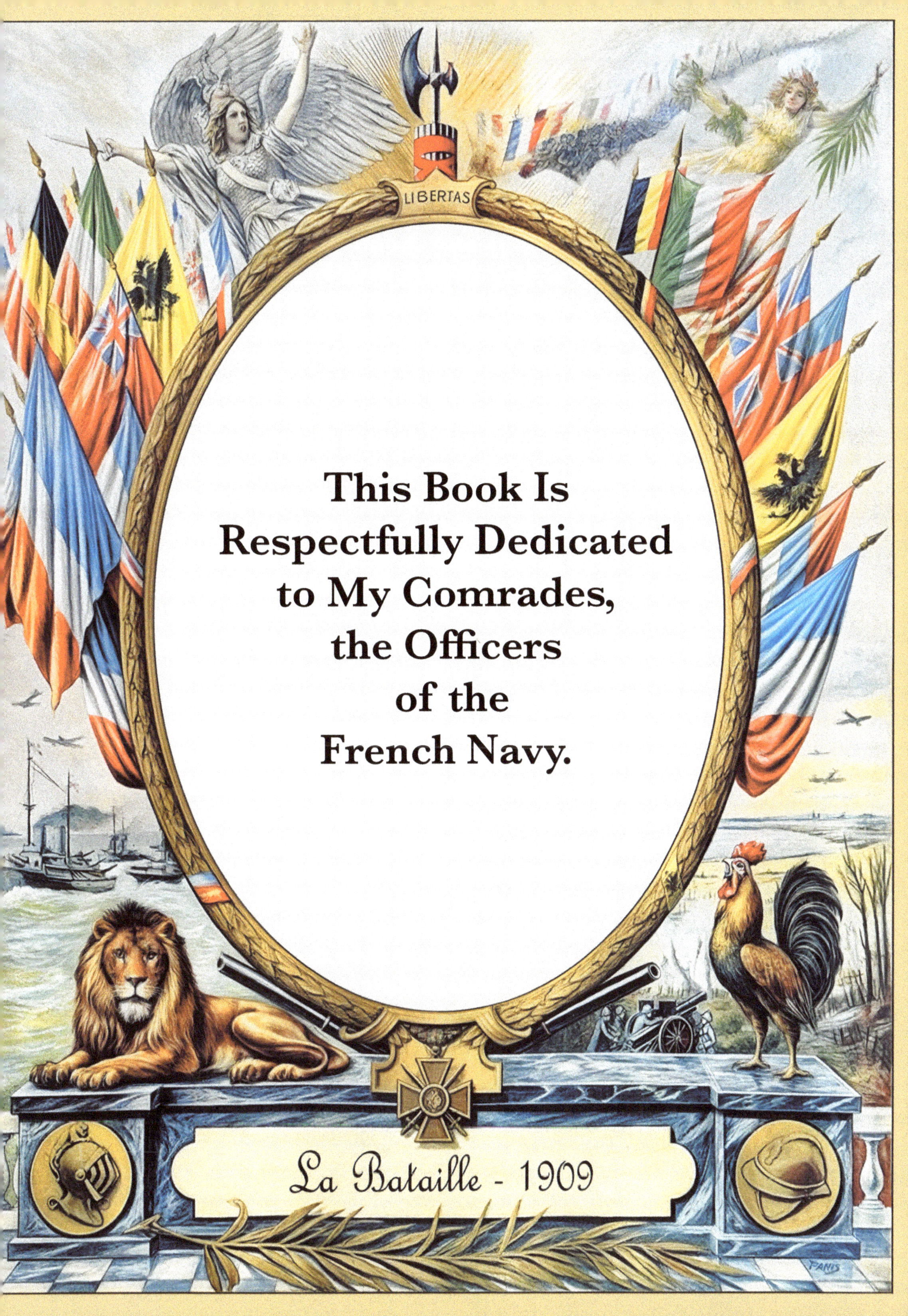

LIBERTAS
This Book Is
Respectfully Dedicated
to My Comrades,
the Officers
of the
French Navy.
La Bataille - 1909

Contents

Appendices

Preface

Idislike the somewhat vain fashion of writing prefaces for one's own books. A new novel is not so fine a figure as to need an introduction to the public by all the rules of protocol. Perhaps if the introduction served some purpose, but what could that be? A book's worth what it's worth, and all the forewords in the world won't change that. An author would be wise, then, to refrain from preliminary explanations, which are at best superfluous. Intent, by the way, is of no consequence here. What matters are the facts, the results, and not a writer's intended meaning. The only thing that counts is what he does in fact say, what he does in fact write. The public can read, and in its view the best, the clearest, the most complete of all prefaces is always the book itself.

That said, here is a preface nonetheless. It is ridiculous, I'm aware, but I'm aware, too, that in this case it is useful, perhaps even indispensable.

The book I'm offering the public today is in fact not a new book. A popular edition was published about two years ago, and this first edition, as I'm pleased to observe without vain modesty, met with fair and general success in France and even abroad.

However, as some may yet recall, and as those who will kindly leaf through the new edition will glean from the first chapter, *The Battle* is hardly a novel in the old sense of the word. It contains hardly any fiction, and scarcely more fantasy, while history and politics are at home in its pages. Moreover, a sinologist has been kind enough to discuss the plausibility of the Chinese puns that embellish some of the dialogue, and an English admiral has congratulated me for having written, as he puts it, "a very good essay on squadron fire in combat." All of this compels me to acknowledge that a great many people, and not the least estimable, have done my book the very rare honor of giving it a more careful perusal than a novel usually gets and ascribing some documentary value to the historical and scientific assertions therein. And so here I am, obliged to explain myself on these matters: for I find it intolerable that erroneous opinions should, by my own doing, have arisen and gained credit among readers too trusting of the literal word. And I certainly find it intolerable that, again by my own doing, nations friendly to France and where my book has found a readership of the curious should remain unconvinced, though they should hold it to be certain, of the high esteem and just admiration I have always had for their rare virtues, belligerent or peaceable, and for the splendid monument of art and civilization that their ancestors have bequeathed to them.

I will therefore explain myself, and the explanation, moreover, will be brief.

As for the purely historical and technical part of *The Battle* — that is, the events of the Russo-Japanese war, from 21 April 1905 to 29 May of the same year — no detail of the story is, I believe, inaccurate. A few minor errors that had slipped into the first edition have been corrected.

And I take this opportunity to extend my very respectful and cordial thanks to the many naval officers who have been kind enough to help me in this part of my task, chief among them Vice Admiral Germinet, Captains Daveluy and Mercier de Lostende, Frigate Commander Ricquer, and Ship-of-the-Line Lieutenant Vandier.

As for the exotic details — manners, descriptions of human beings and things, conversations and chat — I do not believe I have often gone astray. I have spoken only of what I have seen, and seen with my own eyes. And I have also checked each of my memories against the testimony of competent men.

I especially ask Ship-of-the-Line Lieutenant Martinie, French naval attaché at Tokyo, to accept here my tribute of heartfelt gratitude for his collaboration, as enlightened as it was friendly.

My dialogue in Chinese and Japanese, finally, is nothing more than a mosaic of ancient or modern texts, literary or popular, all authentic, and   ، whose translation into French I have verified myself. But, that said, I must address the restrictive chapter.

In *The Battle* a significant part of the novelistic fiction presents, I dare say, a symbolic interest, which, of course, alters the literal truth of the fiction.

For example, the three most important Japanese characters — Marquis Yorisaka, Marquise Mitsouko, and Viscount Hirata — are much less photographic portraits than very general paintings; the brushwork is intended to approximate a resemblance to an entire Japanese caste, whose essential features alone have been selected, and exaggerated, to make the composition more perceptible to European eyes. Shall I clarify?

Well, to cite only a fact or two, I am convinced that no Japanese
marquise has ever granted her final favors to a British officer, nor did
any Japanese ship-of-the-line lieutenant slice open his gut the evening of
the glorious victory of 27 May 1905. — But I am also convinced that to
vanquish Russia and Europe in full all of the Empire's men and women
were ready to sacrifice a thousand, nay, ten thousand cherished things,
manly honor and womanly virtue included, even if it meant later washing
away such glorious stains in the blood of their own disembowelment.

That is what I wished to say. Nothing more, nothing less.

And now that I have said it my preface is done.

C. F.
Paris, this 10 Muharram 1329*

Claude Farrère

(born Frédéric-Charles Bargone)
27 April 1876 – 21 June 1957

Career French naval officer, writing as Claude Farrère, expertly blended his
experiences at sea with literary creation. His extensive global travels, particularly

in the Far East and the Ottoman Empire, provided
authentic inspiration for his prolific output.

Farrère he first gained renown by winning
the prestigious Prix Goncourt in 1905 for *Les
Civilisés*, a novel exploring French colonial life in
Saigon. In 1909, his success continued with *La
Bataille*, his historically accurate novel set in the
Russo-Japanese War. Today, his work is celebrated
for its evocative descriptions of exotic places, naval
adventures, and explorations of different cultures.
Farrère's significant contributions to French
literature, spanning dozens of novels, stories,
and essays, earned him election to the Académie
Française in 1935.

---

* Approximately AD 12–13 January 1911. Noted for his Turkophilia, Claude Farrère dated his
early works with the Islamic Hijri calendar. This preface was absent from the original 1909 edition
of *The Battle*. Its date and content (mentioning the book's release "about two years ago") suggest
it was written for a 1911 edition. It was also reprinted in later versions, the 1925 deluxe limited
edition illustrated by Charles Fouqueray included.

THE BATTLE
MMXXV

LA BATAILLE

[Méng tzèu iue :

« Où wéi wênn wàng ki êul tchéng jênn tchè iè; houang jou ki i tchéng t'ien hià tchè hôu. »]

(*Mencius dit* :

« *Je n'ai jamais entendu dire que quelqu'un eût réformé l'Empire en se déformant soi-même; encore moins, qu'il eût réformé l'Empire en se déshonorant soi-même.* »)

孟子曰
吾未聞枉己、而正人者
也、泥辱己、以正天下
者乎。

— Catherine, Catherine!... Lis-moi
l'histoire de Brutus!...

ALFRED DE MUSSET.

[*Mêng Tzu jih:*

"*Wu wei wên wang chi, erh chêng jên chê yeh, ni ju chi, i chêng t'ien-hsia chê hu.*"][1]

(Mencius said:

"I have not heard of someone who bent himself, and at the same time made others straight; — how much less could one disgrace himself, and thereby rectify the whole empire?")[2]

孟子曰
吾未聞枉己, 而正人者也, 泥辱己, 以正天下者乎。

"Catherine, Catherine!... Read me the story of Brutus!..."[3]
—Alfred de Musset

---

1 In Pinyin: *Mèng jié rì: Wú wèi wén wǎng jǐ, ér zhèngrén zhě yě, ní rǔ jǐ, yǐ zhèng tiānxià zhě hū.*

2 Confucius, James Legge (trans.), *The Four Books*, The Works of Mencius, Book V, Wan Chang, Part I, Chapter VII, ¶ 7.

3 From Alfred de Musset's (1810–57) play *Lorenzaccio*, which, though written in 1833, was not performed until 1896. This line reveals Lorenzo's obsession with tyrannicide and his internal conflict as he plots to assassinate his cousin, the Duke. Lorenzo's request to hear the story of Brutus, the assassin of Julius Caesar, underscores his moral ambiguity and the difficult choices before him. His repetition of "Catherine," the name of a woman of ambiguous social standing and intimate acquaintance, further underscores his turmoil and isolation. Catherine's role as a confidante yet not a clear lover or servant adds to the play's atmosphere of intrigue. With this quotation Farrère no doubt seeks to frame the Battle of Tsushima within a broader context of historical tragedy and moral complexity.

I

The White Peril

In front of a towering bamboo fence that bordered the left side of the path the *kuruma* came to a sudden stop, and the kurumaya, the man-runner —horse and coachman in one[4] — lowered the lightweight shafts to the ground.

Felze — Jean-François Felze, of the Institut de France[5] — stepped out.

"*Yorisaka kōshaku?*"[6] he inquired, not so sure he'd been understood earlier, before climbing aboard, when he'd mumbled, in his pidgin Japanese, an address learned by heart: "To Marquis Yorisaka's, at his villa on Stork Hill, near the great Suwa Shrine, above Nagasaki..."

But the *kurumaya* prostrated himself, bowing deep in utmost respect.

"*Sayo de gozaimasu!*"[7] he replied.

And Felze, recognizing this most courteous conjugation, not always employed with Barbarians, recalled the persistent veneration that modern-day Japan has retained for its aristocracy of yore. The *daimyo* are no more, but their sons — the princes, marquises, and counts — have kept their

---

4 *Kuruma* means car, carriage, wheel, or, as here, rickshaw. *Kurumaya* means vendor of wagons, cartwright, or, as here, rickshaw-puller.

5 France's academy of arts, letters, and sciences.

6 Marquis Yorisaka. "Marquis" (侯爵, *kōshaku*) was the second-highest rank within the *Kazoku* (華族), the hereditary peerage system of the Empire of Japan (established 1869/1884, abolished 1947). Ranking below Prince/Duke and above Count, Viscount, and Baron, the title of Marquis was typically bestowed upon heads of the most prominent former *daimyō* (feudal lord) families or certain high-ranking court nobles (*kuge*), signifying elite status within the Meiji-era social structure and granting automatic membership in the House of Peers.

7 So honorably it is. (Yes.) [Author's note.]

feudal prestige intact.[8]

Jean-François Felze had meanwhile knocked on the villa's door. A Japanese maid, bedecked in a robe with a big belt, opened up and, in proper fashion, all but dropped to all fours before the visitor.

"*Yorisaka kōshaku fujin?*" said Felze this time, asking not for the marquis but for the marquise.

To which the maid replied with a phrase that Felze did not understand but evidently corresponded to the Western phrase "Madame is receiving."

Jean-François Felze proffered his card and followed the Japanese woman's short, hopping steps through the courtyard.

It was about square, this courtyard, though less deep than wide, and they trod on its surface of tiny black pebbles, as clean and shiny as beads of marble. Astonished, Felze bent down to pick one up:

"My word!" he muttered into his mustache, letting the pebble fall, "they must wash each one every morning with soap and hot water!"

❉

The veranda of this broad, low wooden house rested on simple polished trunks. Between two of these rustic columns, at the top of a small porch, a door opened, and an expanse of spotless white mats spread from the threshold.

Felze, versed in the customs, began to remove his shoes, but the servant, already prostrate again, with forehead to the ground, respectfully stopped him.

"Huh," Felze now mumbled in surprise. "Shoes on in the house of a Japanese marquise?"

His taste for the exotic vaguely disappointed, Felze resigned himself to removing nothing but his hat. This was a light, broad-brimmed felt in the style of Van Dyck, and it crowned the head of an impenitent old man, an enthusiastic if gray head, the head of a true artist who had won fame but remained an apprentice.

Bare-headed and shod, Jean-François Felze entered the drawing room of Marquise Yorisaka.

----

8   The *daimyo* were powerful Japanese feudal lords who, from the tenth century to the early Meiji period, in the mid-nineteenth, ruled most of Japan from their vast, hereditary landholdings. They were subordinate to the Shōgun and nominally to the emperor and the *kuge* (a Japanese aristocratic class). The term is derived from *dai*, meaning large, and *myō*, an abbreviation of *myōden*, meaning private land.

… A very elegant, very fashionable Parisian boudoir that would have been banal as could be were it not three thousand leagues from the Monceau plain.[9] Nothing in it suggested Japan. The very mats — the tatami, a national institution, thicker and softer than any rug in the world — had given way to carpets of deep wool. The walls were clad in Pompadour tapestries and the windows — with glass panes! — draped in damask curtains. Chairs, armchairs, a wing chair, and a sofa had taken the place of the classic mats of rice straw or dark velvet. Cluttered up one corner was an Erard grand piano, and facing the entrance door was a Louis XV mirror, no doubt surprised now to be reflecting the darling little miens of yellow *mousmés*,[10] rather than of French girls.

The little servant performed for a third time her reverence on all fours and then left, leaving Felze alone.

Felze took two steps, looked to the right, looked to the left, and spat an oath:

"Good God! Why be sons to Hokusai[11] and Utamaro,[12] grandsons to the great Sesshu![13] ... why belong to the race that sired Nikko and Kyoto,[14] to the genial race that covered the unspoiled land of the Ainu[15] with palaces

---

9 In 1778 the future Philippe-Égalité purchased an expanse from several landowners in the village of Monceaux and had it transformed into a park, in the English style, called La Folie-de-Chartres. About half of this "land of illusion" was in 1861 transformed into what is now the Parc Monceau, one of the most fashionable parks in Paris.

10 From the Japanese *musume*, meaning young girl, daughter, or sometimes, in colonial context, mistress.

11 Katsushika Hokusai (1760–1849), known simply as Hokusai, was a Japanese artist of the Edo period (1603–1868), active as both a painter and printmaker. He is best known for the woodblock print series *Thirty-Six Views of Mount Fuji*, which includes the iconic print *The Great Wave off Kanagawa*. He is also renowned for his erotica; for example, *The Dream of the Fisherman's Wife* depicting a woman, evidently an *ama* (shell diver), enveloped in the sexual grip of two octopi. Farrere was an admirer as well. In his 1905 Prix Goncourt-winning novel, *The Civilized*, his protagonist Fierce keeps a collection of Hokusai's erotic prints in his cabin aboard the *Bayard*, a copy of *The Dream* included. See pp. 77–78 in *The Civilized–Decadence and Damnation in French Indochina*, DatAsia Press, 2025.

12 Kitagawa Utamaro (c. 1753–1806) was a Japanese artist primarily known for his *ukiyo-e* woodblock prints, specializing in *bijin-ga* (pictures of beautiful women). He is best known for his *ōkubi-e* ("large-headed pictures") from the 1790s, which focused on the subtle beauty and details of female subjects.

13 Though not as famous as Hokusai or Utamaro, Sesshu (1712–84) is one of the most influential *ukiyo-e* painters of the mid-Edo period. There is no evidence that Hokusai or Utamaro was directly related to Sesshu or his family.

14 Nikko and Kyoto are cities of historical and cultural significance. Nikkō, in Tochigi Prefecture, north of Tokyo, is home to the famous Toshogu Shrine, dedicated to Tokugawa Ieyasu, founder of the Tokugawa shogunate. Kyoto, in the Kansai region, was Japan's imperial capital for over a thousand years (both *kyo-to* and *to-kyo* mean capital city or emperor's residence) and is known for traditional arts and crafts, such as pottery, textiles, and lacquerware.

15 The Ainu are an indigenous people believed to have lived in Hokkaido, Sakhalin, and the

and temples, creating from scratch a new architecture, a new sculpture, and a new painting! ... why have the unheard-of good fortune to live ten centuries in the most splendid isolation, free of all the despotic influences that have gelded our Western originality, free of the Egyptian yoke, free of the Hellenic yoke![16] ... why have had China to serve as an impenetrable rampart against Europe, and Confucius[17] as a watchdog against Plato![18] ... why indeed have had all this only to stumble at the end of the race, only to end up plagiarizing and aping, only to end up here, in a cage fit for the worst parrots of Paris and London, or even of New York and Chicago?...

He stopped short. An idea flitted across his mind. He went to a window, drew aside the curtain...

Kuril Islands for thousands of years before the arrival of the Japanese. Distinct in language, culture, and traditions, they lived as hunter-gatherers and fishermen.

16   As Felze observes, the Japanese developed outside the influence of the ancient Egyptian and Greek (Hellenic) civilizations that gave rise to Western philosophy, literature, art, architecture, and science.

17   Confucius (c. 551 – c. 479 BC), a fundamental Chinese philosopher, associated with the *Analects*, a collection of sayings attributed to him and his disciples. Confucian interpretations of China's classics served in imperial times to train the lettered men who ran the bureaucracy and to transmit the ancient sacrificial system (*Stanford Encyclopedia of Philosophy*).

18   Plato (c. 427/24 – c. 347 BC), Greek philosopher and author of the Socratic and other dialogues.

And through the glass, under his feet, he saw a Japanese garden.

A true Japanese garden: a small square, ten meters long, fifteen wide, and pressed against the house by three high, high walls, but a square of real symbolism, presenting to the eye mountains and plains, forests, a waterfall, a torrent, caves, and a lake — all it, of course, in miniature. The trees, then, were of those dwarf cedars, no taller than an ear of grain, that only Japan can properly shrink, or tiny cherry trees, in bloom as the season required, for it was April 15; the mountains were molehills cleverly fashioned into jutting sierras, and the lake of red fish, set, for verisimilitude, between picturesque shores green or rocky.[19]

Astounded, Felze looked on wide-eyed. Within him, however, the painter had the first word:

"With gardens like this, it's no wonder that when it comes to perspective these people, these prodigies of drawing and color, have always gone off the rails into pure fantasy!"

He considered the baroque silhouette of the tiny rocks and the tiny trees, seen from above, foreshortened.

But soon he shrugged. Phooey! This garden hardly counted. Indeed, the more he thought about it the less real it seemed. It was too small, too separated from the outside world, from the real and living world that flourished around it… It was like a simulacrum, a shadow of the Japan of yesteryear, abolished, proscribed by the will of the present-day Japanese…

Yet when you peered over the walls and surveyed the surrounding countryside, glanced down the slope of Stork Hill, to admire the distant view in full, the hills splendidly arrayed in green camphor and snowy cherry, with temples on their summits, and villages on their flanks, and you saw, at the edge of the fjord, the brown and bluish town, its countless houses dotting the shore all the way to the blurred horizon of the last cape — oh! then you no longer found the Japan of yesteryear to have been abolished or proscribed … for the city and the villages and the temples and the hills bore the indelible ancient mark, and looked like — could indeed have been confused with — some old print from the time of the Shōgun, some meticulous *kakemono*,[20] where the brush of

---

19 Japanese gardens reflect Japan's ancient philosophical ideal of harmony between man and nature, and are often laid out for viewing from a particular angle. In traditional Japanese houses the garden is located in the center, visible from every room, and considered an extension of the living space. Its design reflects the house's aesthetic and blurs the line between interior and exterior.

20 A *kakemono* (literally "hanging thing"), more commonly referred to as a *kakejiku* ("hung scroll"), is a hanging scroll used to display a painting, calligraphic inscription, or other design. It is usually

an artist dead for centuries had eternalized the wonders of a Hojo or Ashikaga[21] capital…

For a long while Felze considered the landscape in silence, then turned back to the boudoir, and the contrast hurt his eyes. The still-untamed Far East and the invasive Far West were here face to face, on either side of the pane.

"Hum!" thought Felze, "perhaps the serious threat to Japanese civilization right now is coming not from Linevich's troops[22] or Rozhestvensky's ships[23] but from this … the peaceful invasion … the white peril…"

He was about to utter a cliché in reverse when a wee voice interrupted him. It was singsong and strange, but also soft, and spoke French with no accent.

"Oh! Dear master!… How flustered I am to have kept you waiting so long!…"

The Marquise Yorisaka had entered the room and was offering her hand for a kiss.

---

mounted with silk fabric edges on a flexible backing, so that it can be rolled up for storage.

21   The Hojo were a clan of samurai, skilled in battle, and rose to power in the late twelfth century. They held sway for centuries, through a system of alliances and strategic marriages, until defeated by the forces of Toyotomi Hideyoshi, in the late sixteenth century.

The Ashikaga, another samurai clan, rose to power in the mid-fourteenth century, established the Ashikaga shogunate (1336–1573), and famously patronized the arts and promoted Zen Buddhism. Its reign, often called the Muromachi period, is known for political instability and such cultural developments as the tea ceremony, Noh theater, and ink painting.

22   This almost certainly refers to Nikolai Petrovich Linevich (1839–1909), the Russian general who succeeded Aleksey Kuropatkin as Commander-in-Chief of the Russian armies in Manchuria in March 1905, holding the command through the end of the Russo-Japanese War. He had previous experience in the Russo-Turkish War (1877–78) and the Boxer Rebellion.

23   Zinovy Rozhestvensky (1864–1927) was an admiral in the Imperial Russian Navy. He saw action during the Russo-Turkish War (1877–78) and later served as a naval attaché in London, where he studied the Royal Navy's tactics and technologies. In 1904 he was appointed commander of the Baltic Fleet and tasked with leading a squadron to reinforce the Russian Pacific Fleet during the Russo-Japanese War. This would lead to the Battle of Tsushima. Rozhestvensky retired in 1917 and, after the Russian Revolution, emigrated to France, where he died in 1927.

II

An Idol or a Trinket

Jean-François Felze liked to think himself a philosopher, and perhaps he was one — inasmuch, at least, as a Western man can be. For instance, it was effortless for him to adopt the customs, manners, and even dress of the peoples he would visit on his travels around the world. A moment ago, at the door of the house, he had wanted to remove his shoes, in keeping with Japanese courtesies, but now, of course, in this French salon, echoing as it was with French words, exoticism would no longer do.

So Jean-François Felze bowed as he would have in Paris and kissed the extended hand.

Then, with his quick and piercing painterly eye, he examined his hostess.

The Marquise Yorisaka was wearing a gown from Doucet, Callot, or Worth,[24] as was plain to see, for this gown — graceful, well-made, even fetching, but also conceived, imagined, invented by a European for Europeans — took on an extraordinary import and volume around the fragile, slender Japanese woman, like a vast frame of gilded wood around a watercolor the size of a hand. To top it all off, Marquise Yorisaka's hair was done up in a manner opposite to tradition: no glossy shell, no wide bands to wrap the entirety of the face, and instead an elongated chignon, with all the hair drawn back to leave her head bare of the classic ebony turban. This made it look tiny and round, like a doll's.

Pretty? … Felze, a painter who loved the beauty of women, wondered with a sort of anxiety. Was Marquise Yorisaka pretty? … A Westerner

---

24 Three contributors to women's haute couture in the early twentieth century.

Jacques Doucet (1853–1929) produced elegant, sophisticated designs with delicate fabrics, lace, and embroidery. His evening gowns, a specialty, were often made with layers of silk and chiffon and decorated with intricate beading.

Madeleine Vionnet (1876–1975), who worked with her sisters under the name Callot Soeurs, was known for innovative designs, bias-cut fabrics, and flowing, ethereal dresses that emphasized the body's natural curves.

Charles Frederick Worth (1825–95), an Englishman, is widely considered the father of haute couture. He founded the House of Worth in Paris in 1858 and became known for opulent and extravagant designs, with luxurious fabrics, intricate embroidery, and beading. He would make historical references in his designs.

would rather have called her ugly, because the eyes were too narrow, and so drawn to the temples as to resemble two long oblique slits; because the neck was too spindly; because of the white and pink expanse of her overly broad cheeks, rouged and powdered beyond the pale. For a man of Nippon, however, Marquise Yorisaka must have been beautiful. And wherever she was, be it Europe or Asia, the same strange charm, at once disdainful and naive, puerile and hieratic, would have emanated mysteriously from this small creature of slow gestures, pensive forehead, and darling pout; one could mistake her alternately for an idol or a trinket.

"Which of the two?" wondered Felze.

He had kissed the little hand, smooth as a bauble of yellow ivory. And now, refusing to be first to sit, he said:

"Pray, Madame, do not apologize… I have not had leisure enough even to admire your salon and garden…"

Marquise Yorisaka raised her hand, as if to fend off the compliment.

"Oh! Dear master!… You tease, you tease! … Our poor gardens are so ridiculous, as we are all too aware! … As for the parlor, it's my husband who deserves your praise. He's the one who furnished the whole villa, before he brought me here … For, as you know, this is not home for us. Our home[25]

---

25   The word appears in English.

is in Tokyo … But Tokyo is so far from Sasebo[26] that naval officers cannot make it out there on leave … So …"

"Ah," said Felze, "so Marquis Yorisaka is on duty at Sasebo?"

"Yes, of course. Didn't he tell you yesterday, when he went to visit you, aboard the *Yseult?* … His battleship is under repairs at the arsenal — or at least I think it is. After all, these aren't the sorts of things that one tells women … As for yesterday, though, I have not yet extended my thanks to you, dear master! It's really too kind of you to have agreed to do this portrait. We know it was most improper to venture all the way to that yacht, where you're not quite at home, and seek you out … It was all my husband could do to muster the courage … And what a portrait! … A little person like me painted by a master like you! … I shall be terribly proud! Just think of it! You've surely never painted a Japanese woman, have you? Never until now? I shall be the Empire's first woman in a portrait by Jean-François Felze!…"

She clapped, like a baby, and in an instant turned serious:

"Above all, I shall be delighted that, thanks to you, my husband will have me at his side, after a fashion, in his officer's quarters, aboard his ship … A portrait is almost a double of oneself, is it not? So a double of me will be going out there, to sea, and might even witness some battles; there is news that the Russian fleet passed before Singapore last Saturday…"

"My God," said Felze, laughing, "we're going to have to execute this portrait in the heroic style! … But I was unaware that Marquis Yorisaka had to return so promptly to the theater of war… And I understand all the better his desire to take along, as you so aptly put it, your double."

The tiny mouth, done up in a deep carmine that served to narrow it further, parted for an unexpected, very Japanese laugh:

"Oh, the desire is somewhat extraordinary, I know! … It's the fashion in Japan to seem not to be in love with one's wife. The Marquis and I, though, we lived so long in Europe that we have become quite the Westerners…"

"It's true," said Felze. "I remember well: Marquis Yorisaka was a naval attaché in Paris."

"For four years! … The first four years of our marriage… We returned only at the end of the autumn before last, just in time for the

---

26 Sasebo is a city in Nagasaki Prefecture with a significant maritime history. Sasebo Naval District, founded in 1886, became the major port for the Japanese navy during the First Sino-Japanese War and Russo-Japanese War, and remained a major naval base through the Second World War.

declaration of war. I was still in Paris for the Salon of 1903, where I so admired your *Aziyadé!*…"[27]

Felze, with the slightest jest, saluted:

"And it was while looking at this *Aziyadé* that you formed the desire to commission a portrait by my hand?"

The Japanese laugh danced again on the small painted mouth, this time concluding in a Parisian pout:

"Oh, dear master! You are teasing again! … Of course not. I wouldn't wish to resemble that pretty little savage you painted in her extraordinary costume, weeping like a madwoman and staring I know not where…"

"Looking towards a door through which someone has gone out…"

"Is that so? … In any case, it's not a portrait! And I saw your portraits as well … the one of Mrs. Mary Garden, the one of the Duchess of Versailles, and especially the one of the lovely Mrs. Hockley…"

"Ah! Especially that one?"

"Oh yes! … Naturally, I never foresaw then that you would one day arrive in Nagasaki, aboard the lady's yacht, but her portrait was so good! I preferred it to all the others for that marvelous gown. You remember, dear master? A princess's gown, entirely of black velvet, with the top of the bodice in *point d'Angleterre* over a diaphanous satin of ivory hue! … In fact, I had this very dress made with Mrs. Hockley's gown in mind, and I've chosen it to pose in…"

Felze arched his brow:

"To pose in? You'd like to pose in that dress?"

"Why, yes? … Is it not suitable?"

"It couldn't be more suitable, but I thought that for an intimate portrait you wouldn't choose a *toilette de ville*,[28] especially as it's going to be less a real portrait than a sketch … We have a fortnight at best, no? Wouldn't you like to be painted in the delicious garb of your grandmothers,

---

27   *Aziyadé* (1879) is a semi-autobiographical novel based on a diary Pierre Loti kept when stationed for three months in Greece and Constantinople (now Istanbul) in the fall and winter of 1876. It tells of 27-year-old Loti's illicit love affair with an 18-year-old "Circassian" harem girl named Aziyadé. Pierre Loti was the pseudonym of Louis Marie-Julien Viaud (1850–1923), a French naval officer and writer of exotic novels and short stories. Our author, Claude Farrère, served under Viaud's command in the navy and developed a lifelong friendship with him.

    The reference to an *Aziyadé* painting at the Salon of 1903 is fictional, but Farrère would have known at least one *Aziyadé* by Jean-Léon Gérôme (1824–1904), whose paintings were widely reproduced. In 1876 he painted a scene from Loti's book in which the French naval officer is seated on a divan and Aziyadé stands behind him holding a hookah. The scene is of a luxurious room, with richly patterned carpets and textiles, and a view of the Bosporus in the background.

28   Literally, attire or dress for the city.

one of those kimonos, emblazoned with your coat of arms, that all our pretty Parisians have begun to borrow from you?"

A peculiar glance slipped through the slit of the all but closed eyelids:

"Oh, dear master! … You are too indulgent towards our old fashions … I but rarely put on the garb of our grandmothers, as you call it … Very rarely indeed!... And then, you understand, it would certainly not please my husband to have my likeness clad in a costume he barely knows — that he barely knows and does not care for … We are quite, quite the Westerners, the marquis and I."

"Very well!" said Felze, resigned.

And to himself he said:

"As Western as she likes, but it will nonetheless be an ignoble affair, this half-European, half-Japanese portrait! Ignoble and, by God, sinister to paint!"

Marquise Yorisaka had in the meantime rung the bell, and two maids — in Japanese garb! — carried in, on a great platter, all the trappings of an English tea: stove, silver teapot and sugar bowl, cups with handles, saucers, napkins, cream pot…

"You will of course take a little cake, or some toasted bread? … It needs to steep a bit … It's from Ceylon, of course."

"Of course," echoed Felze, docile.

He was thinking of the light, delicate green tea one drinks without sugar or milk in village *ochaya*[29] while nibbling a slice of a never-hardening cake called *kasutera*.[30]

But he drank down the brown, thick, astringent British drug and ate the Viennese pastry.

"And now," said Marquise Yorisaka, "as you were so kind as to have your paint box, easel, and canvas sent here yesterday, we shall start whenever you like, dear master. Let's see. Shall we work out the pose right away? Is the light good here?"

Felze was going to answer, but the opening door did not give him time.

"Oh," exclaimed the marquise, "I forgot to warn you … Would you mind an encounter here with our great friend Commander Fergan — Commander Fergan of the British navy, a most intimate friend? … He was supposed to come for tea today, and here is my husband leading him in."

---

29 The patrons of an *ochaya* (teahouse) are entertained by geisha. Today, *ochaya* refers to geisha houses in Kyoto, but it sometimes denotes establishments outside the old capital.

30 Also known as Castella, a traditional Japanese confectionery. The batter is poured into large square or rectangular molds, baked in an oven, and cut into long rectangles. *Mizuame*, a type of sugar syrup, gives Castella a moist texture.

III

Honeycomb…or Mystery?

"**M**itsouko, would you introduce the commander to Mr. Felze?" Marquis Yorisaka had stepped aside at the parlor's threshold to let his guest enter. His voice, a bit guttural but clear and measured, seemed to command rather than request, despite the courtesy of his words.

And Marquise Yorisaka gave a small nod before obeying:

"Dear master, if you please, this is Commander Herbert Fergan, aide-de-camp to His Majesty the King of England. And, Commander, this is Mr. Jean-François Felze, from the Institut de France! … Pray, sit down, all of you."

She turned to her husband:

"Have you had a pleasant walk, with the fine weather?"

"Yes, most pleasant. Thank you."

He had taken a seat next to the English officer.

"Please, Mitsouko … the tea," he said.

She hastened to serve.

Jean-François Felze looked on.

The scene, playing out in European decor, was decidedly European. The two men — Englishman and Japanese, the latter in a black, gold-buttoned uniform, patterned after the uniform of every other Western navy, the former in the civilian dress of an afternoon, as he would have worn in London or Portsmouth — could have been taking tea at the house of any lady whatsoever, and the young woman was an adept and quick hostess, graceful as she leaned in to offer a brimming cup… Felze no longer saw the Asian face but only the line of the body: almost the same, under the Parisian dress, as the body of a petite French or Spanish woman… In truth, nothing suggested Asia, not even Marquis Yorisaka's flat, yellow face, plain as it was to see, and shown to advantage in the harsh light from the glazed windows; here again was Europe, touching up this Japanese face, raising the hair to a scissor-cut bristle, lengthening the coarse moustache, broadening the neck in an ample detachable collar. Marquis Yorisaka, former student of the French Naval Academy, and ship-of-the-line lieutenant in the very modern squadron that had just defeated Makarov[31] and Wright,[32] and was in preparation to fight Rozhestvensky,[33] had tried so hard to resemble his teachers of yesterday, and even his opponents of today, that to the curious eye of Jean-François Felze he was all but indistinguishable from the English naval captain sitting next to him.

And this very Englishman, with his courteous and familiar air of a man of the world on a visit to friends, made it plain that this house was indeed no exotic and bizarre dwelling — the dwelling of two creatures without a drop of Aryan blood coursing through their veins — but the normal, banal house of a couple whose sort was to be found by the million on the earth's three continents, a cosmopolitan and civilized couple, in whom the leveling work of centuries had erased all racial character, all singularity of origin, and all vestige of the provincial or national customs of the past.

"Mr. Felze," said Commander Fergan, the first to speak, "I've had the honor of admiring several beautiful paintings of yours, for you cannot be unaware that you are even more famous in London than in Paris… Though it's true, too, that I lived for a long time in France, where I was a naval attaché at the same time as the marquis… Pray, accept my congratulations nonetheless on the charming portrait that your stopover in Nagasaki has procured for you. I believe, in truth, that at this point in its history the

------

31   Stepan Makarov (1849–1904) was an admiral in the Imperial Russian Navy known for his pioneering tactics and the development of torpedo boats and minesweepers. Makarov saw action in the Black Sea During the Russo-Turkish War (1877–78) and was later appointed commander of the torpedo-boat flotilla. He also served as a naval attaché in France and played a key role in the development of the Russian torpedo-boat fleet. In 1904, during the Russo-Japanese War, Makarov was made commander of the Russian Pacific Fleet and fought in the Battle of Port Arthur. He died in April 1904, when his flagship, the *Petropavlovsk*, struck a mine and sank.

32   Appearing as Witheft in the original text, an apparent misspelling referring to Walter Withers Wright (1869–1954), an officer of the British Royal Navy who saw action during the Boxer Rebellion in China (1900) and served as commander of the battleship *HMS Superb* during the Russo-Japanese War. He played a key role in the destruction of the Russian battleship *Rostislav* during the Battle of the Yellow Sea. During the First World War Withers Wright continued to serve in the Royal Navy and was promoted to rear admiral. He retired from active service in 1924.

33   Zinovy Petrovich Rozhestvensky (1848–1909) was an admiral in the Imperial Russian Navy. During the Russo-Japanese War (1904–05) he commanded Russia's Second Pacific Squadron, steaming the battleship fleet over 18,000 miles (29,000 km) to engage the enemy in the decisive Battle of Tsushima.

In 1906, along with all of his surviving battleship commanders, Rozhestvensky faced a court-martial for the disaster. Some faced prison or even the firing squad, for losing the battle or surrendering on the high seas. The Tsar commuted the captains' death sentences to short prison terms and pardoned the remaining officers. Rozhestvensky lived his last years as a recluse in St. Petersburg, dying of a heart attack at age sixty.

women of Japan are the most interesting and attractive that the female sex can offer us today… And I envy you, Mr. Felze: you who are to employ your wonderful talent to capture on canvas the face and gaze of one of these superior ladies, superior to their elder sisters in Europe or America… Do not protest, madame, lest you force me to reveal all to Mr. Felze, and especially to compliment him on his greatest stroke of luck: having for his model not this or that of your most seductive compatriots but you yourself, the most seductive of all…"

He was smiling, to mitigate with an air of mirth his overly direct praise. He was impeccably polite and correct as a man, and the status of aide-de-camp to a king seemed, as it were, visible on his person. He had the neat, masculine elegance of the Englishman of good breeding, and his shaved lip, his flat forehead, his bright eye, and the touch of irony in his smile ranged him in a separate category from that of the ale drinkers and raw-beef eaters. The English School has painted such portraits of baronets and lords, sons of eighteenth-century Tory gentlemen to rival our French counts or dukes.

The officers are much younger in the British navy than in ours, and this one, despite his rank and the probable importance of his mission to Japan, seemed an absolute youngster. Marquis Yorisaka, a mere ship-of-the-line lieutenant, was only slightly younger. Felze, by instinct, drew a comparison, and thought that perhaps Marquise Yorisaka too had compared them.

"Mitsouko," asked the Marquis, "is Mr. Felze satisfied with your attire? How will you be posing?"

Felze recalled accordingly that Marquis Yorisaka had no fondness for the old Japanese fashions:

"I am quite satisfied," he said with a hint of irony, "quite satisfied. And I hope to carry off a portrait that will look nothing like an ordinary painting… As for the pose, let us leave that aside for now. It is my habit, even with a hurried job like this, first to sketch my model from all sides and in all attitudes. In this way I produce twelve or fifteen drafts that serve as a kind of a living repertoire, where I can always, and quite naturally, find the most apt and best pose. Have no concern, then, for your painter, madame… Sit, chat, rise, walk, and pay no heed to the album doodler who from time to time gives a stroke of the pencil while looking at you."

He had opened a notebook of grey canvas and was already drawing on his lap as he spoke.

"Now, *here*, Mitsouko," observed Marquis Yorisaka with a smile, "is a way of posing that is bound to please you."

Felze had paused, pencil in the air:

"Mitsouko?" he inquired. "Excuse an ignoramus who knows not three words of Japanese… Is Mitsouko your first name, madame?"

She seemed almost apologetic:

"Yes!… Something of a strange name, is it not?"

"No stranger than any other. A pretty name — and, above all, most feminine. Mitsouko: it has a sweet sound…"

Commander Fergan concurred:

"I agree completely, Mr. Felze. Mitsouko… Mitsou… The sound is very sweet, and so is the meaning, because *mitsou* in Japanese means 'honeycomb.'"

Marquis Yorisaka set his empty cup on the tray.

"Yes," he said, "'honeycomb,' or, when written with another Chinese character, 'mystery.'"

Jean-François Felze looked up at his host. Marquis Yorisaka was beaming a kindly smile, and there was certainly not the slightest insinuation behind it.

"As for me," he added right away, "my name is Sadao, which means nothing at all."

Felze thought:

"Sadao… But his wife is careful not to address him so familiarly, and no doubt employs the famous honorific mode even in private. This might mean something."

He could not withhold an offhand remark:

"Sadao?… Just now, when Marquise Yorisaka was addressing you, I thought I heard…"

A chuckle preceded the reply:

"Oh no, you did not hear… A good Japanese woman hardly ever addresses her husband, for fear that she will be impolite… A remnant of old custom! We were not formerly a very feminist nation. In the days of old Japan, before the Great Change of 1868,[34] our spouses were almost slaves. As you can see, they still remember in the mouth, only in the mouth…"

He laughed again, and gallantly kissed his wife's hand. As Felze observed, however, the gesture was stiff and somewhat awkward. Apparently, it wasn't every day that Marquis Yorisaka kissed Mitsouko's hand.

Perhaps noticing his guest's overly keen eye, the marquis suddenly turned loquacious:

"Life has changed so much in Japan over the past forty years! Books have of course explained this transformation to you Europeans, but

---

34 Before, that is, the Meiji Restoration, when samurai from the Chōshū and Satsuma domains overthrew the Tokugawa shogunate, which had ruled since 1603. Emperor Meiji's government brought feudalism to an end, established a constitution, and reformed the economy and the military. It also abolished the samurai class and, in general, opened the country up to Western influence.

books will explain while showing nothing. Can you imagine the life of
a daimyo's wife in my grandfather's time, dear master? The poor thing
was a prisoner in the depths of a feudal castle: a prisoner and, what's
worse, a servant to her own servants — the samurai gentlemen, the
least of whom would have blushed to humiliate his two swords before a
mirror…[35] In France you would say before a distaff. Just think: *bushidō*,[36]

---

35   "The mirror is woman's soul, just as the sword is the warrior's." Japanese proverb. [Author's note.]

36   Literally "the way of the warrior." The samurai code of Japan's feudal era. A blend of

our ancient code of honor, set women lower than dirt and men higher than the heavens. In the prison-castle where she dwelled a daimyo's wife could meditate at her leisure on this uncontested axiom. The prince would be absent all day, and sometimes at nightfall would barely deign to enter the conjugal chamber. The princess slave, under constant neglect, would busy herself obeying her husband's mother, who would never fail to abuse the authority granted her, without appeal or limit, by the Chinese rites. To such a fate would the wife of daimyo Yorisaka Sadao have been condemned forty years ago — a fate escaped today by the wife of a mere naval officer, your servant, who himself strives not to yearn for the barbarous times! ... It is more comfortable to rejoice in the company of learned and indulgent guests, even in a hovel like this, than to languish in solitude and ignorance at some Tosa or Chōshū[37] manor."

He dropped the old illustrious names with disdain.

"...And it is also more honorable to serve aboard a battleship of His Majesty the Emperor's than to rove the countryside at the head of some band of pillaging warriors in the Shōgun's pay — the Shōgun's or a common clan leader's."[38]

Pausing, he picked a box up off the tea table, opened it, and offered the Turkish cigarettes within to the two Europeans.

"It is after all entirely to you, gentlemen, that we owe the progress we now enjoy every day. We shall never forget. Nor shall we forget the patience and good grace you have shown as educators. Your student was without a doubt thoroughly backward, and his intelligence, gone numb with centuries of routine, struggled mightily to accept Western teaching. Your lessons have nonetheless borne fruit. Perhaps the day will come at

---

Confucianism and Zen Buddhism, it was shaped by centuries of warfare and conflict. Moral and intellectual development — loyalty, honor, self-discipline — were as important as martial skill. Samurai were to embody *bushidō* in all aspects of their lives.

37   Two powerful domains of the feudal era. The Tosa domain, on the southern coast of Honshu, Japan's main island, produced swords of high quality and was home to many skilled samurai. During the Meiji Restoration many of these samurai sought to overthrow the Tokugawa shogunate and establish of a new government under Emperor Meiji. The Chōshū domain, in western Japan, was militant and xenophobic, and also helped overthrow the Tokugawa shogunate, many of its samurai leading the charge against the shogunate's forces.

38   The term *shōgun*, meaning "general," refers to the military leaders who ruled Japan during its feudal era, from the twelfth to the mid-nineteenth century. Originally appointed by the emperor to lead military campaigns, the Shōgun grew in power and, with the support of samurai, came to exercise political control over Japan, through a system of feudal domains. The most famous shogunate was the Tokugawa (1603–1868). The shogunate was abolished in 1868, with the Meiji Restoration, when the emperor was restored to power.

last when a new, truly civilized Japan will do its masters proud."

He had approached Marquise Yorisaka, to present the Turkish box to her as well. She seemed to hesitate for a moment, then, quickly, grabbed a cigarette and lit it herself, without his ever thinking to offer her a light. He was bringing his tirade to a close, and cast at Jean-François Felze a sharp glance whose gleam was suddenly veiled by the flutter of yellow lids.

"Imperfect as we remain, you are already, out of extreme kindness, applauding our victories over Russia's armies… From the start you have rendered us able to fight with advantage for our independence."

He concluded, bowing a bit lower than a Westerner would have done:

"To say Russian is to say Asian, and we Japanese intend soon to become European. Our victory, then, is as much yours as it is ours, for it is the victory of Europe over Asia. Take it as tribute, and suffer to accept our most humble gratitude."

IV

Comrades in Arms, Brothers…

Mr. Felze," said Commander Herbert Fergan, "you're no doubt on your way back to the American yacht." The painter had finished his first session and was taking leave of the Yorisakas. "I'm headed that way. If you'd like to make way together?…"

And so together they left, on foot, walking side by side.

The road snaked along the hillside. Suburban country houses clustered ahead, at the foot of the slope, their roofs the color of dead leaves. To the left the Suwa gardens hid the great temple under the deep verdure of fir and cedar, and the mauve and pink snow of peach and cherry clad for spring, while to the right, beyond the breeze-rippled blue fjord, and the bush-covered mountains of the far shore, a setting red sun beamed its rays as on the standards of the Empire and made its slow descent to the western horizon.

"We shall have to walk a bit," Fergan had said, "for we won't find any *kuruma* before we reach the streets that lead to the temple stairs."

"So much the better!" Felze had replied. "It's good to walk on such a lovely April evening."

The path smelled of geraniums.

"Well," broke in the English officer, "you've seen the household of a Japanese marquis and his wife — a pretty rare sight for a *baka tōjin*, a brutish foreigner, which we both qualify as. Quite rare, yes, and quite curious too. What's your impression, Mr. Felze?"

Felze smiled.

"My impression is excellent! The Japanese marquis is a most courteous man — even, to judge by his remarks today, towards *baka tōjin*; and his wife is a pretty woman."

Satisfaction shone in the Englishman's eyes.

"Isn't she, now? … Quite the pretty woman — so much better, indeed, than three-quarters of her compatriots! And so young, so fresh! It doesn't strike one right away, because of the pink and white make-up that fashion requires. Must have the color of European women! And it's a shame, because the skin underneath is no yellower than new ivory, and a softer satin is scarce to be imagined. She's barely twenty-four years old, Marquise Yorisaka!"

"You know her well," observed Felze, teasing a little.

"Yes! … That is… I'm on quite intimate terms with the marquis."

The clean-shaven face had blushed.

"…Quite intimate terms… We've campaigned together. As you must surely know, my mission in this country requires me to follow the war, and I am a spectator aboard the same battleship that Marquis Yorisaka serves on."

"Really?" said Jean-François Felze, surprised. "On a Japanese battleship? And the Mikado government allows this?"

"Oh, it's made a true exception. I've been dispatched by our king on a special and unofficial mission … for it's not even official. England and Japan are allies, and the alliance permits many things… I'm delighted, incidentally. Nothing, you understand, is more interesting than this war. I was before Port-Arthur on the tenth of August and witnessed the whole battle — from the Marquis's turret, to be exact. This is why we are now close, as I've told you … comrades in arms, brothers … two fingers on the same hand. You understand?"

He was laughing now, mischievous and cordial. He continued in a confidential vein:

"Even that sly fox Yorisaka — for he's no fool, Yorisaka Sadao — yes, that sly fox Yorisaka wanted to me to blab. The Japanese are surely better at sea than the Russians, but they haven't yet reached perfection. They could learn something spending some time with a navy like ours. So our excellent friend there sought to learn, and spent a lot of time around your servant … He did not learn, or not much. Remember your French proverb? 'To a Norman a Norman and a half.'[39] Well! A Japanese is a Norman's equivalent, so I played the Norman and a half. It had to be done. To be proper I must remain neutral; we're at peace with Russia… Ah, here we are! — *kuruma*!"

Two runners were walking up, trailing their empty little carts, and rushed over on catching sight of the Europeans.

"To the Customs docks, right, Mr. Felze?" asked Commander Fergan.

"No," said the painter. "No, I'm not going back aboard the *Yseult*, or not right away. I plan to dine alone tonight, in the Japanese style, at an inn."

---

39 "*À Normand Normand et demi.*" Anyone dealing with a Norman (a man from the French region of Normandy) must expect stubbornness, and so to prevail must do worse than the Norman.

The Englishman raised a finger.

"Aha, Mr. Felze! An inn and a dinner in the Japanese style! You know, you can get all that down by Yoshiwara."[40]

Jean-François Felze smiled and pointed to his gray hair.

"Have you failed to notice the snowfall up top, dear sir?"

"What snow? You're a young man, Mr. Felze. To take you for forty years old one must reflect well over your glories!"

---

40   Established in 1617, Yoshiwara was a famous *yūkaku*, or red-light district, in Tokyo. In 1893 the district had more than 9,000 women, many of them, it is supposed, suffering from syphilis. Here the word is a metonym referring to Nagasaki's own red-light district.

"Forty years old! I'm up to fifty, alas, and will admit to no more."

"Admit nothing. I'll do you the injury of not believing you! But you're decidedly not headed to the port, so I'll be taking my leave. May I be of service before I go? Shall I translate your orders to the *kuruma* runner?"

"Yes, if you please! You're most kind. I'd like to dine first, as I've told you, and then…"

"And then?"

"And then be taken to a quarter called Diou Djen Dji."[41]

"All right."

There followed a few phrases in Japanese, punctuated by the runner's affirmative "*Hai!*"

"Done. Your man won't lead you astray, rest assured. You'll be dining at an *ochaya* on Manzai-machi street. From there you'll be taken to your quarter of Diou Djen Dji, perched halfway up the hill with the large cemeteries. And — what was I telling you? — you'll have to cross a section of Yoshiwara to get up there. There's no escaping it in Japan, Mr. Felze. Goodbye, and may the pretty *oiran*[42] please your eye from behind the gate's bamboo!"

---

41 Almost certainly Farrère's rendering of Jūzenji (十善寺), meaning "Ten Virtues Temple." This hillside district in Nagasaki, near prominent temples and cemeteries, was famously described by Pierre Loti (the author's mentor and friend) in *Madame Chrysanthème* (1888), Loti having stayed in the Jūzenji area during his time in the city.

42 A collective term for the highest-ranking courtesans in Japanese history, who were considered to be above common prostitutes, for their more refined skill in entertainment and the traditional arts. Though by definition *oiran* too engaged in prostitution, certain high-ranking *oiran* could to some degree choose their clients; the highest class of *oiran*, the *tayū*, engaged in no sex work at all.

V

The House of Three Lanterns

The staircase, worn, mossy, rickety, climbed straight up the hillside, between two small Japanese walls, interrupted here and there by wooden houses standing dark and silent. With its deserted gardens and mute cottages, the sleep-bound district seemed a foretaste of the vast city of the dead, the dense welter of a cemetery whose countless tombs descend in tight ranks from all the surrounding summits, encircling, pressing in on, besieging the less-vast city of the living.

At the top of the stairs Jean-François Felze got his bearings.

He had left his *kuruma* down below: no road fit for a carriage leads to Diou Djen Dji. And now, alone on the mountain paths, he wondered which was the right way. "Three lanterns," he muttered, "three purple lanterns at the door of a low house…"

There was nothing of the kind in sight, but a steep path took up where the stairs left off and zigzagged through the shadows to a sort of plateau. From up there the eye could no doubt peer at leisure down the various lanes. Felze resigned himself to scaling the path.

The night was clear as could be, but dark. A reddish crescent moon had just vanished behind the mountains to the west. The gong of a temple beat faintly in the distance.

"Three purple lanterns," repeated Jean-François Felze.

He stopped to get his watch to chime.[43] Dinner had not taken very long at the *ochaya* on Manzai-machi street, but Felze had afterwards been

-----

43 A passing reference to an early-twentieth-century mechanical device. Felze is carrying a minute-repeater watch, a complex and expensive timepiece. Its mechanism allows the wearer to learn the time audibly, even in the dark, by actuating a slide or pusher on the case. Tiny internal hammers then strike tuned gongs to chime the hours (usually low tones), quarter-hours (often high-low pairs), and minutes past the quarter (usually high tones). Repeating watches (chiming hours and quarters) emerged in England in about the 1680s, pioneered by rivals Edward Barlow and Daniel Quare, but the key refinement of substituting resonant wire gongs for bells, which enabled slimmer designs, is credited to master watchmaker Abraham-Louis Breguet in the 1780s. Requiring hundreds of hand-assembled parts, the minute repeater was at once a practical tool (in the days before electric light), a pinnacle in mechanical watchmaking, and a luxury item. A Patek Philippe minute repeater pocket watch from about 1900 sold for nearly $25,000 in 2006.

unable to resist the pleasure of a long stroll through illuminated, sparkling, buzzing, feasting Nagasaki, through the crowds of roaming pedestrians, the babbling *mousmé*, and *kuruma* galloping along in Indian file. And now it was late: his watch chimed ten o'clock.

"Damn," muttered Felze. "This is no hour for a ceremonial visit."

He surveyed the suburb scattered at his feet and, lower down, the city huddled at the gulf's edge. Here he gave a sudden shout: the three purple lanterns were there, close by, at the foot of the steep path he had, not without effort, just scaled. They were just then emerging from a obscuring clump of trees.

Felze went back down the path and made his way around the clump. The low house stood out against a starry sky. It was purely Japanese and made of common brown wood, without ornament. Under the porch, though, an ornamental beam served as a pediment, and this pediment, sculpted, carved, cut, filigreed, and gilded like the paneling on a pagoda, stood in violent contrast to the absolute simplicity of the Japanese roof it had been laid into. The three lanterns too, the three purple lanterns, clashed strangely against the clean, bare facade they illumined: they were three monstrous masks of oiled paper, three masks with a titter as frightening as a skeleton's grin and a color like that of rotting flesh.

Jean-François Felze considered the three cadaverous lanterns, and the carved-ingot of a pediment. Then he knocked, and the door opened.

VI

The Vessel and the Treasure

A very tall servant, dressed in blue silk and shod in black silk, appeared at the threshold and sized up the visitor.

"Zhou P'ei?"[44] said Felze, and held out a long strip of red paper, covered in black characters.

The servant saluted in the Chinese manner — head bowed low, fists joined and shaken over the forehead — and then, respectfully, took the paper and shut the door.

Still outside, Felze smiled.

"The etiquette hasn't changed," he thought.

And he waited patiently.

A gong sounded within. He heard the patter of hurried footsteps and the swish of a mat dragged along the floor. Then, once again, there was silence. But the door did not reopen, not yet. Five minutes dragged by.

There was a fair chill. Spring had come not yet four weeks ago, as Felze remembered, the northeast wind slipping in under his coat.

"The etiquette hasn't changed," he repeated to himself. "But on a night so fertile for the cold, bronchitis, and pleurisy it is no less hard to freeze for so long under the porch while a host mindful of proprieties prepares a proper reception. To judge by the ambient chill, I'm inclined to say that in this case Zhou P'ei does me a bit too much honor…"

At last, however, the door reopened.

Jean-François Felze took two steps in and bowed, as the servant had bowed, in the Chinese manner. The master of the house, standing before him, bowed in turn.

He was a gigantic man, sumptuously dressed in a brocade robe and capped with a toque with a solid ball of coral red, the mark of the highest class of Chinese mandarin. Two servants held him up under the armpits, for he was at least seventy years old, and his enormous body was too heavy

---

44 Zhou Pèi in (the now-standard) Pīnyīn. — The romanizations of Chinese in the text are in the Wade-Giles system, so as to preserve the flavor of the original novel, which appeared decades before Pinyin was developed.

for his old man's vigor; from the age when one becomes a lettered man,
moreover, rank and title had condemned him to horses and palanquins; so
much so that he had probably not taken a stroll on foot for half a century.

For Zhou P'ei — former ambassador and former viceroy, eminent
tutor of the sons of the first imperial concubine, member of the Nei-Ko

Supreme Council, member of the Chün chi ch'u[45] Sovereign Council —
was one of the twelve great dignitaries of the Chinese court. Jean-François
Felze had met him in the past and become a close friend, but it was not
without surprise that he had received, that very morning, an invitation from
Zhou P'ei asking him to come "to a most miserable dwelling and drink as in
old times, with indulgence, a warm cup of bad wine." Zhou P'ei outside of
Peking? What an extravagant turn of events!

Yet it was indeed Zhou P'ei. At a glance Felze recognized the strange,
hollow-cheeked figure, the lipless mouth, the meager tin-colored beard, and
especially the eyes — eyes without form or hue, drowned in the depths of
puffy lids, almost invisible, but emitting such piercing beams that one could
never be run through with them and forget.

Having bowed, Zhou P'ei leaned on the shoulders of his two servants
and took four steps, so as to emerge completely from the house and come
before the visitor. Then, bowing again, and showing the left side of the
door, he spoke in accord with the rites:

"Pray, be so good as to enter first."

"How could I dare?" replied Felze.

And he bowed lower. For in former times he had studied the *Book of
Ceremonies and Outer Demonstrations*,[46] which are, said K'ung Fu-tzu,[47] "the
garb of the heart's sentiments" — an indispensable study, to be certain, for
whosoever desires the genuine friendship of a Chinese scholar.

Zhou P'ei, hearing the correct response, smiled with satisfaction and
bowed a third time.

"Pray, be so good as to enter first," he repeated.

And Felze repeated:

"How could I dare?"

After this, and a final plea, he accepted the invitation and entered.

Four steps at the far end of the antechamber led to a first room. Zhou
P'ei crossed it at a slant, walking on the east side, and, as courtesy required,
asked his visitor to walk on the west.

"If you would be so good," he said, "pray, pass in honor."

"How could I dare?" replied Felze.

And this time he added:

---

45 Jūnjīchù in Pinyin.

46 Probably the *Book of Etiquette and Ceremonial* (*I Li* — or, in Pinyin, *Yili*)

47 Confucius. Kǒng Fūzǐ in Pinyin.

"Are you not my elder brother, most wise and old?"

Zhou P'ei protested:

"You raise me too high!"

But Felze cried out in protest, as he ought.

"Most assuredly not! How could such a thing be? And, as for elderliness, I have heard from all quarters that your glorious age exceeds seventy-three years, while I, your mere little brother, have lived a very vain fifty-two."

Zhou P'ei struck at the ornaments on his belt:

"Here," he said, "is a jade tablet that is new. And in olden days I had an alabaster tablet, which was old. Now, one day, the philosopher of the principality of Lou,[48] speaking to Tzu K'ong,[49] explained why the wise hold jade but not alabaster in esteem. Is it not certain that this new tablet is precious and the old was vile? I compare you, rightly, to the tablet of jade, and myself to the one of alabaster."

"I am unworthy!" Felze averred.

After three refusals, however, he took the west side and climbed the steps, "in honor."

The first room, empty and bare, in accord with Japanese taste, they crossed lengthwise. At the far end an opaque curtain concealed the second room.

Zhou P'ei took the edge of the curtain in his right hand and lifted it:

"Walk very slowly," he said.[50]

"I shall walk very fast," replied Felze.

But after crossing the threshold he took only one step and came to a halt.

The second room, upholstered, furnished, and decorated wonderfully to Chinese taste, offered no floor to walk upon, for the tatami had vanished beneath a splendid heap of velvets, brocades, crepes, watered silks, and cloths of silver and gold. The whole room was in fact but a divan, a daybed vast and princely.

The four walls were clad in yellow satin, all embroidered from ceiling to floor with long philosophical periods written vertically in characters of

---

48   K'ung Fu-tzu (Confucius), born in the country of Lou. [Author's note.]

49   Tzu K'ong (子貢; Pinyin: Zǐgòng), personal name Duanmu Ci (端木賜), was one of Confucius's most prominent and eloquent disciples, often featured in dialogues with the Master in the *Analects*.

50   Walking slowly is permitted only to important persons. Walking quickly is considered a mark of respect. [Author's note.]

black silk. From the roof beams hung nine violet lanterns, their light that of
stained glass. A bronze Buddha, larger than a man, smiled amid sticks of
incense in the north corner, above a dazzling coffin studded with precious
metals and gemstones. Three guéridons — of ebony, ivory, and red lacquer
— carried an incense burner, a vase for warm wine, and a prodigious tiger
of antique faience. And at the center of the silk-strewn floor, on a tray of
mother-of-pearl, stood a pedestal of chiseled silver, which in turn carried
an opium lamp, its flame, veiled by butterflies and flies of green enamel,
sparkling like an emerald. The pipes, the needles, the pipe-bowls, the boxes
of horn and porcelain were set out around it. And the sacred drug's scent
reigned over all, sovereign.

Zhou P'ei extended his arm:

"Pray," he said, "be so good as to choose a place to have your mat
unrolled."[51]

"All of the places are too flattering," replied Felze.

Two young boys kneeling by the opium lamp promptly arranged,
one atop another, three mats finer than sheets of linen. Felze made as if to
remove one, in protest of this excessive honor, but Zhou P'ei hastened to
stop him.

The two young boys then arranged the mats for the master of the
house, in parallel to the visitor's. Next they added to each set, beside the
mother-of-pearl tray, several small pillows of hard leather. And after this
they withdrew, still on their knees, each holding with respect a pipe in his
left hand and a needle in his right.

But before settling down on the mats Zhou P'ei made a sign, and
another servant — of higher rank, as was manifest in the turquoise ball of
his cap[52] — took up the vase from the ivory gueridon and filled a cup with
warm wine.

"Pray, be good enough to drink," said Zhou P'ei.

The cup was of jade: not of green jade, *yao*,[53] but of diaphanous
white jade, *yü*[54] — the jade that the rites reserve for princes, viceroys,
and ministers.

---

51 Even in a room strewn with carpets the rites require that the guest be offered one or more
mats, to sit or lie on. [Author's note.]

52 Mandarin of the third class. There are nine classes of mandarins in the Empire. Zhou P'ei,
minister of the state, has for his aides-de-camp civil and military officers of the rank of prefect or
colonel. [Author's note.]

53 *Yáo* in Pinyin.

54 *Yù* in Pinyin.

"I shall drink," said Felze, "from the unadorned wooden cup."

He drank nonetheless from the cup of jade, once the master of the house had thrice insisted. And then, Zhou P'ei having drunk after his guest, both lay down face to face, with the mother-of-pearl tray between them.

The ceremony was complete. Zhou P'ei spoke:

"Fenn Ta-Jen,"[55] he said, "just now, when your illustrious card was presented to me, my heart beat with joy. It has been thirty years since we first met, at that school in Rome I had wished to visit — I, a most humble traveler, curious to see in your magnificent Europe something other than soldiers and machines of war. It has been fifteen years since we met a second time, in the city of Peking, which you honored with a long sojourn during the learned pilgrimage that in your wisdom you made to all the lands where men dwell. The first encounter revealed to me an adolescent courteous, sage, and pensive as old men rarely are, and the second a philosopher worthy to be likened to the masters of ancient times. Another fifteen years have passed. We meet again, and I rejoice, knowing that in your company I shall get a taste of the unutterable good fortune of Tseng-Tzu,[56] the tiny disciple, who with a zither vibrating at his fingers joined his timid harmony to the precepts of the great K'ung Tzu.[57]

He spoke a French of fair purity, but his muted, hoarse voice paused at length between the sentences, for he was thinking in Chinese and translating his speech as he went along. He continued:

"So I listen, and I await your words as the farmer awaits the harvest of the wheat in the first month of summer and of the sticky millet in the first month of autumn. However, let us both smoke first, that the opium might uncloud our intelligence, purify our judgment, render our ear more musical, and banish the tyrannical sensation of heat and cold, source of many gross errors. I know that the men of this country have, in their singular despotism, banned opium under severe penalty of law, but this house, modest as it is, obeys no law. So let us smoke. This pipe here is made of eaglewood — *ki-nam*. Its soothing virtues make it precious

---

55 The Chinese language has no sound equivalent to the French name "Felze," and therefore no character to represent the name in writing. To write the name of his friend with a brush, then, Zhou P'ei must resort to some character of similar pronunciation. The best is the one pronounced "Fenn." Zhou P'ei, writing "Fenn," naturally pronounces what he writes. — Ta-Jen is an honorific appellation to be given to all officials of the first and second rank, and generally to all grand persons. "Ta-Jen" literally means "considerable man." [Author's note.]

56 Zengzi.

57 Confucius again.

to smokers in your noble West, a more nervous lot than the sons of the obscure Central Nation."[58]

Silent, Jean-François Felze accepted the pipe being offered him by one of the kneeling young boys, and with all the strength of his lungs inhaled the gray smoke, while the child held over the lamp the little brown cylinder stuck to the hole of the pipe-bowl. The opium sizzled, melted, evaporated. And Felze, having exhausted the full pipe in one draw, rested his two shoulders on the mats, the better to expand his chest and prolong the intertwining of the philosophical and benevolent drug's volutes with his own fibers.

After a minute, though, and while Zhou P'ei smoked in turn, Felze did as he had been asked and spoke:

---

58   Chung Kuo — Empire of the Middle. Central Empire — China. The name *China* is incomprehensible to the Chinese. [Author's note.] — Zhōngguó in Pinyin.

Ta-Jen P'ei,"[59] he said, "your overly indulgent mouth has uttered harmonious and reasonable words. It is indeed reasonable to ascribe folly to the young and good sense to old men, even if, like me, they have lived in vain. Yet I recall the times you speak of; I recall the School of Rome, and your city of Peking, famous among all cities. And only now do I come to see the folly of my present days, the folly I have fallen into as an old man, assuredly worse than when I was young, worse even than when I was a child."

He paused to smoke a second pipe, presented to him by the kneeling servant.

"Ta-Jen P'ei," he continued, "in Rome I was a stupid schoolboy, but I studied the tradition of the old masters with respect. In Peking I was an unintelligent traveler, but I strove to open my eyes to the spectacle of Heaven, Earth, and the Ten Thousand Created Things. Now I no longer study, my eyes can no longer see, and I live like the wolf and the hare, letting chance and immodest passion guide my steps. The lettered men and civil servants of my nation have been mistaken to confer upon me so many awards and honors, all undeserved. For a few crude and artless paintings these men devoid of judgment have brought me the attention of the people and the admiration of the ignorant. My head was weak. The warm wine of glory befuddled it. Then came all the impurities and all the degrading pleasures. I was powerless to repel them. And I am their slave. Out of respect for the chaste house of my host, I shall say no more. Permit me simply to compare the modest ship of my old journey to the happy junk of a fisherman or merchant, the one and the other being content to face the sea in hopes of acquiring riches, and the sumptuous ship that today brings me back to the Middle Kingdom to one of those ornate, intricately carved, gilded boats to be seen on the river of Guangdong, and within which the debauched complete their degradation."

"It is absolutely impossible for me," ruled Zhou P'ei, "to approve of your severity towards yourself."

He made a sign, and the servant kneeling nearby substituted a pipe of brown tortoiseshell for the eaglewood pipe.

"It is impossible," Zhou P'ei repeated, "for me to approve of your severity, because no man is without fault, and because only very virtuous

---

59   Zhou is the family name, P'ei the first name, which the Chinese, like the Japanese, place after the family name. A Chinese gentleman always has two first names, one familiar, the other official. The latter is to be used in conversation, the former being reserved for close relations and hierarchical superiors. For the sake of propriety, the author has refused in this book to write the familiar first name of Zhou P'ei, a man of more than seventy years. [Author's note.]

men have the courage to accuse themselves without limit. Furthermore, your caution accords with the rites: for it is written in the *Li Chi*:[60] 'What must be said inside the apartments shall not be said outside the apartments.'[61] And the lettered man who observes decorum in his words cannot break it by his actions."

He smoked the pipe of brown tortoiseshell and blew out through his nostrils a denser, stronger-smelling smoke.

____

60 *Li Ki* in Pinyin.

61 "The apartments": that is to say, the women's quarters. A well-educated Chinese man never speaks of women except in an abstract way — for example, in citing a philosophical maxim. Zhou P'ei congratulates his guest for having contrived to convey, without unnecessary details, that women have played, and still play, an exaggerated role in his life. [Author's note.]

Felze shook his head:

"My elder brother, very wise and very old, has not plunged into the muddy swamp where his little brother flounders in dishonor. My elder brother has not seen with his own eyes, and is in ignorance."

"I am not in ignorance," said Zhou P'ei.

Felze propped himself up on his right elbow to scrutinize his host. The Chinese eyes, all but invisible behind the puffy lids, sparkled with a penetrating, ironical gleam.

"I am ignorant of nothing," said Zhou P'ei. "For I am here by august order of the Son of Heaven. And in this realm of imperfect civilization I, his insignificant subject, must see all, know all, and render an exact account of all. And so, having accomplished my task with little discernment but much zeal, I know that you arrived in Nagasaki yesterday morning on a white ship with three copper funnels. I know that you have long been traveling on this white ship, pleasant to the eye. I know that this ship flies the flowered banner[62] of the American nation, and that it belongs to a woman. I am ignorant of nothing."

Felze blushed slightly, laid his cheek on one of the leather pillows, and considered the opium lamp. The two kneeling children hastened to cook the large tar-colored drops, kneading them against the pipe-bowls, the flame gradually lending them hues of gold and amber.

"Pray, be so good as to smoke," counseled Zhou P'ei.

Other servants had in the meantime entered silently, carrying a teapot of simple brown clay and two marvelous bowls of old pink porcelain.

"This tea," said Zhou P'ei, "is the tea that the August Elevation[63] obliged me to accept upon my departure from Peking."

It was limpid water, with the slightest green tint and small, narrow, long leaves floating in it. It smelled strong and fresh like a flower in bloom.

Zhou P'ei had drunk.

"Imperial tea," he said, "should be beaten in the water of a rocky spring once that water has been boiled over a hot fire. It is best to use a teapot of the

---

62   The flowered banner — *Koa Ki* — is the nickname that the Chinese give to the American flag, for its multi-colored design. [Author's note.]

63   The August Elevation, Hoang Chan; the August Sovereign, Hoang Ti; or the Son of Heaven, Tien Tzeu, are the three appellations in current use among the Chinese to designate their Emperor. [Author's note.]

sort laborers use, in imitation of the Emperors of old, who would beat their tea in the water of rocky springs before the art of enamel was known.

He had closed his eyes, and now his parchment-yellow face seemed stony, indifferent, almost asleep.

The young boy kneeling next to him, however, obeying an imperceptible sign, switched the tortoiseshell pipe for a pipe of chiseled silver.

The opium den was slowly filling with a fragrant fog. Already the room's scattered objects had lost their sharp contours, and the fabrics on the walls and the floor shone with faded colors. Only the nine purple lanterns hanging from the ceiling still shed the same light, because opium fumes are heavy and float near the ground, never rising…

For the fourth time Felze smoked the chiseled-silver pipe… For the fourth time, or the fifth?… He was not very sure… And the brown tortoiseshell pipe how many times before then?… And what about the eaglewood pipe?… He could not remember at all. A light dizziness was creeping over him… In the past, in Peking, and then in Paris, he had used the drug with fair regularity… His best paintings dated to that period. But when approaching the age of fifty even a robust man must choose between opium and love. Felze had not chosen opium.

And now neglected opium was taking its discreet revenge. Oh, this was no drunkenness in the crude sense that drinkers of alcohol lend the word. It was a muddled sensation of marrow and muscle: the muscle diminished and dissolved, as it were, but the marrow teeming with quickened, swelled, multiplied life; Felze, motionless, his eyes closed, could no longer feel the heft of his body sink into the mats. And thoughts flashed through his brain, while several of the veils that swaddle human intelligence tore to bits around him….

The slow, hoarse voice of Zhou P'ei broke the silence.

"Fenn Ta-Jen, the rites forbid the visitor to question the host, and your wise courtesy has heeded the rites, but the host must in return open to the visitor, after the door of his house, the door of his soul… Only with women is it proper to listen without answering. Fenn Ta-Jen, when your illustrious card was presented to me my heart beat with joy. And this joy was not just the selfish pleasure of seeing my venerated brother after fifteen years; it was more the hope that I could be of humble use to him in a kingdom perturbed by a culpable madness and offering to the philosopher's eye a disconcerting and painful spectacle."

Felze slowly raised his left hand and, through his spread fingers, looked at one of the nine purple lanterns.

"P'ei Ta-Jen," he said, "I know not how to thank you as I should, but your light shall in truth serve wonderfully to illuminate my darkness. This is but my second Japanese night, yet Japan has already shown me many things that I have not understood, and that you will explain to me, if your perspicacity deigns to serve my purpose."

Zhou P'ei's lipless mouth stretched into a half-smile.

"Japan," he said, "has already shown you a man who has forgotten filial piety and a woman who neglects feminine modesty."

Surprised, Felze scrutinized his host.

"Japan," Zhou P'ei continued, "has shown you a hearth from which the ghost of the ancestors is excluded, and a roof under which ten thousand unreasonable novelties have taken the place of tradition and compromise the harmonious future of the family and the race."

"So you know," asked Felze, "that this afternoon I paid a visit to Marquis Yorisaka Sadao?"

"I am ignorant of nothing," said Zhou P'ei.

He too raised a hand toward the lanterns hanging from the ceiling, and violet rays played on the nails of disproportionate length.

"I am ignorant of nothing. Have I not told you that I am in this place in obedience to the imperial order of the August Elevation?"

He explained:

"At Yorisaka Sadao's house you found, seated on the west side,[64] a foreigner from the Nation of Red-Haired Men.[65] This foreigner has been sent here by his prince, who was eager to know with what weapons and by what strategy the little kingdom of the Rising Sun strives to conquer the vast empire of the Oros.[66] A mystery of small interest, in fact, and one that no sage of antiquity bothered to solve. With better inspiration from Heaven, the August Elevation has sent me, his subject, to determine how far these new weapons and strategy are likely to distort a civilization that until now has been ruled in accord with the Central Nation's philosophical precepts. It is to this examination that my clumsy efforts are applied. To make up for my inadequacies I must gather a great deal of information. Many loyal spies serve as my eyes and ears, and are tirelessly wearing out their hearts to help me in my task. Thus all the secrets of this city and this kingdom are revealed here, on this mat. And thus I am ignorant of nothing."

Felze laid his cheek on the leather pillow:

"P'ei Ta-Jen," he said, "your words have a hidden meaning. How does Yorisaka Sadao fail in his filial piety?"

The sparkling eyes closed again, and the hoarse voice solemnly spoke:

"It is written in the *Ta Hsüeh*:[67] 'Man must first study the nature of things, then develop his knowledge, then perfect his will, then regulate the movements of his heart, then correct himself exactly, then establish order in

---

64   The west is the cardinal point reserved for visitors one wishes to honor. [Author's note.]

65   "Red-haired Men" (*Hung mao Jen*), nickname the Chinese give to the English. [Author's note.]

66   "Oros," Russians. [Author's note.]

67   The *Ta Hsüeh* (*Great Learning*) [*Dàxué* in Pinyin] is the first of the four classic books. [Author's note.]
     The book identifies personal ethical development (curiosity, learning, sincerity, rectitude, cultivation) as the root of social order. This in turn serves to regulate the family, govern the state, and bring peace to the world. Relying on this core Confucian concept, Zhou P'ei argues that by adopting Western ways and neglecting tradition (personal/family/state cultivation rooted in ancient rites) Yorisaka compromises the entire moral and social structure, regardless of military or political necessity.

his family. Only afterwards shall the principality be well governed and the Empire enjoy peace.' In his commentary on these eight propositions Tseng-Tzu teaches us that they cannot be separated. Indeed, man, his family, his principality, and the Empire are but one. Filial piety extends to all ancestors, to the entire community, to the entire country. In denying the memory of his ancestors, and thus compromising his country, Yorisaka Sadao fails in his filial piety.

The child kneeling near Felze held out a ready pipe. Felze took in hand the heavy pipe of dark shell and pressed his lips against the browned ivory end. The opium bubbled over the lamp, and the gray smoke rolled over the mats in heavy clouds.

And now, with the bold drug mixed into his being, Felze dared object to the philosopher:

"P'ei Ta-Jen, when the Empire is under threat must one not repel the barbarian invasion before observing the rites? The treasure of ancient precepts is priceless, it is true. But is the Empire not the vessel that contains the treasure? If the Empire is subjugated, the vessel shattered to bits, will the treasure of ancient precepts not be dispersed forever? … Filial piety extends to all ancestors, to the entire community, to the entire country. Does Yorisaka Sadao truly fail in his filial piety if he denies, perhaps in appearance, the memory of his ancestors and modifies the rules of his community for the higher purpose of saving his country's independence?"

Zhou P'ei smoked in silence.

Jean-François Felze concluded:

"P'ei Ta-Jen, when necessity compels a husband to stray from the straight path does his wife truly neglect female modesty if she too takes the detour, so as to walk in the footsteps of the man she has promised to follow, step by step, until death?"

Zhou P'ei pushed away the chiseled-silver pipe, but only to point an index finger at a pipe of black bamboo with ends of jade. He remained silent.

Jean-François Felze now raised his two shoulders from the mats and propped himself onto his elbows, facing his host:

"P'ei Ta-Jen," he broke in, "I have smoked more pipes tonight than I can count. And perhaps the opium has raised my feeble intelligence to the comprehension of many things that in everyday life are indecipherable to me… Yes, I saw today a hearth from which the spirit of tradition is excluded. But is it not written that men shall be judged by their intent

rather than their actions? He who
diminishes himself, even debases himself,
to serve and exalt the Empire — should he
not be absolved?"

The pipe of black bamboo was ready. Zhou
P'ei drew on it at   length, and engulfed himself in a thick, odorous cloud.
Then, gravely, he spoke.

"It is better," he said, "not to judge men. We shall therefore neither
condemn nor acquit Marquis Yorisaka Sadao. We shall neither acquit
nor condemn Marquise Yorisaka Mitsouko. But one day the philosopher
Mencius, answering Wang Chang's questions, said he had never heard of
anyone's reforming others by distorting himself, let alone reforming the

Empire through his own dishonor."[68]

"By your reckoning, then," said Felze, "the efforts of the Japanese are vain and the Rising Sun must inevitably succumb in its struggle against the Oros?"

"I do not know," said Zhou P'ei, "and it is in any case of little import."

He let out a strange, sonorous laugh.

"Of no import. We shall speak again and at leisure of this trifle when the time comes."

The child kneeling next to Felze was sticking a thin cylinder of opium onto the bowl of the bamboo pipe.

"Pray, be so good as to smoke," concluded Zhou P'ei. "This black bamboo was once white. Only the good drug has given it this color that you see, after a thousand and ten thousand smokes. No eaglewood, ivory, shell, or precious metal can match this bamboo…"

They smoked together for a long time.

Above the opium fog, growing denser by the hour, the nine violet lanterns shone now like stars on a November night.

And the sizzle of brown droplets as they evaporated above the lamp made the absolute silence more perceptible.

The cold that precedes dawn was already falling over the countryside when a distant cock crowed.

Felze now dreamed aloud:

"The whole real world truly, truly lies within these walls of yellow satin. Outside is but a bit of illusion. I no longer believe in any white yacht with copper funnels, aboard which lives a woman who has made me her plaything…"

68　This quote from Mencius (Mengzi), a major Confucian philosopher, emphasizes the principle that legitimate influence and effective reform stem from one's own moral integrity and adherence to right principles (the 'Way' or 'Dao'). It argues against compromising oneself or using expedient, potentially dishonorable means (like abandoning core cultural values, in Zhou P'ei's view) to achieve external goals, such as political or military success against perceived threats. Zhou P'ei uses this to question the validity and long-term wisdom of Japan's Westernizing path.

VII

Mrs. Hockley's Three Dazzling Halos

Miss Vane, have you rung for lunch?"

"No…"

"Oh, how lazy of you!"

And Mrs. Hockley reached for the electric bell.

The yacht's dining room was enormous, and of a luxury so brutal and aggressive that one could tell at a glance it was meant to dazzle, blind, and crush. One seemed to be anywhere but aboard a ship. The excess of cornices and caryatids, the piling up of paintings, sculptures, and gilding, recalled the foyer of some royal or imperial opera house, or even the roulette rooms of an extravagantly sumptuous Monte Carlo. Mrs. Hockley, owner of the *Yseult*, was a millionaire eighty times over, and would have no one in the world doubt it.

A majordomo, in admiral's uniform, carried in on a vermeil tray an early breakfast in the American style: ginger jam, cookies, toast, and black tea.

"Why only two cups?"

"Madam, Mr. Felze is not yet back aboard."

"That's none of your business. Three cups this instant."

Mrs. Hockley delivered her orders in a perfectly calm, nonchalant voice. But, of course, her pile of eighty millions raised her far above domestic humanity.

She would nonetheless deign to serve sugar and cream to the young girl she had named Miss Vane, and who was officially only her reader.

❊

Now they were having lunch face to face, Mrs. Hockley and Miss Vane. They drank much tea, ate much toast, and spread ginger on a good dozen savory biscuits. This Anglo-Saxon appetite stood in amusing contrast to Mrs. Hockley's delicate grace, and especially to Miss Vane's almost ethereal charm. Indeed, Miss Vane was a veritable lily, a miracle of slenderness and white, a wavy lily of supple and fragile long stem. Figuring this stem were the tapered legs, the narrow hips, and the small waist, and from it the nude flesh of her bust emerged like a corolla just now parting in bloom. Miss Vane wore a strange garment, half ball gown and half blouse, wide open and flowing, its sea-green silk bringing out to perfection her seaweed eyes and jet-black hair.

Mrs. Hockley was less flower and more woman, and, if one may say so, more animal. To look at her, one would have compared her to nothing at all, except to what she was: a thirty-year-old American, of marvelous, irreproachable beauty. This flawless beauty served as the first and most dazzling of Mrs. Hockley's three halos, the second being her enormous fortune and the third her rowdy adventures, of which the two most notorious had been her divorce and the suicide of her ex-husband. Many a princess of New York or Philadelphia would have been famous just for possessing the most splendid yacht afloat, and just for the triumph of going about in the company of a Jean-François Felze, enslaved. But to lay eyes on Mrs. Hockley was to forget that she was rich, and that she had reduced to servitude, after ten other well-known or illustrious men, perhaps the noblest artist of the century. One would forget it all to admire a body, a face, whose every line attained perfection. Mrs. Hockley was tall and blonde, and svelte though muscular. Her eyes were black, her skin golden and luminous. But none of the features characterized the whole, which belied detail and found its value in balance and harmony. Mrs. Hockley was beautiful through and through, and no other adjective could specify. To paint her, and capture on canvas the seductive power emanating from the forehead, the mouth, the waist, the hips, and the ankles, Felze had had to fashion a portrait of everything, down to the dress.

❉

Miss Vane, having finished her thirteenth ginger biscuit, reclined in her swivel chair.

"It's quite late," she murmured, indolently.

Mrs. Hockley looked at the time on her bracelet.

"Yes … a quarter past nine…"

"The master is in no hurry."

Mrs. Hockley made no reply but rang with a somewhat nervous hand. A valet parted the curtain of crimson velvet.

"Bring in Romeo."

"Ugh!" said Miss Vane. "How can you always be touching that horror with your fingers?"

The curtain let through a grey beast with twisted legs, pointed muzzle, bushy tail — a lynx. Mrs. Hockley would not resign herself to a mere dog or cat, vulgar animals.

"Come here!"[69] ordered Mrs. Hockley.

The same instant the velvet curtain parted again, this time to let through a man, Jean-François Felze.

"Good morning," he said.

He went to Mrs. Hockley, to bow before her and kiss her hand. But the hand was stroking the rough fur of the lynx, and Jean-François Felze, forehead low and back bent, had to wait until the lynx had been petted.

❀

Felze had taken a seat and was gulping down the cup of cooled tea.

"You lost track of time, dear," observed Mrs. Hockley.

"Yes," he said, "and I beg your pardon. But you knew where I was, and I thought you wouldn't worry or get cross."

She examined him.

"Did you really smoke opium?"

"Yes. All night long."

"It doesn't show at all … Does it, Miss Vane?"

Miss Vane, silent, gestured her agreement. Mrs. Hockley continued to study Felze's face like a naturalist before a zoological phenomenon.

"And yet it does! It shows a little … in the iris of your eye, which is brighter and more fixed … and also in your complexion, which is more livid … corpse-like, I would say…"

"Thank you…"

"Why 'thank you'? You're not vexed, are you? It's just an observation … a curious observation… I'd like to understand why your complexion has changed. Opium has no effect on the circulation of the blood, does it? It attacks the nervous system exclusively, and paralyses the reflexes… So I couldn't even guess… Can you explain?"

"No," said Felze.

"You haven't even an inkling as to the cause?"

"Not even an inkling."

"But would you be curious to know?"

"Not in the least."

"How extraordinary! You're astonishingly French! The French take

---

69 English in the original French text.

no pleasure in noticing things… Tell me, what is the nature of an opium smoker's sensual pleasure?"

Irritated, Felze rose to his feet.

"It's quite impossible for me to put it into words for you," he said.

"Why?"

"Because this sensual pleasure, to borrow your term, would be inaccessible to an American woman. And you are surprisingly American!"

"That I am, yes. But how are you coming to this sudden discovery?"

"By way of your questions. You are the opposite of a French woman. You take too much pleasure in noticing things … no, in trying to notice things."

"Is this not the natural instinct of a creature endowed with a capacity for thought?"

"No. It's more like the mania of a being who lacks the capacity to feel."

Mrs. Hockley did not grow cross. The slight furrow in her brow was a mark of intense reflection. Miss Vane, still reclining in a swivel chair, burst into impertinent laughter.

"What is so funny?" asked Mrs. Hockley, turning to her reader.

Miss Vane replied, continuing to laugh afterwards:

"It's truly funny to see you, excitable as you are, accused of lacking the capacity to feel."

"Please," said Mrs. Hockley, "do not interrupt a serious conversation with a joke!"

She turned back to Felze:

"Tell me, dear: this Chinaman of yours, the mandarin you know from before, and whom you've rediscovered here in so romantic a way — is he an out and out savage? I mean a primitive, a backward person?"

Felze tilted his head forward and stared into Mrs. Hockley's eyes.

"Out and out," he confirmed. "Rest assured, there is not a single common idea between you and this Chinaman."

"Really? Hasn't he traveled, though?"

"But of course."

"He's traveled! And here he is in Japan, a country now shaking off its ancient barbarity! … Could this Chinaman be as backward as you say? As foreign to civilization? For instance, here, in Nagasaki, in his house, does he not even have a telephone?"

"He does not."

"Incomprehensible! And you find it congenial to be in such a man's company?"

"As you can see, I lost track of time at his house."

"Yes…"

She was reflecting as before, with the slight furrow in her brow.

"The French," interjected Miss Vane, judiciously, "are themselves very ignorant of modern progress."

"Yes," agreed Mrs. Hockley, content with the explanation. "Yes, they know nothing of it, and disdain it, too. You're right, Elsa."

She had risen to her feet and gone over to Miss Vane, giving her two hands a somewhat effusive shake. Felze, turning away, laid his forehead against the glass of one of the bay windows that stood in for portholes.

A valet was bringing in two sprays of orchids. Mrs. Hockley took them and began to arrange them in the large bronze vases that adorned the monumental fireplace.

"Japanese?" asked Miss Vane, pointing to the flowers.

"No. These are still from the Frisco supply. Ice preserves them perfectly."

Felze had collected a fallen corolla from the floor and was stretching the petals between his fingers.

"No scent," he said.

He suddenly remembered Stork Hill:

"At this season all of Nagasaki's cherry trees are in bloom. Wouldn't you prefer lovely pink branches that are alive to these artificial-looking orchids?"

Mrs. Hockley refused the discussion.

"It's truly surprising and shocking that a delicious painter like you should have such popular ideas."

Jean-François Felze opened his mouth to reply, but at the same moment Mrs. Hockley raised her hands, full of gathered stems, towards the bronze vases.

The long, slender legs,
the wide thighs, the flared hips, the narrow
torso, the round shoulders sprouting a robust,
slender neck, under a heavy mass of golden hair,
between outstretched, upraised arms — the entirety
of this womanly body was of such splendor and
harmony that Jean-François Felze made no reply.

Meanwhile Mrs. Hockley arranged her orchids.

"But, dear," she broke in, "I believe you've told us told us nothing
about this Japanese marquise whose portrait you're to paint… What's her
name? I've already forgotten."

"Yorisaka."

"Yes! Is she in fact a marquise?"

"Very much so."

"Of old lineage?"

"The Yorisaka were once *daimyo* of the Chōshū clan, on the island of Hondo. And I don't believe they've ever intermarried."

"*Daimyo* — that's to say, feudal lords?"

"Yes."

"Feudal lords! That is truly fascinating. Since you enjoy the idea of painting her, though, I imagine this Japanese marquise must be a complete savage, like the Chinese mandarin."

Felze smiled:

"Not quite."

"Oh! She has a telephone?"

"I don't know, but I'd wager she does."

Miss Vane interjected:

"Many Japanese have a telephone."

"Yes," retorted Mrs. Hockley, "but I'm surprised the master has agreed to paint the portrait of a Japanese woman who has a telephone."

She laughed, then turned serious again.

"Truly, now, is this Marquise Yorisaka a modern creature?"

"Fairly modern, yes."

"She didn't receive you while kneeling on mats, in a small, windowless room, between four paper screens?"

"No. She received me sitting in a wing chair, in a Louis XV parlor, between a grand piano and a gold-framed mirror."

"Oh!"

"Yes. I have every reason to believe, moreover, that Marquise Yorisaka has the same dressmaker as you."

"You're joking…"

"I am not joking."

"Marquise Yorisaka was not dressed in a kimono and an obi?"

"She was dressed in a very elegant tea-gown."

"I'm dumfounded… And what things did Marquise Yorisaka say to you?"

"Things such you yourself say when receiving a stranger."

"She speaks French?"

"As well as you."

"Why, she's a truly fascinating woman! François…"

"Jean-François, if you'd be so kind…"

"No, never! There you go again with your popular tastes! François by itself is much more noble. So I say: François, dear, would you kindly

introduce me to Marquise Yorisaka, please?"

Felze, who was smiling, felt an imperceptible shudder.

"Oh!" he said in a changed voice, harsh and almost bitter. "Betsy, don't you have enough in your aviary with this popinjay?"[70]

His gave a contemptuous nod towards Miss Vane.

Miss Vane did not flinch.

But Mrs. Hockley burst into laughter.

"Popinjay! Oh! I find that word truly amusing. My goodness, what jealousy! Are you so ridiculous, dear, that you cannot suffer the presence even of women around me?"

She was looking straight at him with those magnificent pale eyes, and her teeth gleamed between the parted lips. Her mirth was like the appetite of a beautiful predator.

He felt a sudden anger, and took a step towards her. Disdainful, she tilted her forehead and, with a kind of defiance, stroked Miss Vane's hair.

He stopped and went pale. Now, in turn, she took a step towards him, slowly. She kept her right hand on the young girl's head, and suddenly offered her left hand to the motionless man.

He hesitated. But she had stopped laughing. A hardness had set into her face, contracting the features. Cruel and sensual, her tongue flitted across her lips.

He went paler still and, humble, bowed to kiss the offered hand.

---

70 *Popinjay* was the original English word for parrot (from Old French *papegai*, ultimately from Arabic *bab(ba)gha'*) and evoked the bird's exotic beauty. By the sixteenth century, however, it had acquired the lasting figurative meaning, as used here by Felze, of a vain, gaudily dressed, talkative, or conceited person, reflective of a parrot's mimicry and showiness.

VIII

Prison *Yseult*

The Yseult had swung at anchor to a southward heading. Propped on his elbows at the porthole of his cabin, situated to port, Felze could see all of Nagasaki, from the great temple of the Bronze Horse, on Suwa hill, to the smoky factories that extend from the city towards the entrance of the fjord.

It was morning, and it had rained. In a gray sky shreds of cloud were still snagged on all the hilltops. The subtly hued greenery of pine, cedar, camphor, and maple seemed all the fresher under this coat of damp cotton wool. The more delicate pink snow of cherry blossoms gleamed. And at the edge of the low clouds were the cemeteries that overlook the city, their rain-washed little steles having gained in clarity. Only the roofs of the houses, still brown and blue but bereft of any play of shadow and light, lay in a muddle, all along the shoreline. Their dull tiles lacked for sunlight.

"In the end," thought Felze, "landscape artists have the same joys as we do. The pleasure is the same whether one paints this wet spring or the face of a sixteen-year-old girl who has spent the day before weeping over her first little heartbreak…"

He left the porthole and took a seat before the drafting table. There were a few sketches on it. He leafed through them.

"Ugh!" he muttered.

He discarded the sketches.

"I had some talent once. I still have a bit … just a bit."

He looked at the four walls, with their paneling of rare woods. The quarters were luxurious, and cleverly arranged to squeeze an upholstered chair of considerable refinement into a small space.

"Prison," said Felze.

Without getting up, he turned his gaze towards the porthole.

"Here I am in an exotic and lovely city, in the midst of a people fighting for its independence, and whose qualities of bravery, elegance, and courtesy are undergoing an unflagging growth and magnification in the exaltation of this combat… Chance has put me in a position to see this people's aristocracy up close and to admire at leisure a fascinating spectacle, as old instincts grapple with a new education. Further chance has reunited me with Zhou P'ei, philosophical projectionist for the whole of this magic lantern that is Asia. And this triple stroke of good fortune, which once would have held me in thrall, shall give me no enjoyment, none at all."

He lowered his head.

"I shall enjoy nothing, because my eyes will persist in seeing the haunting image of a woman, interposed between me and the outside world."

He rested his forehead in his hand.

"The image of a stupid, pedantic, vicious woman, but a beautiful one, with the skill now to grant me, now to refuse me her mouth. Such skill that I'm now done for, poor imbecile that I am…"

He had risen to his feet. He unfolded the *Nagasaki Press*, which a valet had just brought him, and read the following at the top of the day's *Reuters* dispatches:

> Tokyo, 22 April 1905.
>
> Confirmation of the passage of forty-four Russian vessels[71] before Singapore on Saturday 8 of the current month. Vice Admiral Rozhestvensky was in command. No sign yet of Rear Admiral Nebogatov's division.[72] Rumor has it that Vice Admiral Rozhestvensky is headed for the French coast of Indochina.
>
> Admiral Togo's instructions remain secret.[73]

The crumpled newspaper fell. Felze once again set his elbows to the porthole.

The wind had shifted, as it often does on rainy mornings in Nagasaki Bay. The *Yseult* had now swung to a northern heading. Felze saw the west coast of the fjord, the one facing the city. There are few houses on that coast. The green-clad mountains trail off there nonchalantly to the sea. And

---

71 In this number — an exaggeration, incidentally — the Japanese press included warships and coal ships, without distinction. [Author's note.]

72 Nikolai Ivanovich Nebogatov (20 April 1849 – 4 August 1922) was a rear admiral in the Imperial Russian Navy, noted for his role in the final stages of the Russo-Japanese War of 1904–05.

73 Tōgō Heihachirō (27 January 1848 – 30 May 1934) served as an admiral of the fleet in the Imperial Japanese Navy and became one of Japan's greatest naval heroes. As commander-in-chief of the Combined Fleet during the Russo-Japanese War of 1904–05 he confined the Russian Pacific naval forces to Port Arthur before winning a decisive victory, in May 1905, over a relieving fleet at Tsushima. Western journalists called Tōgō "the Nelson of the East." He is revered as a national hero in Japan, with shrines and streets named in his honor.

these mountains — more jagged, more bizarre, more Japanese than those on the other shore — more perfectly evoke the image of the landscapes that old whimsical painters would paint on the rice paper of their *makimono*.[74]

On this west coast, however, lies a valley between two hills, a black and sinister valley from which the opaque smoke of forges and the noise of anvils and hammers rise day and night. This is the arsenal. It is here that Nagasaki manufactures its share of ships and war machines, making its contribution to the Empire's defense.

Felze looked at the flowered mountains and the arsenal at their foot, and had a literary thought:

"Perhaps this will save it…"

He smiled with melancholy.

"Still, what a pity! Back when this didn't exist I would have painted Marquise Yorisaka Mitsouko in a triple robe of Chinese crepe, emblazoned with silver and belted with purple…"

---

74 *Makimono* is Japanese for a scroll: i.e., a long roll of paper with writing or illustrations.

IX

Seeking Immutable Japan

Palette round his thumb, Jean-François Felze took two steps back. Against the brown background of the canvas the portrait was coming swiftly along, robust and delicate. The chignon was too long and too low, but the face, with its stretched eyes and a mouth more narrow than tall, had a Far Eastern smile, mysterious and disquieting.

"Oh, how magnificent, dear master! How can you create such beautiful things so fast, as if with no effort?"

Marquise Yorisaka joined her little ivory hands in her enthusiasm. Felze, dismissive, made a face.

"So beautiful, oh! … You are too kind, madam."

"Are you not satisfied?"

"No."

He looked back and forth between model and effigy.

"You are much, much prettier than I have been able to convey in paint. This … my God … This is not bad in the absolute … When he returns to sea and locks himself into his cabin for the evening, alone with this portrait, Marquis Yorisaka will certainly recognize the features he finds so pleasing, uglified as they are… But I had dreamed of a better imitation of reality."

"You are most demanding! In any case, you are not yet finished: you can touch things up."

"Never in my life have I touched up a sketch without ruining it."

"Well, believe me, dear master, this one is a delight!"

"No!…"

He had set down his palette and, chin in hand, was with extreme, obstinate, one might say obsessive attention considering the young woman who stood before him.

This was the fifth posing session. A familiarity was beginning to arise between the painter and the model — not that idle courtesies had given way to genuine conversation, let alone confidences. Marquise Yorisaka was simply beginning to treat Jean-François Felze more like a friend than like a stranger.

Felze, though, snapped up his brush again.

"Madam," he broke in, "I would very much like to make the most indiscreet of requests…"

"The most indiscreet?…"

"Yes, and without a word of encouragement from you I shall never dare."

She fell silent, surprised.

"I shall dare nonetheless… Pray, accept my apologies a head of time. Now, listen. To refine the study you see before you I shall need another four or five days. Would you be so kind, once I have finished, as to grant me a few additional sessions? I would like to try to make another study of you, for myself… Yes, another study of you, but one that would not be a portrait in the strict sense… This here is a portrait. I have tried to bring out the woman that you are, the very Western, very modern woman, as Parisian as she is Japanese… But I am haunted by a notion, the notion that had you been born a half-century earlier you would have had the same face and the same smile, though you were solely and purely Japanese… And this smile and face, which you get from your mother and your ancestors, and which are of Japan, immutable Japan — I feel a stubborn desire to paint them a second time, in a different setting… You do have, do you not, some robes of yore, beautiful robes with flowing sleeves, noble robes embroidered with your family's crest, kept in some old chest in the room for precious items?… You would don the most sumptuous of these, and I would imagine that before me stood not a marquise of the year 1905 but the wife of a *daimyo* before the Great Change."

He fixed her with an anxious gaze. She seemed embarrassed, and at first could only laugh, in the Japanese way, as she laughed when she was caught off guard and had no time to prepare her European voice, the less childlike one.

"Oh, dear master, what an extraordinary idea! Truly…"

She hesitated:

"Truly, my husband and I would be only too happy to accommodate you. We shall have a look… A robe of yore — I don't think that… But we can undoubtedly nonetheless…"

He was careful not to insist right away.

"Your husband — I have not forgotten him… Will I not have the pleasure of seeing him today?"

"No… He is out for a walk in the company of our friend Commander Fergan. They go out like this, quite often… And today they will not be back for tea."

"Just yesterday I was reading, in the *Nagasaki Press*…"

He stopped. The *Nagasaki Press*, supplementing its report on the Russian fleet, still at anchor off the coast of Annam, had announced Admiral Togo's imminent departure for the south. Perhaps Marquise Yorisaka was unaware. How considerate would it be to inform a young woman out of the blue that her husband was about to leave for war?

But Marquise Yorisaka, serene, was already completing the sentence he had cut off.

"In the *Nagasaki Press*? Ah! I know! The forthcoming departure of our battleships? I too have read that. It may not be immediate, but it surely won't be long."

She smiled with evident assurance. Felze, surprised, asked:

"Will the Marquis not be going back aboard his ship for the departure?"

She widened her narrow eyes.

"But of course! All of the officers will be, naturally."

He asked again:

"Do you think there will be no battle?"

She was grazing her hair with her fingertips, nonchalant as could be.

"We hope there will be a battle, a great battle…"

Felze was now painting with deft, precise strokes.

"You will be all alone, madam, after your husband's departure…"

"Oh, this will not be the first time he has left me like this… And so many Japanese women are in the same situation as I these days!…"

"Will you be returning to Tokyo?"

"No, because I would like to remain near Sasebo until the war is over."

"But I believe you have no friends in Nagasaki, no one to provide some company, and spare you from solitude…"

"No one. We see no one but you, and Herbert Fergan. And he will be leaving at the same time as my husband."

Felze hesitated before replying.

"I myself will not be leaving… Though my hair be white, I shall not dare to impose my visits on you during your husband's absence. Unless I am mistaken, custom absolutely forbids it."

"Absolutely? No… But it is true that a Japanese woman must under such circumstances enter into some degree of seclusion. During the war with China a princess of the blood appeared too often in public with a woman, a foreign ambassador who was her friend, and found herself repudiated by

order of the Emperor."

"Repudiated!…"

"Yes."

"But today custom is less strict?"

"A little less."

There was a moment of silence. Felze was still painting, his hand perhaps somewhat distracted. Marquise Yorisaka, seated, and completely still, kept her pose.

After a few minutes, however, she stirred and clapped. The "*Hai!*" of the Japanese servants sounded through the door.

"You take tea, do you not, dear master? *Ocha o motte kite kudasai!…*"[75]

To speak Japanese she had switched to her very light soprano voice.

"I shall take tea," said Felze. "However, I must confess, dear madam, that your English tea, black, sweet, and bitter, delights me far less than the small cups of fragrant water that I drink in all the country *ochaya*, where I stop to quench my thirst on my walks."

"Oh? What is this you're saying?"

She was so surprised that she forgot to laugh. The slant of her eyebrows arched with intense curiosity.

"You like Japanese tea? Really?"

"Very much."

"But you do not drink it aboard your yacht! Your hostess, Mrs. Hockley, must prefer the tea of her country…"

"Yes. But she has her tastes, and I have mine."

Marquise Yorisaka rested her cheek on a little clenched fist.

"Is Mrs. Hockley enjoying Nagasaki?"

"Most assuredly. Mrs. Hockley is a great one for excursions, and there are a great many walks to take in Kyushu."

"So you are not yet thinking to continue your journey. Where will you go once you leave Japan?"

------

75   Be so good as to bring the tea. [Author's note.]

"To Java, probably… Mrs. Hockley, you know, would like to travel around the world."

"I know… She is quite an extraordinary woman — so daring and resolute … and so marvelously beautiful."

Felze smiled with a shade of melancholy.

"Do you know that she has a strong desire to meet you?"

He had hesitated to utter this sentence, and mumbled the last words, as though regretting that he had opened his mouth. But Marquise Yorisaka heard him.

"Oh, I myself will be delighted… My husband and I were in fact thinking of extending her an invitation, but we were afraid to intrude…"

The door slid in its groove, and the two servants entered carrying the English tray, twice as long as their arms.

"Come, dear master. Take a cup of black tea nonetheless!… As Mrs. Hockley will be coming here, we must get accustomed to her favorite drink."

Marquise Yorisaka, Parisian as could be, held out the sugar bowl in one hand, the cream pot in the other. There could of course be no irony in her words, or ulterior motive in her mind.

X

The Witchcraft of War

A tiny park sits above the great Suwa Shrine and runs to the top of Nishi Hill.

A tiny but true park, dense and deep, a miracle of mystery. The Japanese can stunt their dwarf cedars and wee plums to the point of implausibility, but they love their huge plums and giant cedars all the more for it. Miniature gardens are pleasant baubles, kept as we would keep a hothouse or orangery. Tall woods are the genuine pride and joy of the Empire.

In the little park of Nishi hill, among the centuries-old camphors, the maples, and the cryptomerias festooned with splendid wisteria, Marquis Yorisaka Sadao and his friend Commander Herbert Fergan were walking along engaged in chat.

The winding lane climbed through the woods. Now and then, at a bend in the path, they would catch a glimpse between the trees: the verdant valleys, the bluish city with its scattered suburbs, and the steel-colored fjord coming suddenly into view below the great shrine's gardens, courtyards, and steps.

The two walkers had halted at one of these terraced angles.

"This is lovely weather," said Herbert Fergan. "Late April is proving to be truly brilliant. Things might change in May."

"Yes," murmured Yorisaka Sadao.

He had given the splendid landscape a mere glance. His sharp, black eye, gleaming with fervent, furtive curiosity, kept to the Englishman's calm face.

"By the way," he suddenly asked, "did you receive any news from your friend, Commander Percy Scott,[76] in yesterday's mail?"

---

76 Admiral Sir Percy Moreton Scott, 1st Baronet, KCB, KCVO (1853–1924). After joining the Royal Navy, in 1866, he quickly gained recognition as an innovative problem solver and engineer, particularly in the modernization of naval artillery. Scott introduced continuous-aim firing and other innovations that greatly increased the accuracy and effectiveness of naval guns. Initially met with resistance, his techniques were eventually adopted and improved tactics and artillery not only in Britain but globally.

"Admiral," corrected Fergan. "Percy Scott was promoted six weeks ago, in February."

"Ah! … I suppose that he is still pursuing his work?… That he continues to revolutionize English naval artillery?"

"Oh, is it really a revolution?" said Fergan.

He showed himself slightly skeptical. But Marquis Yorisaka insisted:

"If not a revolution, at least a total reform! Your admiralty has of course been working hard over the past twelve years… I've been keeping up with the advancements in your materiel. Your cannon are now beyond reproach, to say nothing of your shells…"

"Yes," Fergan calmly said. "You've adopted them, after your rather unsatisfactory trial with less-powerful shells last year, on the tenth of August…"

"This is true… And this is why I shall say nothing about it… Ha!… Your materiel, then, is excellent, and credit must go entirely to your admiralty. But *à la guerre*…, no?[77] In war materiel is nothing, personnel everything! And if your personnel is today perhaps the finest in Europe credit must go to Admiral Percy Scott."

Herbert Fergan consented with a nod.

"Good cannon and good shells," professed Marquis Yorisaka Sadao, "are all very well, but good men at the sights, good men at the rangefinders, and good artillery officers are better! And this is precisely Percy Scott's gift to England! … And England, moreover, has aptly rewarded Percy Scott. Was it not an emolument of eighty thousand yen[78] that Parliament recently bestowed on him?"

"Eight thousand pounds sterling, to be exact. It was fair compensation. Had he had sold his patents to industry Percy Scott would certainly have earned more."

"No doubt! … Eight thousand pounds does not cover such a man's genius! Our emperor would probably give more to have a Japanese Percy Scott."

"What need?" said Fergan, with a shade of irony. "You have the English Percy Scott! … England and Japan are allies. You have benefitted, you can still benefit, very freely from all our work."

For a moment Marquis Yorisaka turned to gaze into the green depths of the wood.

---

77 Short for "*à la guerre comme à la guerre*": literally "in war as in war," which means something like "You've gotta do what you've gotta do" or, if we add a martial twist, "When in Rome.…"

78 Two hundred thousand francs. — Historical figure. [Author's note.]

"Very freely," he repeated.

His voice had gone hoarse. He coughed.

"Very freely, true. Oh, we are most obliged to you! Yet we have benefited most from the work of your admiralty: we now possess your turrets, your casemates, your projectiles, your armored steel… We do not yet possess your men, or their wonderful secrets — those secrets of Admiral Percy Scott's invention."

"There are no secrets," Fergan averred. "Besides, weren't you victorious at the battles of the tenth and fourteenth of August?"[79]

"We were victorious, but…"

The thin lips pressed together in contempt beneath the bristly mustache.

"… But these were pitiful victories, as you know. You were at my side aboard the *Nikkō* on the tenth of August."

The Englishman, courteously, bowed:

"I was there," he said. "And, by Jupiter, I hereby testify that the tenth of August was a glorious day!…"

"No!" exclaimed the Japanese. "O Fergan *kimi*,[80] review your memory!

Remember the slowness, the indecision, the general disorder! Remember the Russian shell that hit the *Nikkō* below the blockhouse, and broke the armored communications tube! All life aboard the battleship came to a halt, like that of a man who's had his aorta severed. Our cannon, though intact, ceased to fire. Our gunners waited in vain for an order that could no longer come! And the *Tsesarevich*, riddled as she was by our fire, slipped away, all because the damage of a single blow had left us powerless![81] *That* was the tenth of August!… And I despair that our next day of battle will be the same, as we do not possess the English secrets."

---

79 During the Russo-Japanese War both battles had implications for the naval strategies employed by the combatants and were of great interest to naval observers worldwide.

    The Battle of the Yellow Sea (10 August 1904), a major engagement, prevented the Russian fleet at Port Arthur from breaking out to join forces with the Vladivostok squadron. The Russian fleet was forced to return to port, to the detriment of its operational flexibility. This battle was a major tactical victory for Japan, highlighting the emerging power of its navy and the increasingly obsolete tactics and equipment of the Russian fleet.

    Four days later (14 August 1904) the Battle off Ulsan again pit the Russian navy against the Japanese. This resulted in the defeat of the Russian Vladivostok squadron, which was attempting a sortie. As in the previous battle, the Russian naval found its capabilities constrained, as the Vladivostok group was compelled to remain at anchor. The Battle of Ulsan showcased the efficacy of Japan's naval strategy and modernized fleet.

80 *Kimi*, "my dear," with a respectful nuance. [Author's note.]

81 The *Tsesarevich* was a Russian *Borodino*-class pre-dreadnaught battleship launched in 1903 and scrapped in 1918. She served in the Russo-Japanese War and served as the flagship of Rear Admiral Wilgelm Vitgeft at the Battle of the Yellow Sea.

"There are no English secrets," repeated Fergan.

They fell silent. They had reached the top of the hill and were now descending by a more westerly path, which led to the very gardens of the great shrine.

"During an exercise when he was in command of the *Terrible*,"[82] Yorisaka Sadao broke back in, "Percy Scott landed eighty percent of his fire on target. Eighty percent! What armor could withstand such an avalanche of iron?"

"Bah!" said Fergan. "Why shouldn't the *Nikkō* fire as well as the *Terrible*? Percy Scott had trained his marksmen with devices that are known to you! Don't you have dotters, loading-machines, deflection-teachers?[83] Don't you have your Barr and Stroud rangefinders?"[84]

---

82   *HMS Terrible* was a big cruiser launched in 1895 and scrapped in 1932. She served in the Second Boer War, the Boxer Rebellion.

83   [The terms are in English. —*Translator*.] The dotter and the deflection teacher are two instruments designed to teach gunners to aim accurately. The loading-machine teaches servants to load quickly. [Author's note.]

84   Barr and Stroud rangefinders are still (1910) the only instruments in the world that afford accurate measurement of the distance from the cannon to the target, for proper adjustment of the elevation. [Author's note.]

"We have all that! And you have taught us how to use it… Oh, we are most obliged to you! But all of this is good for peacetime fire. In war the element of unpredictability is so great! Remember the shell of the nineteenth of August."

He searched the Englishman's eyes, like a hunter searches the bush from which the game is to emerge.

"The British fleet has fought so many times, for so many centuries! And it has been everywhere and unfailingly victorious! How? By what witchcraft? This is what we would like to know! What did Rodney, Keppel, Jervis, and Nelson do never, ever to be defeated?"[85]

"How should I know?" said Fergan, smiling.

They reached the gardens. The park came to an abrupt end at a long, narrow terrace planted with a dozen cherries in quincunxes. There stood an *ochaya*, next to an archery range.

"Look!" said Fergan, happy to talk of something else. "Mr. Jean-François Felze!"

The painter was seated in front of the *ochaya*, before a cup of tea. He stood, courteous.

"How are you?" asked Fergan.

Marquis Yorisaka saluted in the French manner, doffing his gold-braided cap.

"You are here, dear master! I thought you at the villa. Commander Fergan and I were just heading back and hoping to find you down there… The marquise could not keep you?"

---

85 The dialogue mentions four prominent figures in the history of the British Royal Navy, each renowned for his strategic and tactical acumen.

Admiral George Rodney (1718–92) was a distinguished British naval officer known for his service during the American War of Independence and the French Revolutionary Wars. His victory over the French at the Battle of the Saintes (1782), through such tactical innovations as "breaking the line," helped secure British naval supremacy during a critical period.

Admiral Augustus Keppel (1725–86) served in many naval campaigns, notably during the Seven Years' War. He was a strong advocate for naval reform and played a pivotal role in improving the conditions and effectiveness of the British fleet. His leadership in such battles as Ushant helped the British maintain control of crucial sea routes.

Admiral John Jervis, 1st Earl of St Vincent (1735–1823), was another British naval officer known for his service during the American Revolutionary War and the Napoleonic Wars. His most famous engagement was the Battle of Cape St Vincent (1797), where he defeated a larger Spanish fleet and boosted British morale and influence at sea.

Admiral Horatio Nelson, 1st Viscount Nelson (1758–1805), is the most famous British naval officer of all time. His tactics and leadership during battles like the Nile, Copenhagen, and especially Trafalgar have cemented his legend. Nelson's audacity, bravery, and innovative tactics ensured British naval dominance during a pivotal time.

"She very kindly tried, but the posing session had already gone on quite a while… The marquise needed some rest, and I some fresh air."

"We shall say goodbye, then… We'll be seeing you tomorrow, no doubt?"

"Tomorrow, definitely."

He had already retaken his seat, after a wave of his hand. Still and silent, he had turned his gaze back to the city and the gulf, there to be glimpsed below the terrace. The six o'clock sun was beginning to redden the bluish mists in the distance, and the sea was bleeding with myriad small reflections of purple, like sparkling wounds.

Fergan and Yorisaka were leaving.

"On foot, right?" asked the Englishman.

He was a good walker. And, besides, Stork Hill is fairly close to Suwa.

"On foot, if you wish."

They had left the garden through the gate opposite the city. They walked in silence as far as the small arched bridge over the northern stream, where the path forks. Yorisaka Sadao, who had been reflecting for a while, came to a sudden stop.

"Oh!" he exclaimed. "I have forgotten my appointment with the governor."

"An appointment?"

"Yes, for this very hour… What to do? Will you excuse me?"

"You're joking!… Go ahead, right away! You'll find a *kuruma* a hundred paces from here, in the streets by the temple… I'll accompany you, of course."

"Oh, no need at all! I shall go and come back. It is a mere military formality. It will be very short, barely an hour. *Kimi*, do go back to the villa on your own, please… Mitsouko is perhaps awaiting us for tea. I'll join you soon, and we'll dine together…"

"All right!"

XI

"When the Cherry Blossoms Fall..."

Striding long, Herbert Fergan was up Stork Hill within ten minutes. He gave three hasty knocks at the door of the villa.

"*Hai!*"

The *mousmé*-servant opened up and prostrated herself before the master's friend. A regular at the house, Fergan patted the fresh, round cheek and went on inside.

The Louis XV parlor was receiving the caress of the setting sun, all its windows open. Slanting sunbeams glowed red on the pompadour drapes.[86]

"Good evening," said Fergan.

Marquise Yorisaka, half-reclining in her wing chair, leaped to her feet as if startled.

"Good evening," she said. "Are you alone? The marquis has left you?"

She spoke English as well as French.

"The marquis has had to hurry to the governor's. I don't know what for. He won't be back for an hour."

"Ah!"

She smiled a somewhat practiced smile. He approached and, with a familiar gesture, simply took her into his arms and kissed her on the mouth.

"Mitsou, dear little thing!..."

She had surrendered, more docile than loving. She returned the kiss, endeavoring to return it as she had received it, in the Westerner way, between parted, aspiring lips.

Meanwhile, Fergan lifted her off the ground and, taking a seat, set her on his lap.

"What have you been doing all day?"

"Nothing... I was waiting for you... I didn't expect to see you alone tonight."

He leaned in and kissed her again.

---

86 A garish style of decoration named for Madame de Pompadour (1721–64), mistress of Louis XV.

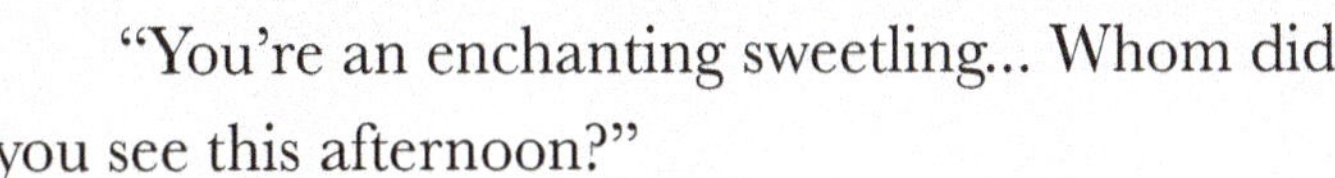

"You're an enchanting sweetling... Whom did you see this afternoon?"

"No one… The painter."

"The painter?… I'm sure he's hoping to woo you!"

"Not at all!"

"Not at all? Most unlikely? All Frenchmen woo all women!"

"But he's too old!…"

"So he says, but he's being cute."

"Too old. And, besides, he's in love with someone else — as you know! That American woman, Mrs. Hockley."

"I'm aware, but, no, he's not in love. He's her slave. He hates her much more than he loves her, but she's got a hold on him… He's French… She's beautiful and vicious…"

"Very vicious?"

"Yes… Oho! Does this interest you?"

He had felt a shudder run through her imprisoned little hand. Perhaps it was an illusion… Her tiny voice was as calm as could be.

"It doesn't interest me. But you know her, this Mrs. Hockley?"

"By reputation, yes. Everyone knows her by reputation."

"I mean, have you been introduced?"

"No."

"Then you shall be."

"How?"

"She's coming here. I've promised to invite her."

"Has she asked for an invitation?"

"No. I proposed it myself."

"Mercy! Why?"

She took a moment to think before answering.

"To please the painter. And also because the marquis would like me to receive European women often."

He laughed and kissed her again:

"Obedient little wife!"

He toyed with her beautiful black hair, supple and yielding in his caressing fingers.

"If you'd kept wearing it like the *mousmés* I wouldn't have the delight of touching your hair like this. This way is much more advantageous."

She looked at him through the narrow slit of her half-closed eyelids:

"I did it on purpose…"

He was growing bold. His eager mouth now pressed the obliging lips, and his hands unhooked the bodice, seeking the warmth of her naked breasts.

"Mitsou, Mitsou!… Delicious little honey-beam !…"

She did not resist. But her arms, motionless, hung down along her body and did not clasp her lover's bust.

❋

"Let me go, now!… I beg of you, Herbert!… Let me go and sit here, like a good boy. Yes, be good… I'd like to play some music for you…"

She opened the piano and rummaged a pigeon-hole.

"I'd like to sing you a song — a brand-new French song. Listen carefully to the lyrics."

She played the first bars, her touch astonishingly deft on the keyboard. She sang, to a sure and expressive accompaniment. Her reedy soprano leant a mystery and unreality to the strange melody.

He told me: "I had a dream last night. Your hair was wrapped around my neck. Your hair was like a black necklace around my neck and on my chest.

"I caressed it, and it was my own; and we were forever joined like this, by the hair, mouth to mouth, the way two laurels will often share a root.

"And so intertwined were our limbs that it seemed to me, little by little, I was becoming you or you were entering into me like my dream."

When he had finished he gently laid his hands on my shoulders, and looked at me with such tenderness that I lowered my eyes with a shiver…

He had listened with great attention.

"It's very pretty," he said, politely.

Like all Englishmen, he had no great ear for music.

"Very pretty," he repeated, "and, best of all, you're perfect in your playing."

She fell silent, hands still set on the final chord. He felt it necessary to show some curiosity.

"Who wrote that?"

She named the poet and the musician. He repeated the illustrious names.

"Mr. Louÿs and Mr. Debussy… Wow, it's really a piece of some significance…"[87]

He had risen to his feet.

---

87 The lyrics above are from a poem called "La Chevelure," from the 1894 poetry collection *Les Chansons de Bilitis*, by Pierre Louÿs (1870–1925), a French poet renowned for emotive prose and stylized Sapphic poetry. Its title is a high-flown term for a head of hair. In the poem Louÿs turns a woman's hair into a symbol of attraction and desire.

In 1897–98 the prominent French composer Claude Debussy (1862–1918) set three of Louÿs's poems, "La Chevelure" included, to music.

He came up behind her and leaned down to kiss the pure amber of her nape.

"You're an excellent artist."

She laughed, incredulous and modest.

"I'm a mediocre schoolgirl. I don't think you can have taken any pleasure in listening to me."

He protested.

"I enjoyed it very much, and I'd like you now to sing another song."

She was coy. He insisted.

"Yes, another song — this time a Japanese one…"

A slight shiver went through her. She paused a moment, settling her voice before making a reply.

"I don't have any Japanese music in the pigeon-holes. And how could I, on a piano?…"

"Play your *koto*."[88]

She looked at him wide eyed. "There's no *koto* here."

He stopped smiling. He was English, with little inclination for daydreams and speculations, but centuries of civilization had nevertheless refined his race, and he was not one to pass life's extraordinary spectacles by with no sense of their grandeur or mystery…

"There's no *koto* here," she had said. The *koto* is a sort of harp, ancient and venerable, whose use was once reserved for the noblest Japanese ladies and for courtesans of the highest rank. With *her* pedigree, Marquise Yorisaka had certainly learned the *koto* in earliest childhood, and had no doubt spent her youth assiduously plucking the sonorous strings with ivory plectrums. But these were now modern times, and "there was no longer any *koto* here."

Shaking off this brief reverie, Herbert Fergan suddenly and once again kissed his mistress on the nape. "Mitsou, my beloved little thing, sing anyway, please…"

She acquiesced.

"I will sing… Would you like… Would you like a very old *tanka*?[89] You

---

88 The origins of the *koto*, national instrument of Japan, go back to the Chinese zither of the seventh to eighteenth century. The *koto* typically has thirteen strings and is strummed or plucked with fingerpicks. Its body is traditionally made from Paulownia wood, and its strings are tuned with bridges moved along the length of the instrument. It produces a distinctive sound that is often described as serene or ethereal, and features prominently in various forms of Japanese music, from court music (*gagaku*) to contemporary compositions.

89 Japanese *tanka* is a classical form of poetry that dates back to the seventh century and was

know, a *tanka*: one of those five-verse poems that the princes and princesses of old would exchange, at the court of the Mikado or the Shōgun…[90] This one dates back more than a thousand years. I learned it when I was only a baby, and I've amused myself translating it into English."

Her fingers ran over the piano, coming up with a sad and bizarre harmony. But she did not at first sing. She seemed to hesitate. To help her through the hesitation, Fergan once again pressed his lips, at length, to her warm, downy neck.

The soft voice now murmured, slowly:

> "The time of the cherry blossoms
> Is not yet done,
> But the flowers must fall,
> Even as the love of their onlookers
> Is at its utmost exaltation…"

The singer fell silent and became still. Herbert Fergan, standing right next to her, was about to express his thanks with another kiss…

But someone spoke from the back of the parlor: "Mitsouko, why are you singing those absurd little refrains?"

Herbert Fergan straightened right up, sweat breaking out on his temples. Marquis Yorisaka had entered, in silence. Had he seen?… What had he seen?…

He had no doubt seen nothing, for he spoke with absolute calm.

"Mitsouko, will you not dine with us this evening?"

She had risen, and replied with her eyes fixed on the ground.

"I am very tired. Indeed, if it is no bother to you, I would like to be served in my room."

"As you wish."

❀

She had left. The door had slid in its groove, without a noise. Herbert Fergan compelled himself to breathe and passed a hand over his forehead.

---

favored by the Imperial Court. Comprising thirty-one syllables, *tanka* are often presented in a single line in the original Japanese, although English versions usually appear as five lines. Unlike *haiku*, *tanka* permit the use of literary devices, like metaphor and personification. While they do not have to rhyme, they must abide by syllable counts. Historically *tanka* were also used for intimate exchanges between lovers.

90   The two principal centers of power in historical Japan. The Mikado is the Emperor, often considered a divine figure, who serves as the symbolic head of state and resides in a court known for its refined culture and traditions. The Shōgun was the military ruler and often the de facto head of the government, with his own, influential court. See notes 37 and 38.

Amicable and insinuating, Yorisaka Sadao took four steps, set his elbows on the piano, and leaned. "We shall dine *en tête-à-tête*, then, *kimi*, and have a chat…"

He paused and looked deep into the Englishman's eyes.

"We shall have a chat. I still have much to learn from you, much advice to ask you for. We must not, must not, restart the battle of the tenth of August. You wouldn't refuse an ally?…"

Herbert Fergan dropped his gaze. His clean-shaven cheeks reddened. Docile, he began to speak.

"The tenth of August… On the tenth of August you were timid, very timid… You didn't know, didn't feel, that you were the stronger combatant. You lacked faith in yourselves. And you fought like people who fear defeat: overly careful, overly clever, from too far away. The only secret of the English is daring. To conquer the sea one must first prepare with method and prudence, then rush in with fury and folly. Such was the way of Rodney, Nelson, and the Frenchman Suffren…[91] In artillery fire, then,…"

---

91   See note 85 for Rodney and Nelson. Admiral Pierre-André de Suffren (1729–88) was a French naval commander noted for his tactical acumen and aggressive strategy. Suffren fought the British in the American War of Independence and is celebrated for his successful campaign in the Indian Ocean against British possessions and his engagements with the British fleet under Sir Edward Hughes.

XII

Shedding the West

The door, without a sound, had slid in its groove. And Marquise Yorisaka had gone out.

Outside the parlor she stopped and listened, attentive.

The voices of Herbert Fergan and Marquis Yorisaka alternated in tranquil phrases. Historic names — Rodney, Nelson, Suffren — passed through the thin partition.

Marquise Yorisaka slowly brought her fingertips to her temples, then with silent steps moved away from the partition.

The room adjoining the parlor was small and narrow, devoid of furniture. Marquise Yorisaka crossed it, crossed the next room as well, and came to the dwelling's far wing.

There a corridor stretched in near darkness between two paper panels of solid color surmounted by openwork friezes. Facing each other at the end were two sliding doors. Marquise Yorisaka slid open the left one.

Behind it lay a sort of alcove, an alcove of simple white wood, finely crafted but utterly bare. Roofbeams were apparent on the low, low ceiling, and the floor, with its tatami, was the color of fresh straw. Three big frames of granulated paper served as windows and panes. Set on the floor in a corner was a dressing table fit for a doll, with a mirror in a black-lacquered frame on top, and before this lay a cushion of black velvet: the only place where one could sit, or rather kneel — kneel in the Japanese style.

Standing at the threshold, Marquise Yorisaka clapped twice, and two servants rushed to her side.

Not a word was spoken. Mouths shut, the *mousmés* first prostrated themselves, then removed their mistress's shoes. Next, in a flash, they undressed her, removing the lace bodice, which slipped quickly down the powdered arms, and the moiré skirt and silk petticoats, and the corset, and the shirt, and the European stockings — toeless, unlike the Japanese variety.

Now naked, Marquise Yorisaka wrapped herself in a kimono of generous floral pattern, slipped her feet through the fabric straps of some sandals, set out from the alcove of white wood, her personal and intimate room, and went to bathe in a tub of scalding water, as all women in Japan do every evening, a little before sunset.

She then returned, let fall her kimono, and pushed the sandals away with her foot. The servants handed her three robes of light crepe and three broad-sleeved Japanese robes, all three of midnight blue, all three soberly peppered with the same strange, hieratic rosette: the *mon*, or crest.[92]

Dressed, Marquise Yorisaka knelt before her mirror. The robes flared out as they should. The broad *obi* cinched them with its magnificent knot. Both hands at work, the hair was detached, parted, smoothed into wide bands that framed the stony face. Marquise Yorisaka rose, walked for a moment through the room, went out into the semi-dark corridor, and suddenly, clapping again, opened the door on the right.

It led to second room, just like the first: same panels of bare, white wood, same frames of diaphanous paper, same beams, same tatamis. Instead of a dressing table and mirror,

---

92 *Mon*, also called *monshō*, *mondokoro*, and *kamon*, are Japanese emblems used to decorate and identify an individual, a family, or (more recently) an institution or business entity.

however, there were two tiny tabernacles flanking an altar of polished cedar, on which ancestral tablets stood in alignment.

Still silent, Marquise Yorisaka first prostrated herself in proper fashion before the tablets, for several minutes keeping her hands flat on the ground and her forehead to the mats.

Then she knelt on a cushion, before a sort of horizontal harp that a respectful servant had just carried in.

This gave birth to a lugubrious, slow music, whose rhythm and harmony in no way resembled the harmonies or rhythms of the West. Mysterious sounds followed in succession, intermingling. Phrases without beginning or end took shape. Reveries, sorrows, and laments quivered amid strange sinister creaks, recalling the rustle of winter's northeast wind or the cry of nocturnal birds. Above it all floated a desperate melancholy…

Kneeling in ancient fashion in her ancestors' room, Marquise Yorisaka played the *koto*…

XIII

"Gold is more precious than silver"

The next week, Jean-François Felze having completed the portrait, Marquise Yorisaka did not fail to invite Mrs. Hockley to "come to tea, without any sort of ceremony, at the villa on Stork Hill and admire the master's beautiful handiwork, before Marquis Yorisaka can carry it off on his battleship."

Mrs. Hockley was careful not to refuse the invitation. She decided to go in the company of the master himself, and insisted that Miss Elsa Vane, her reader, come along.

"Are you not bringing Romeo the lynx?" asked Felze, as the caravan set out from the *Yseult*.

"How droll you are!" retorted Mrs. Hockley.

It was the first of May. Despite the doom-saying news spread every morning by the *Nagasaki Press*, Japanese officers on leave had not yet received the order to rally at Sasebo.

Marquis Yorisaka went to the garden gate to greet his guests. As always, he was wearing his gold-braided black uniform. Mrs. Hockley, favorably impressed, remarked that there was no difference between this uniform and that of the officers in the grand American navy. Marquis Yorisaka declared himself both ashamed and proud.

Inside the villa the Louis XV parlor had acquired the air of a gala. The Sèvres vases[93] were bursting with flowers, and the easel bearing the painting was elegantly draped in liberty satin.[94] Marquise Mitsouko, in a dress of soft guipure, paid her respects to her visitor and, the better to

---

93   France's Manufacture Nationale de Sèvres, often referred to simply as Sèvres, is one of the most prestigious porcelain manufacturers in the world, known for exquisite and artful designs. Established in 1740 in Vincennes, it moved to its current location in Sèvres, near Paris, in 1756. Over the centuries, it has been patronized by French royalty and the elite.

94   A type of high-quality, soft, lightweight satin fabric, likely made of silk, popular in the early 20th century. It was known for its excellent drape and lustrous finish, making it suitable for both elegant decorative purposes (like draping) and fashionable clothing, particularly flowing gowns that required less rigid structuring than earlier styles. The name strongly associates it with Liberty & Co. of London, a store renowned for its influential fabrics linked to the Aesthetic and Art Nouveau movements.

honor her, insisted on speaking nothing but English.

"The master will forgive me if today I am unfaithful to his beautiful French language, but I am sure that aboard the *Yseult* he himself has the gallantry to speak as you do, madam!"

Charmed, Mrs. Hockley was unsparing in her praise, and even in direct compliments. Marquise Yorisaka was a true enchantress! And how graceful, and pretty, and cultured! The old peoples of Europe confine their women to frivolous or household matters, but young nations have other ideas and other ambitions. Mrs. Hockley appreciated the superiority of her own compatriots over Europeans, and rejoiced to see Japanese women follow superbly in the footsteps of their American counterparts.

"You speak English, French, perhaps German?…"

"A few words…"

"Japanese, naturally. Chinese too?"

It was Marquis Yorisaka who answered no.

"You have received a thoroughly Western education! Have you been to New York?"

Marquise Yorisaka had not but regretted it with all her might.

"How perfectly this Parisian gown suits you!… And your hand is a jewel!"

Felze, rather dour, said not a word, and Miss Vane, disdainful, imitated his silence. Despite the hosts' zeal, despite Mrs. Hockley's expansive cordiality, the reception might have sputtered were it not for Commander Herbert Fergan's timely arrival. Marquis Yorisaka received him with a great show of friendship, and Felze was obliged to cheer up a bit so as not to be rude, for the Englishman was in high spirits.

"Mr. Felze," he had begun by saying, "do you recall a certain passage from Thucydides, perhaps the most profound passage anywhere to be found in the psychological literature, whatever the country or century? Pardon me for being pedantic: we English are very strong in Greek… Indeed, it is this strength that in practical matters makes us so pitifully inferior to Mrs. Hockley's compatriots… Anyway, in year III of the eighty-seventh Olympiad, at the height of the famous plague that devastated Athens, Thucydides assures us, the city, in all its mourning and agony, was swept up in a veritable madness for pleasure.[95] This does

---

95 Thucydides (1. 460/455 – 399/398 BCE), the ancient Greek historian, chronicled the Plague of Athens (429–426 BCE), which killed 75,000 to 100,000 people, in his *History of the Peloponnesian War*. At II.vii.3–54 he notes (in P. J. Rhodes's translation):

"…the plague marked the beginning of a decline to greater lawlessness in the city. People

not surprise him, and even seems to him quite natural — in accord with human instinct. Yes. — Well, Mr. Felze, Thucydides is not wrong. This morning I who am in Nagasaki as the Athenians were in Athens — under the threat of unexpected and sudden death, I mean — I woke up with the desire to live life to the fullest!…"

Jean-François Felze had raised an eyebrow.

"You are under threat of death?"

"I am under the threat of a Russian cannonball. I too must soon report to Marquis Yorisaka's battleship, and shall be attending the next battle. A magnificent spectacle, Mr. Felze, but rather perilous. Have you ever seen a gladiator match? I am about to see one. Nothing could be more exciting! There is a small inconvenience, however: there are no stands around the circus, and so I shall be forced down into the arena!"

---

were more willing to dare to do things which they would not previously have admitted to enjoying, when they saw the sudden changes of fortune, as some who were prosperous suddenly died, and their property was immediately acquired by others who had previously been destitute. So they thought it reasonable to concentrate on immediate profit and pleasure, believing that their bodies and their possessions alike would be short-lived."

Illustration: "Plague in an Ancient City," ca. 1650–52 by Michael Sweerts (1618–64).

He was laughing. And Marquis Yorisaka, debonair gladiator, joined him in the laughter, with the best grace in the world.

Herbert Fergan then addressed to Mrs. Hockley an adroit compliment on her yacht. The American took pride in the vessel, and was pleased to have it repeated that she owned what was without question the most beautiful pleasure craft in existence. However, despite the value of a compliment from a ship's captain, and aide-de-camp to the king of England, Mrs. Hockley was listening with half an ear and did not turn away from Marquise Yorisaka, who held all her attention.

Both seated on the sofa, side by side, the American and the Japanese seemed the picture of intimate friendship. Mrs. Hockley had taken hold of her new friend's hands and was speaking to her confidentially, making a tireless inquiry into her childhood, her youth, her marriage, her tastes, her pleasures, the books she read, her religious notions, and her philosophical opinions. She poured into the inquisition all the exasperating curiosity of the women of her race, who train from girlhood in the sport of asking countless and useless questions, questions without interest or purpose, and spend their lives packing their brains with thousands upon thousands of bits of information, thousands upon thousands of documents — laboriously obtained, laboriously classified, sorted, and tagged, never absorbed, never understood…

But Marquise Yorisaka, unaccustomed to this, willingly endured her visitor's indiscreet onslaught. She answered every question obligingly and never tired. She was giving Mrs. Hockley, who was, of course, incapable of weighing it, good proof of the docility of Japan's women. And with imperceptible coquetry she suffered her little fingers of silken ivory to lie in the grasp of the white Western hands: also pretty, but immense by comparison.

Miss Vane, at the far end of the parlor, had discouraged the attentions of Herbert Fergan and even of Marquis Yorisaka himself. Still and nonchalant in the depths of a wing chair, she would on occasion cast a brief glance at the sofa. And Felze smiled, with a bit of irony and a bit of bitterness.

Tea was being served. All of the windows were open, and one could see, beneath a mottled sky, the saw-toothed mountains that line the gulf's two shores, and below them the green cemeteries that ring the brown and blue city. It was mild out, as the sun, still high, continued to temper the humid spring's cool.

"Mr. Marquis Yorisaka," Mrs. Hockley said at last, "I feel I've developed a great affection for your wife, and would like to form an intimate friendship with her. I fear, too, that once you depart for the war she might grow bored all alone, and I hope that my very frequent visits will keep her entertained. I shall extend my yacht's stop here, if necessary, but I will not suffer so beautiful and interesting a woman to languish here in sadness awaiting her husband's glorious return. François Felze, in any case, would like to paint the marquise a second time — in a kind of costume, I believe. I shall accompany him, to ensure that the correct customs are properly respected. And I shall not leave Nagasaki before you have vanquished the Russian savages."

Marquis Yorisaka bowed very low. He was about to reply when the door opened to reveal an unexpected person.

This was an officer of the Japanese navy, an officer in uniform, identical head to foot to Marquis Yorisaka: same age, same rank, and same bearing. Yet the two faces differed in one detail: Marquis Yorisaka's bore a mustache, in the European style, while the newcomer's bore a shaved lip.

He entered and first saluted in the old way, with a bow from the waist, hands on his knees. Then, walking towards the marquis, he saluted Yorisaka in particular, before addressing to him in Japanese a ceremonial compliment, to which the marquis replied with great deference.

Commander Fergan had meanwhile approached Jean-François Felze:

"Observe closely, dear sir. Old Japan is paying us its respects!"

Marquis Yorisaka had taken his visitor by the hand and turned to face the room.

"I have the honor to present my most noble comrade Viscount Hirata Takamori,[96] like me a ship's lieutenant aboard the *Nikkō*. Pray, be kind enough to excuse him, for he does not speak English … or French."

All bowed. Once more Viscount Hirata's rigid body broke in two at the waist, and after he had paid a few courteous but brief tributes to Marquise Yorisaka, who received them in semi-prostration, he took the marquis aside and spoke to him for quite a while, and with considerable insistence.

"I met this Viscount Hirata during the last campaign," Fergan explained to Felze. "He is a most curious man, lagging a scant forty years behind his century — and in Japan, as you know, once you go back further

---

96 The Viscount, important to the action at the end of the book, is a fictional character.

than the revolution of 1868 forty years might as well be four hundred. Viscount Hirata is, like our host, the son of a *daimyo*, but while the Yorisaka are of the Chōshū clan, with origins on the island of Hondo, the Hirata are of the Satsuma clan, with origins on the island of Kyushu. This makes for a prodigious difference. The Chōshū were once men of letters, poets, and artists. The Satsuma were strictly warriors. During the famous revolution, which the Japanese call the Great Change, the Satsuma and the Chōshū took up arms together for the Mikado against the Shōgun, and their military victory led to their feudal disaster, because once it was rid of the Shōgun the Mikado had no more pressing business than to abolish the clans, the *daimyo*, and their samurai. The Chōshū resigned themselves right away to the new order of things, but the Satsuma did not. Marquis

Yorisaka's parents modernized themselves in the blink of an eye, and for the Empire's reorganization the emperor had no more docile or intelligent assistants than they. For nine years Viscount Hirata's parents locked themselves into their lair at Kagoshima, and when they emerged, on the seventeenth of February 1877, it was sword in hand, to make a rush at the imperial troops, under the leadership of the old rebel leader Saigō. They were defeated. All of them died… Yes, Mr. Felze, the very father of the officer you see there was killed fighting the emperor, the emperor who reigns today! And I have every reason to believe that Viscount Hirata Takamori holds exactly the same opinions as all of his ancestors!…

"The funny thing is, he's nonetheless an excellent officer, very familiar with the most recent weapons. Aboard the *Nikkō* he's in charge of the electric machines, and few European engineers could match his skill."

Just then Marquis Yorisaka, who had been listening in silence to Viscount Hirata Takamori's speech in Japanese, turned to his guests:

"My most noble comrade informs me that the two of us…" — he corrected himself, looking at Fergan — "…the three of us are recalled to Sasebo tomorrow."

A sudden silence fell. Jean-François Felze looked towards the sofa. Marquise Yorisaka, no doubt with a shudder, had pulled her hands away from Mrs. Hockley's.

Herbert Fergan was then the first to speak.

"What was I just telling you about Thucydides, Mr. Felze?!… Whatever happens to me in this adventure, I shall be happy to share aboard the *Nikkō* whatever fate awaits this beautiful work…"

He was gesturing toward the portrait, whose presence Mrs. Hockley had not yet thought to remark. Thus reminded of the reception's real pretext, the American woman rose to consider the picture of her Japanese friend.

Viscount Hirata, four paces off, had noticed the painting. His eyes made a quick comparison between the Asian face painted on the canvas and the Western face of Mrs. Hockley, who had approached to get a better look. Speaking low, he uttered some words in Japanese that Commander Fergan alone caught.

"Is he making an artistic judgment?" Felze asked, curious.

"No, dear sir! A good Satsuma rarely utters artistic judgments… Viscount Hirata has expressed a mere ethnological opinion — a rather delicious one, as it happens. Permit me to translate as follows: 'Our skin is yellow, theirs is white; gold is more precious than silver.'"[97]

---

97 Before Commander Herbert Fergan, Mr. André Bellessort heard a samurai from Kagoshima utter a very similar sentence. — C. F. [Author's note.]

XIV

A Flash in a Long Night

Mrs. Hockley's cabin on the Yseult had been modeled after that of H.M. the Empress of Russia's on the *Standart*.[98] The furniture was English, with an abundance of pale woodwork, water-green lacquer, and tone-on-tone marquetry. The copper bed had no curtain except a muslin with a brocade of large irises. The carpet was of short pile, and nailed down. And there were photographs in lieu of works of art. In this exact imitation of a sovereign with austere tastes Mrs. Hockley indulged both her democratic vanity and her instinct for comfort. Genuine luxury, the luxury of gold, marble, old-master paintings, antique statues, was to be lavished with pride in salons and halls. Intimate apartments were better served by the soft simplicity of British upholstery.

Midnight had just struck.

Lying on the bed, elbow on a pillow and cheek in hand, Mrs. Hockley, dressed in nothing but her rings and a shirt of surah silk, much more transparent than lace, was listening to Miss Elsa Vane's evening reading.

A correct reader, Miss Elsa Vane was sitting on a straight-backed chair, and had not removed her dinner dress: this dress, incidentally, was more indecent as a dress than Mrs. Hockley's shirt was as a shirt — it was the difference between the unbuttoned and the nude — but was a dress all the same. The habit makes the monk, as everyone knows, and Miss Vane, in her clothing and in her attitude, served to correct whatever bit of daring there was in Mrs. Hockley's attitude and attire.

Such, in fact, was the ceremony every evening. Mrs. Hockley would never deviate, detesting any breach of protocol.

And this evening Miss Vane was reading chapter eleven of the volume in which on the eve she had read chapter ten.

98　The *Standart* was an Imperial Russian yacht built by order of Emperor Alexander III and launched in 1896 as the largest imperial yacht afloat. The ship was ornately fitted out, with mahogany paneling, crystal chandeliers, and other amenities. After the Russian Revolution the ship was placed in drydock until 1936, when she was converted to a minelayer. During the Second World War she took part in the defense of Leningrad.

The voice — slightly nasal, like all Yankee voices, but of good timber, and very low for a young girl — laid stress on the final words:

"'And yet — strange contradiction for those who believe in time — geological history shows us that life is but a brief episode between two eternities of death, and that in this very episode conscious thought has lasted, and will last, but a moment. Thought is but a flash in a long night.

"'But this flash is everything.'"[99]

❋

"Mr. Poincaré," declared Mrs. Hockley, "is an original writer."

Miss Vane, tired, was drinking the traditional lemonade, lemon squash, prepared in advance.[100]

"Original," repeated Mrs. Hockley. "Philosophical to be sure. A bit superficial, don't you think? Too French and lacking German depth…"

"Yes." said Miss Vane. "The Germans adapt to every subject a particular language that is pleasant to know and understand, because it serves to fix the mind. Mr. Poincaré speaks in everyday language, and there's a tendency to frivolousness in it."

Mrs. Hockley, nonchalantly, reclined on her back and took a knee into her clasped hands.

"Frivolous, in truth. You're right, Elsa. Besides, the vulgar language creates a danger of atheism. It's improper for the uneducated to read such books, which to them would seem irreligious."

"You think these books are in fact not irreligious?"

"Certainly. I think so. They are clearly but a paradoxical speculation. They shake no faith."

The hands clasped on the knee slid down the leg and, at the bottom of the slightly rolled-up shirt, took hold of the exposed ankle. In this new pose

---

99   The passage is from *La Valeur de la science* (1905), by Jules Henri Poincaré (1854–1912), a French mathematician, theoretical physicist, engineer, and philosopher of science. As the book was not published in English until 1913 (*The Value of Science in The Foundations of Science*, The Science Press, New York), we must assume that Miss Vane was reading the French original in the author's 1909 book.

100   (Appears as *lemonsquash.* —*Translator.*) This is a sweet, tangy non-alcoholic drink made from lemon juice, sugar, and water. The origin of lemon squash can be traced back to the late nineteenth century in the United Kingdom, where it was first sold as a bottled concentrate by the Robinsons company. The company's founder, Matthew Robinson, had been experimenting with fruit syrups and concentrates since the late 1800s, and lemon squash quickly became one of its most popular products.

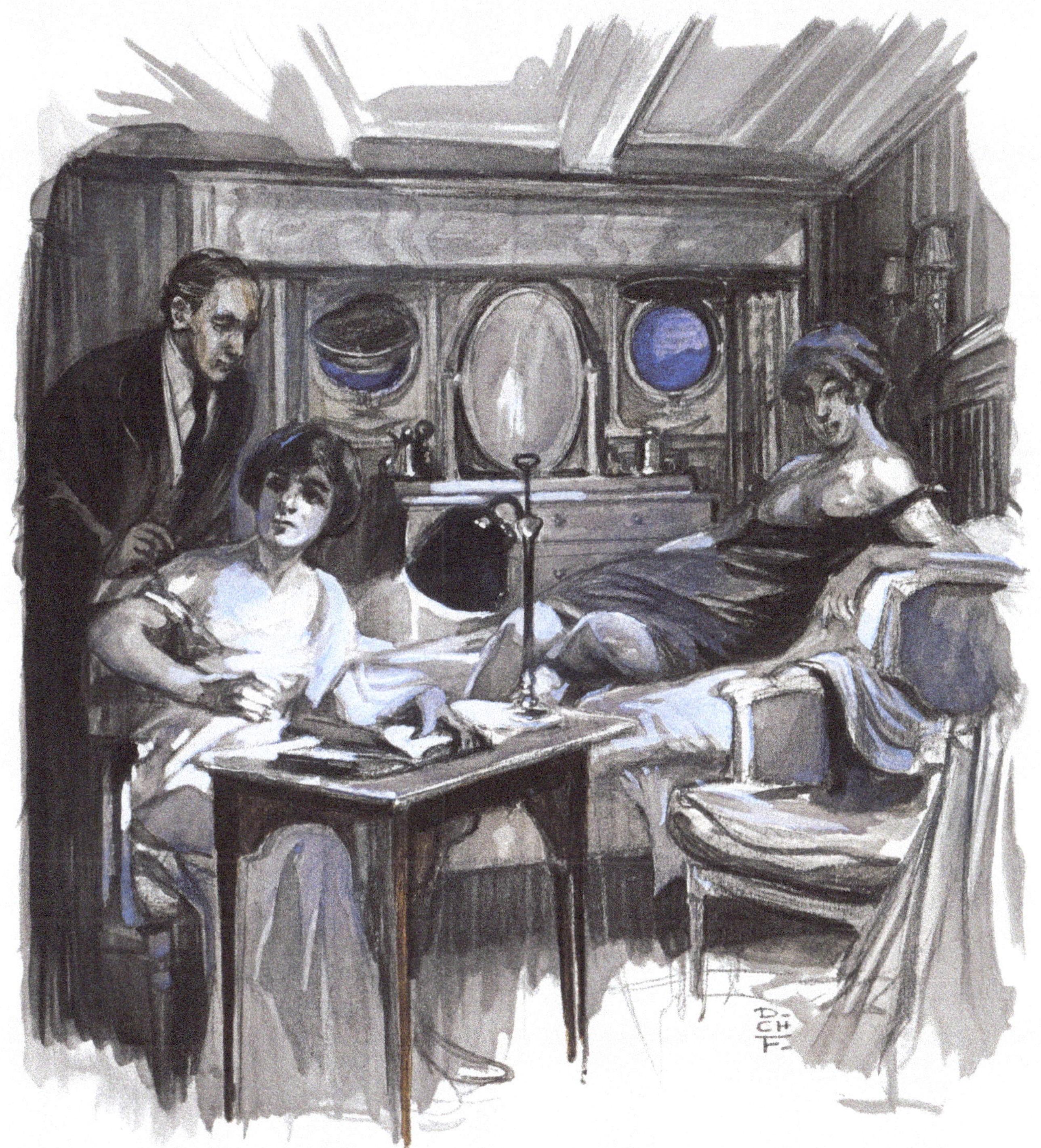

Mrs. Hockley undertook to complete her thought:

"The Holy Bible…"

But two knocks at the door interrupted the exordium.

"Is it François?"

"It's me," said Felze.

He entered, and looked at the two women: Miss Vane still seated, the book beside her, and Mrs. Hockley lying on her back, her hands, knotted together, now gripping her bare foot.

"You were talking theology, if I've heard right?"

He pronounced the word *theology* with all suitable respect.

"Not theology but philosophy, because of this book…"

To point to the book in question Mrs. Hockley had released her foot, and the leg, suddenly free, slid on the bed and laid itself out straight, very white, outside the black shirt.

Felze considered this leg for a moment, then turned his gaze to the still-open volume.

"Good lord," he said, "do you do some lofty reading!"

He bent down and read in a low voice:

"'Thought is but a flash in a long night. But this flash is everything…' Well, now! I'll repeat this affirmation to a Chinaman I know, who will approve… Come to think of it, was it to counter the terrible Poincaré that you were calling upon the Holy Bible to succor you?"

Disdainful, Mrs. Hockley slowly waved her hand, right to left, its diamonds glittering.

"That would have been superfluous. Besides, Poincaré is not terrible. Miss Vane, reasonably, was just deeming him frivolous."

Felze widened his eyes but remembered just in time a sentiment he had recently heard beneath the philosophical light of nine violet lanterns: "Only with women is it proper to listen without answering." And Felze did not answer.

Mrs. Hockley was already asking him:

"Did you go to the station?"

"Yes. And I bade Marquis Yorisaka farewell in your stead."

"So he has left. Has the English commander also left?"

"Yes. And Viscount Hirata Takamori with them."

"I have little interest in this Viscount Hirata, because I believe him to be little civilized. Tell me, though: have you seen the marquise?"

"No."

"So she wasn't at the station… It seems to me, then, that she's not in love with her husband, wouldn't you say?"

"I'm slower than you to observe such things."

"I shall find out her true feelings, in an case. What day do you intend to start the portrait-in-costume?"

"Tomorrow or the day after. I'm in no hurry. But don't you think that this word *costume* is rather disparaging of Marquise Yorisaka when you apply it to the national costume of Japan's women?"

"Why disparaging, since the marquise no longer wears this national costume? You're ever the funny one. Ah!… Now, if you'd be so kind — what whim kept you from coming back aboard for dinner? You are of course quite at liberty, but I received your note at an astonishingly late hour."

Felze pursed his lips.

"What whim?… I don't know. The station is very far away. The sun was about to set when the train left. I crossed half the city. Under the lilac sky the streets were gleaming as though paved with amethysts. I lacked the courage to continue on my way and stopped to get a better look. And when the last reflection had reached full bloom I suddenly felt so tired and sad that I preferred not to inflict my presence on you."

Mrs. Hockley, attentive, had raised her blond head from the lacy pillow.

"My," she said, struck with his words, "how extraordinarily poetic!…"

She fell silent, seeking perhaps to conjure a picture of variegated streets in the twilight, and probably failing. Then, reclining once more:

"But *then* what did you do?"

"I went to greet my Chinese friend Zhou P'ei."

"How strange this pleasure you get from that ridiculous man's company… Have you smoked opium this evening?"

"No."

"Why?"

"Because… because it was my intention to return here, early."

He now looked at her intently. She burst into laughter.

"Miss Vane, I find there's a very Japanese odor coming in through that porthole, and I know you don't care for it. Would you grab the vaporizer?… Yes, vaporize all over, please, and also the bed … and me."

Obedient and silent, Miss Vane pressed the golden bottle's little piston. Under the cool caress of the perfume Mrs. Hockley had stiffened and arched her entire body, and the tips of her breasts stretched the transparent surah.

Felze twice ran a hand over his forehead, then closed his eyes. Mrs. Hockley's laughter rang out again, clear.

"That's enough. Put the vaporizer back, Elsa. I'm quite all right now. What time is it?"

"Half past midnight."

"I imagine you'd both like to turn in."

There was no reply. Miss Vane was slowly setting the gold bottle back on its shelf. Felze, immobile, had not reopened his eyes.

"Yes!" Mrs. Hockley cut in. "You must be tired. Good night!"

One after the other, docile, they approached the bed. Mrs. Hockley held out her right hand, open. Miss Vane, unexpectedly, kissed the palm. Felze just brushed the tips of the nails.

"Good night!" repeated Mrs. Hockley.

At the door Felze stepped aside to let the young girl pass.

"François!" Mrs. Hockley called, suddenly. "Stay a moment, you alone…"

Miss Vane was outside. She closed the door, no doubt with a clumsy hand, as its bolt gave an almost violent click.

Felze, still inside, as per the summons, took three steps forward, and the electric lamps shed a pink light on his somewhat pale face.

Mrs. Hockley was smiling:

"I'm genuinely sorry to keep you when you're so exhausted... You'd best go to bed, like Miss Vane..."

He was right near the bed. He knelt down, took the dangling hand, and, passionately, pressed his mouth to the warm arm's flesh.

"O Betsy! Will you make an exception tonight and not make me suffer too much?"

She tilted her head towards him:

"Are you certain you wouldn't rather go back to your room and paint a picture of those amethyst-like streets?... No?..."

XV

Nipponese Diplomacy

The very next day Mrs. Hockley accompanied Jean-François Felze to Marquise Yorisaka's house — or, rather, led him there.

As was her custom, Marquise Yorisaka gave her visitors the most gracious reception, but the visit did not serve its official purpose: there was no question of starting the "in costume" portrait. Though aware of their coming, the marquise was dressed in her prettiest Parisian gown. And when he reproached her and demanded the promised Japanese attire Felze was met with the reply that at the last moment the necessary courage to don an old relic had been found lacking.

"I am in fact glad that you should have lacked the courage," said Mrs. Hockley, approving, "for you are no doubt much more fetching in that tea-gown."

And there ensued two hours of idle chatter. It pleased Mrs. Hockley to no end to hear English words issue from the narrow, made-up mouth of an Asian lady. And with a singular blend of indulgence and coquetry Marquise Yorisaka obliged her new friend in her effusions.

Felze, sullen, contributed only monosyllables to the conversation, but when the time came to leave he insisted on scheduling the next appointment, which this time would be a genuine posing session.

It was Wednesday, third of May. The next appointment was set for Friday the fifth, but things worked out on Friday as they had on Wednesday. That very morning Marquise Yorisaka had received, by French ocean liner, a shipment from her favorite couturier and, naturally, hadn't been able to resist showing Mrs. Hockley "the latest creation from Rue de la Paix."[101]

"I think," said Mrs. Hockley, "that no woman of Paris or New York is as resplendent in this latest creation as you are."

Felze, twice disappointed, said nothing but was so grim in the face that as they were taking their leave Marquise Yorisaka pulled him aside:

"Dear master," she said in French, "I am truly sorry to have broken my word to you once again. I see that you are cross with me. Yes, yes, I can see it,

---

101 Rue de la Paix, in the second arrondissement of Paris, flourished at the dawn of Haute Couture fashion during the Belle Époque of the early twentieth century. See the illustration of one designer's fashion house: "Cinq Heures Chez Paquin" ("Five Hours at Paquin"), Henri Gervex (1852–1929).

and you are right. I am in the wrong… But I will make amends. Listen: come alone, as you came for the other portrait… Come tomorrow. And I swear that this time I will pose as you wish."

Mrs. Hockley approached: "Are you telling a secret?"

"Oh no! I was just apologizing to the master, because I feel that I would never dare appear before you in a simple Japanese robe; it would be very ugly, and you would dislike it. So, to receive the master's forgiveness, I was offering to pose for him as he wishes, but on a day when you yourself are not here!…"

"Tomorrow," said Felze.

And he admired the Nipponese diplomacy. Mrs. Hockley, most flattered, smiled.

"Yes. That is an excellent idea, because I too prefer to see you in nothing but beautiful gowns. So the master shall come here tomorrow, and I shall not. The day after, though, I shall come and he shall not. That way things will be equal."

She thought for a moment:

"I am convinced, too, that the painting will be perfect in spite of the barbaric costume, because François Felze's talent inclines toward the bizarre."

She thought some more:

"But is it correct, and in accord with the customs of this land, for a man to enter your house alone, while your husband is at war?"

"Pshaw!" said Marquise Yorisaka, carefree.

XVI

The Daimyo's Daughter

Would you like…" asked Marquise Yorisaka, suddenly blushing under her makeup — "would you like for me to pose like a genuine lady of the past? I shall do it to make you happy, and because you have promised to keep this portrait hidden away in your Paris studio, never showing it to anyone… Yes, I believe there is a *koto* here, and I could pretend to play it while you paint. In the *kakemonos* of old the wives of *daimyo* are often shown playing the *koto*, as it was an instrument of very noble reputation… If this would please you, then…"

Her hair styled in broad, smooth bandeaux, her dress made of dark-blue crêpe de Chine, with the white rosettes of the *mon* in hieratic relief, Marquise Yorisaka stood between the piano and the Pompadour mirror of her Parisian parlor, looking like one of those priceless archaic statues that the emperors of legendary centuries would commission to ornament their palaces of pure gold, and which today grow old in the banal gallery of some European museum, between a curtain of red cotton and three walls of painted plaster.

And Felze painted, silent, enthusiastic.

The model had struck her pose and was holding it with Asian stillness. Her knees rested on a velvet cushion, the flared dress spread out around her folded legs, and from a sleeve as wide as a skirt a bare hand, armed with an ivory plectrum, touched the strings of the *koto*.

"Are you not tired?" Felze asked, after a long half-hour.

"No. In times past we were accustomed to kneeling like this, indefinitely…"

He continued to paint, his initial ardor unflagging. A sketch, quite lovely, had taken shape over the half-hour.

"You should play for real," he broke in, "rather than pretend. I need you to play, to get the expression on your face…"

She shuddered:

"I do not know how to play the *koto*."

But he looked at her:

"When one kneels so well on an Osaka cushion I cannot, in truth, believe that one cannot play the *koto*."

She blushed again, and lowered her eyes. Then, yielding to the magnetic power of this will she was subject to, she gently plucked the sonorous strings, which bit by bit produced a strange harmony.

Eyebrows furrowed, lips dry, Felze pushed his brush with a sort of violence across the already luminous canvas, and the sketch seemed to come alive under the magician's touch.

Now the *koto* achieved a more powerful reverberation. The emboldened hand lent itself to the ardor of the mysterious rhythm, so different from all the rhythms known to Europe. And little by little the tilted face took on the disturbing smile of the contemplative idols that ancient Japan would sculpt in ivory or jade.

"Sing!" commanded the painter.

Docile, the narrow, made-up mouth sang. The song was almost indistinct, a sort of chant that would begin and end in a murmur. The *koto* prolonged the muffled notes, its twang laying emphasis on some of the incomprehensible syllables. For several minutes the strange music lasted. Then the musician fell silent, in apparent exhaustion.

"Where," Felze asked in a near whisper, never lifting his head, "did you learn that?"

The answer came, as it were, from the depths of a dream.

"Down there … when I was little, very little … in the old castle at Hoki,[102] where I was born… Every winter's morning, before dawn, once the servants had opened the *shoji*,[103] and the icy mountain wind had roused me from my sleep and driven me from the thin little mattress that was my bed, they would bring me the student *koto*, and I would kneel at it and play until after sunrise. And then, barefoot, I would go down to the big courtyard, often white with snow, and watch my brothers train at their fencing with sabers, and I myself would train with the halberd, because the rule so ordered.[104] The long bamboo blades would clack as they collided. We would have to endure in silence as the blows stung our arms and hands

---

102   Hōki was a former province in what is today the western half of Tottori Prefecture in the San'in region of Japan. In 1871, after the Meiji restoration and the abolition of the *han* system, Hōki became part of Tottori Prefecture. It is unclear which castle the marquise is referring to.

103   *Shoji*, mobile partitions consisting of thick paper stretched over a frame. [Author's note.]

104   The halberd is an archaic weapon typically consisting of a battle-ax and pike mounted on a staff about six feet long.

and the snow bit into our legs… When the lesson was over the servants would put me in ceremonial dress, and then I would first go bow before my father, whom I would always find in the women's quarters… He would take me along to receive the salute of the samurai, the squires, and the other servants. The folds of the beautiful silk robes would drag, and the lacquered sheaths for the sabers would brush against the lacquered sheaths for the daggers. And I would wish in my heart that it would all stay the same for a thousand years…"

The brush had stopped, and the painter, still, had closed his eyes, the better to hear.

"And I wished in my heart to suffer a thousand deaths rather than to live a foreign or different life. But faster than Mount Fuji changes color at twilight the face of the earth underwent a metamorphosis. And I did not die…"

Dreamy fingers plucked at the strings of the *koto*, stirring melancholy sounds. Like a song's refrain the tiny voice repeated:

> *I did not die… did not die… did not die…*
>
> *And a new life enveloped me, as the net of a bird-catcher will
> envelop a trapped pheasant…*
>
> *Pheasants caught in a trap and kept too long in narrow cages
> forget how to spread their wings, and forget their former freedom…*
>
> *The koto wept, faintly.*
>
> *In my own cage, where I have been imprisoned by many skilled
> and wise bird-catchers, I fear that I too shall gradually forget the
> old life…*
>
> *I already no longer remember the precepts I once learned from the
> Classical and Sacred Books.*[105]
>
> *And sometimes — oh, sometimes! — I no longer wish to
> remember…*

Three notes burst like shrieks from the koto.

> *…I have no desire anymore.*

––––––––––––––

105 The Chinese books that were once the basis of Japanese education.

And then…I don't know anymore, not anymore…

Perhaps I ought to forget.

The precepts they teach me today are different…

How am I to taste hot rice while preserving the taste of raw fish on my tongue?…

I think I ought to forget…

The hand had let go of the strings, and fell, mute, into the folds of the silk sleeve.

…In Hoki the snow in the big courtyard was very cold to my bare feet, and the bamboo swords very painful to my tender arms

…Now the swords and the snow are gone, and the servants no longer open the shoji of my bedroom until the sun's warmth has awakened me…

She burst unexpectedly into a gentle, high-pitched laugh, like the tinkle of a fissured drinking glass.

…It is certainly better to forget…to forget it all.

And I shall…Oh!…

The *koto*, which she had kicked by accident, resonated like a gong.

Marquise Yorisaka did not draw back her foot right away. Her eyes were glazed and kept staring off somewhere, into the void. And she remained still, like a kneeling statue. At last she pressed her thumbs to her temples, as if suffering from a migraine, and then once again laughed, more gently still.

"Heh," she said, "I believe I've been boring you with a lot of very foolish talk…"

Jean-François Felze had started painting again, and made no reply.

"Yes," Marquise Yorisaka went on. "I spoke without hearing my own words. I do beg your pardon. Women are often completely unreasonable."

She brushed the *koto* with a fingernail.

"It was this old, old music that put my head in a muddle… You mustn't ever repeat any of this to anyone, all right? Never. Because it's shameful to talk nonsense…"

Felze kept painting in silence.

"You won't repeat it, I know. Your friend, Mrs. Hockley, would get cross. And I believe she would hold me in contempt. She's so charming! I admire her, and I would like to become like her…"

Felze took two paces back and brandished his victorious brush toward the canvas. The portrait, though unfinished, was now alive, alive with a personal and powerful life. And its eyes — eyes from the Far East, deep, secretive, obscure — cast a singularly ironical gaze upon Marquise Yorisaka, admirer of Mrs. Hockley.

XVII

Pheasant in the Claws

I s it in fact incorrect for you to attend the garden party I wish to throw on the yacht?" Mrs. Hockley had asked.

"Oh, it is such a small matter, and I so wish to attend!" Marquise Yorisaka had replied.

And so attend she did.

❀

Wherever she called on her sea voyages Mrs. Hockley would without fail throw a sensational party aboard the *Yseult*, inviting, as the case may be, the diplomatic or consular corps, the foreign colonies, European and American alike, and the local high society, if there was one. The upper classes of Japanese society do not abound in Nagasaki, an ancient city of the shogunate. It has never had a home-grown aristocracy and is populated only by little people, shopkeepers, artisans, and an unimportant bourgeoisie. The Westerners who live within the Concession[106] have little to do with these native plebeians, from whom they differ as much by education as by race. And so, the governor and the commander of the arsenal having excused themselves on military grounds, the entirety of the Japanese element at Mrs. Hockley's garden party was reduced to Marquise Yorisaka alone.

Naturally, this only brought her more attention.

The upper deck of the *Yseult*, the spar deck, which reigned supreme from fore- to aft-mast, and served as a terrace above the reception rooms, had been transformed into a veritable garden, with flower beds, lawns, and a great copse of cherry trees in bloom. A hundred laborers, of the Japanese kind, each worth six of ours in ingenuity and delicacy of skill, had worked all night on this pastoral creation, which seemed rather to derive from magic. It lacked for nothing, not even a reflecting pool: a miniature lake,

---

106 Also called the Nagasaki foreign settlement, or the Oura foreign settlement, this was an area settled by foreigners as Japan opened its doors to Western trade. It was established by treaties between the West and Japan in the mid- to late 1850s, and remained an important center of Western life in Japan until the outbreak of the Second World War. The enclave was home to Japan's first international telegraph and saw Japan's first use of a steam locomotive, the Iron Duke, on a short track.

with marble shores, rocks, lotus, and
the monstrous carp of the Far East,
horned, barbeled, and whiskered.
On a raised, grassy platform towards the ship's poop were
to be found the orchestra and the corps de ballet: twelve *geisha*[107] in dark
robes, playing tambourines or the Japanese rebeck known as the *shamisen*;[108]

107   *Geisha* (also known as *geigi*, or *geiko* in Kyoto and Kanazawa) are a class of female Japanese
performing artists and entertainers trained in traditional Japanese performing arts, such as dance,
music, and singing; they are also proficient conversationalists and hosts. They are distinguished by
their long, trailing kimono, traditional hairstyles, and *oshiroi* make-up. Geisha entertain at parties
known as *ozashiki*, often for a wealthy clientele, and perform on stage and at festivals.

108   The rebeck is an ancient European bowed musical instrument with a pear-shaped body, a
slender neck, and (usually) three strings. The *shamisen*, also known as *sangen* or *samisen* (all meaning
"three strings"), is a three-stringed traditional Japanese musical instrument derived from the

and eight *maiko*, bright as rainbows, who, in series or in groups, danced the picturesque and charming steps of old Japan.[109]

In contrast with this delicate exhibition of national elegance and grace Marquise Yorisaka wore a dress of liberty satin inlaid with Venetian guipure, and four ostrich feathers in her huge Italian cloche of straw.

※

This miraculous garden was soon crowded with Mrs. Hockley's admiring but noisy guests. It was for the most part an American crowd, and even in Japan, the very home of courtesy and refinement, the American remains what he is everywhere else: a rather brutal barbarian. The guests of the *Yseult* trampled the flower beds and, for fun, snapped the lower branches of the flowering trees. Then, after a glance or two at the dancers, who fluttered like big, many-hued butterflies on the grassy stage, they hastened down into the yacht's apartments and laid siege to the dining room, where there was a buffet.

Less hurried, perhaps less hungry, a few groups lingered under the pink shade of the cherry trees, in front of the *geisha* and *maiko*. These were the Europeans, and the civilized elite of the Yankees, Yankees from Boston or New Orleans. Without being too amazed at the show and the concert, both familiar to every Far Eastern eye and ear, these less-primitive persons paid courteous attention to the festivities on offer, and paid court to the mistress of the place, as was her due. Mrs. Hockley had taken a seat on the grass and was to every guest remarking the bizarre and fairy-like contrast of a garden suspended over the waves and the enveloping maritime landscape. The idea had been Felze's.

"I thought it would be a most curious thing," said Mrs. Hockley. "You must look from here to make out the horizon between those two clusters of verdure."

Marquise Yorisaka, to gain the right perspective, was leaning over her friend's shoulder. Uneasy with the noise and the crowd, she had instinctively sought refuge by the only woman who was not a stranger to her. Mrs. Hockley, for her part, took pleasure in showing her guests a Japanese marquise in

---

Chinese *sanxian*. It is played with a plectrum, called a *bachi*.

109   The *maiko* are apprentice geisha in Kyoto. Their job is to sing songs, dance, and play the *shamisen* or other traditional Japanese instruments for visitors during banquets and parties, known as *ozashiki*. *Maiko* are usually aged 17 to 20, and graduate to geisha status after a period of training that includes traditional dance, the *shamisen*, and *kouta* ("short songs"). In Kyoto they must also learn the Kyoto dialect. Apprentice geisha elsewhere in Japan are known by other names (in Tokyo, for example, they are called *hangyoku*, "half jewel," in reference to a geisha's wages, or "jewel money") and can differ considerably in appearance or in the structure of their apprenticeships.

Parisian attire, and did not pass up the occasion to make as many introductions as she could. But for many of the attendees — tourists, merchants, industrialists — the difference was slight between the terms *Japanese* and *savage*. Many people from America and even from Germany or England whom Mrs. Hockley had not without pride led before her treated the heiress of the ancient *daimyo* of Hoki more like a curious animal than like a worldly woman.

There were, however, exceptions.

There was even one that Marquise Yorisaka seemed flattered by.

Three days earlier a visitor had gone up the *Yseult*'s gangway to request the honor of admittance before Jean-François Felze. It was a common occurrence. Many foreigners sought to meet Mrs. Hockley's illustrious friend, and these tributes served to feed Mrs. Hockley's vanity. She would oblige Felze to accept, and then draw benefit when the painter, ever anxious to keep such interviews short, would get rid of his admirers by making an offer they could hardly refuse: that of an introduction to the yacht's owner.

All sorts of people would present themselves in this way, usually out of simple curiosity, but this time it turned out to be an important figure: no less than an Italian gentleman of excellent lineage, Prince Federico Alghero, of the Genoese Algheros. And Mrs. Hockley, an avid

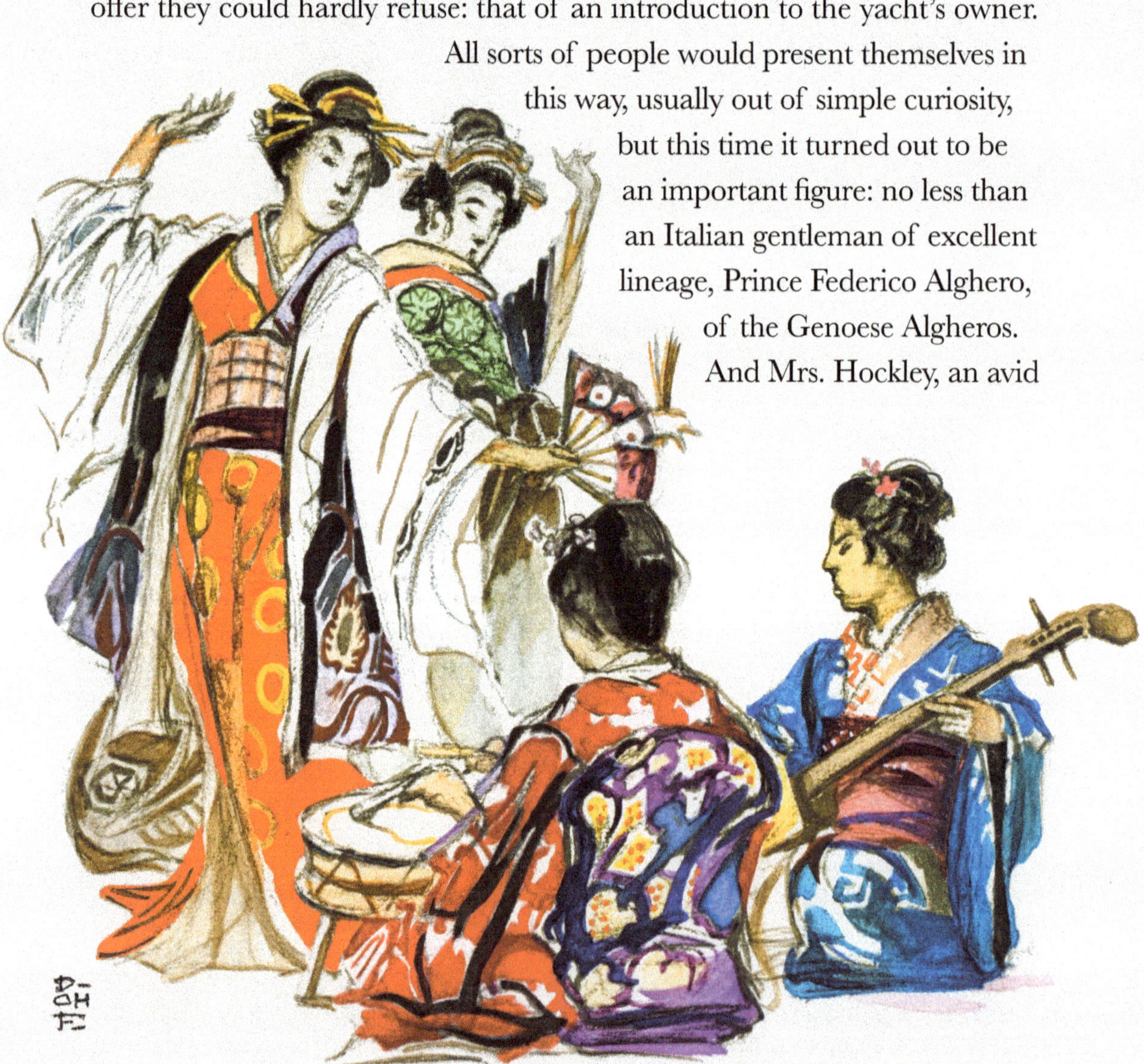

reader of the *Gotha*,[110] was not unaware that the Alghero princes had three authentic doges[111] among their ancestors. She had a fitting appreciation for a lord of such high lineage, especially as Prince Federico turned out to be a man of fine aspect and impeccable distinction.

Invited, he had come to the garden party. Introduced, he bowed before Marquise Yorisaka, as he would have bowed before the noblest of Italian ladies, and with great ceremony kissed her hand.

"I have just come from Tokyo," he said, "and had the honor two weeks ago, madam, to hear you spoken of at the Cherry Blossom Festival, at Her Majesty the Empress's palace."[112]

His English was very pure, but, soon discovering that the marquise knew French, he continued in French:

"I am sure, madam, that you would rather speak French than English… and would prefer still more to speak Italian."

"Why?"

"Because every nation prefers to speak its own language, the one that takes shape naturally in the image of its character and genius. The difference between the Japanese and the English nations is so great that you cannot help but make an effort to translate your Japanese thoughts into English. The effort is less for a French translation, and it would hardly exist for an Italian one, because Italy and Japan bear a close resemblance."

"Close?"

"Yes. Like us, you are brave, courteous, chivalrous, and subtle. Moreover, your poets and ours have sung of the same love: heroic and delicate."

Marquise Yorisaka was smiling, in silence.

"Oh!" said Prince Alghero, "I know what you are thinking … and you

---

110 The *Almanach de Gotha* is a directory of Europe's royalty, high nobility, and major governmental, military, and diplomatic corps. It also contains statistical data by country. Published from 1763 to 1944, it came to be regarded as an authority in the classification of monarchies and their courts, reigning and former dynasties, princely and ducal families, and genealogical, biographical, and titular details.

111 The doges, or dogi, were elected lords and heads of state in several Italian city-states, notably Venice and Genoa, during the medieval and Renaissance periods. Such states are referred to as "crowned republics."

112 Known as *hanami* in Japan, this long-standing tradition celebrates the transient beauty of nature, specifically in the blooming of cherry blossoms, or *sakura*. The practice dates back to the Nara period (710–94), where the capital's elite would enjoy *ume* (plum) blossoms, but by the Heian period (794–1185) *sakura* had overtaken plum as the blossom of choice. *Hanami* literally means "viewing flowers," but it implies picnicking and relaxing with friends and family under a blooming *sakura* or *ume* tree. The event is celebrated with songs, dances, and sake. The short blooming period symbolizes the transience of life, a key concept in Buddhism.

are correct: it is true that our poets have sung for the most part of the passion of men for women, and yours, in keeping with Asian custom, of the passion of women for men. But what does it matter? It only goes to show that in our two lands it is not the same shoulders that bear modesty's useless burden…"

He laid upon the marquise's eyes the gaze of his own, Italian, warmly gentle eyes.

"It would be most amusing if for this reason a Japanese woman deigned to allow herself to be loved by an Italian…"

And he began to flirt, rather adroitly.

Most of the guests were now spread all over the yacht, even paying visits to the cabins, with that fabulous uninhibitedness of those who are not sailors and can never convince themselves that a ship is a private residence, where certain quarters are as intimate as a dressing room and lavatory or a bedroom.

Felze, who abhorred such invasions, had at the first assault holed up in his quarters, and there, with the bolt securely in place, he had opened the mysterious box that hid from every profane eye the now-finished portrait of Marquise Yorisaka dressed as a Japanese princess of yore. He took solace in contemplating this marquise, as it would keep him from having to see the other, the Marquise Yorisaka disguised as a Western woman.

Several tables had been arrayed in one of the parlors, and bridge and poker had gathered their faithful. Card playing is prevalent in the Nagasaki Concession, as it is in Shanghai's, and as it is in Yokohama's and Kobe's — as it is anyplace in the Far East where Europeans grow rich and bored. The players were many. Women, even young girls, would mingle with the men and swell the ranks, casting all caution aside as they raised and countered. Gold and banknotes skittered over the gaming tables.

Mrs. Hockley, meanwhile, had left the lawn and was guiding to the buffet the guests who had not wanted to leave her side. Marquise Yorisaka accepted Prince Alghero's arm.

"Oh," said the prince, "most unforgivable of me. You must be dying of thirst, madam… But in chatting with you I have utterly forgotten the time…"

He gently squeezed against his side the tiny hand that had come to rest on his arm.

Won over, Marquise Yorisaka laughed, not without coquetry.

A major-domo approached.

"A glass of champagne?" the prince proposed.

"Yes, please … but in rather a large glass, with water … plenty of water … and ice."

Off he went to produce mixture himself. She tasted:

"Oh!… But … you haven't put in any water at all."

"Yes, but only a little… Mrs. Hockley wouldn't permit any more. And besides, madam, a European woman like you is not going to play the Japanese here and ask for water or tea!…"

She laughed again, and drank. The prince, on the sly, had added whiskey to the champagne.

Mrs. Hockley approached.

"Mitsouko, darling, I'm so happy that you're here! Hasn't she done well?" she asked, taking Prince Alghero as her witness. "Hasn't she done well to discard the absurd old rules of this country and come to the garden party, as if the marquis were present to escort her?"

The prince approved but nonetheless asked:

"Marquis Yorisaka is at war?"

"Yes. In Sasebo. He will soon return in glory, and I declare that he will be pleased to learn that in his absence his wife has led the free and joyful life of an American or European woman. Yes, he will be pleased, because he is a most civilized man. And I'd like immediately to drink to his success against the Russian barbarians!"

Ginger cocktails were circulating. Marquise Yorisaka was obliged to take one from Mrs. Hockley's hand.

Prince Alghero had taken the small ungloved hand back into his arm.

"An officer with the good fortune to partake in combat," he said, "would surely not suffer his wife to be sad while he himself wins his battles…"

"That is very well said!" averred Mrs. Hockley.

And she called for more cocktails.

A little later Marquise Yorisaka, still in the grips of Prince Alghero, entered the gaming room.

She had for some time been walking about in a sort of daze. She felt hot, and her temples throbbed as though with a singular fever. Gaiety had for no reason welled up within her, and would burst forth occasionally in unexpected laughter. Now when she felt on her nude hand the cajoling pressure of the arm she was leaning on she would respond complaisantly with her fingers and palm.

Japanese ladies would at times drink the national drink of sake, but sake is so sweet a liquor that it is drunk as we would drink sweet wine, steaming in full bowls; a man will gladly swallow two or three dozen cups in one night. Yankee cocktails are of a less-benign humor, and even French champagne when spiked just a bit…

Amid the bridge and poker tables some very cosmopolitan players had improvised a game of baccarat.[113] A baccarat game without a banker,

---

113   Baccarat is a card game often played in casinos, involving a player and a banker. The game has three popular variants: *punto banco*, baccarat *chemin de fer*, and baccarat *banque*. In *punto banco*, the most common version, the outcome is determined purely by chance, with players betting on which of the two hands — the player's or the banker's — will have a point total closest to nine. The variant in the novel is Europe's *chemin de fer*, which allows for more strategy and participation. Players take turns serving as the banker, and the game is a contest between each player and the

a little *chemin de fer* that made its pleasant way around the table, and along the way stripped the reckless to the benefit of the prudent. As Marquise Yorisaka made her entrance the luck of the draw was focusing general curiosity on this game of baccarat. Indeed, play was verging on one of those impassioned moments when the game ceases to be fun and becomes a struggle. Two young women, German and English, the former seated and holding her cards, the latter standing and placing her bet, were facing off, with a great pile of banknotes between them. The Englishwoman had just lost five hands in a row, and now her five doubled stakes were by themselves, as per the rules of *chemin de fer*, supplying the thick bundle that was the obligatory stake of the sixth hand, if it went through.

Ironic and a bit aggressive, the German woman was counting.

"Fifty, one hundred, two hundred. There are four hundred yen."

Stubborn, the Englishwoman threw down the gauntlet.

"Banco!"

They glared at each other, civilities set aside. Their fingers touched as they seized their cards; they seemed to want to claw at each other.

"Card?"

"Eight!…"

A commotion: the German had won again.

Nothing is more foreign to a Japanese woman than gambling, as we understand it when we apply the word to baccarat. Japan's notion of cards is limited to a special tarot deck, with delicate illuminations of birds and flowers. Girls use it to play among themselves, with the same innocence our little girls have in playing pigeon-vole or ferret.[114] Although, as she would sometimes boast, she had lived in the city for four years, Marquise Yorisaka had glimpsed in the diplomatic salons of

---

banker, the object being, once again, to achieve the closest total to nine. Players can "stand" or receive a third card to improve their hand.

114 Traditional French children's games. In pigeon-vole (known also as "flying pigeon") children stand in a circle and toss a handkerchief or small object to one another while chanting "Pigeon flies over the town; who will she poop on?" When the chant ends the child who has caught the object must try to tag, or "poop" on, another child before this other child can run around the circle and take the first child's spot. *Furet* (meaning "ferret," and known also as "weasel in the henhouse") is believed to have originated in the Middle Ages as an adult drinking game. The children sit in a circle. One child is chosen to be the ferret and rises to his feet. The others close or cover their eyes and sing a song. During the song the ferret deposits a handkerchief behind one of the sitting children. When the song ends the seated children look behind them, and whoever has the handkerchief behind him must stand and chase the ferret round the circle. If the ferret manages to go around the circle twice and regain his old spot the chaser becomes the new ferret.

Paris only one or two whist[115] tables, silent and serious as could be.

"We're at eight hundred yen," the German lady proclaimed, not without some insolence.

Her defeated rival remained silent.

"No banco this time?"

The challenge brought an excessive blush the English lady's cheek, but eight hundred yen amount to eighty pounds sterling: a hefty sum, especially for one who has already lost the equivalent. The English lady undoubtedly no longer had eighty pounds sterling, for she turned to the gallery, to make a plea for partnership.

"Half with me?"

"Would that amuse you?" Prince Alghero asked Marquise Yorisaka.

"Yes," she answered at random.

"The marquise shall go halves," he announced, placing his own billfold on the table.

All turned to the newcomer, the English lady with a grateful smile, the German with a glare.

The cards had already been dealt.

"Take them, madam," said the English lady, most graciously.

Marquise Yorisaka took the cards, and, lacking skill, handed them to her cavalier.

"What must I do?"

Alghero took a look and laughed:

"You must shout: 'Nine!…' You've won!"

And he himself laid the hand on the table.

Triumphant in turn, the English lady avidly raked in the pot and then separated out four hundred-yen bills:

"Here is your share, madam."

Marquise Yorisaka took the bills, widening her long oblique eyes.

"Four hundred yen," she said to the prince, who was leading her away, "but had I lost I would have lost four hundred yen?"

"No doubt…"

"Ah!… But I didn't have them in my purse!…"

"No matter! *I* had them, and you would have permitted me to lend them to you."

----

115   Widely played in the eighteenth and nineteenth centuries, whist is a classic English trick-taking card game. In the 1890s a variant known as bridge whist became popular, and eventually evolved into contract bridge.

She laughed.

"I would have permitted … yes … but…"

"Are we not friends?"

They were alone in a vestibule abounding in the tall cycas, which served to separate the gaming room from a library. The prince suddenly leaned in.

"Friends … and perhaps even … a bit more?…"

He had touched her painted little mouth with his lips.

Marquise Yorisaka did not get cross, nor did she retreat. She was simply suffocating with the heat, and her head felt by turn as heavy as lead and as light as cork. Amid this assault of dizziness, after the champagne, the cocktails, and the baccarat, a kiss was no serious matter. Besides, the Italian mustache was silken and fragrant … with an unknown, befuddling, ardent scent…

An orchestra that was no longer that of the *geisha* broke in with a waltz. Mrs. Hockley, keen to get her willing guests to dance, had not failed to hire violins. And in an instant the last of the *Yseult*'s salons, large and designed for the purpose, was filled with twirling couples.

"You must waltz," demanded Prince Alghero.

"But I don't know how…"

Even more than our gambling, our dances are incomprehensible to Japanese women, incomprehensible and scandalous. Japan is no country where prudery reigns supreme, but no man or woman there would ever think to push indecency to the point of a public embrace, waist to waist, chest to chest — to produce before all eyes the infamous spectacle of a kind of coitus…

But, seized by Prince Alghero, Marquise Yorisaka neglected a few principles more and, without much resistance, allowed herself to be led into the impudent whirl.

"How enchanting!" judged Mrs. Hockley, watching from the dance hall's threshold as Marquise Yorisaka Mitsouko waltzed breathlessly past, her hair disheveled, her face flush, her body squeezed in the arms of the Italian prince like a little Yamato[116] pheasant in the claws of some great bird of prey from overseas.

---

116   The Yamato ethnicity accounts for more than 98 percent of Japan's population. Mrs. Hockley uses it as a synonym for *Japanese*.

XVIII

The Abyss

The last rays of sunshine, brushing the western mountains above the old village of Inasa, streamed through the wide-open porthole to strike Jean-François Felze in the face. Jean-François Felze rose from his armchair, closed his sketch box, and carefully unlocked his door. The dance orchestra had piped down a good quarter-hour ago.

"The chummy bacchanalia is perhaps over," said Felze with hope.[117]

And he ventured out of his room.

Most of the guests had gone. A privileged few remained, kept on for dinner by Mrs. Hockley, and were chatting under the garden's cherry trees, not far from the grassy lawn that had served as a stage for the *geisha* and *maiko*. Approaching, Felze first noticed a couple set apart from the main group and flirting quite intimately, and his eyes went wide at the sight of them.

Mrs. Hockley, having given some orders to the servants, was just returning to her guests. Felze stopped her on the way:

"I beg your pardon," he said. "I must be seeing things… Is that not Marquise Yorisaka leaning on the railing over there?"

Mrs. Hockley raised her lorgnette:

"You are not seeing things. That is the marquise."

Felze exaggerated his feigned astonishment.

"What?" he said. "So the marquis is back from Sasebo?"

"Not as far as I know."

"Oh? That's not him there, kissing his wife's hand?"

"How droll you are! Can't you see that it's Prince Alghero? You yourself introduced him to me."

---

117 Felze references ancient Roman festivals celebrating Bacchus (the Greco-Roman god of wine, fertility, and ecstasy), adapted from earlier Greek Dionysian rites. These events became associated with ecstatic states, music, dancing, and often excessive wine consumption. Amid concerns (perhaps amplified by Roman authorities like the historian Livy) about moral disorder, alleged crimes, and potential conspiracies linked to the secret rites, the Senate officially suppressed the Bacchanalia in 186 BCE. The term is used here, as often in modern usage, to describe any wild, potentially drunken or debauched revelry.

Felze took a step back and crossed his arms.

"So," he said, "not content to have dragged the poor girl to your party, or to have seriously, perhaps dangerously, compromised her, or to have no doubt exhibited ten thousand things indecent or revolting to her eye, you've topped it all off by casting Marquise Yorisaka, whether she liked it or not, into the arms of this Italian, so that he could treat her as he'd treat some coquette from Rome or Florence, or even New York?"

Mrs. Hockley, having listened attentively, burst into laughter.

"How extravagant! I think it does you no good whatsoever to stay locked up in your room too long, because when you emerge you speak utter nonsense. Nothing indecent or revolting has been exhibited here, I beg you to believe me. And the marquise herself denied that it was incorrect for her to attend the garden party. She has come freely, and she has freely flirted. I find your indignation totally ridiculous, because the marquise is a civilized lady, and any civilized lady would flirt as the marquise flirts. It could not be more innocent…"

"You are right," cut in Felze.

He laid stress on the word *right*. He repeated:

"You're right. Still, are you quite sure that Marquise Yorisaka is a civilized lady like any other?… Like you?…"

"Why wouldn't she be?"

"Why? I've no idea. She is not: that's the fact of the matter. Let's keep things short and not ask why, if you please. I tell you simply this, with no vain discussion or endless philosophy: you do not know Marquise Yorisaka, and you are prodigiously mistaken about her. You believe her made in your image, or in the image of that silly girl, your Miss Vane. Well, no! Marquise Yorisaka does not affect a Wagnerian first name,[118] and she does not type her correspondence. She does not put on a black silk shirt to discourse on mathematical physics. She is mistress to no tame lynx and does not speak only through questionnaires and lectures. Yet she is what you say: a civilized lady… *more* civilized than you, perhaps, but civilized *like* you? No. You both wear dresses that look alike, but underneath your bodies and souls bear no resemblance… You smile? You're wrong to. I assure you, the abyss between the marquise and you is even wider, much wider, than the Pacific Ocean separating Nagasaki from San Francisco! So stop trying to force a difficult comparison. And leave the poor girl in peace. As a Japanese, she has no use for your American — your all too American — examples."

He had spoken somewhat nervously. Mrs. Hockley replied in the calmest tone — academic controversy being her forte:

"I don't think so. I believe that an American woman is no different from a Japanese woman when they are creatures of the same education and equal culture. Moreover, I contend that I do know Marquise Yorisaka, because I have seen her often and we have had intimate, impassioned conversations together. I say, too, that the abyss between the marquise and me has been filled, thanks to steamships, railways, the telephone, and other sensational inventions that have made the world smaller and shrunk the distance between its different peoples. All your arguments are therefore refuted… Besides, how could you understand Marquise Yorisaka better than I? She is a woman; you are a man. And, as all psychologists proclaim, men and women can never reach a reciprocal understanding."

Felze interrupted a second time:

"Let's have no psychology, I beseech you! The great workings of the human heart have nothing to do with this. Let's not deviate from the matter at hand. We're talking about Marquise Yorisaka Mitsouko, who, a mere ten paces from here, is enduring the pleasant groping of a gentleman of whom she knew nothing two hours ago and whom she has met in your house, through your doing. It is through my doing that you yourself have made the

---

118 Wilhelm Richard Wagner (1813–83), German composer of grand operas, and notably of the *Ring* cycle, a retelling of the Norse Sagas (*Nibelungenlied*), with their tales of gods.

acquaintance of said marquise — through my doing and at the house of her husband, Marquis Yorisaka Sadao. I therefore feel some responsibility for whatever unpleasantness might result for said marquis from said groping. And, though my hair be white, I am young enough to believe it less than honorable to encourage a woman's misconduct while her trusting husband is away at war. And so I implore you to spare me this distasteful duty, and spare yourself at the same time. You will, as soon as courtesy allows, show your remaining guests to the door — especially this Prince Alghero, whom I wish I'd never met. Afterwards you'll prevail on me to escort Marquise Yorisaka home, as any lone woman ought to be escorted at night, for fear of disrespectful encounters. We are agreed, are we not?"

"We can reach no agreement on this," said Mrs. Hockley.

Calmly, she explained:

"Your scruples are as absurd as can be. However, it's true that you arranged my introduction to the marquise. And so I would like to do as you wish, to show you my gratitude, but a little while ago I asked the prince and the marquise, along with the other people you still see over there, to stay and dine aboard the yacht, the better to finish off the evening. In fact, I positively promised to place the prince next to the marquise at the table. So I must keep my word. In consolation, though, I will seat you too next to the marquise, on the other side."

"Thank you, no," said Felze.

He rose to his feet, brusque.

"No. I know you well enough not to insist. If that's how things are to be I'll dine in town."

"Oh!" she said, with irony. "I think I can guess: you're jealous. It's a habit of yours, so I'm not surprised. Tell me, though. Are you jealous of the marquise because of the prince or of me because of the marquise? Because you've already and often shown a very French quirk for quarrelling with me because of my intimate friendship with Miss Vane!..."

Felze had blanched:

"You will understand," he said slowly, "if I decline to answer an injurious question. For now, farewell."

She looked at him, worried:

"Farewell? Oh! Do you really intend to dine in town?"

"As I've said."

"Where?"

"Anywhere. Elsewhere. At a table that will not bring Marquise

Yorisaka and Prince Alghero together under your obliging protection."

He took his leave and turned around. She hesitated for half a second, then shot out her hand and held him back by the sleeve.

"François! Please! No sulking!"

Rarely indeed did Mrs. Hockley let it slip that, even for an American lady of abounding beauty and abounding millions, it was no mean feat to possess in a cage and display before all and sundry the least unworthy heir of the Titians and the Van Dycks[119] — Jean-François Felze. This evening, however, she forgot herself. The truth was, capricious Felze had ill-chosen his moment to rebel: at the very hour of a dinner he would no doubt have elevated with his presence!

"François, I beg you! Be reasonable! Listen! I cannot on a whim of yours send away a great many people I have pleaded with to stay… But I'm very sorry to have upset you, even if I don't understand how, and I promise to do whatever you wish to win your forgiveness. Yes, whatever you wish … as early as tomorrow … or even tonight."

She fixed Felze with her eyes, and pursed her lips as if making a sensual offer.

But Yankee instinct had led her astray: the ruse was too coarse. Felze was French, and, as the cleverest of the great corrupters, Walpole, had already observed three hundred years earlier, negotiations for the purchase of a French conscience must be delicate indeed…[120]

Felze, pale a moment ago, turned redder than the western sky, rearing up violently.

"Egad, woman!" he said. "Why not write me a check while you're at it? But I'm afraid you won't have enough in your coffers to make good!"

Taken aback, she fell silent. He continued, colder:

"Enough. This scene has gone on too long, anyway. Misfortune compels me, then, to offer you my apologies if I am letting you down at the last minute. I'll return tomorrow, once I'm certain the yacht is clear of this couple you've fashioned and whose bringing together I find so displeasing."

---

119   The Italian painter of the High Renaissance Titian (1488–1576) is known for his mastery of color and emotion. His paintings include portraits, religious scenes, and mythological subjects. The Flemish painter Sir Anthony van Dyck (1599–1641) is known for his elegant and detailed portraits of European aristocracy. He was also a prolific etcher and produced a large number of prints.

120   Probable reference to Horatio (Horace) Walpole, 4th Earl of Orford (1717–97), who in a letter to Mary Berry (7 November 1793) writes: "methinks they have no reason to dread the terrors of conscience in any Frenchman!"

He was leaving for good. She in turn grew cross.

"Very well, then! Go! But be warned: you'll be no more certain tomorrow than today. Yes, it's very possible I'll invite back aboard this couple that so displeases you, but that pleases *me*!…"

"Ah!" he said, sarcastic. "So the *Yseult* is to become a boat for trysts, is it? Thanks for the warning. It won't be tomorrow, then, that I come back aboard."

"That will be fine, if you so prefer. It would certainly be better if you vented your ill humor someplace else. You are free, and what if in fact you decided never to return?"

She was defying him, well aware that on this ground she could draw

strength from his weakness. And, indeed, he lowered his eyes, and his voice, to make his reply.

"I shall be glad to return once I never again run the risk of seeing what I am seeing right now…"

He was nodding toward the two silhouettes leaning on the railing, all too near each other.

"This is your house. Do as you please. Me, though, I'll at least ignore what I cannot prevent."

He set off abruptly, avoiding her eye, leaving her standing there, bitter and furious. The sun had set. Night was growing dark over the sea.

XIX

"…Free of hunger, fear, and sleep"

The sampan carrying Felze moored at the stairs to the Customs House. Felze leapt ashore and wandered onto Motokago-machi, the inevitable street, headquarters for tourists and curio merchants. It is all but impossible to avoid when you set forth from the docks to explore the city. And the guides and *kuruma* will never fail to invite you to admire the only storefronts in Nagasaki yet to have acknowledged the new Japan's craze for Western fashions.

Only a thin strip of sky now glowed with the red of twilight, beneath another, scarcely wider strip, like some prodigious sash of emerald green. The rest of the firmament was night blue, and already sparkling with stars.

Noisy, tumultuous, crowded with onlookers, variegate with lantern light, Nagasaki was coming to nocturnal life. *Kuruma* ran past in single file. *Mousmés* strolled about in files of their own, laughing and chattering, their high voices and little wooden clogs filling the street with the music of a baroque concert, half flutes and half castanets. Japanese men in European suits and a greater number in the national kimono came and went, trotted along, met in greeting, with nary a collision or jostle, for there is a wonderful difference in courtesy between Japanese crowds and ours. The stores and bazaars teemed with buyers, they and the merchants exchanging a thousand bows on all fours. Shops open to the wind displayed bizarre victuals, and at the top of their lungs vendors sang of their goods. The few

foreigners peppering this opaque crowd seemed lost like boats mid-sea.

Pensive, Felze shuffled along. He had gone two-thirds of the way down Motokago-machi before figuring out where exactly he wished to go. At the door to a tortoiseshell carver's, however, he had to stop and make way for six English sailors, who, slow and grave, filed into the narrow shop, no doubt to buy the trinkets on display — penholders shaped like sampans, inkwell holders shaped like *kuruma*. Felze sized up the men, all of them tall, pink, and blond. They were as exotic in this

Japanese crowd as six Japanese sailors would have been on Regent Street.[121] Felze now remembered that he had just left the *Yseult* intending not to return for a while, and that he was in Nagasaki, with dinner still ahead.

"Well, now," he said aloud, "I've got to get a handle on this flight of mine, and find myself some supper, and a bed…"

He looked to the adjacent lanes, which scaled the mountain's lower slopes. Up above lay the suburb of Diou Djen Dji, and the hospitable house of the three purple lanterns, with its opium den, draped in yellow silk and redolent of the good drug. Felze recalled the Hindu proverb, known from one end of Asia to the other: "Whosoever smokes opium breaks free of hunger, fear, and sleep." But he no sooner thought of this than shook his head.

"Were I to knock on that door I'd spend the whole night at Zhou P'ei's, and by dawn the pipes would have so consoled me as to color my life rosy, and I would return to my cage in such spirits as to accept and approve of it all. No! Not that!…"

He turned around and surveyed the bustling street:

---

121   One of the major shopping streets in London's West End.

"Sup? Sleep? Easy enough. There are hotels aplenty. But I have little baggage, and I don't care to send aboard for a nightshirt… What I need is some tidy country inn, with washermaid-servants and kimonos for travelers… Such inns are to be found…"

He thought back to the *ochaya* and *yadoya*[122] of the village to which the roads and paths happen to have led him on his walks over the previous weeks. The island of Kyushu[123] is but a vast garden, the earth's prettiest, greenest, and most harmonious. In three moments three radiant landscapes came once more before Felze's eyes: the Himi pass,[124] more a-shimmer than a Swiss valley; the Kouannon waterfall, with its black cedars and russet maples; and the lovely terrace of Mogimachi, overlooking a Mediterranean gulf between two Scottish mountains.[125]

Jean-François Felze abruptly hailed a passing empty *kuruma*.

The eager man-horse pulled his vehicle up to the sidewalk.

"Mogi!" said Felze.

"Mogi?" the *kuruma* runner repeated, in surprise.

Indeed, tourists seldom choose the dark night for a countryside excursion. And a trip out to Mogimachi is more like two excursions than one, for it is a rough, rough road and at least two *ri* long: eight or nine of our kilometers.

---

122   *Ochaya*, teahouse. *Yadoya*, inn. [Author's note.]

123   Home to the city of Nagasaki on the west side, Kyushu (meaning "Nine Provinces") is the third-largest island of Japan's five main islands and the most southerly of the four largest islands. It is mountainous and home to Japan's most active volcano, Mount Aso.

124   Himi is a city in the far northwestern Toyama Prefecture, with mild summers and cold, snowy winters.

125   Mogimachi (or, simply, Mogi) is a coastal area about ten kilometers southeast of Nagasaki. Historically a fishing village, Mogi became famous for its seafood, especially *kamaboko* (fish cake), and picturesque harbor views. The town was also instrumental for trade and communication with the outside world during times of limited foreign interaction. During the country's period of isolation (*sakoku*) the nearby port of Nagasaki was among the few to trade with foreigners.

"Mogi!" insisted Felze.

Having duly heard, the *kuruma* runner, philosophical by trade, made no further objection.

But, as the light carriage set off, Felze suddenly thought of a letter he wished to write, and observed that he was getting hungry, and so had the man stop first at the nearest European restaurant.

He dined, he wrote, and then he repeated his first order: "Mogi."

A second runner had come up to help the first, as was proper for a strenuous route. It was a cool night, and Felze wrapped his legs in the brown wool blanket, sank into the cushions, and looked at the stars. With the four bare legs, yellow and muscular, going at a fast trot, the little conveyance had soon left the outskirts of the city and was rolling down an empty road.

The moon, almost at its zenith, shone white in the night sky, like a crescent of jade in the jet-blue hair of a *mousmé*. Pearly clouds floated all around, driven, deformed, and metamorphosed by an incessant breeze. Felze watched their shifting flight, a magical wind-drawn, moon-hued tableau. Pale, blurry figures wavered against the starry firmament's backdrop, their muddled gestures seeming the mysterious reflection of other gestures, the real, human gestures that living beings were no doubt performing at the same instant, somewhere, beneath the infallible mirror of the skies.

Three big black birds, storks or cranes, streaked across the milky dome, in hurried flight from the eastern to the western mountains. But Jean-François Felze did not see them.

Jean-François Felze had closed his eyes, obsessed with the bizarre aspect of a great cloud stretching itself out, like a half-naked woman lying on a bed. Two other, nearby clouds stood out, like two other women seated next to the first, in a pose of extraordinarily intimacy…

XX

Heart under the Door

Zhou P'ei, sprawled on three mats in the middle of the fragrant den, was smoking his sixtieth pipe when a servant with an alabaster-ball cap[126] parted the curtain at the door and, with a rule-bound bow, head low, fists joined and shaken over the forehead, entreated his master to deign to receive a message that had just arrived from a foreigner.

In Zhou P'ei's left hand was the bamboo of a pipe that a child kneeling by the tray was guiding over the lamp. Zhou P'ei went on with what he was doing, making no signal with his hand, but he closed his eyes, in silence, to assent.

In an instant the curtain at the door parted again and there entered the private secretary, an old, old man whose cap bore a carved ball of coral. He began with the proper courtesy, undertaking to prostrate himself, but affable Zhou P'ei hastened to stop him.

On his feet, the private secretary delivered the message. It was a European letter, under seal in an envelope. Zhou P'ei gave it but a glance.

"Open it," he said politely, "and permit me to bore and fatigue you; lend me your light."

The servants present, with proper discretion, quickly stepped back. Only the child manning the pipes kept his place, because opium supersedes all rites.

Respectful and prompt, the secretary was already searching his belt. Producing his stylus, he slit open the envelope.

"I humbly follow Ta-Jen's order," he murmured.

He unfolded the letter, and his oblique eyes narrowed.

---

126 The author correctly identifies the significance of the alabaster-ball cap mentioned here as indicating mandarin of the sixth class, and the carved ball of coral, mentioned below, as signifying mandarin of the second class. During the Qing Dynasty (1644–1912), officials wore hat finials (*dingdai*) with material and color indicating their rank within a nine-rank system. In descending order from the highest rank the finails are: Rank 1: Ruby (translucent red); Rank 2: Coral (opaque red); Rank 3: Sapphire (translucent blue); Rank 4: Lapis Lazuli (opaque blue); Rank 5: Crystal (clear); Rank 6: White Shell/Tridacna (opaque white, like alabaster); Rank 7: Plain Gold; Rank 8: Worked Gold; Rank 9: Worked Silver.

"The noble characters," he announced, "are in the language spoken by the *Fu-lang-sai*."[127]

"Read with your learning," said Zhou P'ei.

The private secretary had once accompanied the extraordinary ambassador to Europe, and his French was not inferior to Zhou P'ei's.

"I humbly follow the most noble order…," he said again.

And with that he began in his hoarse voice, unaccustomed to Western sounds:

Letter from foolish Fenn to his elder brother, most old and most wise, Zhou P'ei, the great scholar, academician, viceroy, and member of the imperial councils.

The small one greets his elder brother from the ground. He asks, with ten thousand regards, for news of his health, and takes the bold liberty of sending him this letter of no account.

The small one dares further to inform his elder brother of a sudden albeit considered determination. It is written in the Lun Yü:[128]

"When the Empire is well governed the Emperor himself regulates the ceremonies and the music."[129]

The small one has this very day, with bitterness, come to know the dishonor that results from dwelling in a principality whose ceremonies are forgotten, whose music is discordant, and whose remonstrances are of no use. It is written in the book of Meng

---

127   Likely Farrère's rendering of 佛郎機, *Fo lang chi* in Wade-Giles, *Fólángjī* in Pinyin: a historical Chinese term used for Western Europeans. It referred literally to the French (*Français*) but often to the Portuguese or the Spanish, encountered on sea routes. It derives from the word *Frank*, used widely in the Middle East and Asia (from Persian *Farang* / Arabic *Faranj*) to denote Western Europeans, particularly after the Crusades. This root spread along trade routes, giving rise to related terms throughout Asia, like the Thai *farang* (ฝรั่ง), the Hindi *firangi* (फिरंगी), and the Malay *ferenggi*.

128   *Analects* of Confucius. *Lúnyǔ* in Pinyin.

129   K'ung Fu-Tzu, Book VIII, Chapter XVI, §2. [Author's note.]

Tzu: "Whoso be entrusted with an office and cannot discharge it must withdraw."[130]

The small one, in the principality where he dwells, has been endeavoring to spare a still-chaste woman the sight of baleful examples, and spare her husband undeserved disgrace. But the effort has proved vain. And the small one, thus unable to discharge his office, has resolved to withdraw. Some distance from this city — fifteen lis off, by the measure of the Central Nation — is a place called Mogimachi. There the small one intends to go and stay for several days. The small one prevails on his elder brother, most wise and old, to deign to excuse him should he cease during this time to knock at the benevolent door over which hang three violet lanterns.

The weak but sincere man who follows his heart can at times win the high favor not to be judged a hateful creature. It is in this hope that the small one has taken up his fumbling brush and permitted himself to direct to his old and illustrious brother such inelegant phrases, bereft of wisdom. For this he most humbly seeks forgiveness.

The small one has yet many more things to say. But he dares not, certain that he has imposed too much already on his most old brother. The small one shall thus shut his heart and refrain from expressing all of the feelings with which it teems.

The private secretary had read.

Zhou P'ei finished the pipe he was smoking, pushed the bamboo aside, laid his neck on the small leather pillow, and, raising his right hand, let the violet light of the ceiling's lanterns play on his long, long nails.

"Ho!" he said in contemplation.

He gazed upon the kneeling child, busy balling up a drop of opium against the hot glass of the lamp, and thought aloud, uttering brief phrases in Chinese:

"Hui, of Liu-hsia,[131] was careless of his dignity. And the charioteer Wang Liang did not take him as a model. One must approve of Wang Liang. — Yet even men of the lowliest people understand that lovely paths

---

130 Meng Tzu, Book II, Chapter II, §5. [Author's note.] — Mencius. Mengzi in Pinyin.

131 A philosopher of antiquity, renowned for his extreme tolerance. Zhou P'ei here quotes from Meng Tzu [Mencius, Book III, Part B, 1] and alludes to a famous anecdote in Chinese annals. Wang Liang [Wáng Liáng in Pinyin], despite the order of the great prefect, refused to drive the chariot of the sickly archer Hsi [Xī in Pinyin]. For this he was praised as having, contrary to Hui's opinions, maintained the whole of his profession's dignity, even against an order dangerous to infringe. [Authors note.]

lead not far.[132] I must consider this, must think of what lies to the right and to the left."[133]

The child stuck a well-cooked pellet on the pipe-bowl. Zhou P'ei once more took up the bamboo, in his left hand, and smoked. He let the last brown particle properly evaporate.

"The man who sets forth on a painful journey," he then solemnly uttered, "will often forget his heart under the door…"

He stopped and burst straight into laughter. In combination, one set below the other, the Chinese characters *hsin* (heart)[134] and *men* (door)[135] form a third character that means "melancholy." Zhou P'ei, subtle man of letters, took fitting delight in his learned pun. Once he had laughed, however, he regained his sententiousness.

"The man who stays behind," he concluded, "must therefore watch fraternally over the forgotten heart, and care for it."

---

132   Chinese proverb. [Authors note.]

133   Very common idiom. [Authors note.] In Pinyin, Zuǒ shēn yòu xiǎng (左身右想). This idiom literally translates to "left body right thought."

134   *Xīn* in Pinyin.

135   *Mén* in Pinyin.

XXI

The Honorable Traveler

The *mousmé* servant — the *nēsan*,[136] her lovely dress cinched with purple satin, her ebony bun sculpted and lacquered — pattered into the closed room and noisily slid the paper-paned *shoji* in their grooves.

Jean-François Felze, who had slept on the mats, between two futons of quilted silk,[137] awoke with a start and got to his feet, draped in a huge kimono of blue and white with great leafy patterns.

In the frame of the now wide-open window appeared the sea, still nocturnal under a sky of fading stars, but the distant mountains of Amakusa[138] and Shimabara,[139] marking the eastern shore of the gulf, were coming into view on the horizon. Dawn was breaking.

"A bit early!" murmured Felze.

He had asked to be woken just in time for sunrise, but the inn doubtless had no clock. The little *nēsan*, having drawn aside her last *shoji*, not without giving it her all and catching her fingers, knelt by the traveler with so candid and polite a smile that Felze thought any reproach would be unpardonably coarse. As she was clearly waiting for his orders, he summoned his best Japanese and, out of pure courtesy, asked:

"*Furo ga dekimashita ka?*"[140]

He was certain that at this hour the answer would be:

"*Mada dekimasen…*"[141]

---

136 Older sister. In this context, a polite term of address for a young female inn servant or waitress, akin to 'miss.'

137 A thin mattress, usually filled with layers of cotton batting and encased in cotton fabric, placed on a floor for sleeping, especially in traditional Japanese interiors, and folded and stored during the day.

138 Amakusa ("Heaven's Grass") is a series of islands off the west coast of Kyushu, the southernmost of the four main islands of Japan, and is visible from Nagasaki.

139 Shimabara is a city located on the northeastern tip of the Shimabara Peninsula, facing Ariake Bay in the east and Mount Unzen (Fugendake included) in the west, in Nagasaki Prefecture, Kyushu, Japan.

140 "Is the bath ready?" [Authors note.]

141 "Not ready yet." [Authors note.]

And so it was.

Soon, however, the undulating rump of the western mountains came into darker relief against the ever-brightening sky. Quick and brutal, dawn was driving away the twilight. Clouds appeared, bluish at first, then stained, in an instant, with blood, as if slashed by some airy saber. Then the red, the gray, and the blue fused into a vivid hue of pure gold. The sea sparkled with eyespots of pink copper and blue steel. And the Rising Sun made its sudden appearance, bounding up from shore and sea to shine over the whole of the Empire; and the whole of the Empire seemed to shiver with joy.

Dazzled, Felze turned away. Still at his side and kneeling, the little servant kept keen watch on the flamboyant spectacle. Felze saw the quick gleam of the emblematic orb in her slanted eyes, and in those humble Japanese pupils it was like a mysterious flash of pride.

"The honorable traveler's bath is ready!"

A second *nēsan* had just entered and was prostrating herself at the door. A third, behind the second, beamed her most welcoming smile. Together, in procession, they led Felze to a vat filled with water at a near boil: the traditional bathtub of every village *yadoya*.

Under the close but innocent gaze of the three *mousmés* the honorable traveler let the blue and white kimono fall to his feet, stepped over the iron-clad rim, and settled into a squat…

His large white-man's body took up three-quarters of the tub, made to fit the typical Japanese body, less voluminous by a half. His pale, transparent skin reddened with the burn of the water. His limbs, still robust and supple, gave him in his nakedness an air of youth, despite his silver locks and beard.

Curious, the three *nēsan* would approach, extend a finger, and touch the extraordinary white skin, to make sure it was in fact natural, not the result of cosmetics, and kindly,

child-like giggles would issue from their painted lips.

The plain wood of the partitions gleamed, so clean it seemed to have been planed the day before. The roofbeams were so clean as to seem new. The blue kimono had barely hit the ground before careful little hands had scooped it up and carried it to the ever-ready washtub. Another kimono, this one purple, fresh from the wash, and fragrant, was waiting for the honorable traveler to complete a proper scalding in his tub… The *mousmés* were already unfolding the lovely soft crepe fabric, and reaching up as best they could, to raise the sleeves high enough.

When Jean-François Felze stepped out of the bath and was wrapped in the purple kimono, fresh from the wash and fragrant, he thought he felt the welcoming caress of old courteous, simple, healthy Japan, real and tangible, on his shoulders.

XXII

Japanerie Beneath Muscovite Boots?

All of the paths around Mogi resemble park lanes.

Felze, having wandered for half an hour, with his back to the sea, reached the end of a dense, winding pass, at the edge of a great wood of bamboo.

The sky was blue as could be, and the sun rather warm. Felze spotted a fallen trunk by the path and sat down.

It was a fine place for weary travelers. Admiring the view spread out at his feet, Felze could not recall having seen a more harmonious or welcoming landscape. It was only a valley hemmed in by a slope, but all of Japan's grace and delicacy seemed to have come together on these lawns and among these groves, to create an incomparable garden, one that no French or English gardener could ever design or plant. The lawns were terraced, and separated by hedges or rockwork. Flowering shrubs alternated with crimson beeches, brown camphor trees, and gigantic cedars, flowing with immense clusters of wisteria. The top of the slope had the roundness of a breast, and on it stood an old gate, consisting of two rustic columns and a stone beam. A staircase ran underneath it, the mysterious portico to some vanished temple…

"The wonderous thing," murmured Felze, "is that this is no garden but a field for cultivation and yield. These lawns are rice fields, and these flowerbeds plots of vegetables. These thickets serve as screens against the August sun and the October winds. And this waterfall here feeds an irrigation canal…"

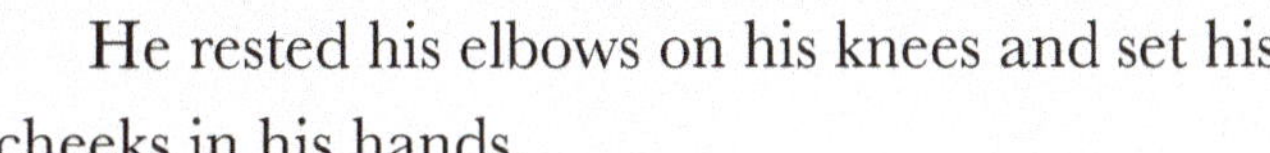

He rested his elbows on his knees and set his cheeks in his hands.

"In Europe fields like these would be hideous, but the farmers of this fairy land do not resemble ours. And I believe them genuinely incapable of steering their plow unless everything around them is first prepared, arranged, calculated to produce the greatest joy to their artistic eye!…"

He listened. The bamboos overhead sang in the wind. These were tree-like bamboo, growing just about nowhere but Japan: thicker than our lindens and taller than our poplars, but with leaves so thin and motile that neither our willows nor our birches could convey an idea of them.

The sun is always all but free to penetrate a bamboo forest, however dense the trunks or tangled the branches. And the shadow there is tenuous, sheer, luminous…

Keeping still, Felze savored the delicacy of the hour and place. Before him, on the road, a *kuruma* passed at a walking pace. A *mousmé*, nonchalant and pretty, lounged within. Her dress was pearl gray and her obi scarlet, with a lining of purple satin. A thousand-ribbed parasol spinning in a pretty amber hand, a fan, and a lengthy bunch of freshly picked flowers rounded out the graceful equipage, which disappeared into the bamboo like some shimmering butterfly into tall grass.

"It would in truth be a pity," mused Felze, "in truth a pity, if all this fine and precious Japanerie were trampled under big Muscovite boots!"[142]

---

142 The author is prescient in his observation of the distinctive qualities of "Japaneseness." There exists an entire literature, *nihonjinron* (literally "theories/discussions about the Japanese"), on Japanese national and cultural identity. Numerous books and articles have been published since the Second World War to analyze, explain, or explore the peculiarities of Japanese culture and mentality, usually by comparison with those of Europe and North America. They delve into such varied fields as sociology, psychology, anthropology, history, linguistics, philosophy, biology, chemistry, and physics. Existing alongside *nihonjinron* are a variety of subgenres, divided up by theme or subject.

XXIII

Little Miss Chastity

For five days Jean-François Felze lived in the Japanese manner at the Japanese inn at Mogimachi. He needed no more to become Japanese himself.

The rustic yet delicate existence of a traditional *yadoya* was a delightful change from the refined yet somewhat vulgar luxuries of an American yacht. Moreover, he had left the *Yseult* in a fit of anger and indignation, and nothing could better soothe him than the pastoral peace he was now enjoying.

Jean-François Felze was not one of those lovers who, to go on living, must cling to their mistress's skirts. First of all, he did not love Betsy Hockley. He desired her, endured her, could not free himself from her. At certain hours he needed her mouth like a thirsty man needs water. — Past fifty years of age people who thirst often gladly make it their custom to drink from a single fountain. — This sensual need, in every way akin to an appetite, left no room for tenderness, but contempt was another matter. Every evening, after a long day of strolls, *ochaya*, snacks of rice and dried fish, and Marivaux-like banter[143] with the *mousmés* at hand, when, behind his closed *shoji*, he would lie down between the two futons of quilted silk and wait for sleep, Felze might feel a sudden, quite painful seizure of the flesh, under the sharp bite of a desire. But the healthy lassitude of being in the open air and walking acted upon him as a narcotic. Chastity is not yet unbearable after five times twenty-four hours.

In five days, then, Jean-François Felze became sufficiently Japanese. On the sixth he became more so…

A violent storm opened this sixth day, with showers, gusts, and great thunderclaps. Then the rain and wind began in earnest, the way they do

---

143 In French: *"de marivaudages avec les* mousmés.*"* The work of French novelist and playwright Pierre Carlet de Chamblain de Marivaux (1688–1763) is known for its wit, humor, and focus on the subtleties of human relationships. *Marivaudage* is wordplay, intricacy of plot, games of love and courtship.

in May on the island of Kyushu, that favorite haunt of spring typhoons. The temperature dropped, and it was soon imperative to relight a few coals in the *hibachi*,[144] for the contrast was harsh between the damp wind and the sun, a sun almost too hot, that had set the night before. A gray mist floated over the gulf, and the mauve mountains of Shimabara and Amakusa vanished from view. The horizon had drawn closer, and the low sky and dull sea began to commingle, blurring their boundary.

Felze, scanning the dripping countryside and the already soaked paths, began to dread the inevitable: the prospect of a lonesome day in his bare room, with the spotty heat of the *hibachi*. But he was not counting on Japanese courtesy. The three *nēsan*, as soon as he had emerged from the vat-bathtub, accompanied the honorable traveler, again in procession, back to his room. And, as he had not expressed a wish to trade right away for his European clothes the morning kimono that he had just been wrapped in, they kneeled politely on the mats and endeavored to entertain the honorable traveler with conversation at once playful and selective.

It is not very difficult to chat, or even flirt, with Japanese girls. With his mediocre Japanese, the honorable traveler managed a near gibberish, but his three partners vied with one another in their benevolent indulgence and sought to understand. The worst of the difficulties were smoothed out, and they spoke of the absent sun, the deplorable rain, the fog, the cold, the storms, the cherry trees, stripped of their pink finery — with all the requisite nuances of regret, indignation, anxiety, terror, and melancholy.

Felze listened, answered, approved, and, above all, kept a fairly close eye on the prettiest of the three *mousmés*, a cute doll, though plump, whose round, fresh cheeks struck an amusing contrast with her pensive eyes and delicate smile.

To find such eyes and such a smile on the face of an inn servant would have been astonishing in Europe, but in Japan the lowliest laborers and humblest peasants often look like princesses in disguise…

"While playing the koto," thought Felze, "Marquise Yorisaka had, of course, a different look… But Marquise Yorisaka rarely plays the koto…"

He closed his eyes for a moment. Then, shaking off the memory, he began resolutely to court the *mousmé*, asking her name and age and paying her all the compliments he knew in Japanese. Seeing this, the other two *nēsan*, discreet, hastened to take their leave under clever pretexts. For in the Far East as in the Far West an inn hostess is by her profession bound to

---

144 The *hibachi*, now in common English usage, is a small cast-iron charcoal brazier covered with a grill, usually used for outdoor cooking.

make many a mysterious accommodation for any honorable traveler who deigns to single her out from her companions.

Alone with O-Setsu san — that was her name, O-Setsu san, "Little Miss Chastity" — Felze, mindful not to be rude, was obliged to make use of this solitude and risk the customary gestures. O-Setsu san, being a young lady of excellent breeding, put up just enough resistance, going on neither too long nor too little. And the adventure came to the same end as all adventures do that have for their setting a locked room and for their actors a man and a woman eager to spare each other all displeasure and humiliation.

❊

Lying in part on the tatamis, with an elbow on the ground and his neck on a fist, Felze looked in silence at his mistress-for-a-minute, who stood before him just as silent.

Even in the moment of abandon she had shown rare restraint and decency. To straighten herself out she had adopted an exquisite pose of true modesty and lovely simplicity.

"Her name is O-Setsu san," thought Felze, "and she is in sum just a clandestine little prostitute. But I believe in truth that Japanese women of all castes, this one included, deserve to be called O-Setsu san."

He continued to look at her, still silent and motionless. She hesitated, wary of displeasing him. What did he want? Should she laugh or remain serious?

Keep silent or speak? She settled on a pout half-playful and half-tender, and for a timid caress from her two outstretched little hands…

❄

They were talking now. Emboldened, she took up the conversation they had interrupted earlier, and, one by one, asked the immutable questions: the ones that yellow, brown, and black girls the world over, offering a smile and the embrace of their naked arms to passers-by, pose to each of their lovers from overseas…

"Where are you from?… What is your country called?… Why have you left your distant house?… The women you loved over there must have been much lovelier and much more clever than me…"

Felze in turn posed questions of his own. Where was she born? Who were her parents? Did she have many lovers, many friends, many girlfriends? Was she happy?" To each question she would reply first with a bow, then with a long, elaborate, usually evasive sentence. At times she would fall silent after the first words and then laugh with a shake of the head, as if to say that it was all of no importance and that the happiness or unhappiness of a simple *nēsan* was not worth looking into.

"Open dress, shut soul!" murmured Felze. "Here's something to upset the morality of the wholesome ladies back home, ever eager to set the intimacies of their psyche on display. In Europe modesty is reserved for external use. Here…"

He smiled, remembering a passage from the *Shih Ching*[145] that Zhou P'ei had taught him:

---

145   The third of the sacred books (*Ching*): *I Ching* (occult sciences), *Shu Ching* (annals), *Shih Ching* (verse), *Li Chi* (rites), *Ch'un Ch'iu* (spring and autumn). [Author's note.] —
The named book is indeed one of the Five Confucian Classics, also known as the *Wu Ching* (Wade-Giles) or *Wǔjīng* (Pinyin), a collection of ancient Chinese texts fundamental to Confucianism. They include (Pinyin below):

The Classic of Poetry (*Shījīng*): A collection of poems and songs dating back to the Zhou dynasty (1046–256 BC) that cover a wide range of topics, including love, nature, politics, and morality.

The Classic of History (*Shujing*): A collection of historical documents covering the period from the mythical Xia dynasty (ca. 2100 BC) to the Zhou dynasty. It includes accounts of important events, biographies of rulers and officials, and records of rituals and ceremonies.

The Classic of Changes (*Yì Jīng*): A divination manual using a set of sixty-four hexagrams (combinations of six broken or unbroken lines) to represent different situations and outcomes. It is used for both fortune-telling and philosophical reflection.

The Record of Rites (*Lǐjì*): A collection of texts describing the social norms, customs, and rituals of ancient China, with instructions on how to behave at weddings, funerals, court ceremonies, and so forth.

The Spring and Autumn Annals (*Chūnqiū*): A historical chronicle of the state of Lu, where Confucius lived, covering the period from 722 to 481 BC. It is named for spring and autumn, traditionally associated with mourning and reflection. Confucius is said to have written the final version of this text.

"Over her garment of embroidered silk she dons a very simple tunic."
Yes! It was the old Chinese fashion, and the *nēsan* still followed it. Elsewhere
the embroidered silk was worn on top.

Still, even the most tightly shut souls will sometimes open a crack when
you apply an unexpected pressure to a secret spring. Felze, in the course
of the conversation, up and mentioned the city of Osaka, where the *Yseult*
had paid a call six weeks earlier, and the mannerly, circumspect girl forgot
herself and gave a start:

"*Hai!*... Osaka?..."

Felze shot her a questioning look. In something of a muddle, she
explained:

"I went to school in Osaka..."

After a spell of silence she continued:

"I was sad when my mother sold me."

Beneath notice, her face had tightened up. Sadness settled like a veil
over her narrow eyes, and an oblique wrinkle formed, running from the
corner of her mouth to the edge of her nostril. In an instant, however, an
astonishing effort buried the pained little grimace and yielded to a resolute
and correct smile.

Felze took the child's hand, a hand in no way ugly, and, not without
respect, laid a kiss on it.

"I have seen old lacquers," he thought, "that had cost an artist ten
years' work. And I have admired those lacquers. But this smile, on this little
servant's face — how many centuries lie behind it of a civilization bent
entirely towards heroism and elegance?..."

Thought after thought flitted through his mind.

"Zhou P'ei," he said, almost aloud, "would perhaps deem this
civilization worth saving, by any means whatsoever..."

XXIV

The Sunshine of Trafalgar

"England expects that every man will do his duty."
—Nelson and Bronte[146]

Two double peals from the flagship's bell: ten o'clock, by the universal convention of sailors. And on all the vessels, from one end of the line to the other, similar bells rang out in response. The fleet — a vice and a rear admiral, two divisions, six battleships — was steaming slowly east. The sky was low, the breeze cold, the sea turbulent, and the horizon shrouded in fog. To starboard loomed the grey mass of the island of Tsu — Tsushima.[147]

A big wave broke in the wind, its spray reaching as far as the aft deck of the *Nikkō*.[148]

Marquis Yorisaka Sadao had been pacing in silence. Struck full in the face, he stopped to wipe his eyes, then started right up again.

The deck, a rounded triangle, was broad and long, flat, without railings or parapets, and slightly inclined at the edges, like the glacis of a fortress.[149] It served in fact as the platform and base of the big aft turret. The giant bores of the twin cannon extended from a double oval embrasure like two recumbent Trajan's columns.[150]

---

146   Admiral Horatio Nelson (1758–1805) sent this message from his flagship, *HMS Victory*, during the pivotal Battle of Trafalgar on 21 October 1805, urging his fleet to valor against the combined forces of France and Spain. Nelson died later that day from a gunshot wound. In 1799 King Ferdinand III of Sicily bestowed the title "Duke of Bronté" upon Nelson for his services. Hence the denomination Nelson of Bronte or Nelson and Bronte.

147   An island of about 700 square kilometers separating the Tsushima and the Korea Straits, about halfway between Kyushu and the Korean Peninsula.

148   No ship by the name of *Nikkō* took part in the Battle of Tsushima. The author, careful to preserve the purely imaginary character of the book's "plot," has of necessity resorted to a battleship that never existed, there to situate characters and adventures that themselves never existed. It goes without saying that all in the ensuing tale that does not directly concern the *Nikkō*, its crew, and its command is of rigorous historical accuracy. [Author's note.]

149   A slope below the walls of a fortress, meant to render attack from any direction an uphill affair.

150   Trajan's Column is a massive (115-foot) triumphal column in Rome, just north of the Forum. Completed in 113 AD, it commemorates Emperor Trajan's victory in the Dacian Wars (AD 101–02 and AD 105–06).

Passing under one of them, Marquis Yorisaka raised a hand to caress the sonorous metal, setting it to vibrate imperceptibly, like a finger brushing a bronze gong.

That very moment someone touched Marquis Yorisaka's shoulder, just as Marquis Yorisaka had touched the cannon's steel.

"How goes it, dear fellow? What news?"

The Marquis turned and gave a military salute after the English fashion.

"Ah! It's you, *kimi*. How are you?"

Commander Herbert Fergan was wearing his British uniform and smoking an Oxford pipe. He had only replaced his embroidered cap with a sou'wester: the same, indeed, as sailors all over the world wear in bad weather.

"I'm quite well," he said. "Is there something in sight over there?"

His outstretched arm was pointing to the southern horizon. Marquis Yorisaka shook his head.

"Too far. They're still south of Mameseki,[151] more than sixty miles away… But they're coming… We're concentrating the army. Kamimura[152] is here, and so is Uryū."[153]

He indicated the southeast.

"All will be set by noon, and then we'll have another hour to wait."

"You made contact last night."

"Yes, by intercepting their wireless telegrams. And then, at five o'clock, the *Shinano Maru* saw them…[154] They were at course 203, on the parallel of Sasebo, eighty miles to the west[155]… They were on course for the strait… Oh, they're coming!… Look here. Kataoka's squadron[156] should be firing on them right now, but it's out of earshot for us… At any rate, a cannonade from cruisers doesn't count for much…"

He again caressed the enormous gun overhead, this one a 305, a battleship gun.[157]

"This here is what counts," said Fergan.

"*Hai!* My thinking exactly."

---

151 There is no Japanese or Korean city by this name, which appears in original editions.

152 Baron Kamimura Hikonojō (1849–1916) was an admiral in the Imperial Japanese Navy, commanding the IJN Second Fleet during the Russo-Japanese War, notably at the Battle off Ulsan and Tsushima.

153 Baron Uryū Sotokichi (1857–1937) was an admiral in the Imperial Japanese Navy during the Russo-Japanese and Sino-Japanese Wars, fighting in the Battles of Chemulpo Bay and Tsushima. After his retirement he served as a member of the House of Peers in the Japanese Imperial Diet.

154 *Shinano Maru* was a 6,388 GRT (Gross Registered Tonnage) merchantman built in Glasgow in 1900 to work a Japan-to-Seattle route. When launched she was 445 feet long and offered comfortable, modern accommodations for 238 passengers (26 in first class, 20 in second class, 193 in third class). At the start of the Russo-Japanese War, in February 1904, the *Shinano Maru* was requisitioned by the Imperial Japanese Navy and converted into an armed merchantman/troopship. On the night of 26–27 May the *Shinano Maru* had the distinction of discovering the first ship of the Russian Fleet, the Russian hospital transport *Orel*, near Tsushima Strait.

155 In navigation a parallel is a line of latitude. The ship, then, is 80 nautical miles west of Sasebo, Japan, on the same latitude as the city, and heading 203 degrees (south-southwest).

156 Baron Kataoka Shichirō (1854–1920) was a distinguished admiral in the Imperial Japanese Navy. At the onset of the Russo-Japanese War he was placed in command of the Third Fleet, a collection of antiquated ships nicknamed the "Funny Fleet." Despite their obsolescence, Kataoka skillfully commanded the fifth and sixth battle divisions from the cruiser *Nisshin* during the Battle of the Yellow Sea, and subsequently from the cruiser *Itsukushima* during the Battle of Tsushima.

157 The 305 is a 305mm (12-inch) naval gun, a standard main battery weapon on early twentieth-century battleships, such as those used at the Battle of Tsushima. These large-caliber guns, firing armor-piercing shells, became prevalent thanks to advances in steel production, smokeless powder, and projectiles and played a decisive role in the era's naval warfare.

Marquis Yorisaka's voice was calm as could be. He was not even nervous, as the bravest Westerners are just before a great battle.

"Well," said Fergan, "I think all will go well. Of course, the first moments will be rough going. The Russians are brave people… But you are much more, especially now… I mean no flattery when I say you've made considerable progress these past few weeks."

"Thanks to you!" said Yorisaka.

He looked at Fergan with irreproachable gratitude. Fergan blushed slightly.

"No! I assure you! You exaggerate greatly… Truth is, your effort has been truly splendid. You've managed to get all the court cards and aces in your hand, and you're about to win the rubber — rightly so… A lovely rubber: this victory will decide the whole war. If Rozhestvensky loses a single trick here, Linevich'll be hit with a grand slam in Manchuria!"[158]

"*Hai*! I hope so…"

They walked together a bit, spreading their legs and bending their knees to counter the roll. The battleships continued to "make" east. Tsushima now showed lengthwise, eight or nine miles behind, and there was now nothing to see in the distance but an iron-grey mist, barely visible among the leaden clouds.

"This doesn't look like the sunshine of Trafalgar," observed Marquis Yorisaka, smiling.[159]

"No," said Fergan, "but at Trafalgar the sun hid as soon as the battle was no longer in doubt, and there was a storm in the evening. Maybe this battle is already won."

"You have too high an opinion of us," protested the Marquis.

The tall funnels would at intervals expel thick black puffs, which the wind would set a-swirl in an instant. And the sea, already dark, reflected the smoke in long, livid streaks.

The English commander backed up to the turret and leaned against it.

"You'll be in this box, Yorisaka?" he said. "This is your combat post, no?"

"Yes. I command the turret."

---

158 Fergan describes the military situation in terms of a card game. "Win the rubber" is from bridge and other trick-taking card games, like whist. A "rubber" is a set of rounds, typically consisting of three games. The team that wins the best of three wins the rubber. Fergan goes on to suggest that if the Japanese navy wins the upcoming naval battle (i.e., wins the "trick"), then the Russian land forces will face a complete defeat (a "slam" or "chelem") in Manchuria.

159 The sunny and somewhat calm weather seemed at first advantageous to the Franco-Spanish fleet at Trafalgar, but Nelson exploited his opponents' weaknesses. His unorthodox strategy and effective use of wind direction led to a decisive British victory, marred as it was by his own death from a French sniper's bullet.

"I'll pay you a visit, if you'll permit me…"

"You would be doing me great honor… I shall count on you… Ah! Here's Kamimura…"

He pointed to the horizon, where other smokestacks, still all but indistinct, were emerging from the sea, two by two or three by three. A moment later appeared their masts and hulls. The two fleets, moving towards each other, nudging their courses south, so as to assume tactical battle formation right away.

"We're staying in the lead, of course?" questioned Fergan.

"Of course. Have you read the preliminary order? A single line: battleships in front, armored cruisers behind. We'll be engaging the twelve ships at once… And, rest assured, we shall not be repeating the tenth of August today!…"

He had lowered his eyes, and beamed now with a singular smile, mordant, with a kind of proud bitterness at the corner of his mouth. He continued, speaking slowly:

"We will not be timid… And we will get in close to fight … as close as necessary… We have learned our lesson…"

He abruptly raised his eyes and fixed them on Fergan…

"We now know that to conquer at sea one must prepare with method and caution, then rush in furious and mad… So did Rodney, and Nelson, and the Frenchman Suffren proceed. So shall we ourselves…"

Herbert Fergan had turned away, making no reply. He seemed to be paying keen attention to the countermarch of the armored cruisers entering the line. There was a heavy minute's silence…

"Would you be so kind as to excuse me?" Marquis Yorisaka suddenly asked. "Our friend Viscount Hirata is signaling to me… I've a small technical matter to attend to…"

Herbert Fergan ceased that very moment to observe the maneuver, as yet incomplete.

"But of course!… Go!… See you soon, dear friend… I myself must head down. Isn't it lunchtime? We shall perhaps be dining late…"

He was phlegmatic through and through, adding a touch of humor:

"Who knows? Later, perhaps, than we shall ever have dined!"

XXV

A Libation of Blood

So the turrets will be running on electricity?"

"Yes, as long as the motors keep operating. If there's a malfunction, we'll switch to hydraulics — and, lastly, to manual operation. That's the order."

"We will obey, then, honorably."

And Viscount Hirata Takamori, having first saluted with military discipline, fingers joined and raised to the visor of his cap, bowed in keeping with the rite of the *daimyo* and the samurai, his body bent to a right angle, hands flat on his knees.

"Permit me now to take my leave…"

And he was leaving when Marquis Yorisaka Sadao stopped him.

"Hirata, are you very pressed for time? It's not yet noon. Would you like to chat a bit?"

Viscount Hirata opened a fan that he carried in his sleeve.

"Yorisaka, you do me great honor. In truth, I dared not impose on the minutes at your noble disposal: hence my discretion. But I am flattered by your condescension. Tell me, then. What do you make of this fine rain, like a melted fog? Don't you think it might become a hindrance soon, on the field of battle?"

Marquis Yorisaka was gazing absent-mindedly at the choppy, foggy sea.

"Perhaps," he murmured.

He then suddenly turned to face his interlocutor.

"Forgive my rudeness, Hirata. I would like to ask you a question."

"If you would so deign, please," said Hirata.

He had closed his fan and leaned his head forward, as if to hear better. Marquis Yorisaka spoke very slowly, in a deep and clear voice:

"Permit me first to recall a few shared memories. Our families, though often enemies over the centuries of ancient times, have most often fought side by side, during many civil and foreign wars. Recently — at the time of the Great Change, I mean — our fathers took up arms together to restore imperial power to its former splendor. And although a little later, during the

events of Kumamoto,[160] our martial fraternity was broken, the blood shed on that glorious occasion did not prevent you and me from establishing a friendship twelve years later, when, on the same day, we entered the Emperor's service."

"Bloodshed, Yorisaka, when not requiring revenge, has only ever cemented the union of two families when both are faithful observers of *bushidō*."

"It is certainly so. We have been like two fingers of the same hand, Hirata. But it seems to me that we are no longer so. Am I wrong? I implore you to give me your thoughts on this matter, with no thought to courtesy."

Viscount Hirata had raised his head.

"You are not wrong," he said, simply.

"Your sincerity is precious to me," replied Marquis Yorisaka, impassive. "Forgive me, then, if I respond with equal sincerity. Although in all circumstances you have continued to show me a thousand courtesies of which I am unworthy, and although no one could certainly have suspected, from your words or attitude, a cooling of our friendship, I can no longer endure even a secret humiliation. I have therefore decided to end it today, and I beg you, honorably, to explain in what way I have failed you. This is my question."

They stared at each other, motionless and alone on an aft quarterdeck dripping with rain and spray, the two cannon of the turret stretching their lengthy barrels overhead, and all around the churn and din of the wind-whipped sea and its topsy-turvy waves.

Viscount Hirata answered even more slowly than Marquis Yorisaka had spoken.

"Yorisaka, you have recalled some of our shared memories. Rest assured, those recollections have not left my mind. Would you now permit me to recall others, memories that have perhaps escaped you? You have spoken of the Great Change. You are correct that during that illustrious era, the dawn of the Meiji era, your clan and my clan together drew the sword

---

160 It was at Kumamoto that Saigō was defeated in 1877, and with him the entire Satsuma clan. [Author's note.] — In 1877 Kumamoto, in the center of Kyushu, Japan's third-largest island, became the primary battleground of the Satsuma Rebellion, a revolt led by Saigō Takamori (1828–77), often referred to as the last true samurai. Once a key figure in the Meiji government, Saigō grew disillusioned with rapid Westernization and modernization, which he felt were undermining the samurai class. He led the Satsuma clan and other samurai in a rebellion against the Imperial Japanese Army. The rebellion's key event was the Siege of Kumamoto Castle, where the well-fortified forces of the Meiji government held out against Saigō's samurai for nearly two months. The rebellion ended, later that year, in defeat for Saigō forces and in death for Saigō himself and the samurai era. The Satsuma clan's defeat led to the complete consolidation of imperial power and accelerated Japan's transformation into a modern nation-state.

for the Mikado against the Shōgun. But have you forgotten the original cause of that struggle? It was no matter of dynastic loyalty. No Shōgun had ever usurped the essential prerogatives of the Divine Emperors, sons of the Sun Goddess.[161] And for seven hundred years the princes of the Fujiwara, the Taira, the Minamoto, the Hojo, the Ashikaga, and the Tokugawa had, without inconvenience, substituted their robust will for the weak will of the Mikado. What changed, then, that so many noble men suddenly wished to destroy an organization of seven centuries? There was, Yorisaka, this: that black ships from Europe had five years earlier bombarded Kagoshima, and that the Shōgun, rather than fight, had signed a shameful peace. Such was the true cause. Japan, having swallowed the insult and not drunk the vengeance, rose in a single bound against the Shōgun, gave forth the cry repeated ten thousand times: *"Death to the Foreigner!"* Death to the Foreigner. Thus had our ancestors cried, Marquis Yorisaka. Thus had they cried on every battlefield, until the Mikado was restored to its original power. Thus had my own ancestors cried; and thus they were still crying on the red day of Kumamoto when, indignant at the new power, which seemed as weak as the old, they marched behind Saigō, who had pledged to wash away the common shame in victory or in death. Thus I myself cry today, for I am legitimate heir to those corpses. Their memorial tablets have never left my belt. For the thirty years that I have lived I have awaited the hour to render unto these tablets what they are owed: a libation of blood. And, hark, the hour is struck!… Yorisaka, forgive the length of my speech. I have no doubt that it has given you full satisfaction regardless. You have certainly not failed me. And of what account to you is the judgment of a tiny *daimyo* of no intelligence? But I have opened my heart to you, and you have read it as you would a book printed in beautiful Chinese characters of the darkest black: I hate the foreigner with all the force of my hatred. You, however, who also hated him once, have love for him today. Have you not little by little adopted his customs, his tastes, his ideas, even his language, which

---

161 Amaterasu Ōmikami, who gave birth to the Mikado dynasty. [Author's note.] — Often referred to simply as Amaterasu. She is the sun goddess and supreme deity in Shinto, Japan's indigenous faith. She is believed to be the ancestor of the Mikado (Japan's Emperor and Imperial Family) and thus grounds the divine legitimacy of the imperial line.

According to ancient chronicles, the *Kojiki* and *Nihon Shoki* included, Amaterasu was born from the left eye of the primordial deity Izanagi as he purified himself in a river. She later took her place in the High Celestial Plain, illuminating the world with her light. One of her most famous myths is the tale of her retreat into a cave, which plunged the world into darkness, and the subsequent efforts of the other gods to lure her out and restore light to the world. Japan's most revered Shinto shrine, the Ise Grand Shrine, is dedicated to Amaterasu.

you are always speaking with that English spy, our supposed ally? I do not presume to cast blame! Far from it! All that you do is, of course, well done. But our opposing sentiments have dug a chasm between us, a chasm that nothing could fill."

Viscount Hirata fell silent. Marquis Yorisaka did not reply right away. He had listened to the end without raising an eyebrow or averting his gaze. At last, after several grave minutes of reflection, he brusquely spread his arms to take in the entire southern horizon, now drowning in a muddle of fog and smoke, and with a stony voice asked:

"Hirata, do you not see something, out there?… Noon has struck, if I am not mistaken… Yes. In that case, those vertical clouds are probably the plumes of Russian funnels. Here comes the foreigner, Hirata, the foreigner you believe you hate so much…"

He smiled, and the half-closed lids narrowed his eyes into two oblique, thin, black slits.

"…The foreigner you believe you hate so much… Now that we're on the subject, Hirata… You've read the secret orders… The tactics have been significantly changed, don't you think?… Especially with respect to the artillery…"

"Yes…"

"Yes! Significantly changed! We will no longer scatter our fire, as before… We will concentrate it on the heads of the enemy columns… Moreover, to guard against failures of transmission, we are giving wide autonomy to isolated sections… It is a bold endeavor. We would perhaps not have risked it if intelligence from a European source — the English — had not convinced the admiral of more than probable success: the certain success that our boldness will earn us. And do you know, Hirata, who has obtained this intelligence — who has won it or stolen it, by force or cunning, with daring and patience, and at great pains? I have, Hirata. It might be that you hate the foreigner as much as you say. And it might be that I love him as much as you believe. But it might also be that an enemy such as you is less deadly to him than a friend such as I."[162]

Viscount Hirata wrinkled his brow.

"Yorisaka," he said, "my stupidity is so great that you could not, I see, grasp the exact meaning of my words. For the Russian fleet you are certainly a more dangerous opponent than I. And never has the injurious

---

162   Prescient of the author, in light of what was to transpire a little more than three decades later.

supposition entered my head that you were in any way unable to do your duty or be of great use in carrying out the Emperor's designs. But you are like those fencing masters who kill without wrath, albeit unfailingly. Today I will kill less well than you, but I will kill with drunken abandon. And my fury can be no friend to your indifference."

Marquis Yorisaka had crossed his arms:

"Do you believe," he said, almost under his breath, "that my indifference is anything but a mask, with a fury possibly more furious than yours roiling underneath?… Hirata, I thought your eyes keener than that!…"

This time Marquis Yorisaka had departed from calm.

"I thought your eyes could read into me! My false face was for the Europeans only. And yet you were fooled — you, a noble Nippon! Viscount Hirata, your ancestors fell at Kumamoto, and you remember them, and you keep their funeral tablets devoutly. But have you not understood the lesson they gave us in their defeat and death? A lesson in patience and prudence! A lesson in cunning! The time is past when battles were won with the sword's blade. To defeat the foreigner we began, you and I, by attending their schools. But the knowledge we learned there amounted to little, and we learned it poorly, besides. Our Japanese brains would not take in European education. And I soon felt the need for us first to acquire European brains, whatever the cost in other domains. I applied myself, and perhaps succeeded: not without fatigue or hard suffering — harsher suffering than anyone will ever know… But it was necessary for the Empire's liberation, for its exaltation. I tell you, Hirata, ten thousand times did my face flush red as, the better to imitate the Western soul, I strove to forget the most rigorous precepts of a *daimyo*'s education. But at such times I thought of the sick whom their doctors dispatch for a plunge in a mud bath, and who emerge cured and hale. I emerge today from my own mud. I emerge cured of my former weakness and hale for the struggle that is about to begin. And I regret nothing. But I did not expect on accomplishing my task to have to endure a former companion's disdain."

Viscount Hirata's eyes sparkled, and his voice took on a cutting tone:

"I have told you, Yorisaka, that there is no question of disdain. I take the extreme liberty of repeating it. I highly appreciate the patriotic concern that has guided you. But, as you yourself have just proclaimed, your brain has ceased to be Japanese and become European. My brain, my thoroughly crude brain, can never imitate yours. It would henceforth be vain of us to make this dual effort to understand each other. Now that everything has been said on this matter do you not think it superfluous to speak further?

"One more thing," said Yorisaka Sadao. "I shall be so bold as to question you a second and last time… Hirata, here, in these straits of Tsushima, we shall soon will win a great victory. Would defeat be preferable to you if all the Japanese of today were still like the Japanese of Kumamoto?"

"I am too ignorant to answer on grounds of wisdom," said Hirata Takamori. "But permit me, most humbly, to question you in turn. Are you certain that we will soon be, as you claim, victorious?! And have you imagined the name that Europe will bestow on us — the Europe that we will have copied to no end, ridiculously — if we are defeated?"

"Yes," said Marquis Yorisaka. "Europe will call us monkeys. But we will not be defeated."

"Yoshitsune himself was. What if we are?"

"We will not be."

"I shall take your word for it. We will therefore be victorious. But what then?"

"Afterwards?"

"After the battle. After the peace is signed. You will return, Yorisaka, to your house in Tokyo, carrying your European brain, and your European ideas, customs, and tastes, along with you. And, as you will be a most glorious hero, the Japanese people will be seduced by your illustrious example, and will imitate your tastes, your customs, your ideas…"

"No," said Yorisaka.

XXVI

The Flag of the Rising Sun

Stem to stern, spar-deck to holds, the grating, strident Nipponese trumpets sounded the call to arms. Yorisaka Sadao, lifting the hatch, entered the rear turret.

"Attention!"

The non-commissioned officer, stiff as a rod, saluted, heels together, hand to visor. The men, quarter-officers and sailors, turned their twelve respectful smiles to their commander.

"Stand easy!" said Yorisaka.

And he commenced a brief but meticulous inspection.

The turret was a low to the head, without door or window, a hexagonal chamber ten meters long, eight wide, and clad in armor of thick steel. The two enormous cannon took up three-quarters of the space, and what little remained was filled with the cradles, the chassis, the gun carriages, the hoists, the ramrods, the swabs, the sights, the scopes, the gunner's levels, the transmitters, and all the piping for pressurized water and compressed air, all the electrical conduits, and the inextricable jumble of iron, copper, and bronze required to operate two naval guns of the largest caliber in existence. From their multiple directions six incandescent lamps bathed and penetrated each mechanism with raw, shadowless light. The daylight added only a sort of bluish halo, filtered through the ring slot of the double embrasure, between armor and cannon.

Yorisaka Sadao circled the two breeches, scrutinizing things one by one and looking every man in the face. Then he made his way to the median ladder, climbed its three steps, and sat on the command saddle. His head now rose past the armored ceiling to stick out of the turret through the central cupola. This cupola, itself armored, served to shield his head. And Yorisaka Sadao, even

as he enjoyed this protection from enemy fire, had a view of the entire
battlefield, through three fairly wide holes in the armor. Also, the cupola's
opening made it easy to communicate with the gunners and to watch the
operation of the guns.

Now that he was seated he first bent down and considered the entirety
of the motionless, attentive turret below. An extraordinary sensation of power
emanated from this fearsome machine and the thirteen men who formed its
living flesh and nerves. The chieftain in command held in his palm a more
terrible thunderbolt than the sky's. Yorisaka Sadao clenched his fists with
pride. Then, instantly restoring his calm, he raised his head and peered,
methodically, through the cupola's holes, the three of them, left to right.

The sea retained its chop, glaucous and furrowed, sinister under a dense
cloak of heavy clouds. The aft quarterdeck, visible below, was but a triangular

raft, besieged by waves and drenched. The fleet had changed course. It was now running west, towards Tsushima, every vessel striving to hold its position and keep to the regulatory four-hundred-meter intervals between ships. The line stretched for nearly three nautical miles, the *Mikasa* leading the way, the *Iwate* bringing up the rear. The *Nikkō* followed the *Mikasa*, the *Shikishima* followed the *Nikkō*, and behind this first division, commanded by old Togo himself, the others advanced in good order, the Kamimura division, the

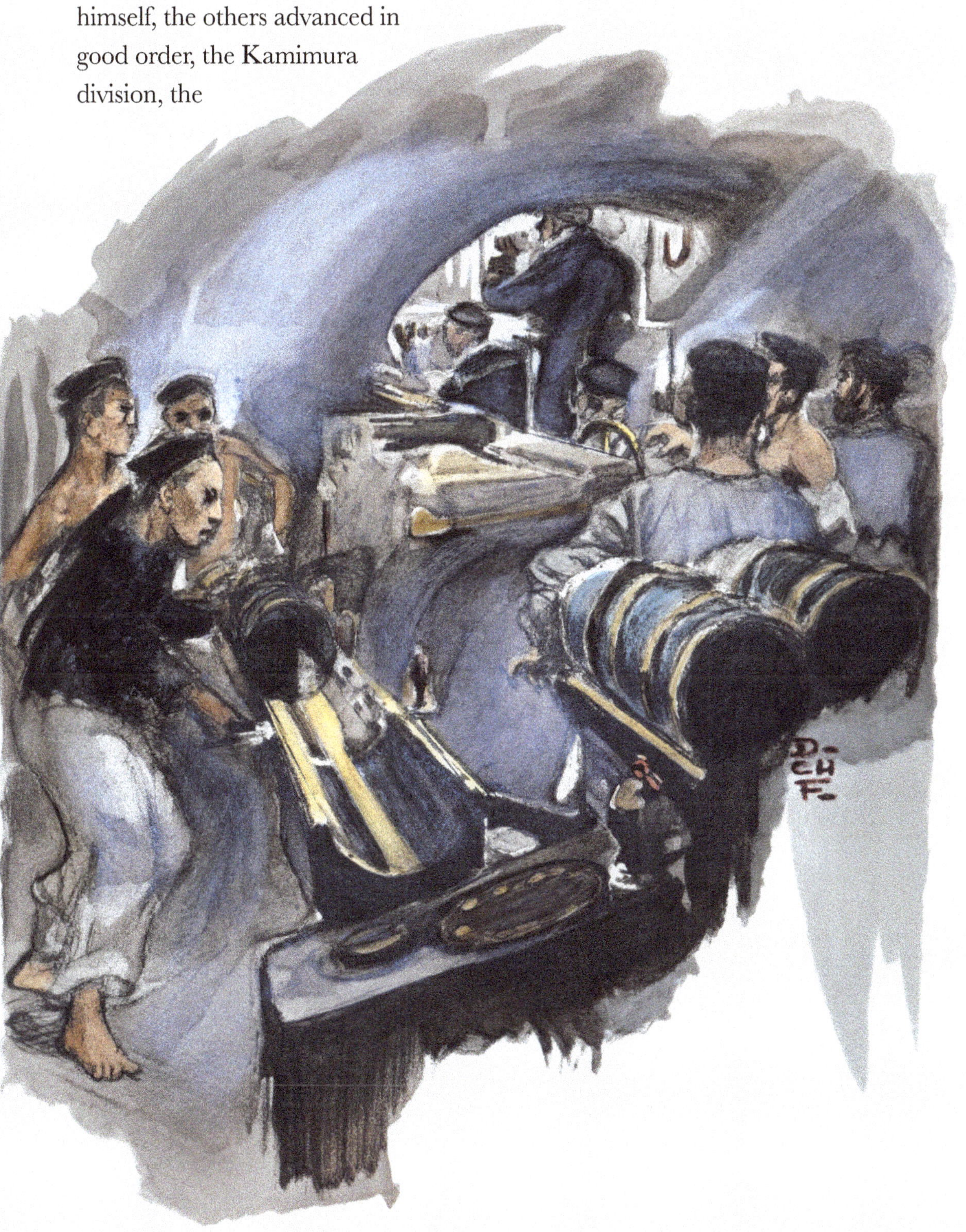

Shimamura division, all the battleships, all the armored cruisers, all of the Empire's vital force. In the flat, foamy wake Yorisaka Sadao watched as the tall gray silhouettes drew near, bristling with cannon leveled for battle. And the flag of the Rising Sun, flying on every mast, fluttering over ships and sea, seemed a glorious presage of the red blood soon to flow…

"Swivel!... Turret left! … Stop! … Turret right!…"[163]

The gunner, seated between the guns, eye to his scope, gripped the firing pistol. A gentle hum rose from the electric motor, and, docile as a toy, the giant turret turned right to left, left to right, carrying along men, machines, cannon, and armor like so much straw, without sound or jolt. Before Yorisaka Sadao's eyes the scene scrolled to the horizon like a conveyor belt on a theatrical set. A distant squadron plumed with smoke appeared to starboard, a squadron of cruisers visibly hurrying towards its battle station — Dewa,[164] no doubt, and Uryū behind him… To port the mist hung like a curtain, and there was yet no sign of the enemy, though he was near.

A double peal on the bell, then a single: half past one o'clock. A trumpet sounded three long notes, then two short ones: "Prepare for battle to port." Yorisaka signaled the order to the gunner. The turret turned to face the presumed adversary.

"Load guns!"

Only the clink of the Galle chains[165] told of the hoists' maneuvering. The servants bustled about mute, their doings miraculously brisk and precise. The two breechblocks opened; two shells vanished into the oily black holes of the powder chambers; two ramrods rolled on their bearings. Distinct sounds — the clang of a projectile hitting a bore's partition, the rustle of silk powder bags pushed against one another under the blows of fists, the clear clap of a closing breech — beat time during the loading... Stopwatch in hand, Yorisaka Sadao smiled: twenty-four seconds, almost a record! The Russians would do better, if they could…

Silence reigned once more. There was still nothing to be seen through the holes in the armored cupola, nothing but fog and sea. Yorisaka Sadao, patient, stopped looking. He took up his rangefinder

---

163 Japanese commands have been translated into equivalent French commands. [Author's note.] — And now into equivalent commands in English. [Translator's note.]

164 Dewa Shigeto (1838–1917), an admiral, is notable for his contribution to the development of the Imperial Japanese Navy and also for his leadership in the Russo-Japanese War, particularly at the Battle of Tsushima.

165 Transmission chains, looped.

and gave it a scrupulous inspection. The mirrors were not quite parallel; he corrected the error. A turret's rangefinder — nothing of surpassing precision, for crying out loud. But if the blockhouse rangefinders were to fail, as they had failed on the tenth of August… Yoshitsune the hero, for lack of a sword, unsheathed a fan…

Yorisaka Sadao set down the rangefinder and once again raised his head. Would the fog not dissipate at last?… Ah! News: a signal rising to the halyards, and the *Mikasa* veered left…

The electric bell rang. Two lamps lit up on the transmitter panel; needles turned on the dials. All of the fleet's trumpets once again sounded their strident notes. Yorisaka Sadao, stiffening in his saddle, issued his orders:

"Prepare for battle to starboard!… Left turret! Fourth gear!"

The turret, already obeying, pivoted.

"Distance, seven thousand three hundred meters! Correction: Right five thousandths! Stop!"

The two long barrels angled up, maws high and on the alert. Yorisaka Sadao leaned in, scanning the blurry line where the sky met the sea... Yes... Over there, dead south ... amid that pile of dense clouds on the horizon ... blackish volutes were rising — three, four, five, at regular intervals ... seven, eight ... and still more ... twelve, fifteen, twenty, thirty...

"Prime! Arm!"

The calm voice did not quaver, not at all.

The telephone rang. Yorisaka Sadao picked up the receiver.

"Hello!... Yes... The admiral's telegraphing?..."

He bent down, looked at the gunners, and repeated, without a word of commentary:

"The admiral's telegraphing: 'The Empire's salvation depends on the result of the battle. Do your duty, all of you!'"

Here the voice, less calm, had quavered a bit, but it was just as soon dry and cold again.

"Eighty degrees! Aim for the head of the line... Yes, to the left, on the ship with two funnels... Stand by!..."

Yorisaka Sadao had grabbed his rangefinder and was checking in succession the distances written on the transmitter panel.

"Seven thousand one hundred!... Six thousand eight hundred!... Six thousand four hundred!..."

He paused for a second. Over there, on the now-distinct enemy hulls, flashes suddenly shone: the Russians were opening fire ... too far, perhaps...

"Six thousand meters!..."

He paused again. Less than a hundred meters from the *Nikkō* a huge splash had just burst up and was now falling in slow rain — the first shell to slap the sea, the first shell to be fired, on this decisive day by the West against the East... Yorisaka Sadao, disdainful, took the measure of the tall white phantom as it vanished into the breeze. That was all it was: a bit of spray raised into the air. They were poor shots...

"Five thousand nine hundred!..."

Other shells exploded here and there among the waves, all short of the target. Yes, the Russians were poor shots. An endless minute elapsed, and at last there came a brutal rumble, like the winged buzz of an enormous bee: the Russians had overshot... In answer, as if this had been the awaited signal for a counterattack, there came a detonation nearby, the first Japanese detonation…

"Five thousand seven hundred meters!"

The voice, still impeccable in its clarity, articulated each syllable separately:

"Commence firing!…"

The bluish halo, the daylight filtering in through the double embrasure between armor and cannon, turned suddenly into a dazzle of purple: the ready maws spat two prodigious flames, twenty meters long and red as blood. A dreadful shock rocked the turret like a gust hitting a reed. A thunderclap such as no terrestrial crash could convey tore through the air, slamming every ear around, leaving every man deaf and all but drunk for several seconds. And the massive breeches, each as heavy as several field cannon, recoiled three feet and snapped back into place, faster than a skilled marksman can spin his revolver's cylinder. The voice of Yorisaka Sadao, icy and serene, was already restoring the servants' lucidity and cool.

"Five thousand six hundred meters!… Rapid fire!…"

XXVII

The Pride of His *Daimyotic* Race

Herbert Fergan shielded his face behind cupped hands and lit a cigarette. He was standing outside the blockhouse, so as not to crowd any further the tight armored cell in which the commander, the helmsman, the gunner, and their aides were bustling about. He was standing on the bridge, exposed, and watching phlegmatically as Russian projectiles exploded all around. He was courageous. Cigarette duly lit, he took up his binoculars again and resumed his study of the two engaged fleets. He made slow, meticulous observations, watching with professional curiosity for signs of fatigue or distress from either of the tenacious combatants. Here a ruptured wall, there a broken mast or superstructures blown to bits. Over there a fallen funnel, a crushed turret, a lopped-off blockhouse. Clean and geometric at the start, the vessels' profiles were distorting, listing off level, fraying with debris and rubble. Now and again Herbert Fergan would set down his binoculars, open his notebook, check his watch, and jot down some episode from the battle. The cannon roared without interruption, so loud that busted ears could no longer suffer. Only from the still-even, blazing glow that ringed the *Nikkō* like a halo could Fergan confirm that the Japanese fire remained vigorous and intact. On the other side, though, the crackle of fire from the Russian ships was already less dense, petering out like the sparks of half-consumed logs.

Herbert Fergan turned on his heels and swept the full circumference of the horizon in one go. The two opposed lines were running parallel to the east: one regular and maneuverable, the other in disorder and on the verge of breaking up. All right, then! Events were bearing out predictions: Rozhestvensky was not "holding out" against Togo. In his notebook the pencil scribbled: "2:35, battle won. *Oslyabya*[166] in distress, giving up. *Suvorov*[167] out of combat. *Nikkō*, no

---

166 The *Oslyabya* was the last of the three *Peresvet*-class second-class pre-dreadnought battleships completed for the Imperial Russian Navy at the end of the nineteenth century. As part of the Second Pacific Squadron sent to the Far East during the Russo-Japanese War of 1904–05, she served as the flagship of Rear Admiral Baron Dmitry von Fölkersam. The *Oslyabya* was sunk on 27 May 1905 at the Battle of Tsushima, and was the first all-steel battleship to be sunk by naval gunfire alone. Sources differ on the exact number of casualties, but over half her crew went down with the ship.

167 The *Knyaz Suvorov* was a *Borodino*-class pre-dreadnought battleship commissioned in 1904.

major damage…" A good prophet, Herbert Fergan smiled — not that his heart was set on a Japanese victory. At best his sympathy went less willingly to the uncouth Muscovites than to these Japanese, whose delicate, sensuous hospitality he had most pleasantly enjoyed… But, as a moment's thought would show, Togo's fleet was in fact an English fleet — built in England, armed in England, trained and tempered with English methods and along English principles. — And British pride took satisfaction in what was, all things considered, a national success…

"All right!"[168] In an hour's time it will all be over. But we must live on until then!…"

A shell — the sixth or seventh — exploded on the spar-deck, shredding a cadaver here and there. Fergan, impassive, leaned over: the

---

As the flagship of Vice Admiral Zinovy Rozhestvensky, she was dispatched to break the Japanese blockade of Port Arthur, but the destination was changed to Vladivostok after the port fell. During the Battle of Tsushima, on 27 May 1905, a shell-hit incapacitated the ship, wounding the captain and Rozhestvensky and killing the helmsman. The battleship was ultimately torpedoed and sunk by Japanese forces; other than twenty wounded officers evacuated by a destroyer, there were no survivors. Rozhestvensky was captured, and later the victorious Admiral Tōgō comforted him at a Japanese hospital with these kind words: "Defeat is a common fate of a soldier. There is nothing to be ashamed of in it. The great point is whether we have performed our duty."

168   In English in the original.

deck, not long ago as clean and polished as a parlor floor, was now just a mess of formless, tangled, tattered, ground-up things. There was streaming blood, and an alternation of severed limbs, open chests, and spilled guts. And fire was devouring these scraps. But water from the fire pumps was still keeping back the flames and, above all, the triumphant cannonade was unspent. Though torn, devastated, and battered, the battleship continued to spit furious death into its enemies' face. And Fergan, having surveyed all these gaping but superficial wounds at a glance, repeated the phrase written a moment before in his notebook:

"*Nikkō*, no major damage…"

As he uttered the last word an officer, rushing out of the blockhouse, bumped into him, and, courteous despite the heat of the moment, bowed to apologize before continuing on his way.

"Eh! Hirata, dear friend! Where are you running off to?"

Viscount Hirata was already descending the ladder to the tween deck, but he stopped, politely, to satisfy the English guest's curiosity with a quick reply:

"To repair communications from the blockhouse to the rear turr…"

Herbert Fergan did not hear the last syllable. Another shell exploded, this time against the blockhouse itself … a shell of large caliber, with fulminate cotton…

Fergan heard a tremendous din, saw an ochre fog that was brighter, much brighter, than the sun…, and struggled, heavy, to get to his feet, agonizing in his legs and arms, and agonizing still more in his brain, a benumbed brain that did not understand, had ceased to understand…

The bridge was no longer there, and neither was the blockhouse. In their place was… there was metal … iron, copper, bronze, blended, amalgamated, fused… shreds, tangles, lacy filaments of metal… It was still fire-red and, in spots,

blackened with ash. Fergan laboriously came to a realization: the shell had carried it all away, melted it all, evaporated it all… And all were dead … all: commander, gunner, helmsman, aides … all but him, Fergan, who, though it had escaped his notice, had only been cast to this spot … here, on the spar-deck, twenty meters from the explosion… He stood and looked around. Right beside him a severed head, lopped clean off, as though with a scythe, lay in a brown puddle. It was smiling, lopped off so fast that the muscles, in sudden paralysis, had lacked the time to erase their smile…

Fergan spoke, surprised that his voice still had a sound.

"Everyone … yes … everyone is dead… Wait! No! Not everyone…"

Atop the still-incandescent wreckage, amid the very flames and embers, appeared a man, fantastical. Clinging to who knew what, who knew how, he was leaning over the acoustic tube that penetrated to the deepest depths of the ship, to the central station, where speaking tubes from the artillery, helm, and machines all converged, and into this gaping tube he was shouting orders, commanding maneuvers that the men below, the sheltered men, executed, surely with no sense of the horrifying state of the man who was serving as their eyes, ears, and intelligence; who lay, every second, under threat of annihilation in an unspeakable furnace and, unmoved, carried on to steer the still-fighting battleship towards victory!…

"Hirata Takamori!…"

Herbert Fergan, still reeling, eyes wide, stared in amazement at the Japanese officer, standing on his terrible pedestal. The shell's explosion had evidently sent him too flying, down from the pulverized bridge… And that was not just reflections of fire reddening his black uniform; it was blood… But no sooner had he been knocked flat than he had dipped into his prodigious energy, into the pride of his *daimyotic* race, more stoic than Zeno and his school,[169] and found the superhuman strength to shed his torpor with a single shake and bound by instinct to the nearest and most perilous battle station…

Fergan felt the heat of humiliation rise to his face: a Japanese had done this, while he, an Englishman, though uninjured, had stayed on the ground, overwhelmed, in a swoon…

Herbert Fergan turned suddenly around and went off towards the rear, walking very slowly and puffing out his chest, anxious, for England's honor, to match the countenance of Viscount Hirata Takamori…

––––––––––––

169 The Stoics, a group of philosophers led by Zeno of Citium (ca. 334 – ca. 262 BC) in Athens. Stoicism asserts that the practice of virtue is both necessary and sufficient to achieve *eudaimonia* (literally "good spiritedness"): one flourishes by living an ethical life.

CHARLES
FOUQUERAY

XXVIII

Mitsou...

"You believe him your dupe: if so he feigns to be, which of you is the greater dupe?"
—La Bruyère[170]

"Four thousand four hundred meters!"

Marquis Yorisaka, eye glued to the scope of the turret's rangefinder, did not turn around when he heard the hatch slam. Herbert Fergan had just entered and, so as not to disturb the gun servants, remained, still and silent, atop the hatch itself.

"Four thousand two hundred!"

The two giant cannon thundered together. Caught off guard, Fergan reeled like a wounded man, and braced himself against the wall...

"Four thousand!"

After thirty minutes of battle nothing here had changed — nothing save that a man alive moments ago was now dead. His corpse lay on the steel floor, his head split open: a wrench, ripped from its hook by a projectile's impact, had done the shattering. Accustomed to the sight of blood, the survivors had been content to wash away the red debris with a bucket of water — lest anyone slip. And, of course,

---

170 Jean de La Bruyère (1645–96), a French philosopher and moralist noted for his satire. The quotation is from *"De la cour,"* in *Les Caractères* (1688), a book of moral and satirical essays depicting the society of his time.

the battle went on — cold, silent, persistent — as if nothing had happened.

"Four thousand three hundred!"

Yet the transmission panel was no longer working, and the turret, isolated and autonomous, fought on as best it could, operating blind on guesswork. At present Yorisaka Sadao thought himself fortunate to have, for master arrow in his quiver, the turret's rangefinder, which alone still enabled him more or less to measure, through the smoke and fog, the variations in distance and changes in correction…

"Four thousand five!"

Again the double detonation. Seasoned now, Herbert Fergan leaned forward and peered out through the ring slot of the embrasure. At the line of sight's end, far, far away, there appeared a shadow puppet against the luminous horizon, the profile of a Russian battleship, a target already riddled. Plumes of water spurted up before it, raised by shots falling short. Fergan suddenly saw two more such plumes, taller than the rest, and realized they were due to the strike of shells fired, short of the mark, by the very turret he was in.

"So…," he murmured, "the Russians have had enough!… They're moving away…"

It occurred to him at the same moment that it would soon be difficult to adjust the fire. No more blockhouse, no more range-finding officer… The enemy, in choosing an abrupt departure from the battlefield, was leaving behind bad conditions under which to achieve an efficient "percent."

For the enemy was indeed moving away; that much was sure. Through the ring slit Fergan had a clear view as the lead battleship came to port. It was steering towards the Japanese tail, no doubt hoping to wrap around and flee north under cover of the fog, still fleecy and floating about. But Togo was already foiling the maneuver, veering left himself. And the *Nikkō*, mimicking the admiral, set course into the *Mikasa*'s waters.

"Cease fire! Right turret!..."

The Russian battleships were overtaking the rear guard. The battle was shifting to port. Firing conditions were naturally to flip, and adjustments to be made from scratch, point by point...

"*Hai!...*"

Two servants released their breechblocks and leapt towards the command saddle. And Fergan, by instinct, leapt with them.

Marquis Yorisaka Sadao had just slid to the ground — without a cry or a moan.

His shoulder, frightfully torn up, was issuing such a flow of blood as to turn his yellow face green. Shrapnel had evidently come in through one of the three holes of the cupola and struck him, though no one inside the turret had heard a thing, what with the ceaseless uproar outside...

With Fergan's help, the men laid out their chief between the two guns. He was not quite dead. He made a sign and spoke, in a very soft but still imperious voice:

"Back to your posts!..."

The two men obeyed. Fergan alone stayed behind, bent over the dying man's face.

And then a singular thing occurred.

The turret's non-commissioned officer had rushed over. The honor fell to him to take the vacant post. He stepped over the supine body and bent down to collect the rangefinder, which had slipped from the bloodied hand. Before climbing into the saddle he spun the instrument in his fingers, with the hesitant air of a man aware of his own inexpertise... And Fergan, despite his sincere sorrow, smiled.

"Lord knows how he'll make use of it!..."

But Marquis Yorisaka, sitting up, raised his right hand and touched the non-commissioned officer, who turned around.

The dying head shook side to side.

"No! Not you!"

And the dimming eyes fixed on the surprised English officer.

"You!"

Herbert Fergan reared back, stupefied.

"Me?"

He hesitated for three seconds, then knelt right next to Yorisaka Sadao and spoke softly — as one speaks to an ailing man as delirium sets in:

"*Kimi*, I'm English … neutral…"

He repeated twice, articulating, with emphasis:

"Neutral … neutral…"

But he suddenly fell silent, because the pallid lips were moving, because a breath was coming out, a hoarse murmur. It was indistinct at first but soon grew clearer, firmed up. It was syllables, words, a song:

> "The time of cherry blossoms is not yet past
> Yet now must the flowers fall,
> While their onlookers' love
> Is at its utmost exaltation…"

Herbert Fergan listened, and a chill shot through his veins.

The nearly dead eyes held their gaze, a steady, somber gaze, with the gleam of something like an ancient vision's reflection. Steeled with some miracle of energy, the voice sang on:

He told me: "I had a dream last night. Your hair was wrapped around my neck. Your hair was like a black necklace around my neck and on my chest."

Paler than Yorisaka himself, Herbert Fergan had taken a step back, and now turned away to avoid the terrible gaze. But he could not escape the voice, a voice more terrible than the gaze:

"I caressed it, and it was my own; and we were forever joined like this, by the hair, mouth to mouth, the way two laurels will often share a root."

The voice resonated like a crystal near to shattering. Blood had little by little returned to Fergan's cheeks, and began now to suffuse the whole of his face with a blush of shame and humiliation, like the mark of a full-on slap…

More pressing now, like an embittered creditor making a sudden, imperious demand for his due, the voice concluded:

"And so intertwined were our limbs that it seemed to me, little by little, I was becoming you or you were entering into me like my dream."

Its life run out, the voice expired. The gaze alone endured, delivering in a final flame a true, clear, irresistible order…

And so Herbert Fergan, head low, eyes downcast, yielded — obeyed. From the non-commissioned officer's hand he took the rangefinder. He climbed the three steps of the central ladder and took a seat on the command saddle…

The Russian battleships were reappearing, one by one, to port. They were moving away, fast…

"A gentleman must pay," mumbled Fergan.

He was working the rangefinder's dial. The target, magnified, specified, came into focus through the scope. The blue cross of St. Andrew's flag showed clear against the white field of etamine.[171] Herbert Fergan, aide-de-camp to the King of England, saw this flag: the Tsar's flag. The Tsar and the King were not enemies…

"A gentleman must pay," repeated Fergan, grim.

He coughed. His voice was hoarse but distinct, resolute.

"Six thousand two hundred meters! Left eight thousandths! Continue fire!"

In the silence preceding the double detonation there was an all but imperceptible noise beneath the ladder. Marquis Yorisaka Sadao had finished dying, without a shudder or a groan, discreetly, decently, properly. Before closing forever, though, his mouth had stuttered two Japanese syllables, the first two syllables of a name never to be completed:

"Mitsou…"

---

171 St Andrew's Cross was the ensign of the Navy of the Russian Empire from 1712 to 1918.

XXIX

Teikoku Bansai!

From atop the mass of debris, sole vestige of the bridge and blockhouse carried off together by the same shell, Viscount Hirata Takamori leaned a last time over the hole that led down to the central station and delivered a last order, the one that ended the day and turned the battle definitively into victory:

"Cease fire!"

From the main mast of the *Mikasa* Togo's signal fluttered and shone, like a radiant rainbow after a storm. At the zenith, amid still-livid clouds, there opened a blue tear in the shape of a soaring winged goddess.

A great cheer went up, passing from ship to ship faster than a northwest gust in the blow of the autumn monsoon: the victory cry of triumphant Japan, the victory cry of ancient Asia, forever freed from the European yoke.

"*Teikoku bansai!*"[172]

"Eternal life to the Empire!"

Hirata Takamori, on his feet, repeated the cry three times. Then, opening with a brisk flick the fan that had never left his sleeve, he swept his gaze south to north and west to east, with a look of inexpressible pride. It was indeed a fine hour, more befuddling than ten cups of sake! Whether he knew it or not, Hirata Takamori had for thirty-three years, since the day his mother gave birth to him, lived only for this moment. But it had not been too long to wait, thirty-three years, for the sublime intoxication that now choked and drowned him as in a sea of pure alcohol.

"*Teikoku bansai!*"

The clamor had barely subsided before it started up again and

---

172   This traditional Japanese patriotic cheer literally means "Ten thousand years for the Empire!" but commonly used as "Long live the Empire!" It combines *teikoku* (帝国), referring specifically to the Empire of Japan (1868–1947), and *banzai* (万歳), a wish for long life or a triumphant cheer akin to *hurrah*. While *banzai* alone has ancient roots derived from the Chinese *wàn suì* (ten thousand years), the specific phrase "Teikoku Banzai!" became strongly associated with Japanese nationalism during the imperial period (Meiji through early Showa eras) and was often used as a victory or battle cry, notably during the Russo-Japanese War and the Second World War.

redoubled. On the other side of the battleships a dispatch boat, the *Tatsuta*, paraded.[173] On the bridge an officer brandishing a megaphone was repeating from ship to ship the order of the day, with which he had been charged:

"The illustrious virtues of the Emperor and invisible protection

---

173   The *Tatsuta* was an unprotected cruiser serving the Imperial Japanese Navy and named after the Tatsuta River, near Nara. Used primarily as an aviso for scouting and the delivery of high-priority messages, the *Tatsuta* saw significant action in the Russo-Japanese War (1904–05). She engaged in the Battle of Port Arthur, assisted with the subsequent blockade, and also took part in the Battle of the Yellow Sea and the pivotal Battle of Tsushima. She helped rescue the crews of the battleships *Yashima* and *Hatsuse*, sunk by mines, and later served as Admiral Nashiba Tokioki's flagship.

of the Imperial Ancestors have given us complete and total victory. Congratulations to all of you who have done your best!"

At that moment the sun appeared, piercing the clouds and fog, at a tangent to the western horizon.

It was all red, like the monstrous ball, dyed with fire and blood, that the Celestial Dragon rolls across the azure plains ... like the dazzling disk that reigns at the center of the Empire's pavilion... And it plunged into the sea, obliquely.

Hirata Takamori was watching. It was like the symbol of the Japanese fatherland, floating there, sweeping its last ray, passing its last luminous caress, over the battlefield, where so much blood had just spilled for the fatherland's greater glory!... And then the allegory came into focus, and was magnified: a Russian vessel, defeated, helpless, on fire, trailing its agony away to the west. The sun suddenly caught up with that ruined carcass, that shadow headed for the depths, and wrapped it round like a shroud of purple and gold. The broken masts, tottering funnels, and torn, listing hull were set into funereal silhouette against the dazzling orb. Hirata Takamori recognized the expiring ship. It was the *Borodino*, one of the ships that the *Nikkō* had fought at close quarters... And the sun, little by little, sank and vanished. And the vessel too vanished, at the same time...[174]

Hirata Takamori turned around. The *Tatsuta* was approaching the *Nikkō* and hailed it.

"Free to maneuver for the night. — Rendezvous tomorrow morning at Matsushima."[175]

"Understood," said Hirata.

"The admiral wishes to know the name of the officer who took command of the *Nikkō* after the blockhouse was destroyed."

"It was I: Viscount Hirata... *Hirata shishaku!*..."

He omitted his first name and repeated his family title, that all the ancestors might have their fair share of the honor bestowed on their descendant.

---

174   The *Borodino* was the lead ship of her class of five pre-dreadnought battleships built for the Imperial Russian Navy in the first decade of the twentieth century. Completed in 1904, after the beginning of the Russo-Japanese War, the *Borodino* was assigned to the Second Pacific Squadron, which was sent to the Far East to break the Japanese blockade of Port Arthur. The Japanese captured the port while the squadron was in transit, and their destination was changed to Vladivostok. The ship was sunk during the Battle of Tsushima (May 1905) when a Japanese shell hit and exploded a magazine. A single member of her crew of 855 officers and enlisted men survived.

175   A group of some 260 small islands (*shima*) covered in pines (*matsu*) in the Miyagi Prefecture of Japan.

The two ships were already separating, carried along by their drift.

"Viscount Hirata," cried the officer of the *Tatsuta*, "I am pleased to announce the admiral's particular satisfaction, and his intention to commend you in his report to the Divine Emperor."

Without replying, Viscount Hirata bowed to the ground. When he rose the *Tatsuta* was no longer in earshot…

A bugler crossed the deck, from one ladder to another. Hirata Takamori summoned him, gave the order to sound the evening call…

"We shall line up the dead on the aft deck, in honor."

Night was now falling, fast. Navigation and position lights were lit. Hirata Takamori, abdicating for a spell the duties of acting commander, left the bridge and made a round through the *Nikkō*'s devastated corridors. The electrical circuits had been hacked through, but ingenuity and skill had restored connections with makeshift circuits, and the lighting was normal almost everywhere.

At the end of his round Hirata Takamori came to the aft quarterdeck, where he saluted twice, in the ancient manner, and proceeded to an inspection of the dead…

They were thirty-nine, and had been laid side by side, in two rows, under the two barrels of the twin cannon. There they slept, the tattered bodies properly gathered and stitched up in bags of gray canvas, their calm heads smiling in the moonbeams.

Two quartermasters, lanterns in hand, shed light on each face. An ensign, in a respectful tone, called the roll. He passed first before three empty bags; no trace had been found of the dead commander or of the maneuvering officer or of the gunnery officer.

Before the fourth bag the ensign called:

"Captain Herbert W. Fergan."

Hirata Takamori bowed. The English officer had been struck by shrapnel below the chin, right at the throat. Both carotid arteries had been severed and the spinal cord reduced to mush.

"Where was he killed?" asked Hirata.

"In the 305 turret."

"Ah!… One can die anywhere at all!…"

This was the entirety of the funeral oration for Herbert Fergan.

Before the fifth bag the ensign called:

"Lieutenant Yorisaka Sadao."

Hirata Takamori stopped short, opened his mouth to speak, and fell silent.

The eyes of the corpse of Marquis Yorisaka Sadao were wide open, and did truly seem still to be looking … looking straight ahead — straight through life itself — looking with disdain, pride, triumph…

❋

At greater speed and with a crisper step Viscount Hirata walked past the sleeping faces, one after another, of both rows.

The ensign, saluting, prepared to leave. The viscount held him back, calling him by his name.

"Narimasa, would you do me the honor of accompanying me to my quarters?"

"I shall, very honorably," the ensign promptly replied.

They descended together. At a gesture from the viscount the ensign knelt. There was no tatami — modern discipline having excluded the rice mats from warships, because too flammable. But Hirata had thrown down two comfortable velvet cushions.

"Forgive my impropriety," he said, "but I must proceed to set forth the night duties before dealing with anything else."

"Pray, proceed," said the ensign.

Subordinates entered, and the viscount gave them his orders. When all these had left Hirata Takamori took the brush and wrote several hundred well-calligraphed characters on two pages of his notepad.

"Forgive me," he said again, "but these matters have their importance."

He tore the two sheets from the notepad and handed them to the ensign.

"This is in fact for you … if you would deign to do me the grace to be the executor of my last wishes."

Surprised, the ensign looked at his superior.

"Yes," said Hirata Takamori. "I am going to kill myself shortly, Narimasa, and I would be much obliged to you, who are of a most noble family of good *samurai*, if you were to assist me in my *hara-kiri*."

The young officer was no longer surprised, and took care to ask no discourteous questions.

"It is an illustrious honor that you do me and all of my ancestors," he said simply. "I am very happy to be able to serve you."

"Here is my sword," said Hirata.

From a lacquered sheath he had drawn a splendid old blade, with a guard of wrought iron in the shape of oak leaves. He wrapped the blade in tissue paper and handed it to Ensign Narimasa.

"I am, respectfully, at your disposal," said the ensign, taking the sword.

Hirata Takamori knelt before his guest and spoke in courteous terms.

"Narimasa, because you deign to serve as my second in this ceremony, it is rightful that you should know my reason. This morning, during a conversation that Marquis Yorisaka did me the honor of permitting, my frail understanding caused me to utter various words that this evening I believe were misplaced. It is, I think, preferable that these words be struck out."

"I shall not contradict you if you so judge."

"Would you be so kind, then, as to wait while I complete the preparations for what remains for us to do?"

"I shall indeed, most honorably."

A sort of washroom adjoined the quarters. Viscount Hirata went in to don the obligatory costume, as immutably set out by the rites. He returned.

"I am in truth," he said, "ashamed to see you carry your indulgence so far."

"I am scarcely abiding by what I must," said Narimasa.

Viscount Hirata had knelt again near his guest. He was now holding in his right hand a dagger: wrapped, like the sword, in tissue paper. He smiled.

"It is a great joy for me to be at liberty today to die as I wish," he said. "Our victory is so complete that the empire can easily do without one of its subjects, especially the least useful."

"I congratulate you," said the ensign, "but I cannot approve of your modesty. I believe to the contrary that nothing could salve the loss that the Empire is about to suffer, if the impeccable example that you bequeath to all were not its near entire reparation."

"I am obliged to you," said Hirata.

He turned away and, very slowly, brought forth the dagger's naked blade.

"Marquis Yorisaka's example is greater than mine," he said.

He was running a finger along the blade's edge. Without a noise the ensign rose from the velvet cushion, and, standing behind the viscount, gripped with both hands the handle of the sword, now bare like the dagger.

"Much greater," repeated Viscount Hirata.

He made the slightest movement. Narimasa, leaning over, saw no more of the dagger's blade. The belly was split open as clean as could be. A little blood was already flowing.

"Much greater, in truth," repeated Viscount Hirata Takamori.

He spoke with the same clarity as before, though with less volume. A corner of his mouth rose slightly, the first sign of atrocious suffering, stonily contained.

Brusque, with his right leg behind him and his left knee bent, Narimasa released the coiled spring of his loins, his chest, and both his arms. The head of Viscount Hirata Takamori, lopped off in a single swipe, fell to the white mats.

The sword came back into view only the moment after, when it was righted again, showing pink.[176]

---

176 *Seppuku* (切腹) and *hara-kiri* (腹切り) both refer to the same Japanese ritual suicide by disembowelment, primarily practiced by the samurai class under their code of honor (*bushidō*). While often used interchangeably in English, the terms differ significantly in formality and origin. See "Honor, Judgment, and Atonement: Viscount Hirata's Bushidō" in the appendices.

XXX

Seven Lives for the Empire

The envelope was long and narrow, and sealed with wax. Breaking the seal, Felze brought forth a sheet of silken paper, folded over twelve or fifteen times. It unfolded the way papyrus unscrolls. The letter had been dictated in French, and its calligraphy, in brush and Chinese ink, revealed a hand more practiced at the characters of Confucius than at the Western alphabet[177] — so much so that, spread to its full length, the strange message bore a fair resemblance to those strips of calico with a flamboyant image printed up top and the verses and refrain of a popular lament printed in line below.

Felze read:

> Letter from ignorant Zhou P'ei to Fenn Ta-Jen, great man of letters and high dignitary of the illustrious Academy of the kingdom of Fu-lang-sai.
>
> Your younger brother, Zhou, greets you from the ground, with ten thousand regards inquires after your health, and takes the extreme liberty of sending you this letter.
>
> The disciple Tseng Tzu, answering the Tzu,[178] expressed a wish: "When spring draws to an end, and the season's clothes are spun and sewn, I would like to go, with my reverie, and bathe my hands and feet in the warm spring of the River I, breathe the fresh air under the Ou iu trees, sing verses, and return. This is what I would like." The Tzu sighed and said: "I approve of Tien's sentiment."[179]
>
> In this year of the she,[180] in the third month of spring,[181] my

---

177   The author describes a Japanese scroll, or *makimono.*

178   The most common name for K'ung Fu-tzu (Confucius). [Author's note.]

179   *Linn Lu.* Book VI. Ch. XI, §25 (Tien and Tseng Si are the first and last names of the same philosopher). [Author's note.] — Tseng Tzu (Wade-Giles), Zēngzǐ (Pinyin).

180   *She* (snake), the sixth of the twelve animals in the Chinese cycle. The year AD 1905 was a year of the *she.* [Author's note.] — *Shé* in Pinyin. 2025, the year of this edition, is also a snake year.

181   May. — The Chinese seasons run about forty days behind ours. [Author's note.]

   The third month of spring in the Chinese calendar would generally be around April in elder brother Fenn Ta-Jen, having performed the rites, went, with his reverie, to bathe his hands and feet in the warm spring, breathe fresh air under the trees, and sing verses. It is now fitting that he should return, so as to abide by the prudent words of the disciple Tseng Tzu.

One mustn't observe in the first month of summer the rules for the third month of spring.

And it profits a man to reread the teaching of the Li Chi:

"In the first month of summer one does not raise great multitudes of men for war. For the sovereign who holds dominion is Yen Ti, the Emperor of Fire."

Reflect on this. Consider it from the right, and from the left. Messengers with news from the sea have arrived at the miserable house over whose door hang three purple lanterns. And other messengers are to come.

I have many things yet to tell you,[182] but I resign myself to finishing this letter unable to express my feelings. And the little one awaits your return with great impatience.

The *shoji* were open, and wind from the open sea entered the room at will. The gulf looked choppy and dark. Waves were breaking as far as the eye could see.

Felze, pensive, had twice reread the strange missive. Lifting his eyes at last, he looked at the sea.

"Bad weather," he thought. "The band of a typhoon passing by… Whatever Zhou P'ei's calendar says, summer is still far off… It's only the twenty-eighth of May…"

He counted on his fingers:

"Yes, the twenty-eighth of May… twenty-eighth of May 1905… And this twenty-eighth of May does resemble a twenty-eighth of March… No matter. It's time to hit the road. All of this deserves clarifying…"

He clapped. In an instant the door slid in its groove, and little O-Setsu san prostrated herself at the threshold:

"*Hai!…*"

Although for three times twenty-four hours she had been joining Felze every night, with a kindly wife's fidelity, and on those occasions had dared

---

the Gregorian calendar.

182 Obligatory formula: I would have many things yet to tell you (but I shall not tell, lest I bore you). [Author's note.]

the most conjugal intimacies, outside the bed the *nēsan*
nevertheless kept to her exact place as a servant. Always
on the lookout, she was prompt to react at the first call,
with a smile and a will to submit.

"I want…," said Felze.

He paused, curious to spy a first emotion
on her face, as it now turned up to attention.
Would it sadden the little one to learn, abruptly,
that her lover was
to up and leave?
The *oirans* of the
Yoshivara,[183] even
when indifferent,
will gladly cling
to the sleeves
of a night's
guest: it is part
of the code of
courtesy.

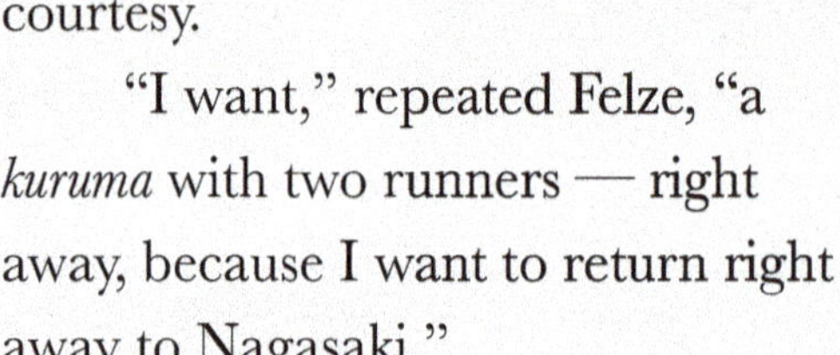

"I want," repeated Felze, "a
kuruma with two runners — right
away, because I want to return right
away to Nagasaki."

"*Hai!…*"

She was still on all fours, and lowered her forehead to the ground
so fast in salute that Felze had no time to read anything in the instantly
concealed black eyes. And when she rose and trotted to the door to carry
out the master's order she had already set the expression on her little face to
match the demands of courtesy. She was now wearing a docile smile, with
the proper touch of sadness.

❀

His *nēsan* had gone out. Waiting for her to return, Felze saw to his
preparations, trading the kimono of fine crepe for a starched shirt, trousers
of stiff cloth, and a narrow-sleeved jacket.

---

183   As noted earlier, *oirans* were high-ranking courtesans. Yoshiwara was a famous *yūkaku* (red-
light district) created in Edo (present-day Tokyo) in 1617. It was one of three such licensed districts
created by the Tokugawa shogunate, the other two being Shimabara, in Kyoto, and Shinmachi, in
Osaka. Here *oirans* and *Yoshiwara* are being used generically.

Once he had dressed the traveler looked outside. The rain had stopped, but the wind was still chasing heavy clouds across the sky, for a heavier downpour over the countryside. Eight or ten intrepid little girls were nevertheless splashing about on the beach, their wooden clogs sinking in the wet sand. The eldest was singing at the top of her lungs the old popular refrain:

> *"Souz'mé, souz'mé, doko itta?"*
> *"Senghé yama é saké nomini.*
> *No mou tcha wan, no mou ftats…"*[184]

"Their fathers or brothers are perhaps fighting today, against Rozhestvensky or Linevich," thought Felze. "But when Japanese men fight Japanese women will sing… Thus the heroine Shizuka when the hero Yoshitsune, a fugitive, was wandering the dangerous wilds of the violet mountains, 'where only boar climb'…"[185]

O-Setsu san, already back, was again prostrating herself on the threshold.

"The honorable traveler's *kuruma* is ready!…"

"Farewell," said Felze.

He leaned over the small kneeling body, bade it to rise, and, with near tenderness, set his lips on the fresh mouth.

Emboldened, the child asked:

"Where are you going?"

Felze thought he would try an experiment:

"To war."

"*Hai!*… To war!…"

The soft black eyes had sparkled.

"To war against the Russians?"

"Yes."

---

184 *Little bird, little bird, where are you going?*
To Mount Sengen, to drink sake.
I'll drink one cup, I'll drink two… [Author's note.]

185 Twelfth-century legend stemming from the history of the civil wars between the Taira and Minamoto clans (1161–1185). [Author's note.]

Farrère is referring to the Genpei War, as recounted in the Japanese classic *The Tale of the Heike* (anonymous, late twelfth – early thirteenth century). Shizuka Gozen, or Lady Shizuka, a renowned Japanese dancer (*shirabyōshi*), is the lover of military commander Minamoto no Yoshitsune, a pivotal figure during the late Heian (794–1185) and early Kamakura (1185–1333) periods. His downfall is emblematic of samurai tragedy. Their doomed romance, marked by a heartbreaking separation, has become a staple in traditional Japanese drama and literature, symbolizing the tragic intersections of duty, honor, and love in feudal Japan.

The *mousmé* had straightened up, almost proud. Observing her, Felze suddenly asked:

"Would you like to come with me?"

The answer came out like a shot:

"Yes!… I would!… I would like to die… and be reborn seven times, giving my life seven times for the Empire!…"[186]

Editor's Note: *This chapter, originally Chapter XXIV in prior editions of* La Bataille, *has been repositioned in this 2025 edition to correct a chronological inaccuracy. In its original placement, this chapter — in which Felze identifies the date as May 28th, 1905 — illogically preceded the chapters describing the Battle of Tsushima, which commenced on May 27th, 1905. You are among the first readers in over a century to experience the author's narrative thread in its proper chronological sequence. A detailed analysis of this editorial decision appears in the appendix article, "Restoring the Timeline in* The Battle: *An Editorial Note for the 2025 Edition."*

------

186   Literal translation of a phrase actually heard from the mouth of an inn servant. [Author's note.]

XXXI

The Morality of Warriors

Jean-François Felze dismissed his *kuruma* at the foot of the stone staircase that went up the hillside to the suburb of Diou Djen Dji and began to climb the familiar steps.

It was raining. Nowhere from Mogimachi to Nagasaki had it stopped raining. For four hours the two running-men had splashed through mud and puddles, never slowing the pace, and interrupting the journey only at the doors of the *ochaya*, for a drink, and before the cobblers' shops, for a change of sandals. They had entered the city at a good clip, splashing both sidewalks of Funadaikumachi.[187] The shopping district was full of the usual crowd. A mass of umbrellas covered the streets.

But the staircase of Diou Djen Dji was, as always, deserted. And Felze, hastening under the downpour, managed to reach the house of the violet lanterns without alerting any passer-by who might watch in surprise as a *ketōjin*[188] knocked on the mysterious door of the great Chinese mandarin, at a threshold that the Japanese themselves would hardly ever cross.

"Noon," observed Felze as he entered the house.

He feared to intrude. An opium smoker typically falls asleep well after dawn and cares not to be awakened before sunset. It is true, however, that rituals have their accommodations for travelers.

"Besides," thought Felze, "it is recommended above all things to obey the will of one's elders. And old, old Zhou P'ei has issued me a clear summons. In that, at least, his letter is unambiguous."

The door first opened to reveal the servant dressed in blue silk, then closed, and finally, after the lapse that courtesy requires, reopened. And Felze, after a wait of exactly the right span, neither too long nor too short, convinced himself that he had arrived at the correct time.

Indeed, Zhou P'ei, having received since the day before a great many

---

187 A "town" or district of Nagasaki.

188 *Ketōjin*, hairy barbarian, or *baka tōjin*, foolish barbarian — foreigner. [Author's note.]

reports and messages, all important, had forsworn sleep for as long as current events continued. He smoked rather than sleep, and thus parried without effort the fatigue of an already thirty-six-hour vigil.

And he came out to greet the visitor, and he received him with all requisite ceremony, such that Felze could discover no trace of weariness or insomnia on the yellow face, with its hollow cheeks and smiling lipless mouth.

Then, in the smoking room hung ceiling to floor with yellow, embroidered satin, with noble philosophical maxims written in beautiful characters of black silk, after drinking hot wine brought in, with all due propriety, by the lettered servant whose cap sported a turquoise ball, Jean-François Felze and Zhou P'ei lay down, amid the silken mass of cushions and fabrics, on three superimposed mats finer than any sheet of linen.

And they spoke, face to face, with the opium tray between their chests. They spoke in observance of the traditional proprieties and rules, while two children, kneeling near their heads, heated over the green lamp the heavy drops hanging from the end of needles, and fixed the well-cooked paste onto the bowls of the silver, ivory, tortoiseshell, or bamboo pipes.

❀

"Fenn Ta-Jen," said Zhou P'ei, the first to speak, "when, in this very place and under my own eye, we sealed the crude, poorly calligraphed letter to you that I had the temerity to dictate to the least ignorant of my secretaries I uttered the customary words: *Yī lù Fú xīng!* — May the Star of Good Fortune be with you on the way![189] For I knew that your heart would prompt you quickly to grant my humble prayer and tie on your travel coat without an hour's delay. You arrive with solar exactitude. And I see that, to my shame, I have caused you some trouble, and thus cannot hope to express the thanks I owe you."

"P'ei Ta-Jen," replied Jean-François Felze, "the magnificent letter I received from you served as a proper reminder of the precepts of philosophy, which I was about to forget, and brought me back in time to the Just and Invariable Middle,[190] from which I was about to depart. Suffer me to accept your kindness with gratitude."

---

189 (路福星): A traditional Chinese blessing for travelers, meaning "May the Lucky Star (Fúxīng) accompany you all the way!" or "May the Star of Good Fortune be with you on the way!" Fúxīng (福星), the Star of Luck/Fortune, is one of the *Sānxīng* (Three Stars), prominent deities in Chinese folk religion and astrology. The Wade-Giles romanization is *I Lu Fu Hsing*. The author's non-standard phonetic rendering of the phrase was *"I lou fou sing"* in the original French text.

190 The Invariable Middle (*Chung Yung*), where Confucius set absolute wisdom. [Author's note.] — *Zhongyong* in Pinyin. In English commonly known as the Doctrine of the Mean.

They smoked. The smoking room was entirely dark. The thick drapes shut out the daylight, so well that it seemed to be the dead the night. From the ceiling the nine violet lanterns shed their stained-glass light. Brutal life seemed banished from this kingdom of infinite peace, where access had been granted only to a superhuman life — attenuated, settled, free of violent and vain passions, free of disharmonious movement.

✻

"It is proper," began Zhou P'ei, "that I should now clear up for you the obscurities of my letter, obscurities due only, as you will certainly have guessed, to the infirmity of my mind."

"It is impossible for me," replied Felze, "to subscribe to your words. In what you please to call obscurities I have seen the wise artifice of an old, old brush, which cares not to entrust a messenger, however faithful, with the stark and reckless truth."

Zhou P'ei smiled and joined his hands in thanks.

"Fenn Ta-Jen, it is delectable to hear the music of your courtesy. Permit me to respond by observing the rule: 'Whosoever is charged with delivering a message or publishing word of something does not let the message or report spend a night in his house. He delivers or publishes it the same day.' Fenn Ta-Jen, this morning, at the second cock-crow, a junk from the Central Nation entered this port, and other junks

followed. Their skippers, men in my service, who wear out their hearts to fulfill the will of the August Elevation, informed me, before anyone else, of what the authorities of this kingdom still did not then know, and I now inform you. Yesterday, not far from an island that the men of Nippon call Tsushima, ten and ten thousand ships clashed at sea. The vast fleet of the Oros succumbed in this battle. Only wrecks remain. And I recalled the precepts of the *Li Chi*, and I took the liberty of recalling them for you in my letter: 'In the first month of summer one does not raise great multitudes of men for war. For the sovereign who holds dominion in this month, Yen Ti, the Flame Emperor,[191] would doom them to extermination.'"

At this Jean-François Felze abruptly sat up. He set his elbows on the mats and almost forgot the proprieties.

"What are you saying, P'ei Ta-Jenn? The Russian fleet defeated? Destroyed?… Is?…"

He checked himself in time, realizing the enormity he was about to commit: that of posing a question to his host. Indulgent, Zhou P'ei hastened to speak, deftly masking the visitor's thoughtlessness.

"I have received many reports. I am now no longer unaware of anything essential. Would it please you to hear an exact account?"

Felze had recovered his composure.

"It would assuredly please me," he said, proper once more. "I shall be pleased to hear all you deem it fitting for me to hear."

"Let us smoke, then," said Zhou P'ei, "and suffer my private secretary, who is not unfamiliar with the noble language of the *Fu-lang-sai*,

---

191 Yán Dì in Pinyin. A figure of legend.

to come lend us his light, and read and translate the pertinent substance of all that has come to pass for us since this morning."

And, from the hands of the child kneeling by his head, he took a pipe, while Jean-François Felze, from the other child's hands, took another. The swirls of grey smoke mingled around the lamp, with its peppering of flies and green-enamel butterflies.

At the smokers' feet the private secretary, an old, old man whose cap bore a ball of carved coral, had lowered himself to a squat and begun to read, his hoarse voice inadept with Western sounds…

✳

"Fenn Ta-Jen," said Zhou P'ei when the long passage had been read, "this perhaps recalls for you a conversation we had, in this place, the very day after your arrival in this city. You asked me then if I thought the Rising Sun was bound to succumb in its struggle against the Oros. I replied that I did not know, and that, besides, it did not matter."

"I remember perfectly," said Felze. "Your condescension deigned even to promise me that when the time came we would speak again of this bagatelle."

"Your memory is without reproach," said Zhou P'ei. "Well! When would be a more favorable time than this? Behold the Rising Sun, far from succumbing, in triumph. It behooves us to examine at leisure the true value of its victory. And should our examination convince us that the value is properly null, we shall have been right formerly to assert that the war now being waged is a bagatelle, and its issue of no consequence."

Felze, having just smoked, was silent. He gently pushed the warm pipe away and, laying his left cheek on the leather cushion, fixed his gaze on his host's eyes. Zhou P'ei himself smoked and began.

"It is written in the book of Meng Tzu. 'You undertake to wage wars; you imperil the lives of the leaders and soldiers; you draw the enmity of princes. Does your heart find joy in this? No. You do these things only to pursue your great design: you wish to extend the limits of your States, and subject even foreigners to your laws. But to pursue such a design by such means is to climb a tree to catch fish. Force opposing force has ever produced only ruin and barbarism. It is proper only to endeavor to exercise beneficence through administration. Then all officers, even of foreign nations, shall seek to hold charges in your palace. All farmers of the land, even from foreign nations, shall seek to cultivate the fields of your countryside. All merchants, wandering or sedentary, even of foreign nations, shall seek to deposit their merchandise in your market. If they are so disposed, who could stop them? I know of a prince who ruled at first over a territory of seventy *lis*, then over the entirety of the Empire.'"[192]

Solemn, Zhou P'ei punctuated the quotation with a sort of exclamation from the depths of his throat.

"It is written in the book of K'ung-tzu:[193] 'The principality of Lu is tipping into decline and is divided into several parts. You know not how to preserve its integrity; and you plan to foment revolt within it. I very much fear that you shall encounter great difficulties not at the border but within your own house.'"[194]

Zhou P'ei repeated his respectful exclamation, then closed his eyes.

"It seems to me that these texts are as apt to the Empire of the Oros, the vanquished, as to the kingdom of the Rising Sun, the victor. Any nation that engages in a needless and bloody war abdicates its ancient wisdom and renounces civilization.

----

192 Meng Tzu, Book I, Chapter I. [Author's note.]

     Mencius, Book 1, Part A, Chapter 7 (1A7). This translation is based on the author's French rendition or understanding of the original Chinese, and may differ from standard scholarly English translations. For comparison, readers may consult James Legge's translation, found in *The Chinese Classics, Vol. II: The Works of Mencius* (Original edition 1861, revised 1895; various reprints available).

193 Confucius.

194 *Lioun Iou*, Book VIII, Chapter XVI. [Author's note.]

     The author's original note is incorrect for this passage, as Analects 8.16 discusses unrelated matters. The quote presented in the text is a thematic paraphrase of Confucius's warning found in Analects 16.1. Readers may consult standard translations, such as James Legge, *The Chinese Classics*, Vol. I, for the precise wording.

"This is why it matters not at all whether the new, barbaric Japan has defeated the new, barbaric Russia. It would have mattered no more if the new Russia had defeated the new Japan. This was a battle between the striped and the ocellated tiger. Its issue is of no interest to men."

He pressed his lipless mouth to the jade of a pipe held out to him by the kneeling child and with a single inhalation drew all the grey smoke.

"Of no interest," he repeated.

Reopened, his eyes swept their discerning gleam right and left.

"My own memory" he resumed after a pause, "is entirely unfaithful and uncertain. But in the course of our conversation the day after your arrival in this city you spoke such memorable words as I have been unable to forget, despite my infirmity. You most ingeniously compared the Empire to a vase containing the precious liquor of ancient precepts. And, not without good reason, you feared for the invaluable liquor, on account of the imperial vase's fragility. Were the Empire indeed subdued, what would become of the ancient precepts? To this most philosophical question the poverty of my intelligence could not right away supply an answer, but I shall answer today, after ten thousand reflections and meditations, as events have at last enlightened me. The ancient precepts' immortality rests not on the Empire's perishable life. The Empire can be subdued: provided that the Son of Heaven has done his duty to the end, observed the rites, kept the five moral laws, and practiced the three indispensable virtues, which are humanity, prudence, and fortitude of soul; provided that every prince, every minister, every prefect, every man of the people have likewise done their duty, observed the rites, kept the five laws and practiced the three virtues, it matters not at all whether the Empire is vanquished or victorious. It matters not at all whether all its inhabitants are dead or alive. If they are dead, their irreproachable example survives them, and their very enemies are compelled to admire and follow it. And the immortality of the ancient precepts is thereby renewed and rejuvenated. On the other hand, the nation that deviates from the Invariable Middle in view of a momentary advantage, a fleeting success, an apparent glory, or a deceptive profit gravely compromises its reputation and honor, and can leave to history only a tainted memory, apt to corrupt by contagion all future nations, to the thirtieth and to the sixtieth generation."

He paused here, to scrutinize the fat pipeful that the child kneeling by the mother-of-pearl tray had just stuck on a freshly cleaned pipe-bowl, then concluded.

"What does the material destiny of a single nation weigh against the moral evolution of humanity as a whole?"

Having reached this judgment, he smoked two pipes, one after the other. And once the drug had poured indulgence into his soul he smiled.

"The kingdom of the Rising Sun, too young, is unaware of these things. It would know if, like the Central Nation, it had lived ten thousand years and if, year after year, it had grown wiser."

Felze had listened in silence. But, as Zhou P'ei had now stopped speaking, courtesy demanded that the visitor break his silence. And the visitor so remembered.

"P'ei Ta-Jen," he said, "you are my elder brother, most old and most wise. And I shall certainly not correct a single word in all that you have said. Like you, I think the kingdom of the Rising Sun a young kingdom. Young kingdoms are like young men: they love life with an exaggerated love. So as not to die, the kingdom of the Rising Sun has deviated from the Invariable Middle. Its excuse lies in the beauty of life and the ugliness of death. P'ei Ta-Jen, love of life is a virtue."

"Yes," pronounced the smoker, "but the practice of no virtue ought to lead men astray from the Invariable Middle, astray from the Primordial Law, foundation and pedestal of society and the world."

He reclined and set the back of his head on the leather pillow. His hand with its long, long nails rose towards the ceiling's lanterns.[195]

"Under the Han dynasty," he said, "an Emperor reigned by the name of Kao.[196] In accord with the rites, he had an empress-wife, called Lu,[197] and a concubine-princess, called Tsi.[198]

"And the former had given him a son, a prince of the first rank, who

---

195　The story that follows recounts events from the beginning of the Han Dynasty (206 BC – AD 220). It is a brutal episode recorded in such Chinese historical texts as the *Records of the Grand Historian* (*Shǐjì* in Pinyin, *Shih chi* in Wade-Giles), by Sīmǎ Qiān (Ssu ma ch'ien), and the *Book of Han* (*Hàn shaltū* or *Han shu*). The core elements — the succession struggle, the cruelty of Empress Lü (Lúhòu or Lü hou) towards Consort Qi (Qī Jī or Ch'i chi) and her son after the death of Emperor Gāozǔ (Kao tsu), and the horror of Emperor Hui (Huìdì or Hui ti) — are documented facts, not folklore.

196　This refers to Emperor Gāozǔ (Kao tsu) of Han (漢高祖). His personal name was Liu Bang (劉邦). "Gāozǔ" means "High Ancestor" and is his temple name. The French "Kao" is a rendering of "Gāo" (高).

197　This is the powerful Empress Lü Zhi (Lúhòu or Lü hou) (呂雉), often known simply as Empress Lü (呂后).

198　This is Consort Qi (Qī Jī or Ch'i chi) (戚夫人) or Lady Qi. *Tsi* is a reasonable French phonetic approximation of *Qi*. She was a favored concubine of Emperor Gāozǔ.

was called Hoéi[199]; and the latter had given him a son, a prince of the second rank, called Joui.[200]

"Now, when his days were many the Emperor summoned his ministers and his great prefects and questioned them to find out whether the philosophers of antiquity had authorized the sovereigns of the Central Nation to change the order of succession to the throne, and thus whether he, Kao, could follow the desire of his heart and bequeath power to the prince of the second rank, Joui, rather than to the prince of the first rank, Hoéi. To this the ministers and the great prefects answered no. So, obeying the philosophers, Emperor Kao bequeathed power to the prince of the first rank, Hoéi, and then fell majestically, into death, as falls the peak of a high mountain.[201]

"At the time the prince of the first rank, Hoéi, was not yet capable of directing the ceremonies in honor of the spirits that watch over land and grains. When he became Emperor he was as yet wearing short clothes,[202] and so the empress-consort, Lu, served as regent.

"She was a hard-hearted woman.

"She first had the concubine princess, Tsi, imprisoned, with a view towards her torture. She then ordered the poisoning of the prince of the second rank, Joui, and sent the poison to the prince's tutor.

"But the tutor, a righteous man, having reread all the sacred books and all the classical books, did not find therein any authorization to kill the pupil entrusted to him by the late Son of Heaven. This is why, rather than obey, he drank the poison himself.

"And when the news reached his ears the child Emperor, Hoéi, full of admiration and pity, took the child prince, Joui, and this prince's mother, Tsi, under his protection. And the regent empress, Lu, did not dare continue right away with her dark designs.

---

199   This is Liu Ying (Liú Yíng or Liu ying) (劉盈), the eldest son of Emperor Gāozǔ and Empress Lü. He succeeded his father as Emperor Hui (Huìdì or Hui ti) of Han (漢惠帝). *Hoéi* is a French rendering of *Hui* (惠, meaning "benevolent"). As the son of the Empress and designated heir, he was indeed the "prince of the first rank," or crown prince.

200   This is Liú Rúyì (Liu ju i) (劉如意). He was the son of Emperor Gāozǔ and Consort Qi. Emperor Gāozǔ favored him and considered making him crown prince instead of Liu Ying, which was the root cause of Empress Lü's intense hatred for both Liu Ruyi and his mother. Liu Ruyi was made the Prince or King of Zhao (趙王). *Joui* seems to be the author's attempt at rendering *Ruyi* (如意, meaning "as desired" or "according to one's wishes"). The "second rank" refers to his status relative to the crown prince or his title as a regional king..

201   Ritual paraphrase to express that a Son of Heaven has died. [Author's note.]

202   Ritual paraphrase to express that a Son of Heaven is not of age. Respect forbids the Chinese to count the age of the Emperor. [Author's note.]

"She waited, as the striped tiger waits when, before he bloodies the flock, he watches for the shepherd to depart. In the third month of summer the Emperor, as it is prescribed, set forth to fish for big sea turtles, and she took advantage of his absence.

"She first killed, with her own hands, the prince of the second rank, Joui, piercing his brain with long needles. She then removed from prison the mother of this prince, Tsi, and cut off her nose, her lips, and all four of her limbs, at the elbows and knees. Finally, she then shrank her ears, with a red-hot iron, into the shape of pig's ears, made her drink a potion that deprived her of intelligence, and condemned her to live on the dung heap, south of the palace, and bear the name of human sow.

"All of these things, of course, springing from a rancorous mind, and cruel.

"Emperor Hoéi, however, was returning, having fished for the great sea turtles. Arriving at the palace by the southern plain, he saw in passing the human sow and, seized with horror at the sight, exclaimed thoughtlessly: 'This runs contrary to humanity. My mother was wrong.'

"Now, this story is told us in all of the annals of the Empire, by all of the philosophers and all of the great scholars.

"And all of the annals, and all of the philosophers, and all of the great scholars are agreement that the regent empress, Lu, was not to blame. Although she had indeed been lacking in the virtue of humanity, she had not overstepped her right as regent empress, absolute mistress in the child Emperor's absence.

"And all of the annals, and all of the philosophers, and all of the great scholars agree that the child Emperor, Hoéi, is to blame. Although he observed the virtue of humanity, he failed to keep the Primordial Law, according to which sons are never to judge their mothers. For it is written in the Nei Tse:[203] 'In the presence of their parents, sons shall obey and keep silent.'"[204]

Zhou P'ei let his hand drop, and fell silent. And this time Jean-François Felze made no reply.

---

203 Tenth book of the *Li Ki*. [Author's note.] — This is the author's phonetic rendering of *Nei Ze* (內則), the title of which translates to "The Pattern of the Family" or "Domestic Regulations." As the author correctly notes, this is indeed the tenth chapter (or "book") of the *Li Ji* (禮記), also known as the *Book of Rites*, one of the core texts of Confucianism.

204 This accurately reflects the strong emphasis on filial piety (孝, *xiào* in Pinyin, *hsaio* in Wade-Giles) and obedience to parents detailed within the *Nei Ze* and central to Confucian ethics. While perhaps not a word-for-word translation of a single line found in all English versions, the principle is absolutely central to the *Nei Ze*. The chapter outlines strict rules for behavior within the family, emphasizing deference to and obedience of elders.

The grey smoke now filled the smoking room with a fragrant fog, and above it shone the nine violet lanterns like stars on a misty November night. Several hours had flowed past, unctuous as milk.

And Jean-François Felze, the sovereign drug bit by bit reconquering him, began to forget all external things and, in good faith, to doubt that there existed, outside these walls of yellow satin, a real world where beings lived and did not smoke…

But Zhou P'ei suddenly coughed twice, and his hoarse voice sounded again, dispelling the visitor's nearly crystallized dream.

"Fenn Ta-Jen, when he has risen to thought's supreme speculations the philosopher does not without effort descend to life's mediocre incidents. K'ung Tzu, however, excelled in this. And it behooves us most humbly to imitate him. Now that you have learned the rest, then, know that several of the men you have met in this country

died yesterday: Marquis Yorisaka Sadao, and his friend Viscount Hirata Takamori, and his other friend the foreigner from the Nation of the Red-Haired Men. All met with glorious death by the morality of warriors."

Too many pipes, one after the other, had imbued Jean-François Felze's soul with their serene virtue. Learning in this way of the total mourning and ruin of the only Japanese house that had received him as a friend, Jean-François Felze was unmoved.

"It is a sad death," he said, simply, "because of the most lamentable loneliness in which Marquise Yorisaka Mitsouko will henceforth live, for she has lost her husband and her dearest friends all at once."

"Yes," said Zhou P'ei.

He spoke in a graver voice:

"Before a blameworthy madness disturbed this kingdom, the rules of mourning were observed therein. The woman deprived of her husband would don a robe of coarse, greyish brown cloth, left without hems, and wore a girdle and headband made of two hemp strands twisted together; — this, for three years. She refrained from elegant speech. She deprived herself of food so as to achieve a suitably pale complexion. Often, she would even enter a convent and there await death."

"Today's women," acknowledged Felze, "have less virtue."

"Yes," said Zhou P'ei again.

His sharp eye scrutinized the visitor.

"Fenn Ta-Jen," he resumed after a while, "I know and you know the commandment of the rites: 'Men shall not speak of what concerns women; what is said and done in the gynoecium shall not leave the gynoecium.' I shall not disobey this commandment. But I imagine that later, although she has often neglected feminine modesty and so violated the Primordial Law, you shall want to observe the virtue of humanity yourself, and with due care tell Marquise Yorisaka Mitsouko of the misfortune that has struck her, a misfortune that she will otherwise learn tomorrow morning from someone other than you, without any preparation. And so I shall tell you, prudently, what you need to know. Not long ago you asked me whether I esteemed that a woman whose husband had strayed from the straight path failed in her duty if she too took the fork, so as to follow the footprints of the one she had promised to follow step by step unto death. I reserved my answer, keeping silent out of ignorance. I answer now, enlightened: it is possible that the woman of whom we were just speaking has taken the fork so as to follow the footprints not of her husband but of another man. And it is perhaps not when learning of the Marquis Yorisaka's death that Marquise Yorisaka will weep."

"Herbert Fergan," Felze murmured, hesitant…

"You have learned what you needed to learn," interrupted Zhou P'ei. "Suffer us now to smoke, as is proper, from the pipe of black bamboo."

And when they had smoked he added:

"The lamp's flame is waning."

A servant hastened over with a flask of oil and a lit torch, and Felze recalled that it is written in the *Ch'ü Li*:[205]

"Rise when the torches arrive."

And, observing all ceremony, he took his leave.

---

205   First Book of the *Li Chi* — *Ch'ü Li* — Small Rules of Decorum. [Author's note.]
    In Pinyin: *Qūlǐ*, first book of the *Liji* (*Book of Rites*).

XXXII

News of the Great Victory

The rain had ceased. The clouds, drained, were relinquishing their livid hues. Shafts of sunlight pierced them here and there. And the countryside, still verdant with fresh water and already gilded with the light, was once again clad in its spring attire.

Jean-François Felze walked slowly, filling his lungs with the earth's vital odors and satiating his eyes with the pure clarity of the day.

At the foot of the stars to Diou Djen Dji he suddenly thought to check his watch.

"Half past three already! High time indeed I headed to Stork Hill: where I'll probably find the door closed to me…"

He hastened towards the busy streets, where *kuruma* were likely cruising for custom.

"What a task! Toilsome, ungrateful task!" he mused. "Poor thing! Whatever it's about, I pity her with all my heart! Whether she weep for Herbert Fergan or Yorisaka Sadao, I'll gladly weep with her!"

He shook his head. He thought back to the garden party aboard the *Yseult*, and to Mrs. Hockley and Prince Alghero…

"Alas!" he murmured. "Europe's alcohol goes quickly to a *mousmé*'s head, be that *mousmé* a marquise!…"

There was no *kuruma* to be found on Megasaki Street,[206] or on Hirobaba Street.[207] Felze made his way to the inevitable Motokagomachi.[208] There was a dense crowd there, pressing and jostling, and one need not

---

206 No Megasaki Street appears on standard maps or in lists of Nagasaki districts (*machi/chō*) from that era. There is a Megasaki Wharf (女神崎) southwest of the central city, but it is remote, and Felze is unlikely to have passed it on a walk from Motokagomachi to Hirobabamachi. A more plausible route would make Megasaki Street a reference to the area near the famous Meganebashi (眼鏡橋), or "Spectacles Bridge," very close to Motokagomachi in central Nagasaki..

207 The author is almost certainly referring to Hirobabamachi (広馬場町). "Hirobaba" means "Wide Horse-Riding Ground." Historically, Hirobabamachi was a district in Nagasaki, notably located near the important Suwa Shrine. Areas named "-baba" often originated from grounds used for horse riding or training, frequently associated with shrines, temples, or castles.

208 Motokagomachi (本籠町) is a well-established historical district in Nagasaki City. Its name translates literally to something like "Original/Base Palanquin Town/Street."

have seen many Japanese crowds to remark at first glance that this one was beside itself and swept up in some extraordinary emotion. News of the great victory of the day before had just spread in Nagasaki. And already every shop, every lodging, every window had been hastily festooned with flags and banners. Brought to a fever pitch, drunk with pride and triumph, the crowd was setting aside restraint and the national decorum and expressing its joy almost in the manner of a Western throng. There were cries, songs, processions. There were quarrels and almost brawls. There were loons and perhaps drunkards. Felze, trying to cross the street and reach the dock, nearly fell. Two *mousmés* had collided his legs, two running *mousmés* shouting themselves hoarse, their beautiful black hair-buns in great disarray, locks fluttering in the wind.

"Alas!" said Felze again. "It truly matters little whether the new Japan has defeated Russia, new or old…"

On the dock, however, the *kuruma* had not lost their old courtesy. And when Felze uttered the magic words, *Yorisaka kōshaku*, there arose great competition between all the trotting folk, for the honor of conveying the most honorable foreigner to the house of the noble marquis, once a *daimyo*…

CHARLES
FOURVERAY

XXXIII

A Sudden Metamorphosis

In the Pompadour boudoir, between the Erard piano and the gold-framed mirror, nothing had changed. Sunbeams entered cheerfully through the panes of the windows, spreading a celebratory air and lending the speckle of variegated gemstones to the flowers in the vases. These flowers, Felze observed, were no longer the lopped cherry-tree branches of before but American orchids…

"Who knows!" he mused, suddenly bitter. "America has been by… Perhaps not even Herbert Fergan himself will get a tear! So much the better, and the worse!"[209]

Gone to the window, he looked at the tiny garden, with its rockeries and waterfalls and Lilliputian forests.[210] A voice he had not forgotten, a sweet, singsong voice, wee as a bird's cry, suddenly repeated behind him the phrase of welcome that had greeted him for the first time in this same salon six weeks earlier.

"Oh, dear master!… How ashamed I am to have made you wait so long!"

And, again as before, a little hand of pale ivory stretched forth for a kiss.

But this time, having touched his lips to the silky fingers, Felze made no reply to the welcoming phrase.

Heedless of the silence, Marquise Yorisaka chattered on cheerfully.

"Ah! Mrs. Hockley and I thought you might soon have had enough of your excursion! Have you gone far? Have you had too much rain? Have you returned with some lovely sketches? Tomorrow I shall be going aboard the *Yseult*, and I would absolutely like you to show me everything!"

---

209   Felze interprets the replacement of traditional cherry blossoms with "American orchids" as a symbol of Marquise Yorisaka's further assimilation into Western culture, which meets his disapproval. The orchids are those Mrs. Hockley boasts, in Chapter VII, were imported ("still from the Frisco supply"), and reinforce Felze's sense that her influence ("America has been by…") is pervasive. He fears that Mitsouko might have adopted a superficial or emotionally detached attitude, under Mrs. Hockley's influence, might not even grieve her lover Fergan's death on hearing the news. His concluding thought reflects this conflict: perhaps "better" if she avoids suffering (a cynical pity), but "worse" if it signifies the loss of that authentic Japanese sensitivity Felze values.

210   In Jonathan Swift's satirical novel *Gulliver's Travels* (1726) Lilliput is an island nation whose inhabitants are only six inches tall.

She spoke more boldly than before. She was wearing a Louis
XV dress[211] in embroidered muslin, pink on pink, as well as a big tulle
capeline[212] with great, knotted ribbons. She was leaning on a furbelowed

---

211   This refers to a style inspired by the elaborate court fashions of eighteenth-century France
under Louis XV, part of the Rococo aesthetic. Such dresses were known for their elegance, with
their flowing lines, ornamentation in lace and ribbons, and silhouettes designed to emphasize a
narrow waist above a full skirt (e.g., the *robe à la française*). The style signifies Mitsouko's adoption of
ornate, historical Western fashion, in contrast with traditional Japanese attire.

212   A capeline is a style of women's hat characterized by a small or fitted crown and a wide,
often soft or floppy, brim.

parasol,[213] pink like the dress. And in this ensemble, designed for the stature of the women one meets at Pré Catelan or Armenonville, she looked tiny, tiny indeed…[214]

Felze coughed three times, then began a sentence:

"I have come back…"

"Ah!" said Marquise Yorisaka, "I am happy that you are back!"

"I have come back," Felze repeated…

And he fell silent, staring fixedly at the young woman.

She was smiling, but Felze's eyes were no doubt at the moment clearer of speech than his mouth. The smile vanished from the pretty painted lips, and the lashes on the thin, oblique eyes fluttered with worry.

"You have come back?…"

Between the large pink tulle ribbons, beneath the frilly capeline, the face underwent a sudden metamorphosis, and was once more intensely Asian.

Four seconds passed, slow as four minutes. The wee voice spoke again; it was no longer in any way singsong, had mysteriously turned monotone, uniform, grey.

"You have come back … to?…"

Laboriously Felze finished:

"To tell you … that yesterday … near Tsushima, a great battle took place…"

There was a rustle of silk. The furbelowed parasol had fallen. It stayed on the floor.

"A very great battle … between the Russian fleet and the Japanese navy… Have you not heard?…"

He paused as if to take a breath. Standing against the wall, motionless and silent, Marquise Yorisaka Mitsouko listened.

"No, you cannot yet have heard… A very great battle. Very bloody, of course… Yes. Many wounded…"

She was not moving, no longer speaking. She was still leaning against the wall, and facing the grim messenger…

"Many wounded… As I understand it, I believe that Viscount Hirata…"

She did not flinch…

---

213 Furbelows are strips of fabric gathered, pleated, or ruffled to create ornamental trim. In this case, the parasol is adorned with such ruffles or flounces.

214 During the Belle Époque both Pré Catelan and Armenonville were famous and fashionable Parisian establishments where the elite would gather to dine and socialize, and the women would dress in the latest fashions: that is, in clothes designed for tall, full-bodied women.

"…and Marquis Yorisaka himself…"
Not a shudder.
"…and Commander Herbert Fergan…"
Not a blink of an eye.
"Are … wounded…"
The words were catching in Felze's throat.
"Wounded … seriously wounded…"

The terrible word would not come out. Four more seconds dragged on.

"Dead," Felze finally said, under his breath.

He had opened his hands and was just beginning to reach out, preparing to bear up the victim. He had often seen women faint in such cases. But Marquise Yorisaka Mitsoko did not faint.

And so he stepped back a bit, the better to see her. She remained motionless and on her feet, as if nailed to her wall — crucified. She was pallid, and seemed of a sudden to have grown in stature.

"Dead," Felze repeated. "They have died in glory."

And he fell silent, unable to find more words.

Now the painted lips moved. In the whole of that fixed, icy face the lips alone seemed imbued with life — the lips and the eyes, the wide-open eyes, well lit like funeral lamps.

"Defeat?… Or victory?…"

"Victory!" averred Felze.

And, emphatically:

"Decisive victory: the whole of the Russian fleet has succumbed. All that remains are wrecks. It is not in vain that so many heroic men have shed their blood. Japan has triumphed, forever!"

A flush, slowly, returned to the pallid cheeks. The narrow mouth spoke again, in the same grey and calm voice.

"Thank you… Farewell…"

And Felze, thus dismissed, bowed and backed towards the door.

At the threshold he paused to bow again…

Marquise Yorisaka had not moved. She remained rigid and stiff, indecipherable, unrecognizable — Asian, Asian from head to toe, so Asian that the Western cast-offs had receded from view. And the silk-covered wall served her as a kind of frame, and within this she now looked tall, tall indeed.

XXXIV

A Singular Procession

For an hour above Suwa Shrine,[215] in the small park on Nishizaka Hill, among the centuries-old camphors, the maples, and the cryptomerias, with their splendid dangling arborescent wisteria, Jean-François Felze had wandered.

His reverie had by instinct led him there as he left the villa on Stork Hill, its door shutting behind him much like a tomb's on the heels of grave diggers. He had felt an immediate need for solitude, shadows, and silence. He had walked, by reflex, as far as the small park, less than a mile away, where the dense lanes and deep wood had enticed him to pause. He had climbed to the top of the hill by the eastern lane, and descended by the western one. He had stopped at the bends in the path to contemplate the green dells in their undulation towards the plain, and the mist-colored city at the edge of the steel-colored fjord. He had gazed down into the grand temple's courtyards and gardens. He had strolled along the southern terrace, with its cherry trees sown in quincunxes...

And everywhere he had seen not the landscape spread before his eyes but the image, burned onto his retina, of a woman on her feet, leaning against a wall...

He had now left the small park. Feeling spent, he wanted to return to the city, get back aboard the *Yseult*, and rest at last, at home, in his cabin, from this long, long journey with its lugubrious end... But a mysterious obsession was leading him astray, diverting him from his path. He had turned right instead of left. And he found himself once more on the flanks of Stork Hill, a scarce hundred paces from the house in mourning...

He had come to a halt here and was about to turn back when the hurried trot of *kuruma* made him look up. He heard his name.

"François! Is that you?"

---

215 The Suwa Shrine is the major Shinto shrine of Nagasaki. It stands in the north of the city, on the slopes of Mount Tamazono-san. A 277-step stone staircase leads to it up the mountain.

About ten *kuruma* were rushing up in single file, loaded with pale dresses and orchid-patterned jackets. All of American Nagasaki was there, with Mrs. Hockley in the lead: Mrs. Hockley, prettier than ever, in a muslin dress, embroidered pink on pink, twin sister to the dress that Felze had seen earlier on Marquise Yorisaka Mitsouko.

Mrs. Hockley's *kuruma* had come to a sudden stop, and all the *kuruma* in tail did their best to stop as well, one bumping into the next.

"François!" said Mrs. Hockley, "are you really back? I'm happy to see you. Come with us. We're all going together on a snack-time picnic in a lovely forest that Prince Alghero knows. We're stopping here to collect Marquise Yorisaka…"

"Will you listen to me first?" said Felze.

She had stepped down. He approached and spoke without preamble.

"I have myself just seen the marquise and shall warn you right away: the marquis was killed yesterday, at Tsushima."

"Oh!" exclaimed Mrs. Hockley.

Her cry had been so loud that the full picnic party stepped right off the *kuruma* to learn the news, and then break into multi-lingual lamentation.

"Poor, poor, poor little darling!… Mitsouko darling!… What a pity!… *O, poverina!…*"[216]

"I think we must right away go and comfort her," said Mrs. Hockley. "I'm going, then, and I shall take along Prince Alghero, who is particularly close to the marquise. Later I'll return to fetch everyone else."

She walked resolutely to the door. She knocked. For the first time, though, the door-keeping *nēsan* did not open up or drop on all fours before the visitor. Again Mrs. Hockley knocked, and knocked harder, and battered the shut door with her fists. And the shut leaf did not yield.

Vexed, Mrs. Hockley retreated as far as the *kuruma* and had her public bear witness.

"It is incredible that nobody in that house should hear or answer. The marquise has surely not been informed. For she would find it sweet and comforting to be surrounded with her friends at this hour. I must think of some way to get her a message…"

"No need," broke in Felze. "Look!"

The door, at which no one was knocking anymore, had just opened, and from it was issuing a singular procession.

---

216 The Italian diminutive of *povera*, "poor woman." It could be translated as "poor little one" or "poor thing."

Servants, maids, all in traveling clothes, all burdened and encumbered with those pretty, well-folded packages, those pretty boxes with the fine joinery, those paper bags that never tear that are the trunks and suitcases of old Nippon, were shuffling away, trotting along one after another, taking the westward path, that one that leads to the station for the railway from Nagasaki to Moji, Kyoto, and Tokyo…[217]

And suddenly, from behind the maidservants and menservants, and itself followed by other servants and maids, a *kuruma* passed through the gate and took the path leading to the station … a *kuruma* pulled by two runner-men … a master's *kuruma*, most elegant… Upon the cushions , a white form was seated…

---

217   Tokyo is more than 1,200 kilometers away, but the marquise would be going only about 780 kilometers to Kyoto.

A white form. A woman in mourning, clothed in the old style, in plain, unhemmed cloth, as the rites prescribe widows should be dressed. A woman who was taking her leave, stiff and hieratic, her head held high and her gaze fixed — Marquise Yorisaka...

She passed. She passed near Prince Alghero, without giving him a glance. She passed near Mrs. Hockley, without uttering a word. She passed near Jean-François Felze…

Down the path she went, slowly, and at all times surrounded by her escort…

Jean-François Felze stopped the last servant and asked him a question in Japanese.

"It is Marquise Yorisaka Mitsouko," the man replied, "Yorisaka *kōshaku fujin*.[218] — Her husband was killed yesterday in the war. She is going to Kyoto, to live in the Buddhist convent for the daughters of *daimyo* — to don the cilice and die — in honor."[219]

Atlantique, 1326 *anno hegirae*.[220]

---

218   While generally meaning "wife," "Mrs.," or "madam," *fujin* (夫人) is often used as a respectful term for the wife of a high-status man, such as a nobleman (like the *kōshaku* mentioned here) or dignitary, akin to the English "Lady" or the title corresponding to her husband's rank (in this case, Marquise).

219   The cilice was a rough garment worn by nuns and monks. Farrère seems to have modeled the marquise's destination on Zuiryūji, an imperial Buddhist convent formerly in Kyoto, near the imperial palace.

In her detailed, 2021 paper, "The Auspicious Dragon Temple: Kyoto's 'Forgotten' Imperial Buddhist Convent, Zuiryūji," Patricia Fister describes how the elder sister of the powerful warlord Toyotomi Hideyoshi (1536–98) founded the convent, in 1597, as a place for aristocratic women — i.e., the "daughters of daimyos" — to take religious vows (p. 34). From the seventeenth to the nineteenth centuries its abbesses came from families like the Nijō, the Takatsukasa, and the Kujō, some of the most elite aristocratic houses related to the imperial family (p. 44).

The head of the convent at the time was Abbess Nichiei (1864–1920), who came from the imperial house of Fushimi and was close with Empress Shōken (p. 46). She traveled around Japan preaching and founded the Murakumo Women's Association to promote Buddhist teachings, virtues, and morality among women, expanding Zuiryūji's influence nationwide (p. 47).

Farrère's reference to a "Buddhist" convent provides further evidence, because Zuiryūji was Kyoto's sole convent of the Hokke/Nichiren sect.

220   1908 in the Gregorian calendar. Farrère dates the book on the Hijri (Islamic) calendar, which begins in AD 622, when Muhammad emigrated from Mecca to Medina.

Appendices

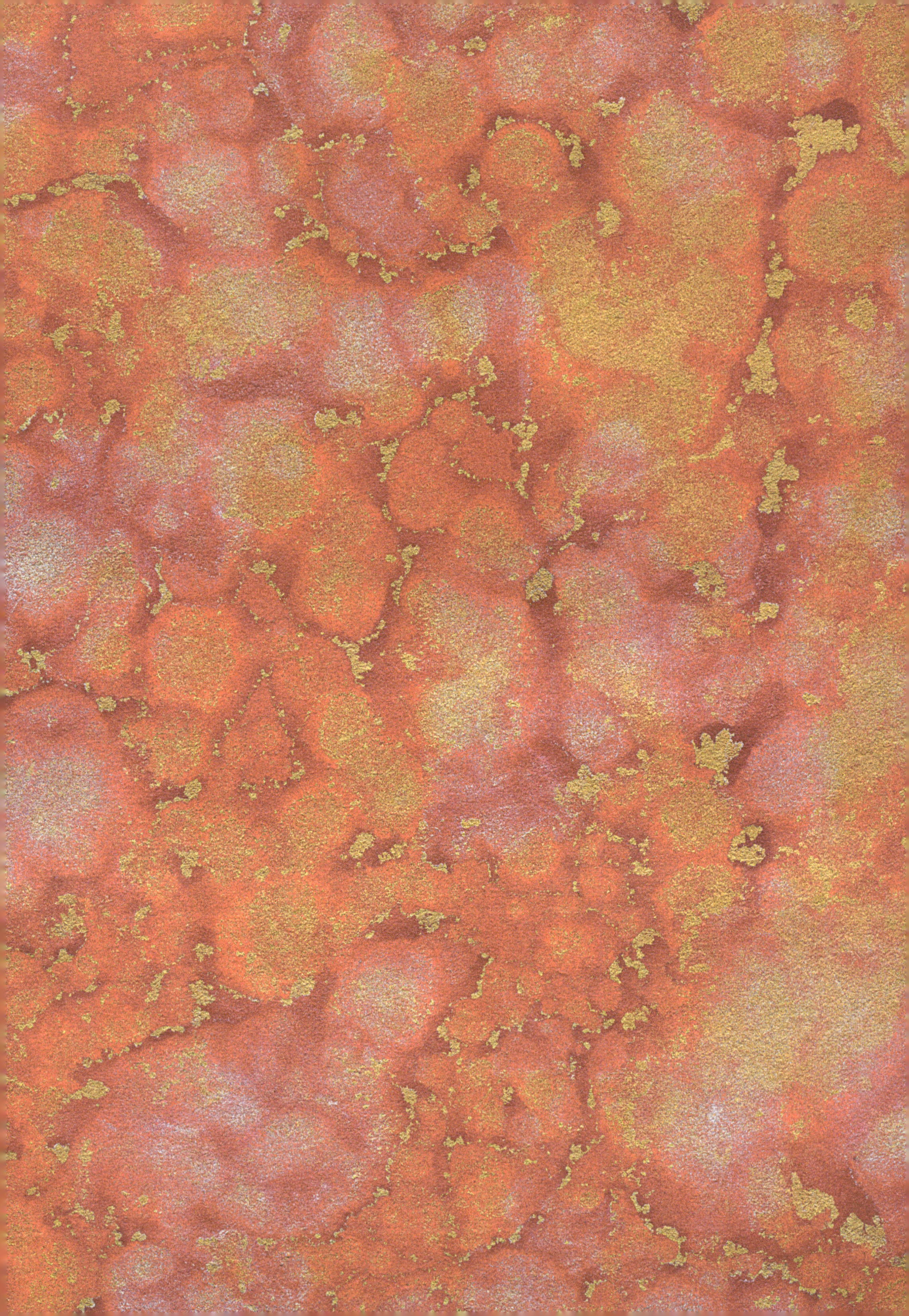

Restoring the Timeline

An Editorial Note for *The Battle* – 2025 Edition

By Kent Davis

Spoiler Warning: *This note discusses details of the plot's structure and timeline. We strongly recommend reading the novel in its entirety before proceeding with this appendix.*

Introduction

During preparation of this first modern annotated English-language edition of Claude Farrère's 1909 novel *La Bataille* (*The Battle*), I identified a significant chronological inconsistency. The sequencing of chapters in the original publication and, remarkably, all subsequent editions, illogically breaks the chronology of events and disrupts development of the narrative.

As the editor entrusted with bringing this classic work to a new generation of readers, discovering a structural anomaly of this magnitude in a novel by an author of Farrère's stature was both baffling and concerning. After careful analysis and consideration, and with absolute respect for both the author's original text and the need for narrative coherence, I have changed the placement of the chapter originally numbered XXIV to fall *after* the battle sequence. This note details the reasoning behind this difficult, but I believe essential, editorial decision and reflects on the puzzling nature of the original error's persistence.

The Chronological Discrepancy

The inconsistency arises between events in Chapter XXIV, and the beginning of Chapter XXV in the original ordering:

1. **Chapters XIX–XX:** After withdrawing from the yacht Yseult, Jean-François Felze, goes to Nagasaki for an immersion in the Japanese lifestyle. He wrestles with the idea of another opium session with his friend Zhou P'ei, but decides against it, instead sending a letter to his friend in Chapter XX.

2. **Chapter XXI–XXIII:** Felze retreats to a traditional Japanese inn in Mogimachi. Chapter XXIII notes that Felse is there for "five days," and that "a violent storm opened this sixth day," distancing him from the main events transpiring in the war.

3. **Chapter XXIV (Original Placement):** Opens with Felze, at the end of his stay at the inn in Mogimachi, receiving a cryptic letter from his Chinese friend, Zhou P'ei. The letter strongly implies that Zhou P'ei (a well-connected Chinese official) has already received significant news about the outcome of the battle via his private network:

4. "Messengers with news from the sea have arrived at the miserable house... I have many things yet to tell you, but I resign myself to finishing this letter unable to express my feelings. And the little one awaits your return with great impatience."

5. After reading this summons, Felze reflects on the weather and explicitly identifies the current date: **"It's only the twenty-eighth of May... twenty-eighth of May 1905..."**. The chapter concludes with Felze resolving to return to Nagasaki immediately. Clearly, Felze is reacting, *on May 28th*, to Zhou P'ei's summons prompted by news of the battle that commenced the previous day (May 27th) and concluded on May 28th (the same day).

6. **Chapter XXV (Original Placement):** This chapter abruptly shifts focus and timeline, depicting events aboard the Japanese battleship *Nikkō* at "ten o'clock" on the morning as the Battle of Tsushima begins. Historically, this was May 27th, 1905. This chapter details pre-battle preparations, fleet movements, and conversations between Marquis Yorisaka and Commander Fergan anticipating the engagement. Chapters XXV through XXX then proceed to narrate the battle and its immediate aftermath sequentially.

7. **Felze's Absence/Return:** Notably, Felze is completely absent from the narrative during Chapters XXV-XXX, which aligns with his established retreat in Mogimachi. He only reappears at the beginning of Chapter XXXI, arriving at the

steps of Zhou P'ei's house in Diou Djen Dji after his journey from Mogimachi.

The original sequence thus presents an unavoidable illogical situation: In Chapter XXIV, Felze is reacting to a letter with news stemming from the battle's conclusion on **May 28th**, yet the narrative then reverts in Chapter XXV to depict the battle *beginning* on May 27th. This disrupts the cause-and-effect relationship, potentially confusing readers about the sequence of crucial events.

My Editorial Decision

As a modern editor inheriting the privilege of working with this manuscript, the discovery of this apparent error was perplexing. Claude Farrère was an intelligent, experienced author and naval officer, deeply familiar with the historical events he depicted. How could such a significant structural flaw – one that fundamentally breaks the narrative timeline at a climactic point – persist through over one hundred documented editions, many published during the author's lifetime?

The question became a central preoccupation during the preparation of this edition. While holding the author and the integrity of the original text in the highest regard, I felt that my primary responsibility editing a new translation must be towards clarity and the reading experience. After extensive review and considering the impact of the inconsistent narrative, I made the difficult decision to correct the chapter sequence for this English edition. I believe that it is essential to present the story coherently and with chronological accuracy to contemporary readers.

The Editorial Solution

To resolve this chronological inconsistency, the chapter originally numbered XXIV has been moved so that it follows all six chapters describing the battle.

The revised sequence in this edition is therefore:

- **Chapter XXIII:** Felze retreats to Mogimachi for five days.

- **Chapters XXIV-XXIX (New Numbering):** The narrative unfolds the events leading up to, during, and immediately following the Battle of Tsushima (May 27th-28th), focusing on the characters involved (Yorisaka, Fergan, Hirata) as Felze remains off-stage in Mogimachi.

- **Chapter XXX (New Numbering - Orig. XXIV):** Felze, still in Mogimachi and totally unaware of the battle that has just taken place, receives Zhou P'ei's letter on the morning of May 28th summoning him to his home to learn the outcome. Sensing the gravity of the situation, Felze orders a *kuruma* to take him to Zhou P'ei's house.

- **Chapter XXXI (Return to original numbering):** Felze arrives at Zhou P'ei's house to learn the explicit details of the battle and its outcomes.

Justification

This restructuring aligns the narrative threads logically. Felze's time in Mogimachi now correctly spans the period of the battle from which he is absent. His receipt of the summons occurs chronologically *after* the events Zhou P'ei is cryptically referencing, and his return journey leads seamlessly into his meeting with Zhou P'ei to learn the details. Furthermore, the detailed review undertaken for this edition of the subsequent battle chapters (now Chapters XXIV-XXIX) confirmed Felze's complete absence from that narrative arc, validating the timeline wherein he remained in Mogimachi until receiving Zhou P'ei's summons after the battle's conclusion (now Chapter XXX). While altering the chapter order of a published work is a significant step, it was deemed essential in this case to correct a clear structural error.

A Persistent Puzzle: Why Was the Error Not Corrected?

The question remains: why did this inconsistency persist for over a century? While a definitive answer is lost to history, several speculative possibilities exist, reflecting the realities of authorship and publishing, especially in the early 20th century:

- **Initial Oversight & Publishing Inertia:** The simplest explanation is a mistake in the first edition (manuscript mix-up, typesetting error) that went unnoticed. Once printing plates were made, correcting a structural issue involving reordering chapters and repaginating subsequent sections would have been significantly more costly and labor-intensive than fixing minor typos. Furthermore, subsequent reprints often become exercises in replication rather than deep re-editing, preserving the established format unless a significant flaw is forcefully flagged. Publishers issuing frequent reprints of commercially successful novels probably prioritized maintaining the existing format over undertaking such a revision.

- **Subtlety of the Error Across Perspectives:** The chronological inconsistency occurs across a significant shift in narrative point of view, time, and location – from Felze determining the date is May 28th in Mogi (Original Chapter XXIV), back to the battleship preparing for action on May 27th (Original Chapter XXV). This structure, while illogical upon close inspection, doesn't present a contradiction within a single continuous scene. Readers deeply engaged with Felze's personal journey, the novel's exotic atmosphere, or the dramatic impact of the battle scenes might not pause to meticulously cross-reference the dates mentioned chapters apart, allowing the discrepancy to pass unnoticed.

- Perhaps even more significantly, *none* of the battle chapters mention the date! One has to be historically familiar with the Battle of Tsushima to understand exactly when this (fictional) battle narrative takes place.

- **Authorial Focus & Limited Revision:** Claude Farrère was a highly prolific author. Having submitted *La Bataille* for publication, his creative energies likely shifted to new projects. While he added a preface for the 1911 edition, this suggests engagement at the level of framing the work, not necessarily a word-by-word, structural re-reading. Authors, especially successful ones, often move on from past works without subjecting them to the same scrutiny as their initial composition, unless undertaking a major, comprehensive revision. Farrère's preface, notably, emphasizes the accuracy of the historical and technical details, perhaps indicating where his own review efforts were focused.

- Moreover, faced with a work by a prominent author — a Prix Goncourt winner, and eventual member of the Académie Française   subsequent editors over the decades may simply have shown obeisance. They might have hesitated to implement such a significant structural change, potentially assuming an obscure authorial intent or prioritizing strict fidelity to the established text, even with its apparent flaw.

- **Editorial Practices of the Era:** Early 20th-century editorial standards, particularly for popular fiction, might not have routinely included the rigorous continuity checks common today. Editors were more focused on linguistic style, grammar, and basic print errors, potentially overlooking larger structural timeline issues.

- **Error Not Flagged:** It is conceivable that, despite the novel's popularity and numerous editions, no contemporary editor, critic, or reader raised this specific chronological problem with sufficient force to prompt Farrère or his publishers to address it. Sometimes even seemingly obvious flaws can become accepted parts of a text's landscape if unchallenged early on.

- **Intentional Disjunction (Highly Unlikely):** While improbable, one cannot entirely discount the remote theoretical possibility that Farrère intended the illogical chronological contradiction for a specific, albeit obscure, artistic effect — perhaps to create disorientation or emphasize the simultaneity of disparate events. However, given the lack of any clear textual support for such an interpretation and the straightforward improvement in narrative logic achieved by the reordering, this remains highly speculative.

Ultimately, without direct evidence from Farrère's correspondence or publisher records, the reason for the error's persistence remains a historical puzzle.

Conclusion

This editorial intervention was not lightly undertaken, but with the conviction to present Farrère's powerful story with the clearest narrative progression that best serves the modern reader. This restructuring preserves the author's plot, character arcs, and thematic development while ensuring internal chronological consistency, allowing the dramatic force of *The Battle* to be experienced without unnecessary confusion.

‘❀’

Mitsouko

Farrère's Symbolic Bridge Between East and West

By Kent Davis

Spoiler Warning: *This commentary delves deeply into the plot, characters, and thematic intentions of Claude Farrère's novel,* The Battle. *The author meticulously structured his narrative to reveal insights and plot twists at the moments he intended. Reading this analysis before experiencing the novel itself will inevitably diminish the impact of his carefully crafted masterpiece. Reader discretion is advised.*

Introduction: Centering the Narrative

How is it that the melodious name of a young Japanese wife, Mitsouko, finds itself sharing the title page of this modern edition of Claude Farrère's epic 1909 military tale, *The Battle*?

The added subtitle, *Mitsouko Amidst a Clash of Empires*, reflects a deliberate editorial choice, guided by Farrère's own preface and narrative structure, to center the reader's attention on the character who serves as the crucial vessel for the novel's most profound themes. Because, while delivering thrilling accounts of naval battle, *The Battle* transcends the genre of a simple war story.

Farrère presents a complex, deeply layered exploration of cultural identity, the tensions between modernization and tradition, the nature of sacrifice, and the resilience of the Japanese national spirit confronting the overwhelming forces of Western imperialism. Through his female protagonist, Marquise Mitsouko Yorisaka, Farrère examines the soul of Japan at a pivotal moment in world history. Paired with the perspective of the French painter Jean-François Felze, whose appreciation for the East mirrors Mitsouko's engagement with the West, her journey becomes a compelling exploration of the profound cultural encounters shaping the modern world.

The author, born in Lyon, France as Frédéric-Charles Bargone (1876-1957), and later writing as Claude Farrère, was himself a career French naval officer. In 1894, at the age of 18, he entered France's prestigious

École Navale, beginning a naval career spanning 25 years. His extensive service, particularly in the Middle and Far East, provided him with firsthand experience of maritime life and combat. His worldview was further influenced by his admiration for the renowned author and fellow naval officer Pierre Loti (under whom he served aboard the *Vautour*), whose own works explored themes of exoticism and cultural encounters. In 1905, Farrère's literary talents exploded onto the scene with his controversial novel, *Les Civilisés*, set in French Indochina, which won the prestigious Prix Goncourt, establishing him as a significant literary voice.[1]

The year 1905 was also marked by the stunning victory of the Imperial Japanese Navy over the Russian fleet at the Battle of Tsushima (May 27-28). This event resonated globally as the first (and arguably last!) major engagement between modern battleship fleets, dramatically upsetting the perceived balance of power between East and West. As a naval officer, the battle's military implications made such a deep impression on Farrère that just weeks later, as he was finishing *Les Civilisés*, he dedicated a late chapter to "The dead of Tsushima." Apparently, however, a seed had been planted; as a novelist intimate with the complexities of the Far East, he saw far more. While numerous contemporary accounts analyzed tactics and outcomes, Farrère embarked on a novelistic exploration of Tsushima's deeper cultural and existential significance. Published in 1909, *La Bataille* was lauded for its naval authenticity and evocative portrayal of Japan. Yet, Farrère insisted the novel's heart lay not just in the conflict, but in the symbolic story woven around it — primarily through Mitsouko as the connective thread of his story.

Farrère's Stated Intent: Symbolism Over Literal Truth

Farrère's original preface (likely added in 1911) is indispensable for understanding his aims. He asserts its necessity, acknowledging the novel blends history and politics with fiction. While proud of the work's technical accuracy, Farrère emphasizes that its core purpose lies deeper: "In *The Battle*," he writes, "a significant part of the novelistic fiction presents, I dare say, a symbolic interest, which, of course, alters the literal truth of the fiction." Farrère identifies the three main Japanese characters – Marquis

---

1   Now available in its first English translation as *The Civilized – Decadence and Damnation in French Indochina*, in an expanded annotated 2025 edition illustrated by Henri Le Riche from DatAsia Press.

Yorisaka, Marquise Mitsouko, and Viscount Hirata – not as realistic "photographic portraits" but as "very general paintings," representing "an entire Japanese caste," their features "selected, and exaggerated, to make the composition more perceptible to European eyes."

To underscore this, he explicitly states that key plot points – Mitsouko's affair with the British officer Fergan, and Viscount Hirata's ritual suicide – are not historical facts but symbolic actions. What truth do they symbolize?

Farrère declares it unequivocally: "...I am also convinced that to vanquish Russia – and Europe in full – all of the Empire's men and women were ready to sacrifice a thousand, nay, ten thousand cherished things, manly honor and womanly virtue included, even if it meant later washing away such glorious stains in the blood of their own disembowelment. That is what I wished to say. Nothing more, nothing less." This is Farrère's interpretive key.

While Mitsouko's complex actions clearly align with the potential sacrifice of "womanly virtue" for national survival, the reference to "manly honor" and subsequent "disembowelment" points complexly towards both Yorisaka's strategic compromises and Hirata's ultimate act of atonement. Mitsouko, therefore, is deliberately crafted as the complex soul of Japan navigating an existential clash.

Bridges Between Worlds: Mitsouko and Felze

From the novel's outset, Mitsouko embodies the central cultural conflict. We meet her through the eyes of Jean-François Felze; a renowned French portraitist whose journey provides a counterpoint to her own. Felze, arriving at Mitsouko's villa near Nagasaki, is immediately struck by the jarring juxtaposition within her home: a meticulously crafted, traditional Japanese garden ("a square of real symbolism, presenting to the eye mountains and plains, forests, a waterfall...") lies just outside a room furnished entirely in the opulent Parisian style, complete with Pompadour tapestries, an Erard grand piano, and a Louis XV mirror. "The still-untamed Far East and the invasive Far West were here face to face, on either side of the pane," he observes.

This physical setting mirrors Mitsouko's own internal state and appearance. Dressed in a Parisian gown "from Doucet, Callot, or Worth," her small frame seems almost enveloped by the European fashion. Felze notes her features might be deemed "ugly" by Western standards – narrow, slanted eyes ("two long oblique slits"), overly powdered complexion – yet possessing undeniable beauty and a "strange charm, at once disdainful and naive, puerile and hieratic" to Japanese eyes. Her very name, Mitsouko, is infused with duality, meaning either sweet "honeycomb" or elusive "mystery". She exists as a fascinating enigma, whom Felze alternately perceives as "an idol or a trinket."

Felze himself serves as her inverse reflection. While Mitsouko, daughter of a *daimyo*, embraces Western fashion, decor, and society, Felze, the celebrated European artist living aboard the luxurious American yacht of Mrs. Hockley, yearns for the authenticity of the East. He disdains the superficiality of his hostess, Mrs. Hockley ("her pile of eighty millions raised her far above domestic humanity"), and her circle. He prefers Japanese tea ("light, delicate green tea one drinks without sugar or milk") to the English blend Mitsouko serves ("the brown, thick, astringent British drug") and persistently requests she pose for a second portrait not in her fashionable gowns, but in the traditional kimono of her ancestors, seeking to capture what he calls "immutable Japan."

His deepest intellectual connections are not with his Western companions but with his enigmatic Chinese friend, the mandarin Zhou P'ei, with whom he discusses philosophy while smoking opium in his hidden Nagasaki den; "three purple lanterns at the door of a low house…" When seeking refuge "from the refined yet somewhat vulgar luxuries of an American yacht," Felze retreats to the simple serenity of a traditional Japanese inn (*yadoya*) in the countryside, finding solace in its "pastoral peace." Together, Mitsouko and Felze represent the complex dialogue between cultures, each drawn to aspects of the other's world while remaining fundamentally rooted in their own.

Navigating Conflicting Demands

Mitsouko's journey involves navigating complex loyalties and cultural pressures, particularly through her relationships with the men around her. Her husband, the Marquis Sadao Yorisaka, shares her Western affinity, having served as a naval attaché in Paris where they lived for four years. Yet, he also seems to encourage, or at least tacitly accept, her intimate connection with the British liaison officer, Commander Herbert Fergan. The nature of Mitsouko's relationship with Fergan – whether genuine affection, strategic sacrifice for intelligence gathering, or manipulation –

remains deliberately ambiguous, aligning with the "mystery" of her name and Farrère's theme of sacrificing "womanly virtue." Fergan himself notes their intimacy when he kisses her and calls her "Mitsu, dear little thing!", while her own responses remain more reserved, more "docile than loving."

Mitsouko's embrace of Western social customs accelerates throughout the narrative. She chooses Parisian gowns over kimonos, even when Felze pleads otherwise. Aboard Mrs. Hockley's yacht during a lavish garden party (Chapter XVII), Mitsouko participates eagerly. She allows the Italian Prince Alghero to flirt with her ("He gently squeezed against his side the tiny hand that had come to rest on his arm"), accepts champagne likely spiked with whiskey ("Yankee cocktails are of a less-benign humor"), plays the Western game of baccarat despite her unfamiliarity ("had I lost I would have lost four hundred yen?... But I didn't have them in my purse!..."), and is eventually swept into the "impudent whirl" of the waltz, a dance Farrère notes is scandalous by Japanese standards ("a public embrace, waist to waist, chest to chest... the infamous spectacle of a kind of coitus...").

This sequence marks a potential descent into Western excess, starkly contrasting with traditional Japanese values, especially as her husband prepares for a life-or-death battle at sea; ultimately an existential fight for the Japanese people. Felze witnesses this with dismay, seeing her as a "little Yamato pheasant in the claws of some great bird of prey from overseas."

Yet, crucial glimpses of her underlying Japanese identity persist, often surfacing through interactions with Felze, the Westerner who values her heritage. It is Felze who encourages her to play the koto, the traditional Japanese zither, leading to a pivotal scene (Chapter XVI). Finally agreeing to pose for Felze in the traditional robes of her ancestors (*jūnihitoe* implicitly, though not named), Mitsouko assumes the kneeling posture of "a genuine lady of the past," looking like "one of those priceless archaic statues." As she plays the koto, the music unlocks a profound, melancholic reminiscence of her childhood training in the "old castle at Hoki," enduring the cold ("the icy mountain wind"), the harsh discipline of halberd practice ("the long bamboo blades would clack... the snow bit into our legs"), and the rigid ceremonies. She reflects on the overwhelming changes brought by modernization: "And I wished in my heart to suffer a thousand deaths rather than to live a foreign or different life. But faster than Mount Fuji changes color at twilight the face of the earth underwent a metamorphosis. And I did not die..."

This poignant confession, juxtaposing the hardships of her past with the comforts of the present, reveals the deep cultural conflict within her, culminating in her lament, "How am I to taste hot rice while preserving the taste of raw fish on my tongue?...". This moment, facilitated by Felze's appreciation for her tradition, underscores the divided soul beneath the Western veneer.

Foils and Counterpoints: Hirata, Fergan, and Hockley

Farrère's characters surrounding Mitsouko all serve as critical foils, representing distinct cultural poles that illuminate her central struggle:

- **Hirata vs. Fergan: Japanese Tradition vs. The West:** Viscount Hirata Takamori embodies the unyielding spirit of traditional *Bushidō*. A descendant of the fiercely resistant Satsuma clan, he represents the samurai past, viewing Western influence with deep suspicion and hatred. His foil is Commander Herbert Fergan, the polished British aide-de-camp to His Majesty the King of England, representing the established Western military power Japan must both learn from and overcome.

- Despite his staunch English heritage, Fergan reveals his intimate knowledge of Japanese history (Chapter VIII) by giving a detailed explanation of Hirata's samurai ancestry to Felze. In his opening, however, he describes Hirata as "a most curious man, lagging a scant forty years behind his century — and in Japan, as you know, once you go back further than the revolution of 1868 forty years might as well be four hundred." Confirming his views, Felze hears Hirata comment on the portrait of Mitsouko he has just finished. Concerned that it may be a criticism of his work, Fergan assures him that Hirata merely expressed an "ethological opinion" stating: "Our skin is yellow, theirs is white; gold is more precious than silver."

- In Chapter XXV, the East-West conflicts also arise in Hirata's tense pre-battle conversation with Marquis Yorisaka, highlighting the irreconcilable ideological chasm between them. Hirata implicitly criticizes Yorisaka's Westernization and friendship with Fergan as a betrayal of their race ("You, however, who also hated him once, have love for him today"), while Yorisaka defends his adaptation as a necessary, albeit painful, strategy for victory.

- Ultimately, Hirata's final act of *seppuku*—atoning for misjudging Yorisaka's methods — stands in stark contrast to Fergan's death in battle while commanding Yorisaka's turret after the Marquis falls, embodying different codes of honor and sacrifice. (For a detailed analysis of Hirata's motivations, please see the appendix "Honor, Judgment, and Atonement: Viscount Hirata's *Bushidō*").

- **Mrs. Betsy Hockley: The Superficial West:** The fabulously wealthy American yacht owner, "a millionaire eighty times over," represents a different facet of the West. She is characterized by her luxurious lifestyle, her casual dominance over Felze (whom she calls "François" despite his preference for "Jean-François," deeming it "much more noble"), her detached, analytical curiosity ("Tell me, what is the nature of an opium smoker's sensual pleasure?"), and her profound cultural insensitivity.

- She treats Mitsouko as a fascinating novelty ("a Japanese marquise in Parisian attire") and fails utterly to grasp the depth of Japanese customs or emotions, exemplified by her suggestion to "comfort" the newly widowed Mitsouko by bringing Prince Alghero along. She embodies a shallower, perhaps more invasive, form of Western influence compared to the established, strategically complex relationship represented by Fergan and Britain.

Denouement: The Victory of the East Within

After the deaths of the Marquis and Fergan during the battle, and before the novel's climax, Felze discusses the unfolding situation with Zhou P'ei (Chapter **XXXI**). His cultured Chinese mentor describes the traditional mourning rites for a Japanese widow ("don a robe of coarse, greyish brown cloth... enter a convent and there await death"), prompting Felze's pessimistic observation, "Today's women have less virtue." Zhou P'ei then subtly hints at Mitsouko's potential infidelity, suggesting she might weep more for Fergan than for her husband, setting the stage for her dramatic final choice.

The novel's conclusion powerfully resolves Mitsouko's internal conflict, triggered by the catastrophic news Felze delivers. When he arrives at her villa (Chapter **XXXIII**), he finds her dressed elegantly in Western attire, anticipating another social engagement. As he breaks the news – "Marquis

Yorisaka himself… and Commander Herbert Fergan… Are… wounded… seriously wounded… Dead" – her reaction is not the fainting or overt emotional display Felze anticipates from a Western woman.

Instead, she stands "motionless and on her feet, as if nailed to her wall — crucified," her face pallid but composed. Her first question cuts through personal grief to national concern: "Defeat?… Or victory?…" Only upon hearing Felze confirm the "Decisive victory!" does a flush slowly return to her cheeks. In this moment of supreme national triumph and profound personal loss, her carefully constructed Western persona shatters.

The final scene (Chapter XXXIV) dramatizes this complete transformation. Mrs. Hockley arrives with her picnic party, intending to fetch Mitsouko, only to witness a "singular procession" emerging from the villa. Servants carry traditional Japanese luggage. Then, Mitsouko herself appears, not in Parisian fashion, but clothed "in the old style, in plain, unhemmed cloth, as the rites prescribe widows should be dressed." Stiff, hieratic, and utterly transformed, she passes her recent Western acquaintances – Prince Alghero, Mrs. Hockley, even Felze – without a glance or word.

A servant explains her destination: "She is going to Kyoto, to live in the Buddhist convent for the daughters of *daimyo* — to don the cilice and die — in honor." This is not merely grief; it is a profound reversion. She sheds her Western identity, embracing the ultimate act of traditional duty and self-abnegation demanded by her lineage and the cultural code Farrère sought to explore. Just as Japan, in Farrère's view, achieved military victory by melding Western means with its core spirit, Mitsouko finds personal and cultural resolution by choosing the path of traditional sacrifice, reaffirming the enduring power of her Eastern soul.

Conclusion: Mitsouko as Farrère's Message

Claude Farrère used the historical canvas of the Battle of Tsushima to paint a nuanced portrait of cultural collision. While accurately depicting military events, his true focus, as stated in his preface and woven through the narrative, was the symbolic representation of the Japanese spirit facing the challenge of the West. Marquise Mitsouko Yorisaka stands as the central pillar of this exploration.

Her journey—from embracing Western modernity, navigating complex personal and potentially political relationships, to her ultimate reversion to traditional Japanese values in the face of tragedy—serves as Farrère's primary vehicle for exploring themes of sacrifice, honor, duty, and the perceived resilience of the Eastern soul. She is not merely a character caught amidst clashing empires; she is the embodiment of that clash, and her final, resolute choice represents Farrère's ultimate commentary on the enduring strength of Japanese tradition, justifying her prominence in understanding *The Battle*.

Perhaps ominously, thirty-five years later, the entire world would learn the extent of this cultural disconnect in an event known as the Second World War.

Kent Davis
Editor and Literary Archaeologist
DatAsia Press – Snead Island, FL, USA
kentdavis@gmail.com

Honor, Judgment, and Atonement
Viscount Hirata's Bushidō

Kent Davis

Spoiler Warning: *This article discusses significant plot points and character fates, including the conclusion of Viscount Hirata Takamori's storyline. We strongly recommend reading the novel in its entirety before proceeding.*

Introduction

Viscount Hirata Takamori's decision to commit ritual suicide by self-disembowelment following the Japanese victory at Tsushima is one of the most arresting and potentially challenging moments in *The Battle*. For modern readers unfamiliar with the stringent demands of the samurai code — Bushidō — his motivation seems unclear at best. Did he somehow hold himself responsible for the death of his comrade, Marquis Yorisaka Sadao? Farrère's text reveals a different, more complex reason rooted in honor, duty, and the profound weight Hirata placed on judging his fellow samurai incorrectly, especially in the crucible of war and national transformation. His act was not one of guilt for Yorisaka's death, but one of atonement for his own perceived failure in judgment.

The Act of Seppuku

Seppuku (切腹) and *hara-kiri* (腹切り) both refer to the same Japanese ritual suicide by disembowelment, primarily practiced by the samurai class under their code of honor (bushidō). While often used interchangeably in English, the terms differ significantly in formality and origin. *Seppuku* (切腹) is the formal, written term derived from the Sino-Japanese readings of the characters: *setsu* (切 – 'to cut') and *puku* (腹 – 'abdomen'), and it is the preferred term in Japanese historical and formal contexts, emphasizing the ritualistic nature of the act.

In contrast, *hara-kiri* (腹切り) is the colloquial, spoken term using the native Japanese readings of the same characters but in reverse order: *hara* (腹 – 'abdomen') and *kiri* (切り – 'cutting'); this term is more widely known in the West but can be considered somewhat cruder in Japan, focusing more directly on the physical act.

This ritual served several purposes: allowing a samurai to die with honor rather than fall into enemy hands, serving as a form of capital punishment for serious offenses, or atoning for shame brought upon oneself or one's family. The ceremony typically involved plunging a short blade, traditionally a *tantō*, into the left abdomen, drawing it across to the right. To ensure a swift death and preserve dignity, a designated assistant (*kaishakunin*) often performed a near-simultaneous decapitation after the abdominal cut was made; this merciful decapitation was an integral part of the formal *seppuku* ritual itself, not a distinction between *seppuku* and *hara-kiri*.

The Bushidō Code

In Chapter III, Farrère introduces Bushidō through a short speech by Marquis Yorasaka who, along with his wife, has strongly adopted many Western values in their own lifestyle. When speaking with his European guests, British Commander Herbert Fergan and French painter Jean-François Felze, the Marquis frames Bushidō, which he explicitly names "our ancient code of honor," through the critical lens of his newly acquired modern perspective, contrasting the freedoms of his present life with what he terms the "barbarous times" of Japan's recent feudal past. Despite his critique, his words offer the reader an initial glimpse into the core tenets and social implications of this complex code, which literally translates to "the way of the warrior."

Yorisaka paints a stark picture of the rigid social hierarchy dictated by Bushidō, emphasizing its particularly harsh impact on women. He laments how the code "set women lower than dirt and men higher than the heavens," illustrating this with the poignant image of a high-ranking daimyo's wife forty years prior. In his telling, she was effectively "a prisoner in the depths of a feudal castle" and "a servant to her own servants," expected only to obey and endure neglect within strict confines dictated by tradition and familial authority. This depiction underscores the inescapable, rigidly defined roles Bushidō imposed upon individuals within the feudal structure.

In sharp contrast to the constrained noblewoman stands the samurai warrior. Yorisaka highlights the samurai's profound sense of pride and status, noting that even "the least of whom would have blushed to humiliate his two swords before a mirror." This sensitivity points directly to a fundamental aspect of Bushidō: the deep symbolic connection between the samurai, his swords, and his honor. The sword was more than a weapon; it was widely considered the "warrior's soul," representing his identity, his commitment to the code, and his personal and familial honor.

Shaped by centuries of warfare and blending elements of Confucian ethics and Zen Buddhist discipline, Bushidō demanded exacting virtues from its adherents. Beyond martial skill, samurai were expected to cultivate absolute loyalty (primarily to their daimyo or lord), rigorous self-discipline, righteousness, courage, and above all, an unwavering sense of personal honor. Within this demanding framework, where honor dictated one's standing and shame could stain entire families, failure to live up to the code—through acts of disloyalty, cowardice, incompetence, or bringing disgrace upon oneself or one's lord—carried immense weight.

Consequently, ritual suicide emerged as the ultimate recourse within this value system. It was a means to atone for failure, to demonstrate final sincerity or loyalty, to avoid the disgrace of capture, or to restore lost honor. While Yorisaka looks back on this past with discomfort, his critical recollections inadvertently underscore the immense pressures of the code he descended from. His speech, therefore, serves as an effective early introduction to the centrality of honor in the samurai world, preparing the reader to understand the motivations behind actions, including the drastic measure of *seppuku*, that might otherwise seem incomprehensible from a purely modern or Western viewpoint.

Understanding Viscount Hirata

Introduced in Chapter XIII as a stark counterpoint to the Westernized Marquis Yorisaka, Viscount Hirata Takamori embodies the traditional warrior spirit of feudal Japan within the rapidly modernizing Meiji era. Commander Fergan explains his background to the painter Felze, vividly describing Hirata as "a most curious man, lagging a scant forty years behind his century." This temporal disconnect is profound in the context of the narrative, as Fergan emphasizes that in post-Restoration Japan, where the "revolution of 1868" (the Meiji Restoration or "Great Change") dramatically reshaped society, receding forty years into the past is akin to traversing centuries. Hirata, therefore, represents a living link to the values and mindset of the recently abolished samurai class.

A fundamental key to understanding Hirata lies in his lineage, which contrasts sharply with that of Marquis Yorisaka. Both men are sons of daimyo, the feudal lords of the old regime, but Fergan highlights the "prodigious difference" stemming from their clan origins. Yorisaka belongs to the Chōshū clan, associated with learning and arts, whose leaders quickly adapted to the new Imperial government. Hirata, however, hails from the Satsuma clan of Kyushu, historically renowned as being "strictly warriors."

While both Satsuma and Chōshū initially allied to restore the Emperor and overthrow the Tokugawa Shogunate, their paths diverged dramatically following their military victory. The Chōshū, including Yorisaka's parents, embraced the Meiji reforms, becoming "docile or intelligent assistants" in the Empire's reorganization. Conversely, the fiercely independent Satsuma, stripped of their feudal power and privileges by the very Emperor they helped empower, resisted the changes. Hirata's own parents retreated to their Kagoshima stronghold before participating in the tragic Satsuma Rebellion of 1877, led by the revered Saigō Takamori. They died "sword in hand," fighting against the Imperial army — a poignant detail Fergan underscores by noting Hirata's father "was killed fighting the emperor, the emperor who reigns today!"

This deeply personal and tragic history shapes Hirata's character. Fergan asserts his belief that Viscount Hirata "holds exactly the same opinions as all of his ancestors," suggesting an ingrained loyalty to the old ways, the samurai ethos, and perhaps a quiet resentment towards the Meiji government he now serves. Yet, paradoxically, this figure steeped in feudal tradition is also described as "an excellent officer, very familiar with the most recent weapons," responsible for sophisticated technology like the "electric machines" aboard the warship *Nikkō*. This highlights a complex reality of the Meiji era: the harnessing of traditional samurai discipline and skills for the creation of a modern military force, even when individuals harbored loyalties to the past.

Hirata's unwavering commitment to his heritage and his distance from Western influence are further revealed in a quiet but telling moment involving Felze's portrait of Madame Yorisaka depicted in Western attire. Unable or unwilling to converse in French or English, Hirata observes the painting and utters a Japanese comment in a low voice. The curious painter asks, "Is he making an artistic judgment?" To which Fergan, fluent in Japanese, replies, "No, dear sir! A good Satsuma rarely utters artistic judgments… Viscount

Hirata has expressed a mere ethnological opinion — a rather delicious one, as it happens." Fergan then translates the remark as follows: 'Our skin is yellow, theirs is white; gold is more precious than silver.'"

Viscount Hirata, therefore, embodies the unyielding spirit of the Satsuma warrior and the enduring tenets of traditional Bushidō within the novel. He is a man defined by his clan's history of martial prowess and resistance, carrying the legacy of his ancestors' loyalty and sacrifice. His adherence to the ancient code, his quiet cultural pride, and his tragic lineage position him as a foil to the adaptable Yorisaka, unable to reconcile the stringent demands of traditional honor with the realities of the modern world.

A Chasm Between Comrades

In Chapter XXV, a pivotal exchange occurs aboard the Japanese battleship *Nikkō* as it heads directly towards its fateful confrontation with the Russian fleet. A tense conversation lays bare the profound ideological chasm between Marquis Yorisaka Sadao and Viscount Hirata Takamori, revealing the conflicting ways two scions of the samurai class grapple with tradition, modernity, and national identity, ultimately illuminating the path that leads Hirata toward his final, tragic adherence to the old code.

Sensing a distance despite Hirata's maintained courtesies, Yorisaka initiates the confrontation, asking Hirata directly to explain the cooling of their former friendship. Stating he can "no longer endure even a secret humiliation," Yorisaka implores Hirata to speak plainly. Hirata's response delves into the historical roots of their divergence, arguing it stems from differing interpretations of the Meiji Restoration and Japan's relationship with the West.

He reminds Yorisaka that the original impetus for overthrowing the Shōgun was not merely loyalty, but fury over foreign insults and perceived weakness, citing the bombardment of Kagoshima and the "shameful peace." The true cry then, Hirata insists, was "Death to the Foreigner!" This fierce spirit animated his ancestors who died fighting Imperial forces at Kumamoto during the Satsuma Rebellion, a legacy Hirata feels bound to honor: "For the thirty years that I have lived I have awaited the hour to render unto these tablets what they are owed: a libation of blood." The core of their rift, Hirata states, is his unwavering hatred for the foreigner versus Yorisaka's apparent embrace: "You, however, who also hated him once, have love for him today," evidenced by Yorisaka's adoption of foreign "customs, his tastes, his ideas, even his language".

Yorisaka counters this accusation with a startling revelation of his own deep-seated, albeit strategically masked, patriotism. He claims his Westernization is merely a necessary "mask," an act of "cunning" endured at great personal cost—including violating traditional precepts and undergoing "harsher suffering than anyone will ever know" —to ultimately defeat the West. He likens the painful process to taking a "mud bath" to emerge "cured and hale" for the real struggle. The goal was pragmatic: Japan needed to "first to acquire European brains" to master the enemy's methods. As proof of his strategy's effectiveness, he points to the vital British intelligence he obtained, crucial for the impending battle, arguing this makes his "friendship" more dangerous to the enemy than Hirata's overt hostility.

While acknowledging Yorisaka's patriotic motives and strategic acumen, Hirata fundamentally rejects the path Yorisaka has taken. The method itself, Hirata contends, has irrevocably altered Yorisaka's identity: "your brain has ceased to be Japanese and become European." This transformation creates an unbridgeable gap; Hirata's own traditional mind "can never imitate yours," making further attempts to understand each other futile. Hirata's concern then shifts to the future, fearing that post-victory, Yorisaka's celebrated "European brain, and your European ideas, customs, and tastes" will become the dominant influence, leading the Japanese people away from their true heritage.

The dialogue thus culminates not in reconciliation, but in the stark illumination of an irreconcilable divide. Hirata confronts the reality that his unwavering adherence to traditional Bushidō, with its emphasis on purity of spirit and fierce xenophobia, is incompatible with the pragmatic, adaptive strategy embodied by Yorisaka—a strategy seemingly proving essential for Japan's survival and victory in the modern world.

Faced with the perceived contamination of Japanese methods, the potential erosion of traditional values in the future, and his own profound existential isolation from the path his nation and former comrade are taking, Hirata is left cornered by his own code. This intense confrontation crystallizes the conflict defining Hirata. The irreconcilable divide revealed in this dialogue confirms his inability to compromise his ideals, setting his course towards an ultimate, tragic adherence to the ways of the past.

Hirata's Final Honor

In Chapter XXVIII, Marquis Yorisaka dies honorably at his battle station, and in Chapter XXIX we learn of the resounding victory at Tsushima, achieved through the very modern tactics championed by the fallen Marquis himself. This sets the stage for Viscount Hirata Takamori's final personal reckoning. In the immediate aftermath, Hirata stands atop the wreckage of the *Nikkō*'s bridge, having assumed command and delivered the order to "Cease fire!" and joining the triumphant cries of "Teikoku bansai!" ("Eternal life to the Empire!"). He experiences a moment of "inexpressible pride" and "sublime intoxication" — the culmination, perhaps, of a life lived awaiting this vindication of Japan against the West. His competent command even earns him the admiral's specific commendation, relayed via dispatch boat.

This moment of national triumph, however, soon forces a deeply personal confrontation with his own judgment and the principles he rigidly upheld. While inspecting the dead laid out in honor on the aft deck, Hirata comes before the body of Lieutenant Yorisaka Sadao. He stops short, unable to speak, seemingly transfixed by the look in the dead Marquis's wide-open eyes—a look of "disdain, pride, triumph." In that silent gaze, Hirata confronts the undeniable truth: the decisive victory validated Yorisaka's controversial methods, his adoption of Western means, and Yorisaka himself had died a hero's death for the Empire.

This realization precipitates Hirata's final decision, executed with the calm formality dictated by his code. He summons a junior officer, Ensign Narimasa, whom he knows to be "of a most noble family of good samurai." After calmly dictating night orders and writing his last wishes, Hirata states his intention plainly: "I am going to kill myself shortly, Narimasa, and I would be much obliged to you... if you were to assist me in my *hara-kiri*." The young ensign accepts without question, recognizing the "illustrious honor" being conferred upon him according to their shared code.

Hirata offers Narimasa a concise, understated justification rooted in his earlier confrontation with Yorisaka: "my frail understanding caused me to utter various words that this evening I believe were misplaced. It is, I think, preferable that these words be struck out." Within the strictures of Bushidō, this admission of flawed judgment, particularly concerning the honor and methods of a fellow samurai like Yorisaka — who ultimately proved both effective and loyal—constitutes a profound failure. Hirata's sharp criticism and assertion of ideological superiority during their pre-battle conversation now appear unfounded, a stain upon his own discernment and honor. His final words before completing the act serve as an explicit retraction and acknowledgment of Yorisaka's vindicated path: "Marquis Yorisaka's example is greater than mine... Much greater... Much greater, in truth."

Hirata's *seppuku* is therefore not an act of despair but a deliberate, ritualized act of atonement and reaffirmation according to the absolute demands of his traditional samurai ethics. It is the only way within his code to "strike out" his misplaced judgment, rectify his failure to recognize Yorisaka's strategic patriotism, and cleanse the dishonor of having misjudged a comrade whose path, however unorthodox, led to Imperial glory.

While the victory proves the effectiveness of embracing modernity, Hirata's final act is an unwavering, ultimate assertion of the traditional values he embodied. Faced with a world that has validated the very methods he scorned, his meticulously performed suicide becomes a final, poignant statement of allegiance to the "way of the warrior," even as the era necessitating such codes draws to a close.

Battle of Tsushima (1905), by Tōjō Shōtarō

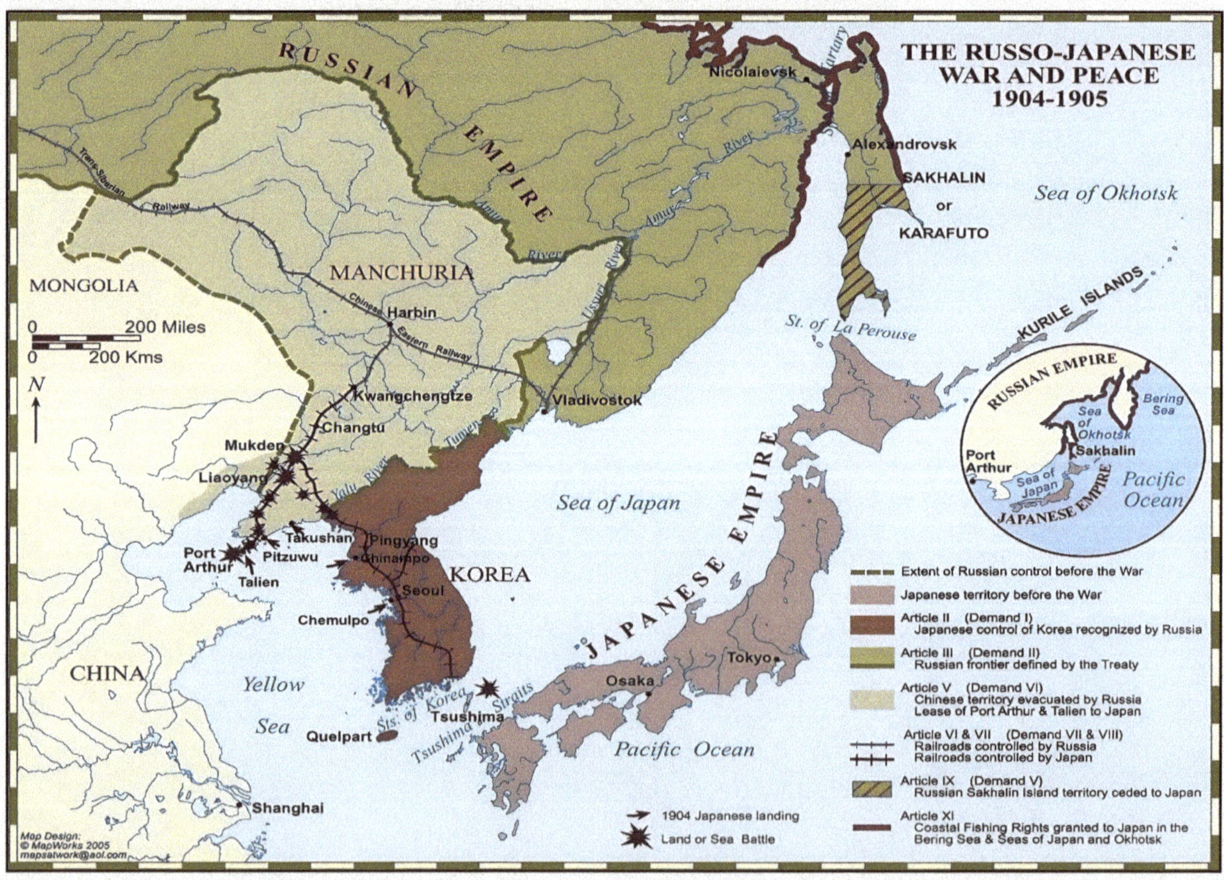

Commissioned by Japan-America Society of New Hampshire for portsmouthpeacetreaty.org

Map Design © MapWorks 2005, MAPSatWORK@aol.com

Tsushima's Ghosts

From Farrère's *Battle* to the Tōgō-Nimitz Enigma

By Kent Davis

In 2025, a reporter conducting man-on-the-street interviews would be hard-pressed to find *anyone* who knew *anything* about the Russo-Japanese War…let alone about the Battle of Tsushima. The conflict is largely lost to modern memory, yet its echoes resonate through history in startling and unexpected ways. Imagine a single naval battle so devastating, so absolute in its outcome, that the repercussions transcended the immediate conflict by reshaping the global balance of power. The Battle of Tsushima was such a battle. This clash of steel and fire between the Imperial Japanese Navy and the Russian Second Pacific Squadron was so decisive that it quickly ended the Russo-Japanese War. It was also a watershed moment in the history of naval warfare, military technology, and international relations.

This paper, however, will go far beyond describing a battle that took place 120 years ago. It delves into the enigma hinted at in our title, uncovering for the first time historical details that weave threads of connection, improbable coincidences, and even echoes of fate linking legendary admirals across oceans of time and multiple generations. Consider this: who would imagine that Admiral Tōgō, hailed as the greatest naval commander of his era, would share a bottle of Russian champagne with a 20-year-old sailor whose future led *directly* to the unconditional surrender of Japan at the end of World War II? But, as you'll soon read, that is precisely what happened.

The flashpoint was on May 27, 1905 when Japanese and Russian fleets clashed in combat in the Sea of Japan. The ensuing melee became a milestone of history: it was the *only* decisive engagement ever fought between modern steel battleship fleets[1]; it was the first time in history

---

1 While major naval battles involving battleships occurred in World War I and World War II, the Battle of Tsushima was unique in its decisiveness and the context of its time.

The Battle of Jutland (1916) in WWI, the largest surface battle of that war, was a major that modern battleships were sunk; and it was the first naval battle in which wireless telegraphy (radio) played a critically important role. British historian Sir George Clark described it as "by far the greatest and the most important naval event since Trafalgar."[2]

Fittingly, the architect of this stunning victory, Japanese Admiral Tōgō Heihachirō, was immediately hailed by Western journalists and admirers worldwide as 'the Nelson of the East.'[3] This wasn't merely a casual comparison; it reflected the immense scale of his achievement and, significantly, Tōgō's own profound, lifelong admiration for the British hero whose Trafalgar tactics he adapted at Tsushima.

When it happened, author Claude Farrère was a twenty-nine-year-old naval officer near the beginning of his prolific literary career. In 1905, his book *The Civilized* was awarded the prestigious Prix Goncourt in France. Four years later, in 1909, Farrère published *La Bataille* (*The Battle*), his own fictionalized account of the fight. While Farrère crafted a novel, he was meticulous in his historical and technical descriptions of the event.

His motive for fictionalization? To present a subtler, more symbolic account capturing the conflict's essence from a Japanese perspective. Farrère portrayed the existential battle as a conflict between East and West, embodied by his characters. In his preface, the author alludes to his Japanese protagonists stating, "I am also fully convinced that, to really defeat Russia and Europe all the men and women of the Empire were ready to sacrifice a thousand and ten thousand cherished things, including their honor as a man and their virtue as a woman, even if it

---

clash between British and German dreadnought battleships, but it was less decisive than Tsushima. Both sides claimed victory, and while the German fleet was damaged, it was not destroyed, and the strategic situation in the North Sea remained largely unchanged.

In WWII, naval warfare evolved significantly with the rise of aircraft carriers, which became the dominant force in naval engagements. While battleships still played important roles, their influence was diminished, and battles like the Battle of the Philippine Sea or the Battle of Midway were largely determined by carrier-based aircraft, not battleship engagements. In contrast, Tsushima stands as the only instance of a clash between two fleets primarily composed of battleships.

2 Sir George Sydenham Clarke, 1st Baron Sydenham of Combe (July 4, 1848 – Feb 7, 1933) was a British Army officer and colonial administrator.

3 The ubiquity of this epithet is detailed by Jonathan Clements in *Admiral Tōgō: Nelson of the East* (London: Haus Publishing, 2010), Introduction. Clements notes its use across numerous international newspapers (e.g., *Western Mail, Glasgow Herald, New York Truth, Newcastle Chronicle*) and observes: "Nelson was Tōgō's hero, a figure who inspired him during his student days in England... Indeed, the concept was soon embraced by the Japanese themselves, who never seemed to tire of styling themselves as the 'British of Asia,' or comparing Tōgō to the victorious admiral of Trafalgar." Tellingly, the poet Doi Bansui later reversed the cliché in a funeral song for Tōgō, referring to Nelson as the 'Tōgō of England.'

meant washing such glorious stains in all the blood of a disemboweled body afterward."

My goal in this article is to objectively examine the facts, analyzing Farrère's accuracy while exploring the incredible, almost uncanny connections that emerged from this conflict — connections Farrère himself never knew. Following the threads suggested by Farrère's era, the most surprising discoveries first involved learning how integral the United States was in ending the Russo-Japanese war, but later revealed how the life of Japanese Admiral Tōgō Heihachirō became intertwined with the destiny of a famous American admiral through a chance encounter.

First, we'll journey back to the turn of the 20th century to see how this conflict arose. Then we'll view the naval battle that stunned the world in detail. Finally, we'll uncover the surprising anomalies and hidden links connecting samurai codes of honor, America's fading Wild West, bleeding edge military technology, American icon Teddy Roosevelt, a quiet resort on the coast of Maine, the preservation of Admiral Tōgō's flagship *Mikasa* — revealing patterns that seem to rhyme with our headlines today. Perhaps you'll be as shocked as I was by some of these discoveries. Let us now explore how all this came to pass.

Weakness in China: Seeds of the Russo-Japanese War

The late 1890s was a period of intense imperial competition in East Asia. China, weakened by Qing dynasty corruption and vulnerable to foreign encroachment, saw European powers, the United States, and the rising Empire of Japan all vying for control. Known as the "Scramble for China" or the "Partition of China," the trend of "New Imperialism" drove outside powers seeking to establish their own exclusive spheres of influence,

Russia had gained significant ground in the north, notably securing control of Chinese territory in Manchuria, thereby establishing a strong regional sphere of influence. Russia enforced its advantage with land-based military troops and the Russian Pacific Fleet based at Port Arthur, a naval base located on the Liaodong Peninsula. Their increasing dominance led to tensions with Japan, which was also expanding its power, particularly in Korea and Manchuria.

On February 8, 1904, Japan confronted the Russian threat directly; destroyers of the Imperial Japanese Navy, commanded by Admiral Tōgō Heihachirō (Jan 27, 1848 – May 30, 1934), launched a surprise attack on

"China -- the cake of kings and… of emperors." This 1898 French political cartoon vividly captures the imperialism of European powers and Japan towards China in the late 1890s. A stereotypical Qing official looks on, powerless to stop the partitioning of a pastry representing "Chine" (French for China). Left to right, we see caricatures of Queen Victoria of the United Kingdom, William II of Germany, Nicholas II of Russia, the French Marianne (diplomatically shown as not participating, symbolizing the Franco-Russian Alliance), and a samurai representing Japan, carefully contemplating which pieces to take.

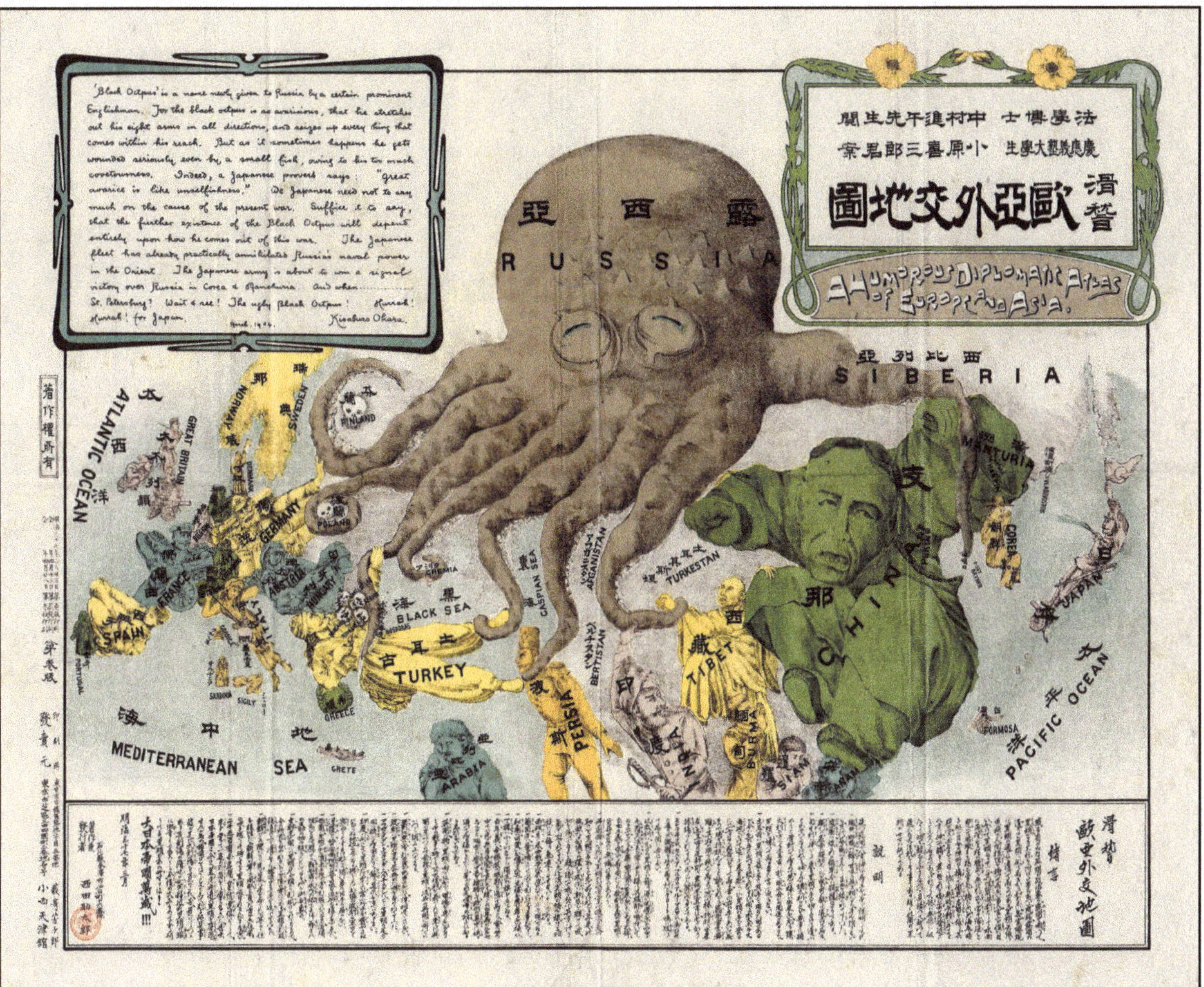

A Humorous Diplomatic Atlas of Europe and Asia:

'Black Octopus' is a name newly given to Russia by a certain prominent Englishman. JOY the black octopus is so avaricious, that he stretches out his eight arms in all directions, and seizes up everything that comes within his reach. But as it sometimes happens, he gets wounded seriously even by a small fish, owing to his too much covetousness. Indeed, a Japanese proverb says: "Great avarice is like unselfishness."

We Japanese need not to say much on the cause of the present war. Suffice it to say, that the further existence of the Black Octopus will depend entirely upon how he comes out of this war. The Japanese fleet has already practically annihilated Russia's naval power in the Orient. The Japanese army is about to win a signal victory over Russia in Corea & Manchuria.

And when....St. Petersburg? Wait & see!

The ugly Black Octopus! Hurrah! Hurrah! For Japan. March, 1904

—**Kisaburo Ohara**

The Battle of Port Arthur (8–9 February 1904), by Kasai Torajiro.

the Russian Far East Fleet anchored in Port Arthur,[4] damaging three ships. This daring strike was the opening salvo of the Russo-Japanese War, with Japan fighting to secure its power, commerce, and communication lines with the Asian mainland. Neutralizing Russian naval power in the Far East was paramount to achieving this goal.

Incapacitating the Russian navy at the beginning of the war allowed Japanese expansion in Korea unopposed. The arrival of Vice Admiral Stepan Makarov (Jan 8, 1849–Apr 13, 1904) briefly revitalized the Russian efforts, and he achieved some success against the Japanese. This resurgence, however, was short-lived. On April 13, 1904, Makarov's flagship, the pre-dreadnought battleship *Petropavlovsk*, struck a mine, detonating the ship's magazine. The ship quickly sank with 27 officers, 652 enlisted men, and Admiral Makarov

---

4   Established as Lüshun Port in the 1880s for the Beiyang Fleet of the Qing dynasty, control of this base changed several times in the first half of the 20th Century: from China to the Russian Empire (1895-1904), to the Empire of Japan (1905-1945), to the Soviet Union (1945-1956), and finally back to China in 1956.

Russian Admiral Makarov.

himself aboard, causing Russian morale at the fort to plummet.

By May 1904, the Japanese had landed forces on the Liaodong Peninsula, and by August, they had begun their siege of Port Arthur. Worse still for the Russians, the Japanese Navy had blockaded Port Arthur by sea, so the remaining Russian battleships and armored cruisers found themselves effectively trapped. Russo-German Admiral Wilgelm Vitgeft (Oct 14, 1847 – Aug 10, 1904), appointed temporary commander after Makarov's death, made one aborted attempt to break out on June 23. Apart from that, the new admiral chose to simply stay at anchor, but his superiors in Russia didn't agree. Faced with an Imperial writ and threat of legal action, Admiral Vitgeft was ordered to sail for Vladivostok.

At 06:15 AM on August 10, 1904, flying his flag in the battleship *Tsesarevich*, the admiral began leading his fleet from the harbor. He was accompanied by the battleships *Retvizan*, *Pobeda*, *Peresvet*, *Sevastopol*, and *Poltava*, the protected cruisers *Askold*, *Diana*, *Novik*, and *Pallada*, and 14 destroyers. Despite his intimidating armada, Admiral Tōgō led the Imperial Japanese Navy's Combined Fleet to intercept the Russians resulting in the Battle of the Yellow Sea. At 18:40 PM that same day, Admiral Vitgeft and his immediate staff were killed instantly when a 12-inch salvo from the Japanese battleship *Asahi* struck the upper bridge of the *Tsesarevich*.

Sinking of the Russian cruiser *Rurik* in the Battle off Ulsan.

The shell also jammed the flagship's steering, throwing the Russian line into confusion. Five battleships, a cruiser and nine destroyers escaped back to Port Arthur;

the damaged *Tsesarevich* and three escorting destroyers sailed to Qingdao, where they were interned by Imperial German authorities under Governor Oskar von Truppel. Four days later on August 14, 1904 the Russians lost the armored cruiser *Rurik* and nearly 1,000 men at the Battle of Ulsan. Russia was in danger of losing all its influence in East Asia.

Summoning the Baltic Fleet

With the First Pacific Squadron neutralized and the Japanese tightening their grip on Port Arthur, the Russians were faced with a fateful decision in September 1904: should they dispatch a significant portion of their Baltic Fleet to the Far East? The ambitious objectives were to relieve Port Arthur, join forces with the remaining squadron, overwhelm the Japanese Navy, and stall the Japanese advance until reinforcements could arrive via the already strained Trans-Siberian railroad.

The Imperial Russian Admiralty Council vigorously opposed this plan, citing the Japanese navy's preparedness, combat experience, and the impossibility of meaningful training during the Russian fleet's long voyage. Worse still, their Baltic crews were woefully inexperienced.

Key battleships had only just completed sea trials weeks earlier. The newest Russian battleship *Borodino* had only undergone sea trials from August 23 to September 13, 1904, Her sister ship, *Knyaz Suvorov*, began trials on August 9, and the *Oryol* even later on September 10, leaving *Imperator Aleksandr III* as the only *Borodino*-class[5] ship fully ready for deployment. The need for thousands of new crewmen for the expanding Borodino-class fleet led to a decline in training quality in general. The Admiralty recommended training in the Baltic until spring.

On August 23, Tsar Nicholas II (May 18, 1868 – July 17, 1918) convened a council at the Peterhof Grand Palace. The Tsar overruled the Admiralty's opinion, backed by Admiral Zinovy Rozhestvensky (Nov 11, 1848–Jan 14, 1909), and Navy Minister Theodor Kristian Avellan. A key factor was a massive, non-cancellable coaling contract the navy had

---

5   The Borodino-class was a class of pre-dreadnought battleships built for the Imperial Russian Navy. These ships, displacing approximately 14,000 tons, represented the last generation of battleships before the advent of the dreadnought.

The term "pre-dreadnought" refers to battleships built before the launch of HMS Dreadnought in 1906. Pre-dreadnoughts like the Borodino-class typically featured a mixed battery of large-caliber guns (such as 12-inch) and smaller caliber guns. The HMS Dreadnought revolutionized battleship design by featuring an "all-big-gun" armament of 12-inch guns and steam turbine propulsion, which made existing battleships obsolete.

THE CZAR'S BALTIC FLEET IS ENROTE TO THE FAR EAST.—NEWS ITEM.

already signed with the Hamburg-American Steamship Line; essential because neutral nations couldn't legally allow Russian warships to refuel in their ports. Perhaps the loss of face Russia had suffered, as evidenced by contemporary cartoons, was an even greater factor.

With the matter decided, the Tsar chose Admiral Rozhestvensky to command the Second Pacific Squadron. Rozhestvensky — an iron-fisted commander affectionately nicknamed 'Mad Dog' — would lead an untested fleet with untrained sailors on the longest coal-powered battleship voyage in history. Soon, 11 of Russia's 13 battleships departed between October 1904 and February 1905, traveling over 18,000 nautical miles (33,000 km) to the Tsushima Strait. Their mission: reach Vladivostok, establish naval control, ostensibly break the Port Arthur blockade, and relieve the army in Manchuria. While numerically superior in battleships, the Russian fleet was older, slower, and outnumbered by the Japanese nearly three-to-one in total ships.

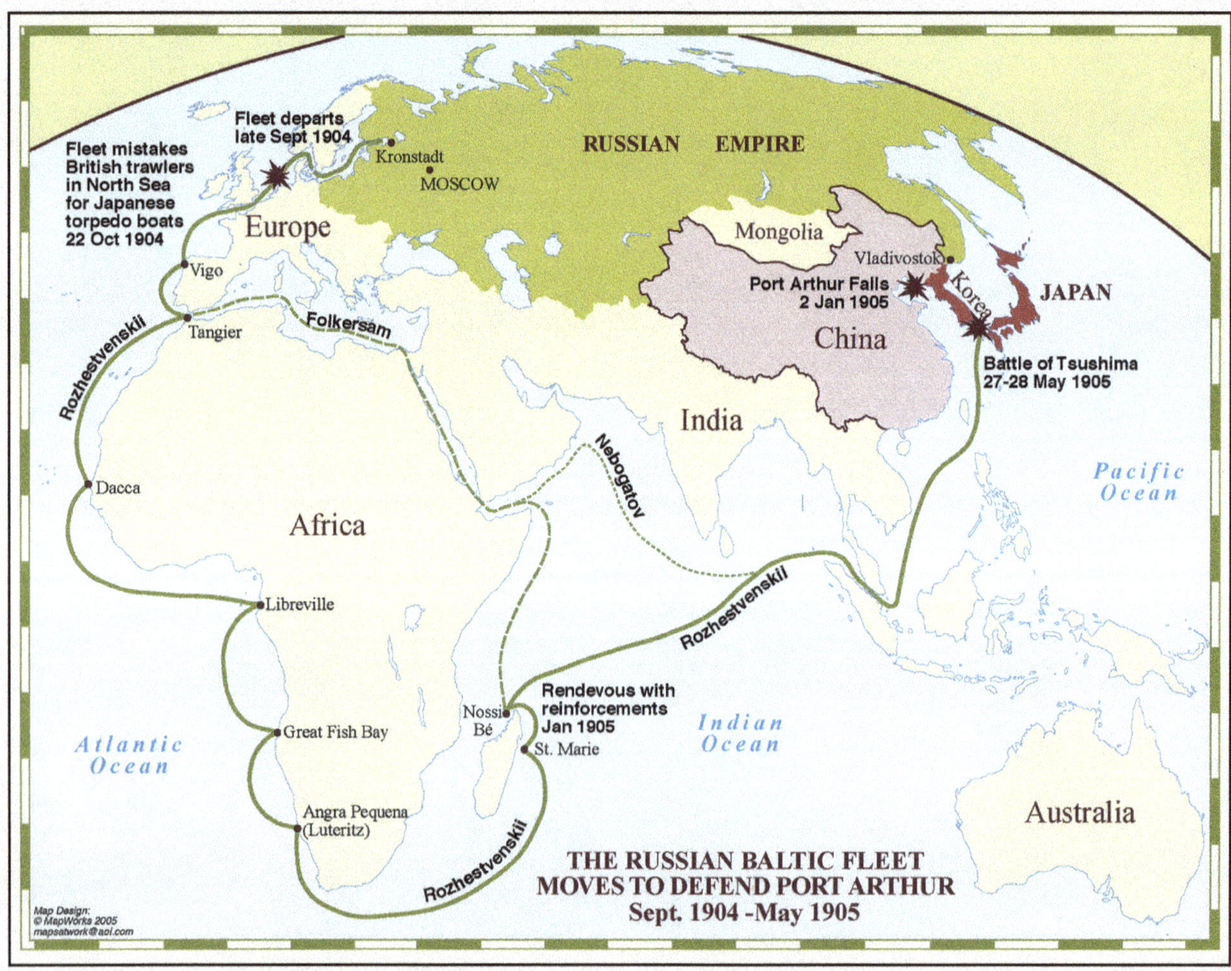

Commissioned by Japan-America Society of New Hampshire for portsmouthpeacetreaty.org
Map Design © MapWorks 2005, MAPSatWORK@aol.com

An Inauspicious Beginning to a Logistical Nightmare

Almost immediately, tragedy struck. Sailing through the Oresund strait[6] into the North Sea, the inexperienced crews were on high alert due to false reports of Japanese torpedo boats lurking in the area. In a moment of panic and misidentification, they mistook British fishing trawlers near Dogger Bank for hostile ships. They unleashed a barrage of fire on the defenseless civilian vessels, killing British fishermen and damaging seven boats. In the chaos, they even fired on two of their own ships, resulting in casualties among their own men.

The firing lasted for a tense twenty minutes before Rozhestvensky ordered it to cease. The British public was outraged, finding it inconceivable that the Russians could mistake fishing trawlers for Japanese warships thousands of kilometers from the nearest Japanese port. Allied with Japan, Britain was nearly drawn into the war. France, seeking to foster an anti-German alliance between Britain and Russia, diplomatically persuaded Britain to refrain from declaring war. The Russians were compelled to remove officers suspected of misconduct to face an International Court of Inquiry in Paris. Ultimately, Russia accepted responsibility for the incident and provided compensation to the fishermen. This "Dogger Bank Incident," as it became known, was a humiliating start to an already daunting voyage.

The fleet's continuing voyage evolved into a logistical nightmare. Newer battleships couldn't use the Suez Canal due to their size, forcing the fleet to split. Rozhestvensky took the newer battleships, cruisers, fast auxiliaries, and destroyers around Africa's Cape of Good Hope, while Admiral von Fölkersahm (Apr 29, 1846 – 24 May 1905) took the older battleships and cruisers through the Suez, rendezvousing months later in Madagascar. Even halfway through their trip, the long journey was taking a heavy toll. Conditions deteriorated with respiratory disease spreading, claiming the lives of a number of sailors. Rough seas led to higher fuel consumption than anticipated, and neutrality laws made obtaining coal difficult, despite their contract. All told, the Russians required an estimated 500,000 short tons of coal and 30 to 40 re-coaling sessions to reach French Indochina!

As Farrère accurately portrayed in *The Battle*, the United Kingdom played a significant role in Japan's conflict with Russia via the Anglo-

---

6   The Øresund or Öresund strait forms the Danish–Swedish border. It is 118 kilometers (73 mi) long and its width varies from 4 kilometers (2.5 mi) to 28 kilometers (17 mi).

Japanese Alliance. Britain provided ships, training, weapons, intelligence, and finance. With its vast network of harbor facilities, shipyards, and coaling stations, Britain also controlled more resources than Russia and its allies (France and Germany), thus obstructing Russian attempts to purchase ships and coal.

France, despite claiming neutrality in the conflict, allowed the Russian fleet warships into Cherbourg and Tangier ports, even after the Dogger Bank Incident. Great Britain formally protested, pointing out that neutral countries could not accept warships of warring nations without internment, and that if France was no longer neutral, the UK would be obligated to support Japan under the Anglo-Japanese Alliance.

Subsequently, the rendezvous point for the Rozhestvensky and Fölkersahm squadrons was changed from the French protectorate of Diego Suarez to the waters around Île Sainte-Marie and Nosy Be in Madagascar. This created a major logistical challenge for the Baltic Fleet's deployment, forcing them to anchor for nearly two months each off Nosy Be in Madagascar, further impacting crew morale. By April-May 1905, the fleet finally reunited in French Indochina, anchoring outside of Saigon and Ba Ngoi in Cam Ranh Bay, but the French prudently denied them port access.

By then, however, the original objective — relieving Port Arthur — had become obsolete; the city had fallen in January 1905 and its battleships were sunk by land artillery. The new goal was simply to reach Vladivostok and reunite with their remaining ships before engaging the Japanese.

Commanders and Forces: A Study in Contrasts

Heading north to Vladivostok, the Russian fleet had three potential routes to cross the Sea of Japan: sailing east of Japan to the Soya Strait, north of Hokkaido; sailing east of Japan and crossing the Tsugaru Strait, to the south of Hokkaido; or taking the shortest and most direct route, through the Tsushima Strait between the Japanese island of Kyushu and the Korean Peninsula. Admiral Rozhestvensky kept his choice a closely guarded secret until May 25, when he ordered the fleet to head northeast towards Tsushima. It was here, in the waters near the Tsushima Islands, that the Japanese Combined Fleet and the Russian Second and Third Pacific Squadrons, now numbering 38 ships, would clash in a battle for naval supremacy.

The opposing commanders, Admiral Tōgō and Admiral Rozhestvensky, were both born in 1848 but shared little else. Tōgō, born

Marshal Admiral Tōgō Heihachiro

Admiral Zinovy Rozhestvensky

to a samurai family two decades before the Meiji Restoration, had been a warrior his entire life. He was one of the few modern warship commanders who had actually seen combat, giving him a decisive advantage. Tōgō had already demonstrated his tactical prowess by commanding the operations that led to the deaths of two Russian admirals: Stepan Makarov outside of Port Arthur in the battleship *Petropavlovsk* on April 13, 1904, and Wilgelm Vitgeft in his battleship *Tsesarevich* in August of the same year.

Before their deaths, Tōgō had chased Finland-Swedish Admiral Oskar Starck (Aug 6, 1846 – Nov 13, 1928), who was also flying his flag in the *Petropavlovsk*. In addition to these skirmishes, Tōgō and his men had gained valuable combat experience in battleship fleet actions at Port Arthur and the Yellow Sea, giving them a significant edge over the less experienced Russians. Moreover, since the beginning of the war, the Japanese fleets had engaged in extensive gunnery practice, utilizing sub-caliber practice guns, honing their accuracy and efficiency.[7]

---

7 Sub-caliber guns are smaller guns mounted inside larger naval guns. They were used for practice to conserve ammunition and reduce wear on the main guns. Sub-caliber rounds allowed for more frequent training, improving the gunnery skills of the crew.

As noted, Russia's Baltic fleet, particularly the new Borodino-class ships, had limited training before their arduous voyage. By the time they reached Tsushima, the fleet was exhausted. Ships carried extra coal on deck and hulls were heavily fouled,[8] reducing speed and maneuverability—a critical disadvantage against the swift Japanese whose well-maintained ships were organized into divisions of uniform speed and range.

New Naval Technologies: The Keys to Victory

Beyond leadership and crew condition, technology proved decisive.

Wireless Telegraphy: Invented in the late 1890s, major navies rapidly adopted the wireless telegraph (radio) and the upcoming Battle of Tsushima was "the first major sea battle in which wireless played any role whatsoever."[9] Japanese Lieutenant Akiyama Saneyuki (Apr 12, 1868 – Feb 4, 1918), a naval attaché to the United States, recognized the potential of wireless telegraphy during the Spanish-American War and urged the Japanese Imperial Navy General Staff to acquire the new technology. Finding the Marconi wireless system too expensive, the Japanese developed their own system under Professor Kimura Shunkichi (1866–1938). By 1901, they achieved transmissions up to 60 miles (97 km) and formally began using the technology. By the start of the Russo-Japanese War, every major warship in the Combined Fleet was equipped with wireless sets produced at the Imperial Japanese Navy Mines Training School in Yokosuka.

On the Russian side, Alexander Popov of the Naval Warfare Institute had built and demonstrated a wireless telegraphy set in 1900, but they lagged behind Germany and Japan in technology and production.[10] Despite Popov's inventions, the Imperial Russian Navy chose to adopt the "System Slaby-Arco" from Allgemeine Elektricitäts-Gesellschaft (AEG) and Telefunken in Germany, widely used by the Kaiserliche Marine. While

---

8   Hull fouling is the accumulation of marine organisms on the hull of a ship, including algae, barnacles, mollusks, and other sea creatures. Historically, copper sheathing was used to prevent fouling, as copper is toxic to many marine organisms. Modern methods include anti-fouling paints that release toxins or create a surface that is difficult for organisms to adhere to. Regular cleaning of the hull is also necessary, which can be done manually or with specialized equipment. Having been at sea for an extended period, the Russian ships' hulls were heavily fouled, reducing both speed and maneuverability, making them less able to evade or engage the Japanese fleet effectively.

9   Evans, David C; Peattie, Mark R (1997). *Kaigun: strategy, tactics, and technology in the Imperial Japanese Navy, 1887–1941*. Annapolis, Maryland: Naval Institute Press. ISBN 0-87021-192-7. Pg. 84.

10   Alexander Stepanovich Popov (Ma 16, 1859 – January 13, 1906) was a Russian physicist who was one of the first people to invent a radio receiving device. In a March 24, 1896 demonstration, he transmitted radio signals 250 meters between different campus buildings in St. Petersburg.

both sides possessed early wireless telegraphy, the Russians used German sets maintained by German technicians, while the Japanese had their own indigenous equipment, maintained and operated by navy specialists trained at the Yokosuka school, giving them a significant advantage in both reliability and operational skill.

Gunnery Fire Control: Until the Battle of the Yellow Sea on August 10, 1904, a gunnery officer assigned to each gun or turret controlled the guns locally. They determined elevation and deflection, issued firing orders, monitored inclinometers for ship roll and pitch, and adjusted aim based on spotters' reports. With the new 12-inch guns extending range to over 8 miles (13 km), these traditional vantage points became inadequate.

Just months before the battle, Japanese Lieutenant Commander Katō Hiroharu (Dec 23, 1870 – Feb 9, 1939), the Chief Gunnery Officer of the *Asahi*, introduced a revolutionary system for centrally issuing gun-laying and salvo-firing orders by voice, inspired by the early mechanical Dumaresq computer.[11] This central system allowed spotters to more effectively identify salvo splashes and track firing, while the 'director' officer on the bridge had a superior vantage point and close proximity to the ship commander for course and speed adjustments.

The Japanese implemented the Dumaresq system on a number of ships, while conducting extensive training and practice while awaiting the Baltic Fleet. Consequently, Japanese fire was more accurate at longer, 3–8 mile ranges (5–13 km), complementing their advantage at shorter distances with the latest 1903 Barr and Stroud FA3 coincidence rangefinders, effective up to 6,000 yards (5,500 m).[12] Russian battleships, equipped with older Lugeol stadiametric rangefinders that had a range of only about 4,400 yards (4,000 m) (Russia had only retrofitted the *Oslyabya* and *Navarin* with Barr and Stroud 1895 FA2), were significantly outmatched in rangefinding capability.[13]

---

11   Invented by British Royal Navy officer Lieutenant John Dumaresq, the Dumaresq was an early mechanical computer used for fire control on ships. It helped calculate gunnery solutions by taking into account various factors such as the speed and course of the target ship, the ship's own motion, and wind conditions.

12   The British optical engineering firm Barr and Stroud developed the FA3 coincidence rangefinder; a state-of-the-art optical instrument used to measure the distance to a target. Effective up to 6,000 yards (5,500 m), the "coincidence" aspect refers to the method used by the operator to align two half-images for range determination.

13   Stadiametric rangefinders are optical devices that measure distance by comparing the known height of an object with its apparent height as seen through the instrument. The Lugeol rangefinders were older technology, limiting the range at which the Russian battleships could effectively target their opponents.

Explosive Chemistry: Explosives composition was a crucial factor for both sides. The Japanese primarily used high-explosive shells filled with Shimose powder (pure picric acid), stabilized using a special lacquer coating. Undiluted Shimose had higher detonation velocity and temperature than contemporary explosives. Used with sensitive Ijuin base fuses,[14] these shells exploded on contact, maximizing damage to upper structures. The Japanese fuses also exploded on hitting the water, creating splashes that destabilized Russian inclinometers. The Russians continued using older armor-piercing rounds with guncotton bursting charges and insensitive delayed-detonation fuses, primarily using brown powder or black powder as propellant. These often didn't detonate on hitting water, hindering Russian range correction as misses were less obvious.

Ironically, it was Vice Admiral Makarov, — killed on April 13, 1904 when his flagship, the *Petropavlovsk*, struck a Japanese mine — who had tried to solve Russia's firepower problem in the early 1890s. As then Chief Inspector of Russian naval artillery, Makarov proposed a new 12-inch gun design and assigned a junior officer, Semyon V. Panpushko, to research picric acid as a shell explosive. On November 28, 1891, Panpushko was filling shells with Melinite when a huge explosion killed him and two assistants. After this, experimentation to make Melinite more stable stopped and high-explosive shells remained out of reach for the Russian Navy. Consequently, Japanese hits caused more damage to Russian ships carrying these unstable high-explosives, than Russian hits on Japanese ships.

Range and Rate of Fire: The late Admiral Makarov's 1890s munitions work also influenced the battle in another unusual way. In addition to his experiments with explosives, he proposed a 12-inch gun design that increased the range of the older 12-inch Krupp guns (installed on *Imperator Nikolai I* and *Navarin*) from 5-6 km to 11 km (at 15-degrees elevation). This increased range, however, came at the cost of a significantly limited amount of explosives in the 332 kg (732 lb) shell. The reload time was improved from 2–4 minutes to a rated 90 seconds, but in reality, it was 2.5–3 minutes. These guns were installed on the *Sissoi Veliky* and the four *Borodino*-class ships.

The four Japanese battleships, *Mikasa, Shikishima, Fuji,* and *Asahi*, had the latest Armstrong 12-inch 40-caliber naval guns, designed and manufactured by Sir W.G. Armstrong & Company. These British-built 12-

---

14 Japanese technology developed by Vice-Admiral Baron Ijūin Gorō, (Sep 29, 1852 – Jan 13,1921) a career Japanese naval officer and engineer.

inch guns had a range of 15,000 yards (14 km) at 15-degrees elevation and a rate of fire of 60 seconds with a heavier 850 lb (390 kg) shell. The Royal Navy was initially hesitant to adopt this gun type due to accidental shell explosions on Japanese battleships up to the Battle of the Yellow Sea, but the Japanese Navy had largely rectified this issue by the time of the Battle of Tsushima with the use of the Ijuin Fuse.

The Russian fleet had 20 of the longer-range 12" guns on five battleships, compared to the Japanese having 16 of the Armstrong 12" guns on four battleships. While the Russians had a 20% advantage in the number of guns, they were significantly disadvantaged by the 60% difference in the rate of fire; the Japanese could fire one shot per minute compared to the Russian's one shot per 2.5 minutes. The range difference (11 km vs. 14 km) also gave the Japanese shells a flatter trajectory, resulting in a better hit rate when both sides were at equal distances of 11 km or less.

The Battle: A Two-Day Clash of Titans

Within hours, an empire was defeated and naval warfare changed forever. The battle unfolded on May 27 as the Russian fleet approached from the south-southwest, maintaining radio silence under fog. At 04:45 AM,[15] the Japanese auxiliary cruiser *Shinano Maru* spotted three lights on the horizon and moved closer to investigate. These emanated from the Russian hospital ship *Orel*, which, adhering to the rules of war, had her lights on. The *Shinano Maru* approached the vessel, noting that she carried no guns and appeared to be an auxiliary ship. The *Orel*, mistaking *Shinano Maru* for another Russian vessel, did not alert the fleet but signaled to *Shinano Maru* in Russian code, which the Japanese ship did not understand. *Shinano Maru* then sighted ten other Russian ships in the mist.

This seemingly minor encounter had far-reaching consequences, as wireless telegraphy played its pivotal role from the very beginning. At 04:55, Captain Narikawa of the *Shinano Maru* sent a wireless message to the Combined Fleet command onboard *Mikasa* in Masampo: "Enemy is in grid 203." By 05:00, intercepted radio signals confirmed to the Russians that they had been discovered and that Japanese scouting cruisers were shadowing them. Admiral Tōgō received the message at 05:05 and began preparing his battle fleet for a sortie, which began at 06:05.

By 07:00, Cruiser *Izumi* relieved *Shinano Maru* of its reporting

---

15 All times following are Japan Standard Time (JST).

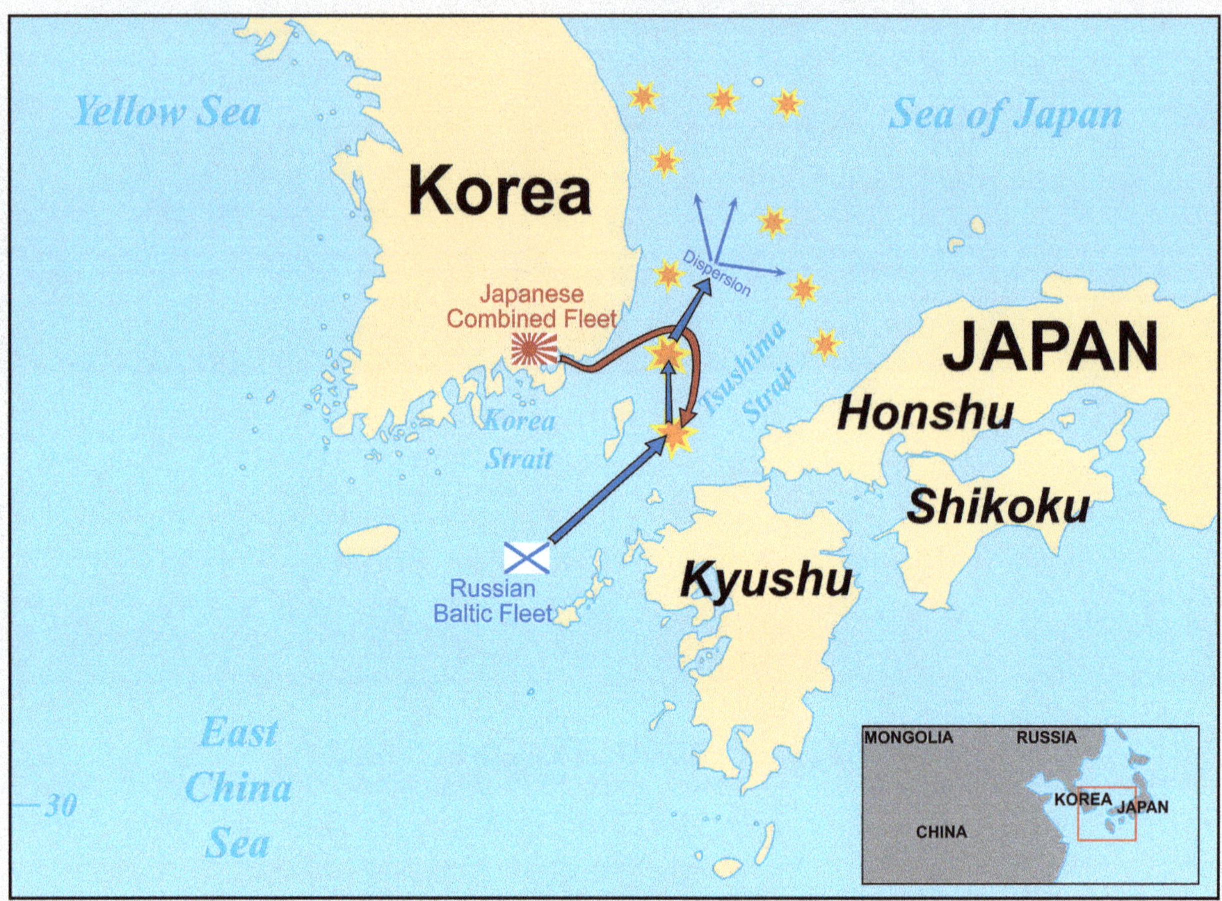

Routes of the Russian and Japanese fleets on 27–28 May 1905.

task, closing in to 10,000 meters of Russian battleship *Knyaz Suvorov*, and shadowing the Baltic Fleet alone. At 10:00, Admiral Tōgō sends a confident wireless message to the Imperial General Headquarters: "Upon receiving its spotting report, Combined Fleet is going into battle with enemy fleet today near Okinoshima Island. Today's weather is fine but waves are high."

Now the entire Japanese fleet was mobilized, steaming from northeast to southwest, with Admiral Tōgō leading over 40 vessels from his flagship *Mikasa*. The shadowing Japanese scouting vessels sent wireless reports every few minutes, providing crucial information about the formation and course of the Russian fleet. Despite heavy fog that reduced visibility, wireless communication gave the Japanese a decisive advantage. In his report on the battle, Admiral Tōgō remarked: "Though a heavy fog covered the sea, making it impossible to observe anything at a distance of over five miles, [through wireless messaging] all the conditions of the enemy were as clear to us, who were 30 or 40 miles distant, as though they had been under our very eyes."

This 1906 painting by Tōjō Shōtarō depicts Admiral Tōgō Heihachirō on the bridge of the Battleship Mikasa. Left to right: messenger Yamazaki Genki, navigator Second Lieutenant Edahara Yurikazu, staff Major Iida Hisatsune, chief navigator Lieutenant Colonel Nunome Mitsuzō, aide-de-camp of gunnery officer Lieutenant Imamura Nobujirō, captain of Mikasa Captain Ijichi Hikojirō, gunnery officer Major Abo Kiyokazu, 4th grade sailor Noguchi Shinzō, chief of staff Rear-Admiral Katō Tomosaburō, measurement officer Cadet Lieutenant Hasegawa Kiyoshi, Commander-in-chief of the Combined Fleet Tōgō Heihachirō, staff Lieutenant Colonel Akiyama Saneyuki, 1st grade sailor Miura Tadashi, cadet Tamaki Shinsuke.

Over the next two hours, the Japanese defined the Russian fleet formation, and by 11:30 their 3rd battle division battleships (*Kasagi*, *Chitose*, *Otowa*, *Niitaka*) were shadowing the Baltic Fleet's left flank.

At 11:55, Tōgō gathered all hands on *Mikasa's* rear deck, describing the situation and saying "Accurate aim on all the shots is the foremost and the only wish I have at this moment." At 12:38, Admiral Tōgō ordered 'Battle stations' on the *Mikasa* as both fleets prepared to engage in the long-

The Japanese fleet heads into battle.

awaited battle. A little more than an hour later, at 13:54, *Mikasa* was 12,000 meters from the *Oslyabya*. Tōgō ordered the hoisting of the Z flag, as seen in the illustration above, the prearranged signal to the entire fleet, proclaiming: "The Empire's fate depends on the result of this battle, let every man do his utmost duty."

At 14:00, Tōgō ordered a 180-degree turn in sequence, aligning the *Mikasa* and his five following ships with Russian's course. At 14:03, *Oslyabya* opened fire from 9,000 meters. Although Tōgō's U-turn (later famously known as the "Tōgō Turn") was successful, the initial Russian gunnery proved surprisingly effective; the flagship *Mikasa* took 15 hits in less than ten minutes. Though Russian shells were hitting the *Mikasa*, she and other Japanese ships began hitting the *Oslyabya*, which immediately lost its front mast and center stack. The superior Japanese gunnery soon began taking its toll, with more Russian battleships suffering crippling damage.

As the Japanese approached, Rozhestvensky ordered his fleet to move from a line formation to parallel columns. At the end of the line, *Oslyabya* was forced to reverse engines to avoid hitting battleship *Oryol* as she maneuvered. Shells continued to inflict heavy damage, knocking out the *Oslyabya's* rangefinder, wounding the gunnery officer, and severing the cables connecting the guns to the fire-control system. Other hits shot away the mainmast, knocked out the forward gun turret, and three of the port six-inch guns. Splinters entered her conning tower, killing the quartermaster and wounding most of the men inside.

This damage caused the ship to fall completely out of line, and she was quickly engaged by six Japanese armored cruisers at short range. Large-caliber shells struck along the ship's waterline, causing major flooding. Her bow opened to the sea, and she began listing to port. Captain Vladimir Ber (the ship's captain) ordered flooding of her starboard forward magazine to counteract the list, but that added too much weight forward destroying the ship's stability. By 14:20 *Oslyabya's* list increased to 12 degrees, flooding the lower turrets. Her funnels touched the water around 15:10, and the captain ordered "abandon ship." The ship sank with her starboard propeller still turning, taking Ber and 470 of her crew with her. Only ninety minutes into the battle, the Russians had lost the *Oslyabya,* marking a grim milestone: this was the first time a modern armored battleship had been sunk by gunfire alone.

The complex battle raged. Admiral Rozhestvensky was taken out of action when a shell fragment struck his skull. At 17:30, the Russian destroyer *Buyniy* rescued Rozhestvensky and from the heavily damaged *Knyaz Suvorov.* At 17:51, the Japanese sunk the Russian auxiliary cruiser *Ural,* before concentrating salvos on *Imperator Aleksandr III,* which caught on fire at 18:16. The Japanese main group then switched to targeting the *Borodino.*

At 19:03, *Imperator Aleksandr III* sank and, one minute later, a shell penetrating its magazines triggered a huge explosion on the *Borodino's* stern, sending smoke billowing thousands of meters into the air. With Rozhestvensky injured, Rear Admiral Nikolai Nebogatov (Apr 20, 1849 – Aug 4, 1922) assumed command of the Russian fleet. One Russian staff officer recounted his harrowing experience:

> It seemed impossible to count the number of projectiles striking us. Shells seemed to be pouring upon us incessantly one after another. The steel plates and superstructure on the upper decks were torn to pieces, and the splinters caused many casualties. Iron ladders were crumpled up into rings, guns were literally hurled from their mountings. In addition to this, there was the unusually high temperature and liquid flame of the explosion, which seemed to spread over everything. I actually watched a steel plate catch fire from a burst.

Torpedo boats attacking the *Sissoi Veliky*.

At 19:20, the *Knyaz Suvorov* sank, taking over 900 souls with her to the bottom. Then, at 19:30, the *Borodino* sank almost simultaneously with the Russian repair ship, *Kamchatka*. By the end of the day, the Russians had lost four battleships — *Knyaz Suvorov*, *Oslyabya*, *Imperator Aleksandr III*, and *Borodino* — while the Japanese sustained only minor damage. The Japanese 1st Battle Division left the battleground and the 2nd and 4th battle divisions headed north to regroup.

As darkness fell, the battle took on a horrifying new dimension. At around 20:00, 21 destroyers and 45 Japanese torpedo boats launched a relentless assault on the scattered Russian forces. Like a school of sharks, the aggressive Japanese maintained their attacks for three continuous hours. The chaos of the night led to numerous collisions between the small craft and Russian warships, further disorienting the already beleaguered Russians.

By 23:00, the Russians seemed to have vanished, but their positions were betrayed when they switched on their searchlights in a desperate attempt to locate the attackers. The old battleship *Navarin* struck chained floating mines and was torpedoed four times, sinking with only three survivors out of her 622 crew members. Severely damaged by a torpedo, the battleship *Sissoi Veliky* was scuttled by her crew the following day. The armored cruisers *Admiral Nakhimov* and *Vladimir Monomakh* were also badly damaged and scuttled by their crews the next morning off Tsushima Island. The night attacks inflicted heavy losses on the Russians, with two battleships and two armored cruisers lost, while the Japanese lost only three torpedo boats.

Surrender at the Bitter End[16]

The following day, May 28, at 05:23, the Japanese scout ship *Yaeyama* spotted remnants of the Russian fleet heading northeast. Within minutes, Tōgō directed the Japanese Combined Fleet to the new location, with the *Mikasa* gaining visual contact at 09:38. Their battleships surrounded Nebogatov's remaining squadron south of Takeshima Island and at 10:31 the *Nisshin* opened fire from 9,000 meters.

Realizing that his guns were out-ranged by at least one thousand meters, and that the Japanese battleships were faster, Nebogatov ordered the four remaining battleships under his command to surrender (*Emperor Nikolai I, Oryol, General Admiral Graf Apraxin*, and *Admiral Senyavin*). At 10:34 they hoisted the international signal of surrender, XGE, but the Japanese navy continued firing; they did not have "surrender" in their code books! Nebogatov hastily ordered a white tablecloth sent up the masthead; Recalling a difficult decision he had made in the First Sino-Japanese War, Tōgō knew this meant a request for a truce or parley, not a formal surrender. As the Russian ships were still moving, he continued firing.

Finally, Nebogatov ordered his crew to lower St. Andrew's Cross, raise the Japanese national flag on the gaff, and stop all engines. Now satisfied that the requirements for surrender were met, Tōgō gave the order to cease fire and accepted Nebogatov's surrender at 10:45. At 10:50, *Mikasa* lowered the battle flag, with all engagement ending three minutes later. The battle was over.

Fully aware that he could face execution for his decision, Nebogatov told his men: "You are young, and it is you who will one day retrieve the

---

16 The phrase "bitter end" has its origins in naval terminology. In British nautical usage, the "bitter end" specifically denotes the ship end of the anchor cable, secured within the cable locker. In stormy conditions, a ship might pay out increasing lengths of anchor cable to improve its hold. Reaching the "bitter end" meant that no more cable could be released, and the ship could only hope its anchor held fast, thus giving rise to the expression "hanging on to the bitter end" to signify a final, desperate point.

honor and glory of the Russian Navy. The lives of the two thousand four hundred men in these ships are more important than mine."

In the confusion, Commander Vasili Fersen of the Russian cruiser *Izumrud* refused to surrender, instead using her speed to break through the Japanese blockade. He turned and fled towards Vladivostok, but ran aground that evening. Her own crew then destroyed her with explosives, later reaching Vladivostok by land.

Capture of the Admirals

Following his surrender, Admiral Nebogatov was the first senior officer to be captured. At 11:53, Commander Akiyama Saneyuki and Lieutenant Yamamoto Shinjirō left *Mikasa* to head for *Nikolai I* on the torpedo-boat *Kiji*. At 13:37, *Kiji* returned to *Mikasa* with Admiral Nebogatov and his staff. *Asama* commander, Captain Yashiro Rokurō, acted as the interpreter in the first Tōgō-Nebogatov meeting.

As noted above, Admiral Rozhestvensky had been wounded the previous day, having been rescued from the burning *Knyaz Suvorov* by the crew of the destroyer *Buyniy*. That morning, the severely damaged *Buyniy* joined the destroyers *Byedoviy* and *Grozniy*, and the slower cruiser *Donskoi*. With his surviving crew, Rozhestvensky transferred to the *Byedoviy* and began heading for Vladivostok with the *Grozniy*. They left the struggling *Buyniy* behind with the *Donskoi*, which finally had to take the *Buyniy's* crew aboard before sinking that crippled boat themselves.

Though the Japanese destroyers *Sazanami* and *Kagerō* experienced mechanical issues during the night battle on the 27th, they made repairs at the Port of Ulsan and were back on the water the next day. On their way to rejoin the Combined Fleet they spotted the two Russian destroyers and engaged them at 15:25. Under shelling from the approaching *Sazanami*, the *Byedoviy* slowed, stopped, and raised a white flag. Meanwhile, the quicker destroyer *Grozniy* outran *Kagerō*, exchanged a few long-distance shots, and became one of only three warships from the main Russian force to reach Vladivostok.

The Combined Fleet command was later astonished when the cruiser *Akashi* rendezvoused with *Sazanami*, and sent a radio telegraph message reporting the capture of Admiral Rozhestvensky. Until then, the Japanese were certain that the squadron commander had perished with his flagship, the *Knyaz Suvorov*, when it sank the previous evening. Cruiser *Akashi*, escorted

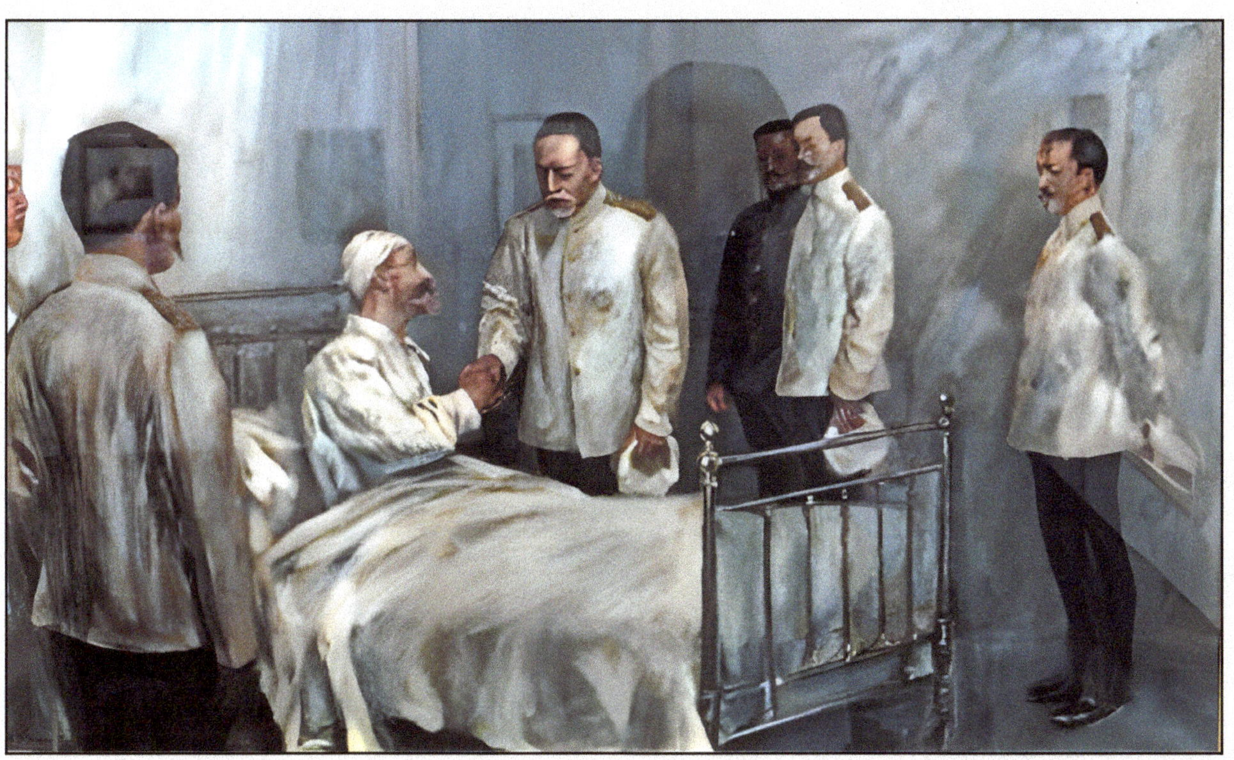

***Admiral Tōgō Visiting Zinovy Rozhestvensky*, by Fujishima Takeji.**

by *Sazanami* and *Kagerō*, arrived at Sasebo port on the morning of May 30 with *Byedoviy* in tow, carrying not only the injured admiral but also the surviving members of the Russian fleet command.

The wounded Admiral Rozhestvensky was taken to the Imperial Japanese Naval Hospital in Sasebo to recover from his head injury. The victorious Admiral Tōgō visited him in plain clothes, stating: "Defeat is a common fate of a soldier. There is nothing to be ashamed of in it. The great point is whether we have performed our duty."

Rozhestvensky was permitted to send a telegram to Tsar Nicholas II who responded saying: "From the bottom of my heart I thank you and all the ranks of the squadron who honestly fulfilled their duty in battle, for their selfless service to Russia. Your feat was destined to be crowned with success, but your fatherland will always be proud of your selfless courage. I wish you a speedy recovery, and may God console you all. Nikolai."

Aftermath of the Battle

The Battle of Tsushima was a catastrophic defeat for Russia with staggering losses of personnel: 5,045 men killed, 803 injured, and 6,016 captured as Prisoners of War. In the humiliating defeat, Russia lost all its battleships and most of its cruisers and destroyers, The Japanese, in stark contrast, lost no

Japanese victory celebrations swept the nation following the Battle of Tsushima, as they did in this image following the Battle of Port Arthur.

heavy ships and suffered only 117 dead and 583 injured.

Admiral Rozhestvensky and other officers met with harsh judgment after being placed on trial in August 1905. Rozhestvensky claimed full responsibility for the debacle and was sentenced to death, as he had anticipated. The Tsar commuted his sentence.

Rear Admiral Nebogatov's troubles began even while he was still a Japanese prisoner of war; the Russian Admiralty dishonorably discharged him and stripped him of all his titles of nobility. On his return to Russia, he and 77 of his subordinate officers were arrested and taken before a court martial in December 1906.

Nebogatov's defense that his defective ships, guns and ammunition would have resulted in the meaningless slaughter of his men was rejected, and Nebogatov and three of his captains were sentenced to death by firing squad on December 25, 1906. Again, by order of Tsar Nicholas, the sentences were commuted to 10 years in prison. Nebogatov was released from the prison fortress of Saints Peter and Paul in May 1909, when he was pardoned on the occasion of the tsar's birthday.

Flag captains Clapier de Colongue (Second Pacific Squadron) and Cross (Third Pacific Squadron), Staff officers Filippinovsky, Leontieff, along with the commanders of the surrendered battleships, Captains Vladimir Smirnov (*Nikolai I*), Nikolai Lishin (*Apraksin*), Sergei Grogoryev (*Senyavin*), and the *Byedoviy* commander Nikolai Baranov, were sentenced to 10 years in prison and dismissed from service. Tsar Nicholas II later pardoned them on May 1, 1909. The executive officer of *Oryol*, Captain 2nd rank K.L. Schwede, and other officers were acquitted.

The Battle of Tsushima stands as a pivotal moment in naval history, showcasing the decisive impact of technological innovation, strategic leadership, and logistical preparation on the outcome of warfare. It marked the rise of Japan as a major naval power and the decline of Russia's maritime might, with far-reaching consequences for the global balance of power in the 20th century.

An Unexpected American Path to Peace

While Farrère focused his novel on cultural dramas leading up to Tsushima, he omitted broader geopolitical contexts; the surprising aftermath involved the crucial involvement of the United States in the peace process. A close examination of events after the conflict also revealed unusual interactions spanning decades that linked two legendary naval figures in ways that almost seems preordained by fate.

Russia's staggering defeat, losing virtually its entire fleet in a single, brutal encounter, effectively ended its will and ability to continue the war. Russia not only faced military humiliation but the rising threat of revolution at home. Japan, despite its stunning string of victories, was economically exhausted, its resources stretched thin. Both nations suffered greatly from the demands of history's first truly modern war – a conflict fought with long-range cannons, machine guns, advanced torpedoes, innovative explosives, radio telegraphy, and armored battleships — and were teetering on the brink. A continuation of the struggle threatened financial ruin and risked dragging other European powers into a wider conflict through tangled alliances, potentially igniting the first global war. The world watched nervously. Who could possibly step in to broker peace between these two diametrically

"GOOD OFFICES"

**Theodore Roosevelt, the peacemaker, standing between Tsar Nicholas II of
Russia and Emperor Meiji of Japan. W. A. Rogers, 1905.**

opposed cultures?

The intervention came from an unexpected quarter, spearheaded by
a dynamic leader half a world away, representing a nation only recently
emerged as a global player: the United States. President Theodore Roosevelt,
a figure already known for his "big stick" diplomacy, saw an opportunity – not
just for America to assert its influence, but to act as a genuine peacemaker
on the world stage. Using sophisticated back-channel diplomacy, Roosevelt
extended an offer. He proposed that the United States host direct, face-to-face
negotiations, respecting both nations' insistence on avoiding the third-party
interference previously imposed by European powers.

Intrigue surrounds even the choice of venue. Eschewing the political
crucible and sweltering summer heat of Washington D.C., Roosevelt

selected the quiet, coastal town of Portsmouth, New Hampshire. He entrusted the complex logistics, security, and diplomatic protocols to the U.S. Navy at the Portsmouth Naval Shipyard in nearby Kittery, Maine. From August 6th to August 30th, 1905, this unlikely setting became the focal point of international diplomacy. The delegates, led by Japan's determined Foreign Minister Komura Jutarō and Russia's formidable former Finance Minister Sergei Witte, were housed at the grand Hotel Wentworth in New Castle, New Hampshire, making daily trips across the Piscataqua River to the negotiations held in the unassuming General Stores Building (Building 86) at the Shipyard.

The talks were fraught with tension. Tsar Nicholas II remained defiant, forbidding his envoys to concede territory or pay reparations. Japan, acutely aware of its financial strain but buoyed by victory, demanded recognition of its dominance in Korea, reparations, and control over Sakhalin Island. For weeks, the delegations hammered out agreements on secondary issues – troop withdrawals, lease transfers, railway control – but remained deadlocked on the crucial points of Sakhalin and financial indemnity. At critical moments when talks seemed destined to collapse, Roosevelt, despite never physically coming to Portsmouth, worked tirelessly behind the scenes, urging compromise.

Simultaneously, the remarkable hospitality of the people of New Hampshire and Maine played a crucial, informal role, hosting social events and creating an atmosphere of goodwill that encouraged the delegates to persevere. Neither side wished to be seen as the first to walk away, disappointing their hosts and risking global disapproval. Finally, after Witte employed shrewd negotiation tactics, including leveraging the American press and threatening to resume hostilities, a breakthrough occurred: Japan agreed to drop its demand for reparations in exchange for the southern half of Sakhalin.

On September 5, 1905, the Treaty of Portsmouth was signed, formally ending the Russo-Japanese War. It established Japan as the pre-eminent power in East Asia and forced Russia to abandon its expansionist policies there. For his masterful, albeit remote, orchestration of the peace process, Theodore Roosevelt was awarded the Nobel Peace Prize in 1906, marking America's arrival as a significant force in world diplomacy. The treaty itself ushered in three decades of peace between Russia and Japan.[17]

---

17 Many of the facts in this section were sourced from the Portsmouth Peace Treaty website: www.portsmouthpeacetreaty.org. Interested readers will find a wealth of information there, including maps, documentation, and period photos.

The Improbable Tale of the Samurai and the Texan

But connecting Teddy Roosevelt to this story is only one thread in this astonishing tapestry. Now we will delve into the unbelievable personal connections hinted at earlier – threads of destiny linking Admiral Tōgō with a unique young American who would one day stand as his counterpart on the world stage.

First, we must rewind our story to Fredericksburg, Texas, on February 24, 1885. While the 37-year-old Tōgō was already a seasoned military officer actively fighting the Chinese at the time, a baby boy was born in the dusty heart of America's fading Old West. His parents named him Chester William Nimitz. For his first 16 years, he wouldn't see a body of water larger than a lake. Then, destiny intervened; after being rejected by West Point, he was accepted into the U.S. Naval Academy and in 1901 he traveled to Annapolis, Maryland, to begin his education.

He graduated with distinction on January 30, 1905, with the academy's yearbook describing him as a man "of cheerful yesterdays and confident tomorrows."[18] Three weeks later, he had his 20th birthday, perhaps while on his way to San Francisco for his first assignment aboard the newly built battleship, the USS *Ohio*. He boarded as a Passed Midshipman and departed on April 1st as the ship set sail for Manila to become the flagship of the American Asiatic Fleet. Weeks later, on May 27, Admiral Tōgō achieved his stunning victory at Tsushima, securing his global reputation as the "Nelson of the East." There wasn't a sailor on the planet who wasn't touched that that event; no doubt Claude Farrère and Chester Nimitz took note as well.

With the signing of the Treaty of Portsmouth on September 5, 1905, the Russo-Japanese War was officially over, and it was time for Japan to celebrate. Emperor Meiji planned a grand triumphal return and reception for Admiral Tōgō at the imperial palace on October 22nd. Coincidentally, the USS Ohio was anchored in Tokyo Bay, so Japanese officials courteously extended an invitation to the ship's officers. The senior officers, however, expressed no interest in attending the affair. While their specific reasons weren't recorded, this cool reception perhaps reflected the complex mix of official diplomacy and underlying racial prejudice common in America at the time; "Yellow Peril" fears, often crudely depicted in political cartoons,

---

18   "Chester William Nimitz," Naval History and Heritage Command, accessed April 22, 2025, https://www.history.navy.mil/research/histories/biographies-list/bios-n/nimitz-chester-w.html.

were intensifying following Japan's unexpected victory over a European power. Nevertheless, the officers decided that an American presence was appropriate. They selected six midshipmen to represent the ship – including the 20-year-old Nimitz. In his biography, E.B. Potter provides a vivid description of the scene:

> Scattered about the imperial palace grounds were two or three hundred tables, each with several bottles of Russian champagne captured at Port Arthur. Because of transportation difficulties, the midshipmen arrived late and were seated at the table nearest the exit.
>
> Toward the end of the party, the Americans saw Admiral Tōgō coming down the path to take his departure. Somewhat flushed with wine, they decided to intercept him, and it was Midshipman Nimitz whom they selected to step forward and invite the admiral to their table. Tōgō smilingly accepted the invitation and came over. He shook hands all around, took a sip of champagne, and chatted briefly in English.[19]

The admiral had perfected his English during seven years of naval training in Britain. Indeed, he always had an affinity for young sailors and probably enjoyed this conversation more than talking with dignitaries at the event. But imagine the scene for Nimitz! A young man from landlocked Texas, barely out of Annapolis, at the emperor's palace sharing a toast with the architect of one of history's greatest naval victories, a figure revered worldwide as an equal to Horatio Nelson. But Nimitz, like Tōgō, was a quiet, humble man; apparently, he didn't mention this brief encounter often, not even to some of his closest associates later in life.

Nimitz would never see Admiral Tōgō alive again…but he *would* see him, and their connection, forged in that brief meeting, was far from over.

---

19 Potter, E. B., *Nimitz* (Annapolis, Maryland; Naval Institute Press, 1976.

The Celebrated Admiral Tōgō

With his battles now over, Admiral Tōgō's star continued to rise. In 1911, he set out on a round-the-world tour, returning to England for the first time in almost 30 years representing the Emperor of Japan at the coronation of King George V. On July 29, he concluded his visit to Great Britain by boarding the *Lusitania* to sail for New York.[20] In the United States, he promoted US-Japan relations, boosting the moral of Japanese communities wherever he appeared. President Taft received Tōgō at the White House, and he visited the grave of George Washington at Mt. Vernon. In New York, ex-President Roosevelt hosted him at his Oyster Bay home, then he headed to Boston, Niagara Falls, Vancouver, and back to Japan.

We pause here to mention another birth that soon ties into our story. On October 5, 1913, Eugene Bennett Fluckey was born in Washington D.C.; he also had an illustrious naval career ahead of him.

Meanwhile, Tōgō's titles and responsibilities continued to grow. In 1913, he was awarded the honorific title of Marshal-Admiral; roughly equivalent to the rank of Grand Admiral or Admiral of the Fleet in other navies. From 1914–1924, Tōgō was put

Admiral Tōgō's triumphal return to Tokyo from the Sea of Japan.

---

20   Less than four years later, the magnificent *Lusitania* met its infamous end. Torpedoed by German U-boat U-20 off Ireland (May 7, 1915), she sank in a shocking 18 minutes, claiming nearly 1,200 lives (128 Americans). Passengers boarding might have noted the German Embassy's chilling newspaper ad — placed right beside Cunard's own sailing notice — warning travelers away from Allied ships in the war zone. Fueling the global outrage was later confirmation that *Lusitania* was in fact carrying rifle ammunition and artillery shell casings. This fact sparked a bitter debate still ongoing: did this contraband fatally accelerate the sinking via secondary explosions, and did it justify the sinking as a military act?

Marshal-Admiral, the Marquis Tōgō Heihachirō of the Imperial Japanese Navy with the Collar and the Grand Cordon of the Order of the Chrysanthemum.

Aboard the Lusitania in 1911: Gen. Verbeck (aka Virbeck), Chandler Hale, Admiral Tōgō, and Frederick Dent Grant.

in charge of the education of Crown Prince Hirohito, the future Shōwa Emperor who would preside over Japan during World War II. When Tōgō's former pupil ascended the throne in 1926, he awarded his teacher the Collar of the Supreme Order of the Chrysanthemum, an honor held only by Emperor Hirohito and Prince Kan'in Kotohito at the time. This rank made Marshal-Admiral Tōgō Japan's most decorated naval officer in history. Take note of that fact. Then on Nov 8, 1926, Tōgō became the first Japanese person to appear on the cover of *Time* magazine, another milestone in his illustrious career.

Captain Nimitz Reunites with Admiral Tōgō

Nearly two decades had passed since Nimitz shared that fateful champagne toast. Yet the invisible threads binding these two men seemed to stretch across time without weakening, although their connections would only become clear long after both men were gone. For Marshal-Admiral Tōgō, that happened at 6:35AM on Wednesday, May 30, 1934, when he died of throat cancer. His funeral was quickly arranged for the following Tuesday.

Coincidentally, *Captain* Nimitz, now in command of his own ship, USS *Augusta*, was already anchored in Tokyo. He made arrangements to attend Marshal-Admiral Tōgō's official lying-in-state ceremony on June 5th. Somehow, the next day, he was also included in the private Japanese funeral rites, held in Tōgō's home, a simple five-room cottage in the forest outside Tokyo. Official Japanese records, preserved in the later-constructed Tōgō shrine, report that, as Nimitz passed Tōgō's body, he quietly said, almost to himself: "I feel the spirit of Tōgō flowing into me."[21]

But Tōgō's influence on Nimitz was far from over. Perhaps, this is when it truly began.

Another Surprise Attack

Roosevelt's concerns over Japan's strength finally proved true as it continued expanding its influence in Asia, and with America seen as the biggest threat to that expansion. Echoing the start of the Russo-Japanese War, the Japanese staged a surprise attack on Pearl Harbor on December 7, 1941, and the United States entered World War II. Just ten days later, President Franklin D. Roosevelt acted to appoint the commander-in-chief of the United States Pacific Fleet (CINCPACFLT); the key person to plan and coordinate America's fight against its enemy across the Pacific ocean: he chose Chester William Nimitz.

Over the next three years, Admiral Nimitz made history in remote corners of the Pacific with names that still resonate today: the battles of the Coral Sea, Midway, Guadalcanal, and the Philippines Sea. The campaigns of the Solomon Islands, New Guinea, the Gilbert and Marshall Islands. Truk Lagoon, Peleliu, Angaur, and Ulithi. And in October 1944, the three-day Battle of Leyte Gulf that finally destroyed much of Japan's remaining naval power. Slowly, Nimitz inexorably turned the tide against the Japanese, and was recognized for his success. On December 19th, President Roosevelt appointed Nimitz to the rank of fleet admiral − the highest rank in the Navy, established by Congress a few days earlier. Thus, he, like his spiritual counterpart Tōgō, attained the highest naval rank in the history of his country.

---

21   This fact, and others following, was not revealed for nearly half a century. While some became known to Commander Eugene B. Fluckey in 1984, even those weren't revealed until Captain Robin William Garson, Commander of the Order of the British Empire of the Royal Navy, published his January 1999 article, "Three Great Admirals − One Common Spirit?" in *The Naval Review* 87, no. 1.

Allied landings, August 1942 – August 1945.
Source: MacArthur, Douglas. Reports of General MacArthur, Vol. 1,
Center of Military History, [1950] pp. p. 432.

Towards the end of the war, another naval hero emerged who earned the nickname Lucky Fluckey. Our 1913 baby grew up to become Lt. Commander Fluckey, who established himself among America's greatest submarine skippers for his success on USS *Barb*. He was credited with the second most tonnage sunk by a U.S. Naval skipper during World War II (after Richard O'Kane) at 179,700 tons: his score included 25 ships with a carrier, cruiser, and frigate among them.[22] Later awarded the Congressional Medal of Honor and four Navy Crosses, Fluckey became the most decorated United States Naval Officer of WWII. But he's featured in this story because of new discoveries he would later make about Tōgō and Nimitz. But first, we must end World War II.

---

22   Detailed in Eugene B. Fluckey's book, *Thunder Below!: The USS* Barb *Revolutionizes Submarine Warfare in World War II.*

Admiral Chester Nimitz signs acceptance of the formal Japanese surrender, representing the United States of America Supreme on the USS MISSOURI in Tokyo Bay. September 2, 1945. Directly behind him are (left-to-right): General of the Army Douglas MacArthur; Admiral William Halsey, USN, and Rear Admiral Forrest Sherman, USN.

From Unconditional Surrender to *Mikasa*

Admiral Tōgō's glorious Japanese victory seemed to come full circle on September 2, 1945. In a way, he even became part of the event through the actions of his admirer. That morning, Japanese officials boarded the USS *Missouri* in Tokyo Bay to sign their unconditional surrender. And who was the official signatory representative for the United States of America? Fleet Admiral Chester W. Nimitz. But even at this apex of his career, Tōgō was evidently on his mind. After the formalities, Nimitz returned to his ship, *South Dakota*, to release his formal statement of the war's end for broadcast throughout the Pacific and the United States. He then went ashore for a final visit while in Japan. His destination? Tōgō's former flagship, *Mikasa*.

Mikasa, named after Mount Mikasa in Nara, Japan, is a pre-dreadnought battleship built for the Imperial Japanese Navy in England where her keel was laid down on January 24, 1899. Launched on November 8, 1900, she was the only ship of her class and served as the flagship of Vice Admiral Tōgō throughout the Russo-Japanese War.[23] A lesser-known fact is that on September 11, 1905, just six days after the Treaty of Portsmouth was signed, a fire in the ship's magazine triggered an explosion that sank the ship killing 251 crewmen. This is more than *double* the number of Japanese sailors who died at the Battle of Tsushima. Salvaged and repaired over the next two years, she was put back into service. In 1922, however, the major Allies of World War I, including Japan, signed the Washington Naval Treaty agreeing to prevent an arms race by limiting naval construction and the size of fleets. This caused *Mikasa* to be decommissioned on September 23, 1923, destined to be scrapped under the treaty. But Japanese officials proposed another idea; preserving the historic ship as a memorial by encasing her hull in concrete and removing all her engines and guns. The signatories agreed, and on November 12, 1926, Mikasa was opened for display in Yokosuka in the presence of Crown Prince Hirohito and Tōgō.

Nineteen year later, Admiral Nimitz himself boarded *Mikasa*, taking in the full extent of the damage inflicted by American bombers. He also learned that his fellow admiral, William Frederick "Bull" Halsey Jr. (Oct 30, 1882 – Aug. 16, 1959), had already been there to confiscate her flag to be presented to the Russians as a war trophy. Nimitz quickly reacted to this news; he immediately ordered a permanent marine guard to be posted aboard *Mikasa* to prevent any additional looting or souvenir hunting.[24] Another faction sought more than souvenirs; they wanted *Mikasa* to be hauled out to sea and destroyed as a weapon of war, forbidden under the unconditional surrender. Apparently, the Russians still had a bit of anxiety over Tōgō's victory in 1905. Through channels, Nimitz saw that attempt defused as well, as he returned to his family in America to resume his duties where he hoped his life could return to normal.

---

23   https://www.kinenkan-mikasa.or.jp/en/mikasa/index.html

24   Potter, *Nimitz*, 306-308.

Chester William Nimitz, Chief of Naval Operations, ca. 1945–1947.
Source: Naval History and Heritage Command 80-G-K-9344; US Navy.

A Lifetime Commitment

Like all returning heroes, Admiral Nimitz was in demand for awards, speeches, parades, and myriad appearances. And who better to assist him than Lucky Fluckey? In November 1945, Nimitz selected him as his personal aid to assist in organizing his obligations. Fluckey returned to his submarine duties in 1947, but the two men became lifetime friends. Nimitz also continued to keep an eye on *Mikasa*, but the news wasn't good. Despite his best efforts, the ship fell into further disrepair under the American administration of Japan.

It's uncertain how long the marine guards lasted, but after the US Navy took over the Yokosuka Navy Base, things went downhill. Supposedly, they salvaged *Mikasa*'s superstructure to be cut up, sold for scrap, and melted down. Mikasa was abandoned for years, until the port was revitalized by the Korean War. Then, members of the Japanese business community built a Quonset hut on the deck named the *Club Mikasa*, as a dance hall, nightclub, and "a cheap boozer/dive providing female entertainment" for US Navy men.[25] The project *failed* (talk about a reality disconnect!), and the ship was again abandoned.

Fast forward to September 1955. After visiting *Mikasa*, a Brit named John S. Rubin wrote a letter to the *Japan Times* expressing his shock at the ship's state of disrepair, as Colin Randall reports in Australia's Naval Historical Review:

> "I saw the Mikasa launched and completed at Vickers Sons and Maxim's Shipbuilding Works at Barrow-in-Furness, England," he wrote, explaining that the ship was built there between 1900 and 1902. Rubin goes on to note that during his visit to Japan he saw the old ship: The outer surface is fairly presentable, but the interior is a shambles and ghostlike in its decrepitude. This letter garnered wide public response and reaction around Japan and helped gather momentum to restore the ship.[26]

Rubin's report became the catalyst for a new restoration campaign, inspiring support from the Japanese public. The narrative now circles back to the man who held Tōgō in such high esteem. In 1958, the preservation committee contacted Nimitz, and he was only too happy to help. He wrote an article for an essay collection supporting *Mikasa*'s restoration, contributing his royalties among the first donations. His visible contribution

---

25   Colin Randall, "Battleship Mikasa – Restoration," *Naval Historical Review*, September 2019.

26   Randall, "Battleship *Mikasa* – Restoration."

motivated more members of the Japanese public to support the cause. Two other battleships being scrapped in Japan in the late 1950s provided parts and, in an unexpected twist, the US navy yard returned original parts from the ship that had supposedly been scrapped, but were kept in storage. The restoration was underway.

On May 27, 1961, — the 56th anniversary of the Battle of Tsushima — Mikasa was rededicated. Invited, but unable to attend, Admiral Nimitz sent his photo with this message:

> To all those patriotic Japanese who helped to restore this famous ship
> *Mikasa*—flagship of Admiral Tōgō—your greatest naval officer—
> with best wishes from a great admirer and disciple.
>
> C. W. Nimitz, Fleet Admiral, U.S. Navy[27]

Ironically, *Mikasa*'s 12-inch forward gun turret now points directly at the US Navy Base.[28]

The Tōgō Shrine and the Final Reunion

Despite the impending war, Admiral Nimitz was probably aware of the 1940 dedication of the Tōgō Shrine, where the Marquis Tōgō Heihachirō is celebrated as a Shinto *kami*.[29] Built four years after his death, but

---

27 Potter, *Nimitz*, 366.

28 Randall, "Battleship *Mikasa* – Restoration,"

29 In Shinto—Japan's indigenous spiritual path often translated as 'the way of the *kami*' — *kami* (神) are not typically 'gods' in the Western monotheistic sense, but rather spirits, divinities, or

destroyed during the bombing of Tokyo in the final years of the war, a small, temporary shrine was erected on the site. By the early 1960s, plans were underway to restore the original shrine, and in 1962 Admiral Nimitz found an opportunity to help.

In the 1950s, Nimitz spent years creating a book on the history of sea power. According to his daughter Nancy, "I think this was one of the exercises that gave him more pleasure after he left Washington than almost anything else. Nothing gave him more pleasure than receiving the chapters of this voluminous book in typescript and going through them."[30] Finally published in the summer of 1960, *Sea Power: A Naval History* went on to be translated into seven languages, receiving favorable reviews worldwide.[31] Refusing any payment for his contributions to *Sea Power* and its subsidiary works, Admiral Nimitz delegated the handling of his share to the book's editor, E. B. Potter, and his former aide, Eugene Fluckey. They subsequently arranged for Nimitz's royalties to be donated to causes supporting the Navy and its personnel.

In 1962, a Japanese publisher was preparing to issue a Japanese language version of *Sea Power*, focused specifically on the war in the Pacific. Who better to write the foreword than Admiral Nimitz himself? The publisher made his request, and Nimitz agreed with one condition; that any payment due to him would be donated to the Tōgō Shrine restoration fund. Seeing a wonderful public relations opportunity, the publisher arranged a press conference at the American Embassy in Tokyo to present the donation. Newspapers gave the event great coverage and, as with the *Mikasa* restoration, Admiral Nimitz sparked

---

sacred powers inherent in nature (like mountains or wind) and, significantly, are embodied by certain revered human beings after their death. Individuals who displayed outstanding character or achievements — such as national heroes like Admiral Tōgō — can be enshrined and venerated as *kami*, becoming objects of respect and remembrance at dedicated shrines like this one.

30   Potter, *Nimitz*, 466.

31   E. B. Potter and Chester W. Nimitz, eds., *Sea Power: A Naval History* (Englewood Cliffs, NJ: Prentice-Hall, 1960).

Admiral Nimitz State Historic Site, Fredericksburg, Texas, USA.

terrific Japanese support for the cause, and donations poured in. Incidentally, as Potter describes,

> the book became a best seller in Japan. Published on December 7, Pearl Harbor day, as *Nimitz's History of the Pacific Ocean War,* it sold out in less than a month. A second printing was rushed through the presses to meet the demand.[32]

The fully restored Tōgō Shrine reopened in 1964, while Admiral Nimitz also saw another tribute devoted to his own life taking shape here in the United States. The newly formed Admiral Nimitz Foundation initiated the creation of the National Museum of the Pacific War in the admiral's boyhood home of Fredericksburg, Texas, The six-acre site was centered on his grandfather's Nimitz Hotel, founded in 1852, with a rich history of uses including a saloon, a brewery, a ballroom that doubled as a theatre, a smokehouse, and a bath-house.

Though Admiral Nimitz saw the realization of the museum, his own final voyage was approaching. Following a stroke in late 1965, the legendary admiral's strength waned. Four days before his 81st birthday, Admiral Chester

---

32 Potter, Nimitz, 467.

Nimitz Museum, Japanese Peace Garden.
Photo: Ed Uthman, Houston, TX.

William Nimitz died on the evening of February 20, 1966. in his home. He was laid to rest with full military honors beside his wife at Golden Gate National Cemetery in San Bruno. His legendary leadership and his service to his country and family secured him enduring reverence, while his profound, lifelong connection to Admiral Tōgō, echoed the spirit of the *kami* he admired.

The Enduring Connection

The momentum of Admiral Nimitz's life continued, even after he had gone. Restoration of his grandfather's hotel progressed, and in 1968 an act of the Texas legislature renamed it the Admiral Nimitz Museum. In 1976, the people of Japan sought to honor the friendship between Admiral Nimitz and Admiral Heihachiro Tōgō with a unique gift to the people of America, through the museum. Japanese craftsmen and gardeners traveled to Texas to build the Japanese Garden of Peace, at the facility, with its dedication on May 8, 1976, the 130th anniversary of the founding of Fredericksburg. In 2000, the expanding complex, — dedicated exclusively to the Pacific

Theater battles of World War II —
was renamed Admiral Nimitz State
Historic Site – National Museum of
the Pacific War.[33]

Next, we return to Japan to
uncover perhaps the most striking
testament to the Tōgō–Nimitz
connection, revealed through an
unexpected source. In the 1970s,
the admiral's friend and post-war
personal aid, Commander Fluckey,
was working on his own book about
his legendary wartime experiences
aboard the USS *Barb*. A stickler for
accuracy, Fluckey delayed completing
Thunder Below! until he could access
original records in Japan.

That opportunity finally arrived
in 1983, when Japanese military
associates arranged for now Rear
Admiral Fluckey to visit Tokyo with full archival access. After completing
his research in 1984, an extraordinary event occurred, later recounted by
Captain R. W. Garson of the Royal Navy. According to Garson's research:

**Rear Admiral Eugene B. Fluckey, USN.
Photo: United States Navy, Photographer's
Mate Second Class Moiz, March 12, 1963.**

> the Japanese authorities closed the 'Tōgō Shrine' at Yokosuka to all
> public visitors and held a banquet there to honour Admiral and Mrs
> Fluckey. During this private visit, and unique tour of the Shrine, all
> the display cases were opened and their guests invited to handle all
> the exhibits.
>
> Margaret Fluckey, glancing through one of Admiral Tōgō's
> personal diaries, was surprised to find they were written in English.
> The Admiral had, of course, been one of the first Japanese Naval
> Officers to be sent to England for Cadet training in the middle of the
> 19th century — pre-Dartmouth — and was later the Japanese Naval
> Attache in Washington.
>
> By chance the following sentence caught Mrs Fluckey's eye:
> **"I am firmly convinced that I am the re-incarnation of
> Horatio Nelson."** Re-reading this fascinating sentence her startled
> exclamation drew the attention of all.[34]

---

33 www.pacificwarmuseum.org

34 Garson, "Three Great Admirals - One Common Spirit?"

This potential discovery is remarkable. While countless books and articles have drawn parallels between Tōgō and Nelson, Garson's account represents the only suggestion of Tōgō *himself* claiming such a direct spiritual lineage, apparently recorded in his personal, English-language diary. Garson's article continues, adding more layers to the Tōgō-Nimitz connection:

> It was then that Admiral Fluckey noticed that the collection included numerous photographs of Fleet Admiral Nimitz at various stages of his Naval career. **This surprised him because, although he had been a personal aide to Admiral Nimitz — and later a close friend — an intimate association with Admiral Tōgō had never been mentioned.** He was, however, fully aware that Nimitz firmly believed Tōgō to be one of the greatest Admirals in Naval history.
>
> Admiral Fluckey enquired of his hosts why were there so many photographs of Admiral Nimitz in the showcases? Adding, as a statement of fact, "He was the one who defeated Japan in World War II rather than General MacArthur." [35]

Their Japanese host then reportedly detailed Nimitz's profound respect for Tōgō — protecting Mikasa during and after the war, raising funds for its restoration, and donating book royalties to the Tōgō Shrine restoration. These revelations apparently surprised Fluckey, highlighting how quietly Nimitz held his deep reverence for the Japanese admiral. Curiously, while Fluckey briefly mentions his research trip to Japan in *Thunder Below!*, he provides no account of this specific banquet or the discoveries described by Garson.

Aftermath and Legacy

The echoes of Tsushima, and the intertwined legacies of the admirals it touched, continue to resonate with compelling force. In a poignant gesture bridging past and present, American sailors volunteered to help repaint the *Mikasa* on August 5, 2009, as a mark of respect. Fittingly, perhaps even inevitably given the history uncovered here, they hailed from the aircraft carrier USS *Nimitz*.[36]

Researching these events in 2025 – a journey sparked while preparing the first annotated English translation of Claude Farrère's 1909 novel, *La*

---

35   Ibid.

36   Amara R. Timberlake, "Nimitz Preserves Ties to Renowned Japanese Warship," Navy News Service, August 26, 2009.

Bataille – became a process of uncovering threads that seem to weave a pattern transcending mere coincidence, hinting at forces beyond ordinary understanding. Assembling this narrative, connecting details overlooked or presented in isolation by previous biographers, has been its own profound experience. One is struck not just by the historical weight of their actions, but by the character of the men themselves.

Both Tōgō and Nimitz achieved global fame, yet both remained profoundly humble men. Tōgō, known for his reticence, lived out his days simply; Nimitz, despite orchestrating the Pacific victory, rarely spoke of his youthful encounter with the celebrated Japanese admiral — a meeting that would surely be a lifelong boast for most. This quiet strength, this seeming indifference to the accolades showered upon them, only deepens the sense of wonder surrounding their connection. They were men secure in their destinies, unbent by the fame they earned.

The Battle of Tsushima itself remains a pivotal moment in naval history; a stark demonstration of the decisive impact of leadership, training, technology, and logistical foresight. It irrevocably shifted the global balance of power, marking Imperial Japan's arrival as a major world power and signaling the decline of Tsarist Russia's maritime ambitions. Tōgō Heihachirō became an international icon, the "Nelson of the East" – a title perhaps closer to his own heart than previously known, if the account of his English diary holds true. His flagship *Mikasa*, saved through the quiet intervention of his American admirer, remains a tangible link to that thunderous clash of empires.

Yet, beyond historical analysis and strategic lessons, stand these remarkable, intertwined destinies. The threads connecting Nelson, Tōgō, and Nimitz – threads potentially encompassing self-perceived reincarnation, reported spiritual transference, quiet reverence, and improbable encounters – add a layer of fascinating, almost mystical resonance. It is perhaps this enduring spirit – the *kami* of determination, duty, victory, and profound humility – that truly compels us. I dedicate my humble effort to their memory and the enduring spirit they represent. Their story reminds us that history is shaped not only by battles fought, but by the quiet strength and perhaps fated connections of those who lead.

෴ ✿ ෴

Bibliography

The sources below are readily available. While foundational, none of them individually present all the connections examined in the article above (e.g. the Tōgō/Nimitz 1905 personal meeting; the specific account of Tōgō diary stating his belief that he was the reincarnation of Admiral Nelson; Nimitz attending Tōgō's public funeral, and personal funeral rites in his home; witnesses observing Nimitz's funeral remark that he felt the spirit of Admiral Tōgō passing into him; Nimitz representing the United States to accept Japan's unconditional surrender and then going directly to the *Mikasa*; Nimitz protecting *Mikasa* from looters and from Russian intentions to destroy the ship; Nimitz initiating fund-raising efforts for the *Mikasa*; Nimitz's personal assistant Fluckey working directly with him for decades yet never hearing about his association with Tōgō, etc.). This article synthesizes information from these and other sources, including Captain R.W. Garson's specific account, to present a more complete picture of these extraordinary links.

✻

Bodley Major R.V.C., *Admiral Tōgō. The Authorized Life of Admiral of the Fleet, Marquis Heihachiro Tōgō*, London: Jarrolds, 1935.

Clements, Jonathan, *Admiral Tōgō: Nelson of the East*, London: Haus Publishing, 2010.

Evans, David C; Peattie, Mark R (1997). *Kaigun: strategy, tactics, and technology in the Imperial Japanese Navy, 1887–1941*. Annapolis, Maryland: Naval Institute Press.

Fluckey, Eugene B. *Thunder Below!: The USS* Barb *Revolutionizes Submarine Warfare in World War II*. Urbana: University of Illinois Press, 1992.

Garson, R. W. "Three Great Admirals – One Common Spirit?" *The Naval Review* 87, no. 1 (January 1999).

Harris, Brayton. *Nimitz*. New York: St. Martin's Press, 2011.

Lloyd, Arthur, *Admiral Tōgō*. Tokyo, Japan, Kinkodo Publishihg Co., 1905.

Portsmouth Peace Treaty website: www.portsmouthpeacetreaty.org

Potter, E. B., *Nimitz*, Annapolis, Maryland, Naval Institute Press, 1976.

Potter, E. B., and Chester W. Nimitz, eds. *Sea Power: A Naval History*. Englewood Cliffs, NJ: Prentice-Hall, 1960.

Randall, Colin. "Battleship Mikasa – Restoration." *Naval Historical Review*, September 2019 edition.

Semenoff, Vladimir. *The Battle of Tsushima: Between the Japanese and Russian Fleets, fought on 27th May 1905*. Translated by Captain A. B. Lindsay. London: John Murray, 1906.

Semenoff, Vladimir. *Rasplata (The Reckoning)*. Translated by L. A. B. London: John Murray, 1909.

Semenoff, Vladimir. *The Price of Blood: The Sequel to "Rasplata" and "The Battle of Tsushima"*. Translated by Leonard Lewery and F. R. Godfrey. London: John Murray, 1910.

Timberlake, Amara R. "Nimitz Preserves Ties to Renowned Japanese Warship." Navy News Service. August 26, 2009. Accessed April 29, 2025.

About the Author

After working and traveling extensively in Southeast Asia since 1990, Davis and his wife Sophaphan founded DatAsia Press in 2005. Since then, Davis has worked as chief editor, translator, and independent scholar pursuing his passion as a literary archaeologist, discovering exceptional books that have slipped into obscurity and become lost over time.

Photo: Anders Jiras

As a publisher, Davis restores the reputations and classic works of forgotten authors who made noteworthy literary contributions, — both fiction and non-fiction, — by reviving out-of-print books as expanded modern editions with added academic analysis, supplemental materials, illustrations, and original modern translations. The 2025 edition of Claude Farrère's 1909 masterwork *The Battle* is a perfect example of Davis's craft.

kentdavis@gmail.com

About the Artist

Charles Fouqueray (1869–1956)

The evocative illustrations accompanying this edition of Claude Farrère's *La Bataille* are the work of Charles Dominique Fouqueray (1869-1956), a French artist whose life journey through art, adventure, war, and extensive travel uniquely positioned him to visualize Farrère's epic tale. Fouqueray's deep connection to the sea, his firsthand experiences in modern warfare, and his fascination with the Orient provided the ideal foundation for illustrating this novel of naval conflict, cultural collision, and human passion set against the backdrop of the Russo-Japanese War in 1905. Understanding his story enriches our appreciation of the 108 vibrant paintings he created for the original 1925 limited edition of *La Bataille*, painstakingly restored for contemporary readers.

Born in Le Mans, France on July 23, 1869, Fouqueray hailed from a family with maritime roots in Fouras (Charente-Maritime). Though seemingly destined for the sea – even attempting entry into the French Naval School (*École Navale*) before being thwarted by his weakness in mathematics – his true calling lay in art. In 1887, he entered the prestigious École des Beaux-Arts de Paris, studying under the academic masters Alexandre Cabanel (1823–1889) and Fernand Cormon (1845–1924). This formal training provided a strong technical grounding, but Fouqueray's spirit constantly sought dynamic subjects found far beyond the studio walls, particularly the ocean and maritime life.

His canvases frequently depicted the rugged Atlantic coast he knew from childhood, and his lifelong passion for the sea received official validation in 1908 when he was appointed an official Painter of the French Navy (*Peintre officiel de la Marine*). More than a title, this was a reflection of his core artistic identity, granting him privileged access to naval subjects. Recognition soon followed, with awards like the Prix Rosa Bonheur (1909), and the Prix de l'Indochine in 1914, foreshadowing significant travels later in his career.

Fouqueray possessed a restless energy, undertaking artistic journeys even before the major conflicts that shaped his era. He traveled to Belgium

Charles Fouqueray, self-portrait (1911)

and the Netherlands, financed by a travel grant following a Salon medal, and spent extended time in Spain broadening his artistic horizons.

The outbreak of World War I in 1914 brought Fouqueray's identities as marine painter and patriot into sharp focus. Learning of the war while in Spain, he returned immediately to France, enlisting with Admiral Ronarc'h's naval fusiliers (*fusiliers marins*) on the Belgian front. Far from remaining in the rear, Fouqueray served as a true painter-reporter (*peintre "témoin reporter"*), experiencing and documenting the brutal realities of combat at Dixmude, the Battle of the Yser (*Bataille de l'Yser*), Nieuport, and later Douaumont. His service extended to the Dardanelles expedition, travels to Greece and Egypt (witnessing the 1915 Suez Canal attack), and missions aboard patrol vessels hunting U-boats. He created thousands of sketches and watercolors – "valuable accounts of battles" – providing powerful visual testimony to the conflict. Some of these works illustrated 1920s publications like *La guerre racontée par ses Généraux* (*The War Narrated by its Generals*) and *La guerre navale racontée par nos Amiraux*.

The end of the war did not diminish Fouqueray's wanderlust. He embarked on extensive voyages, first a four-month Mediterranean tour covering Italy, Greece, Turkey, Lebanon, Syria, and Palestine (1919). This was followed by a pivotal journey eastward around 1921, encompassing Ceylon (Sri Lanka), French Indochina (Vietnam, Cambodia, Laos), China, and the Red Sea region. He continued traveling extensively in the Middle East and Arabian Peninsula until 1924. This profound immersion in diverse cultures and landscapes—from European battlefields to Mediterranean coasts and the vibrant scenes of Asia—gave him an exceptionally rich visual palette.

It was this unique combination of naval understanding, wartime experience, and firsthand knowledge of the Orient that made Fouqueray the ideal artist to illustrate Claude Farrère's *La Bataille*. Farrère, himself a naval officer, set his 1909 novel during the Russo-Japanese War (1904-1905). In 1921, the publisher Ernest Flammarion commissioned Fouqueray to produce black and white illustrations for an edition of the novel. Recognizing the power of Fouqueray's dramatic interpretations, publisher Auguste Blaizot then commissioned the 108 full-color paintings that define the lavish 1925 limited edition. Far more than decorations, Fouqueray's illustrations became integral visual counterparts to the text, powerfully conveying the intensity of the naval battles, the exoticism of the Japanese settings, and the emotional depth of the characters, underscoring the novel's themes of duty, sacrifice, and cultural encounter.

Fouqueray's talent extended far beyond this landmark project. He was a sought-after illustrator for a host of literary giants of his day, including Rudyard Kipling, Pierre Loti, George Groslier, Joseph Conrad, Jack London, Léon Daudet, Pearl S. Buck, Maurice Larrouy, Pierre Benoit, and others, as well as five other books by Farrère himself. His artistic versatility also shone in advertising, notably creating the iconic "See Britain First" poster series for the Shell Company in 1925. As a decorator (*décorateur*), Fouqueray left his mark on numerous public buildings, including the town halls (*hôtels de ville*) of Vincennes, Montreuil, Le Bourget, Niort, Fouras, and Paris's 20th arrondissement, as well as international commissions like the Congress Palace in Buenos Aires (1932) and the Cathedral of Gaspé in Canada (1933).

His service continued even into World War II; despite being 70 years old, he undertook naval missions (1939-1940) and was appointed head of fleet camouflage services (*chef des services de camouflage de la flotte*) in Nantes in 1940. His contributions earned him significant honors, including the Chevalier de la Légion d'honneur in 1920 and election to the prestigious Académie des Beaux-Arts in 1947. He was also President of the Société Coloniale des Artistes Français and a founder of the Société des Beaux-Arts de la Mer.

Charles Fouqueray died in Paris on March 28, 1956, characteristically active until the very end, working on a decoration for the Le Bourget town hall. He left behind an immense and varied body of work, celebrated for its dynamism, skilled draughtsmanship, and narrative power. While his works are preserved in institutions like the Musée de la Marine and the Musée du quai Branly (related to African and Oceanic Arts) in Paris, his illustrations for *La Bataille* remain one of his most accessible and compelling legacies. Through these restored images, Fouqueray's unique artistic vision, forged in a life of extraordinary experiences, continues to illuminate Farrère's masterpiece, offering contemporary readers a powerful visual journey into a dramatic past.

The Battle

Dramatis Personae

This also includes historical figures referenced by the author in his fictionalized story. Note that the author states in his preface, his "three most important Japanese characters — Marquis Yorisaka, Marquise Mitsouko, and Viscount Hirata — are much less photographic portraits than very general paintings; the brushwork is intended to approximate a resemblance to an entire Japanese caste, whose essential features alone have been selected, and exaggerated, to make the composition more perceptible to European eyes."

Chapter 1

- **Confucius**: A fundamental Chinese philosopher who lived ca. 551 – ca. 479 BC.
- **Hokusai and Utamaro**: Renowned makers of *ukiyo-e* woodblock prints in the late 18th to early 19th centuries.
- **Jean-François Felze**: A renowned French painter in his mid-50s, frequently engaged by high-society subjects. Distinguished, worldly, and appreciative of Japanese heritage and culture, he loves women and is loved by them.
- **Linevich**: Ivan Linevich (1854–1918), an officer of the Russian Imperial Army, appointed commander of the Russian forces in Manchuria in 1904.
- **Marquise Yorisaka**: An attractive, sophisticated 24-year-old Japanese noblewoman who, along with her husband, favors Western culture and décor.
- **Plato**: A classical Greek philosopher who lived ca. 427/24 – ca. 347 BC.
- **Rozhestvensky**: Zinovy Petrovich Rozhestvensky (1848–1909) was the admiral in the Imperial Russian Navy charged with relocating the Baltic Fleet to the Pacific during the Russo-Japanese War (1904–05).

Chapter 2

- **Commander Herbert Fergan**: A masculine officer in the British navy, aide-de-camp to His Majesty the King of England, and a friend of Marquis Yorisaka.
- **Marquis Sadao Yorisaka**: An influential Japanese nobleman, educated in naval studies in France and Great Britain, who is the husband of Mitsouko, the Marquise Yorisaka.

Chapter 3

- **Makarov**: Stepan Makarov (1849–1904) was an admiral in the Imperial Russian Navy.
- **Mitsouko**: The Marquis Sadao Yorisaka's affectionate name for his wife, meaning 'honeycomb,' or 'mystery' when written with an alternate Chinese character.
- **Wright**: Walter Withers Wright (1869–1954), an officer of the British Royal Navy who saw action during the Boxer Rebellion in China (1900) and served as commander of the battleship HMS Superb during the Russo-Japanese War.

Chapter 6

- **Zhou Pèi**: A close friend of Felze, formerly a Chinese ambassador, viceroy, eminent tutor of the sons of the first imperial concubine, and one of the twelve great dignitaries of the Chinese court.

Chapter 7

- **Mrs. Betsy Hockley**: A tall, blonde, slim, and attractive 30-year-old American woman, "eighty times a millionaire", who is the proud owner of the luxurious yacht, *Yseult,*
- **Miss Elsa Vane**: A young guest on Mrs. Hockley's yacht who assists as her friend as a "reader."

Chapter 8

- **Admiral Tōgō**: Tōgō Heihachirō (27 January 1848 – 30 May 1934), admiral of the fleet in the Imperial Japanese Navy and became one of Japan's greatest naval heroes.

- **Rear Admiral Nebogatov**: Nikolai Ivanovich Nebogatov (20 April 1849 – 4 August 1922) a rear admiral in the Imperial Russian Navy.

Chapter 10

- **Jervis**: Admiral John Jervis, 1st Earl of St Vincent (1735–1823), a British naval officer known for his service during the American Revolutionary War and the Napoleonic Wars.
- **Keppel**: Admiral Augustus Keppel (1725–86) served in many naval campaigns, notably during the Seven Years' War.
- **Nelson**: Admiral Horatio Nelson, 1st Viscount Nelson (1758–1805), the most famous British naval officer of all time.
- **Percy Scott**: Admiral Sir Percy Moreton Scott, a British admiral who gained recognition as an innovative problem solver and engineer, particularly in the modernization of naval artillery.
- **Rodney**: Admiral George Rodney (1718–92), a distinguished British naval officer known for his service during the American War of Independence and the French Revolutionary Wars.
- **Suffern**: Admiral Pierre-André de Suffren (1729–88), a French naval commander noted for his tactical acumen and aggressive strategy.

Chapter 13

- **Thucydides**: An ancient Greek historian (ca. 460/455 – ca. 399/398 BC) who chronicled the Plague of Athens (429–426 BC).
- **Viscount Hirata Takamori**: A Japanese lieutenant aboard the fictional battleship *Nikkō*, descended from a samurai family and who adheres to traditional values.

Chapter 14

- **Mr. Poincaré**: Jules Henri Poincaré (1854–1912), a French mathematician, theoretical physicist, engineer, and philosopher of science.

Chapter 17

- Prince Federico Alghero: An Italian noble from a prominent Genoese family who attends Mrs. Hockley's yacht party.

Chapter 18

- **Titian**: Titian (1488–1576), a preeminent Italian painter of the High Renaissance.
- **Van Dyke**: Sir Anthony van Dyck (1599–1641), a Flemish painter.
- **Wagnerian**: Referring to Wilhelm Richard Wagner (1813–83), German composer of grand operas.
- **Walpole**: Probable reference to Horatio (Horace) Walpole, 4th Earl of Orford (1717–97).

Chapter 20

- **Fenn Ta-Jen**: Zhou Pèi's way of addressing Felze. Ta-Jen is an honorific that means "considerable man."
- **Hoéi**: (discussed) A son of Emperor Kao and his concubine-princess, Tsi, in the Han Dynasty

Chapter 23

- **O-Setsou san**: A young girl, whose name means 'Great Chastity,' working in the Japanese inn at Mogimachi who becomes Felze's lover.

Chapter 25

- **Kamimura**: Baron Hikonojō Kamimura (1849–1916), an admiral in the Imperial Japanese Navy.
- **Kataoka**: Baron Kataoka Shichirō (1854–1920), a admiral in the Imperial Japanese Navy.
- **Nelson and Bronte**: A title of Admiral Nelson, previously bestowed upon him by King Ferdinand III of Sicily for his services.
- **Uryū**: Baron Uryū Sotokichi (1857–1937), an admiral in the Imperial Japanese Navy.

Chapter 30

- **Narimasa**: An ensign aboard the battleship *Nikkō*, who assists Viscount Hirata.

৪০ ❀ ୯৪

Books by George Groslier – the Khmerophile

A romance of colnial Cambodia.
ISBN: 978-1-934431-16-0

A romance of colonial Cambodia.
ISBN: 978-1-934431-94-8

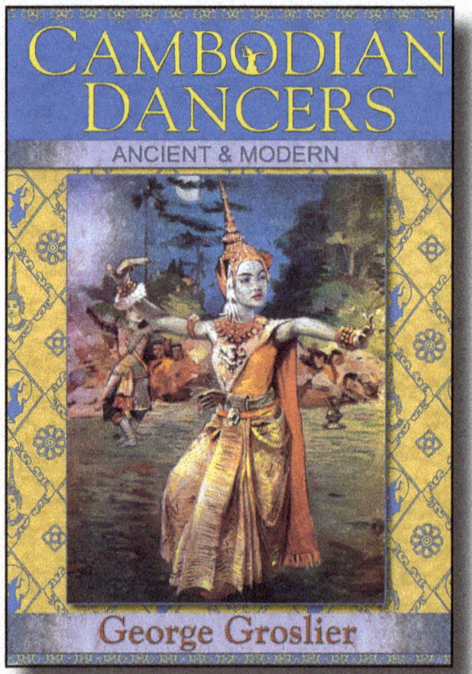

First Study of Cambodian Dance.
ISBN: 978-1-934431-12-2

1912 exploration in Cambodia.
ISBN: 978-1-934431-90-0

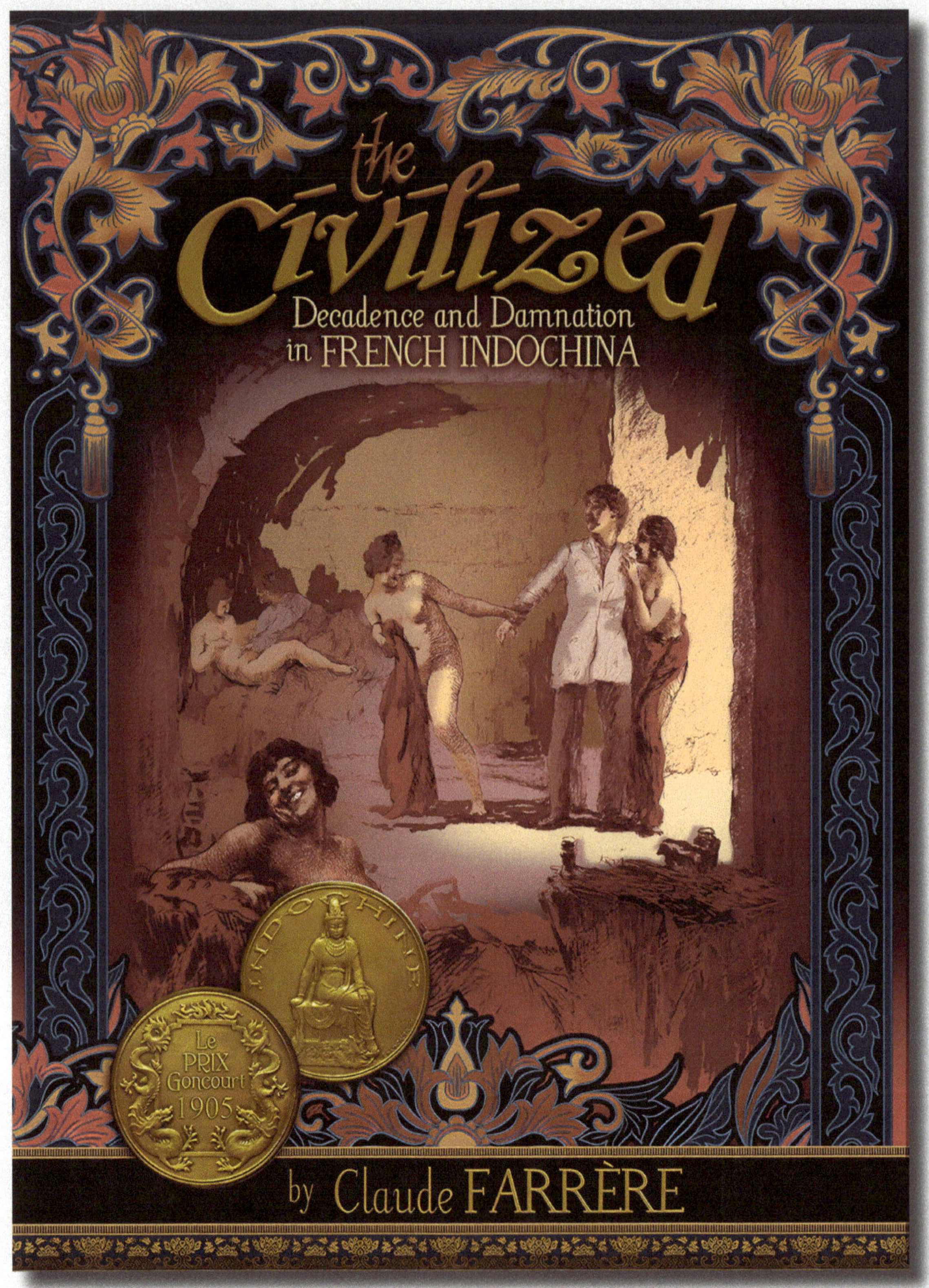

"One of the most magnificently daring books that contemporary literature has produced" —*Gil Blas*, 1905

"Sumptuous rot…pornography…an atmosphere of amiable corruption… a silly, childish and pretentious novel." —*Courier saïgonnais*, 1906

ISBN: 978-1-934431-75-7